THE
Barefoot
BRIDES
COLLECTION

7 Eccentric Women Would Sacrifice All—Even Their Shoes—for Their Dreams

THE
Barefoot
BRIDES
COLLECTION

Lori Copeland
CJ Dunham, Cynthia Hickey, Maureen Lang,
Cathy Liggett, Kelly Long, Carolyn Zane

BARBOUR BOOKS
An Imprint of Barbour Publishing, Inc.

Barefoot Hearts ©2018 by Lori Copeland
The Castle Made of Sand ©2018 by CJ Dunham
A Teacher's Heart ©2018 by Cynthia Hickey
Between the Moments ©2018 by Maureen Lang
Promise Me Sunday ©2018 by Cathy Liggett
Lady's Slipper ©2018 by Kelly Long
Hope's Horizon ©2018 by Carolyn Zane

Print ISBN 978-1-68322-682-6

eBook Editions:
Adobe Digital Edition (.epub) 978-1-68322-684-0
Kindle and MobiPocket Edition (.prc) 978-1-68322-683-3

All scripture quotations, unless otherwise noted, are taken from the King James Version of the Bible.

Scripture quotations marked niv are taken from the HOLY BIBLE, NEW INTERNATIONAL VERSION®. niv®. Copyright © 1973, 1978, 1984, 2011 by Biblica, Inc.™ Used by permission. All rights reserved worldwide.

This book is a work of fiction. Names, characters, places, and incidents are either products of the author's imagination or used fictitiously. Any similarity to actual people, organizations, and/or events is purely coincidental.

Published by Barbour Books, an imprint of Barbour Publishing, Inc., 1810 Barbour Drive, Uhrichsville, Ohio 44683, www.barbourbooks.com

Our mission is to inspire the world with the life-changing message of the Bible.

Member of the
Evangelical Christian
Publishers Association

Printed in Canada.

Contents

Barefoot Hearts

by Lori Copeland

Chapter 1

On the banks of the White River
Edgar's Cove, Arkansas, 1876

Annie Lawson adored three things: the St. Louis Browns, sourdough toast smeared with blueberry jam, and baseball.

The latter was harder to come by here in sleepy Edgar's Cove, a tiny Arkansas community that sat along the banks of the White River. Between Frank Otter, who owned the cove's small press that produced the monthly *Town Crier*, and Ben Grison, the town barber, she was able to keep up with latest news from the major professional teams. But baseball and jam were the last thing on Annie's mind this morning. This morning, her weekly elderly charges' outing was her only concern.

She stepped into Main Street and thrust her right arm straight out, erecting a physical barricade for passing vehicles. The barefoot girl, dressed in worn overalls and with her loose, waist-length auburn hair whipping in the breeze, lifted a whistle to her lips and blew hard.

The wheels of buckboards, two carriages, and a hay wagon ground to a shuddering halt.

Two more shrill blasts filled the air before Annie, through narrowed eyes, was convinced the path was safely cleared. She waved the group forward, and one by one, a half-dozen men and women shuffled, rolled in chairs, and reeled across Main Street.

The sight of Annie herding her familiar entourage was as common as mosquito bites on a hot summer night. The tiny community sat tucked in a cove on the lower branch of White River. Summers promised hot, humid days, and winters could be as fickle when daytime temperatures dropped as much as thirty degrees in a matter of hours. While only a few chose to live in Edgar's Cove, those that did were loyal to the core to neighbors.

Giving Mrs. Helprin's cat, Big'un, a gentle foot nudge, Annie urged the large American Bobtail to fall into step. The cat eyed her as though he'd like to protest but didn't. A second nudge. "C'mon. You can do it."

The cat blinked as if to say, "I am thirty pounds overweight. I hate walks."

Annie recognized the cat's combative eye language. Yes, Big'un was most likely the hugest cat on earth, but a walk was beneficial for anybody. Annie paused and focused sharply on the animal.

Impatient buggy drivers and riders sat and watched the impasse.

"Stand up," Annie ordered.

Big'un stared.

"Now. I am not carrying you across the street this morning. You are going to walk on your four paws. You might as well get it over with."

The cat's mouth puckered with defiance.

Annie's tone turned to one of finality. "Pouting won't change a thing. Get on your feet—are you rolling your eyes? Stop it."

A buckboard eased forward a bit. "Do something with Big'un, Annie! I'm getting older by the minute!" a man's voice called.

Annie acknowledged the detainees growing impatience. She turned back to Big'un. "See what you're doing? You're upsetting folks. Fine. Sit here in the blistering sun." Annie wiggled her bare toes. The hard-packed ground was starting to scorch her toes. "Very well, have your way. I'm crossing with the others." Annie turned and fell into line with those who were gradually reaching the other side. "If you're hit and flattened it's your own fault." Of course, she knew she would never let anything happen to Mrs. Helprin's cat, and Big'un did too, but the threat sometimes worked.

The cat's amber-colored eyes focused on the line. When Annie was nearly to the opposite side of the street, Big'un slowly got to his feet and started moving.

Groans erupted from the waiting traffic. A lone rider approached in the distance, the sound of hoofbeats prominent in the muggy air. Annie turned when she noticed the approaching rider had not appeared to slow. Turning marginally, her eyes located Big'un, who was sluggishly crossing the street.

She raised her hands to cup her mouth, "Walk faster!" Ask anyone in town, and they would assure you that Big'un wasn't known for speed. The cat's sheer size made a faster gait impossible. It wasn't that Mrs. Helprin, who Annie worked for at the mercantile, overfed the animal. On the contrary, Annie had to coax food down both Mrs. Helprin and her cat. Ada's fading appetite was due to advancing age; Big'un's trouble was due to a glandular disorder, or so old Doc Blue said about a month before the jolly white-haired physician retired to go live with his son in Arizona.

Annie shouted louder. "Now! Pick up the pace, Big'un!"

Flying hoofbeats drew closer. Whoever was riding that horse was in one big hurry. Annie glanced at the cat and then back to the looming rider. Probably one of those wranglers fresh in from a round-up in an all-fired hurry to get to town to waste his month's pay at the Tired Monkey, the cove's one and only local watering hole.

With a last desperate glance, Annie turned and lunged for the pet. In her haste to save the cat, she lost her grip on the furry feline and shoved the pet farther into the line of danger. The rider swept by in a boil of dust, obviously unaware of the cat or of the onlookers staring in horror at the tragedy playing out.

Annie felt the hot air off the lathered horse as the big gelding swept past, nearly trampling her in the process. Horse and rider hurtled toward the edge of town where the bar sat, ignoring the cat's frantic howls.

Annie caught her breath and rolled to her side, terrified to look. Poor Big'un. He never knew what hit him. Tears sprang to her eyes. Mrs. Helprin! How would she tell her employer, friend, and landlady that the thing she lived for most in life, Annie had recklessly destroyed?

She felt hands lifting her, anxious voices surrounding her. "Are you all right, honey?"

"My, that was a close one. You could have been killed!"

"Why, that man ought to be horsewhipped coming through town like a freight train!"

"I tried. . ." Annie whispered. Her head spun like a top. "I dove to save Big'un but—"

Mrs. Holly's voice reached her. "Big'un's fine, hon—or I think he is." Annie battled to focus on Verdeen, who crouched to her left, cradling the cat. "Poor baby. You might have had eight of your nine lives scared right out of you." She paused. "There's a drop or two of blood here behind your tail on the left leg. Wouldn't hurt none to let the doc check you out." Her voice lifted. "Same for you, Annie Girl. You took a hard spill."

Shepard, the ferry operator, stepped up to help Annie to her feet. She leaned on his strength while the small entourage crossed the street.

In the cove, having a doctor was short of a miracle. Ray Burrows, town black-smith, usually did the patching up around here on animals and humans, but last week the stage broke an axle in Flippin, the nearest town to Edgar's Cove, and was stranded for a full day. One of the riders was a doctor, fresh out of school and on his way to St. Louis to start a new practice. The doctor had wandered to the cove to kill time.

By the time the stage pulled out of Flippin the following day, the self-appointed mayor of the cove, Maynard Pulse, had offered twenty-five dollars a month, all the eggs and chicken the young doctor could eat in the winter, his laundry washed and ironed, and all the summer produce he could eat if he'd stick around until the cove could find a new doc. He only needed to stay a few weeks, just until the town could hire medical help. The young man, for some reason, agreed to the terms.

Annie limped toward the doctor's office, clinging tight to Shepard's arm. Her muddy dress clung to her body and her shins were skinned raw. She turned to Shepard. "Did everyone make it safely across the street?" Her charges were elderly but apparently made of better stock than she. She and Big'un were the only casualties.

Dr. Gabe Jones stepped to the office window as the party approached and lifted the freshly laundered curtain. The racket of the last ten minutes finally caught his interest. Something had the community in an uproar. His gaze focused on half-a-dozen men and women heading his way. An elderly black man supported a young, barefoot woman. Instinct told him she was the cause of the ruckus. He reached for his suit coat and slipped it on, a garment he hated. Would he ever forget the natural feel of a cotton shirt and denims? Once he set up his St. Louis practice, the coat would go. Father might have felt a need to look the profession, but Gabe didn't. The pain in his left hand momentarily distracted him. He reached for a bottle and popped a couple of pills under his tongue.

The front door flew open, and a group of elderly residents rushed him, everyone talking at once.

"We need your help, Doc."

"Oh lordy, lordy. The cat's been hurt."

"Do you think it's anything serious with Annie?"

"There's nothing wrong with me," the young woman denied. "Have him check Big'un first."

Gabe's eyes switched from one outburst to the other, rattled by the sudden confusion. He swallowed the pills, nearly choking.

The loveliest eyes of robin's-egg blue he had ever witnessed lifted to meet his gaze. "Check Big'un first, please. I'm fine, really."

"Who's Big'un?"

"The cat."

"Come in." Gabe opened the door wider to allow the group full access to the office. He focused on the young girl, trying to guess her age. He wasn't good at the game, but he'd say older than sixteen and younger than twenty-five. Maybe early twenties. His gaze shifted to her bare feet and scraped knees. Not the most ladylike woman he'd seen in a while. Tomboyish. Her overalls had seen better days, and her shirttail bunched at the waist. His eyes moved to her face. Cute. Winsome—a sprinkle of freckles across the bridge of her nose. Dark auburn hair with a fair amount of red sprinkled through it hung to her waist.

"Put the lady on the table." His gaze moved to the huge cat a woman was cradling in her arms. "Put—"

"Big'un," the woman supplied.

"Yes. Large animal." He had never seen a cat that size. Looked more like a giant crab with crocodile eyes.

Annie smiled. "We think we have a world's record, but of course, we don't know for certain."

He focused on the animal and the spot of blood on the cat's left leg. "What happened?"

He cleaned and dressed the cat's insignificant wounds as he talked. "Doesn't appear to be anything broken." His hand gently moved over the animal, exploring. The young woman frowned with anxiety. He turned to smile at her. "How are you doing?"

"Upset—but better now. I should have carried Big'un across the street."

"By the looks of his size, Big'un should have carried you across the street." The doctor grinned. "Unless there's something I'm not picking up, he doesn't appear to have any threatening injuries." He finished with the cat and turned to her. "Now let's see about you." Practiced hands gently explored, touched, felt. When he came to her knees he paused. "Can you lift your cuffs?"

She drew back, hesitant. She wasn't the kind who lifted her cuffs to just any man. His grin widened. "I need to get a better look at those cuts and bruises."

With a hesitant glance toward the men in the crowd, she slowly complied. Lifting the denim, she showed him the wounds. "This is a lot of fuss over some tiny scratches."

"How did you say this accident happened?"

She explained the incident, the insensitive rider, the scare that Big'un had been seriously hurt.

"Big'un is your cat?"

"No, he belongs to Mrs. Helprin, the lady I work for—she's my friend and landlady. I take a small group of seniors for a walk three times a week, and of course Big'un needs the exercise."

He glanced at the cat, who was sleeping now, purring.

Annie continued. "It's glandular—his size. Or so we've been told."

"Big cat."

"Yes sir. Mighty big, and Mrs. Helprin would die if anything happened to him."

"Well then, we can't let anything happen to him." He glanced up and met her eyes. "Can we?"

"No sir, we can't."

"Gabe. Call me Doc Gabe." After a bit, he straightened. "All superficial wounds. Nothing to be concerned about." He set about cleaning and dressing the injuries. Her leg was petite and shapely. He hadn't been around a woman for so long, he'd forgotten the pleasure. School had filled his time the past few years, and frankly he hadn't missed the experience. For a long time, he hadn't enjoyed his own company. He saw no reason to bring a woman into his misery.

The young lady spoke. "Big'un is fine too?"

Something flipped in his stomach. Something he'd rarely felt. Something he didn't necessarily want to feel—not yet.

He firmly set the dainty foot back in place, but the instinct inside of him persisted. "Big'un is fine—for now."

She peered up at him. "For now?"

He nodded to the others crowding the office. "May I have a few words in private with the cat's guardian?"

Rounds of friendly agreement followed, and the group trailed out of the office, closing the door when they left.

"Big'un is really fine, isn't he?" Annie persisted.

"Do you live close, Miss. . ."

"Call me Annie. Everybody does. I rent a room in Mrs. Helprin's upstairs. I'm a block away."

He paused, contemplating his next words. "It wouldn't be an imposition to bring the cat by the office in the morning? I'd like to check him again."

Her brows lifted. "Are you worried?"

"Not worried. Simple caution. Perhaps for the next few mornings you could bring the cat by the office, and we'll make sure nothing shows up that shouldn't."

"Something. . .like what?"

"Like what?" He weighed the possibilities, fully aware that what he was about to say was sneaky. Not dishonest. Sneaky. The way a man would react to a pretty young woman because he wanted to see her again. "There's always Briny Fever and Gray-Tongue Madness to consider. Rumble Dementia—a strange, deep-throated purring that's often instantaneously lethal. Then I can't completely rule out the Whiskered Chill, an even more worrisome prospect—"

She interrupted. "Oh my—then rest assured. I will bring the cat over first thing every morning."

Guilt engulfed him. Misleading someone was not like him. Maybe the cove's isolation had gotten to him. "Miss—Annie. Will this be putting you out—is there any reason you can't bring Big'un by? Because if there is, we can make other arrangements."

"None." She slid off the examining table and bent to roll her cuffs. This site presented an enticing and exquisite view. Gabe quickly focused on a chart hanging on the wall. "You aren't employed?"

"Only to Mrs. Helprin. She visits her son in Phoenix during the winter. Of course I take my friends for a walk three mornings a week, take Mr. Pierson his evening meal from the restaurant, dust the church pews on Wednesdays and Saturdays, do Mrs. Owens' laundry when her lumbago is acting up, and tidy up where I'm needed. Other than that, I don't have a thing." She flashed a winsome smile that reminded him of an innocent child but also took his breath. "How much do I owe?"

"Owe? I hesitate to charge you anything. Everything was minor."

Her jaw firmed. "I wouldn't dream of permitting you to treat me without compensation. Do you like rhubarb pie?"

"Sorry, I hate the slimy stuff." He thought for a moment. "Do you make preserves?"

"What kind? Cherry—I make delicious cherry preserves, and the crop was very good this year. I have several jars in the cupboard right now."

"Fair enough. One jar of cherry preserves." They shook hands on the agreement. When she left, he stepped to the sill, watching her cross the street. Other than a slight limp, she seemed unfazed by the accident. His mind returned to their earlier conversation.

Briny Fever. Rumble Dementia.

Whiskered Chill?

Where were his ethics? He wasn't prone to extending visits with female patients. He'd made up every one of those "supposed" dangers on the spot. There wasn't a thing wrong with the cat. By tonight Big'un would be eating like a lumberjack.

Chapter 2

A ctually," Annie said as she bent to take a bubbling rhubarb pie out of the oven and set the dish on the kitchen counter, "I've been taking you to see the doctor for three days now and you are doing fine. There hasn't been a sign of the Whiskered Chill, whatever that is, and you're eating well. Yet the doctor insists that he still needs to see you every morning."

As far as she could tell, the cat had shown nary a sign of anything worrisome relating to the accident, but if she allowed anything to happen to the animal, Mrs. Helprin would never forgive her. She set the pie, that she intended to take to Pastor Sterling on her way to clean the church this morning, in the warming oven. Henry enjoyed warm pie, and if she ever took him one even slightly cool, though polite, she would see his nose curl with disappointment.

Big'un lay at her feet, purring softly. "Remind me to stop by to see Mrs. Owens on the way back and get her laundry." The Widow Owens had such a small dab of soiled clothing that Annie could allot almost a full week without stopping by for a visit. She had to admit that the visits with the new doctor weren't entirely an imposition. They were an exciting journey, and she'd begun to look forward to the fleeting encounters. Yesterday, when she'd handed him the jar of cherry preserves, something changed in their relationship, and the doctor insisted that she join him for a cup of coffee. They'd sat on the office front porch and drunk the bitter brew he'd poured from the speckled pot that sat on the woodstove in the office corner. The room was sparsely furnished. Three hardback chairs, a coat rack, and a spittoon. Gabe apologized for the heat radiating from the woodstove, but they'd have no coffee otherwise. The sacrifice made the room stifling, so they sat outside and visited.

After a sip or two, she learned that he was born and raised in St. Louis. His father was a physician, his mother taught French at the University of St. Louis, and after a brief interval of Gabe chasing his childhood dream, he'd enrolled in University of the Pacific, located in San Francisco. She was embarrassed to tell him that she'd never been any farther than Flippin, some twelve to thirteen miles away.

He glanced down at her bare feet. "You don't wear shoes. Any particular reason why?"

"Because I don't want to. Mr. and Mrs. Helprin barely had the money to feed and clothe me, and any shoes they could provide were hand-me-downs from others." She sighed. "I had numerous blisters on my feet from wearing shoes that were too small or much too large for me, so I stopped wearing them."

"What do you do in the winter?"

"Well. . .I guess I pray for an early spring?" She flashed an impish grin. "I have shoes now, but given the choice, I don't wear them unless absolutely necessary."

"So you plan to be a barefoot schoolteacher. I gather you plan to teach in Edgar's Cove?"

"Of course. When the cove is big enough to warrant a schoolhouse. Right now, the children take the ferry to Flippin."

"And if the position here wasn't open? I wouldn't think Edgar's Cove would need two teachers."

"Suppose not. But if I'm not married by then, I'll fight for the position."

He chuckled. "Seems that you have your life perfectly planned out. Every *t* crossed and *i* dotted."

"The rest of my life? I can't honestly say that's true. If God's plans agree with mine, then I suppose I do, but I can't imagine living anywhere but Edgar's Cove—though your life appears to be very exciting."

His gaze had focused on the almost silent street, and she was reminded of how nothing noteworthy ever happened in the cove, but that's the way she liked it. The town baseball game held each fall was the only significant event for the residents. She supposed he'd lived a thrilling, breathless life in St. Louis, and she told him so.

"No, I've never been much into excitement or the social scene," he said. "Been too busy completing my education."

Her gaze slid slyly sideways. "Too busy to marry?" Very blunt of her to outright ask, but they had established a comfortable camaraderie during the brief morning visits.

He chuckled. "Way too busy to consider commitment. What about you? Surely sewing, a cat, and taking care of your elderly charges doesn't consume all of your time."

"Haven't you noticed? Time is meaningless here. Each day is like the other—except for the change of seasons."

"And that doesn't bother you?"

"Not in the least." She smiled. "I suppose I'm not much into excitement or social life."

He was about to answer when Edie Smith's lumbago took priority over the conversation. "Good-morning, Edie." Annie stood up and helped the elderly woman up one step, experiencing an odd sense of letdown. She hadn't finished her coffee, and the doctor was good company.

Edie heaved her body upward. "Thank you, dearie. You're ever so kind." The older woman turned to face Annie, her face glistening with early morning heat. "We are having Keno at three?"

"Yes ma'am." Edie asked at least twice a week about the Keno game. Her memory for coming events wasn't exactly intact anymore.

Edie flashed a smile. "I'll be there, lumbago or not. I intend to play two cards this afternoon."

"Now Edie." Annie wagged a stern forefinger. "You know two cards are against the rules."

"Rules. Who needs them?"

Annie knew if Edie had been eighty years younger she would have stomped her foot. The old curmudgeon could be a handful when it came to games and fairness. The latter had no place in the woman's social life.

"Edie, we have been through this conversation every Keno day. Two cards are too confusing for the others." Edie was the oldest person in the cove, and while her memory for new dates and events might be a little shaky, she had a mind like a steel trap when it came to playing games she'd known all her life. And Edie loved to win—whatever the cost.

"One card, Edie. And no fussing with Adelaide today." She glanced at Gabe. "Miss Edie likes to divert Adelaide's attention from the game."

"I do not!"

"You do, Edie." The rebuke was soft but carefully aimed.

"Shoot fire!" Edie brushed past Annie and entered the office, slamming the door behind her. Annie could still hear her complaining. "Just cause others are old tarts don't mean that I'm one."

Annie glanced at Gabe and felt heat color her cheeks. "I'm sorry. She can be. . ."

"Difficult?"

"You've noticed?"

His features gentled. "I gather competitive deceit greatly upsets you."

Annie smiled and cocked her head. "Doesn't it you?"

"Sure—intended deceit does."

"Is there such a thing as false deceit?"

"No but there's kidding—jokes—toying with someone in a good-natured way. I'm sure Edie doesn't cheat."

"She certainly does, every chance she gets. I take folks at their word, and one's word is their honor." She offered another amiable smile. "You better go. Edie doesn't like to be kept waiting."

Annie and Big'un wandered off, but Gabe's remark stuck in Annie's head. Deceit bothered her. Mr. and Mrs. Helprin had taught her that if a man gave his word, that word was to be honored. What others thought didn't matter, unless someone accused Annie of deceit. Never once in her life had she been dishonest with anyone—unless you count the time she told Mrs. Helprin she didn't look fat in her new Sunday-go-to-meeting dress. That morning she had flat out lied.

The flowery swans in the fabric stretched over Mrs. Helprin's jiggly hips like a sprouted potato. Those ugly birds jumped up and down like puppets on a string when Mrs. Helprin walked across the floor. Annie had been torn about telling the truth and bruising Ada's feelings. She worked so hard on the dress.

In the end, deceit tipped the scale, but Annie never again used the excuse of hurt feelings from telling the painful truth.

Her footsteps slowed. Folks told her that she was a good judge of character. She could read folks like a book, so she'd already decided that Gabe was a good person, not one to lie or spin tales. Her gaze focused on Big'un. The doctor wouldn't fib about anything.

Would he?

Pastel rays of pink, yellow, and blue streaked the sky the following morning as Annie untied her apron and stripped it off. She draped the flour-stained garment over a kitchen chair and paused to scrape a bit of rhubarb off the fabric. Seemed she took extra care lately to look presentable. "Big'un? Are you coming?" She had to drop the pie off at Pastor's home and then walk back to the doctor's office. She grinned. If business was slow, Gabe might invite her to sit a spell on the porch with him. Butterflies swarmed her stomach. Silly girl. The doctor was far too sophisticated to notice her in any way but a professional duty, but he had taken extra time with her yesterday.

Doctor was sitting on the porch when she approached. The small office was empty. Her eyes strayed to the two cups of steaming coffee waiting on the steps.

"Ah, there you are." She met Gabe's disarming grin. "Good morning."

"Have time for a cup of coffee?"

She checked her small pocket watch. "Why yes, I believe I can spare a few minutes. Thank you."

A full hour passed before she could blink. They'd discuss everything from the weather to making cherry jelly while the pastor's pie cooled.

She finally checked the time. "Oh my, I've kept you too long."

He glanced at the empty street. "Seems no one is in need of my services this morning." He lifted a dark brow. "More coffee?"

A full half hour later he said, "Now that you know all about me, what about you, Annie Lawson?"

"Me?" Annie shrugged. "My parents are dead. They, and my little brother, died in a boating accident when I was seven. Mr. and Mrs. Helprin took me in and raised me. Whit Helprin passed away several years ago. At that time, I had been preparing to take an exam to become a schoolteacher, but Mrs. Helprin needed help in her sewing business, so I stayed on. I live in my childhood bedroom. For now, I'm content to stay with Mrs. Helprin until the good Lord calls her home."

"And after that?"

"After that, I might pursue my dream of becoming a teacher. Or not. I'm very content with my life."

"You don't have dreams of falling in love, marrying, starting a family of your own?"

"Certainly I have those dreams, but I figure all will come in time. Until then, I'm happy."

"Well, not many folks can say that."

"Oh, all folks have dreams. But I'm content to wait until mine come true." She studied her bare toes. "Where else but Edgar's Cove could I go barefoot and no one care?"

His gaze focused on her toes. "And if the dreams don't show up?"

Annie caught the sight of Pete Minot approaching the office. The beautiful time with Gabe was over. "Then what have I lost? I love exactly where I am."

His smile slowly faded. "Best not to have dreams. They can let you down sometimes."

"Not have my dreams? What would life be without dreams?" Even though Annie was fully aware that dreams were hard to achieve in this little community, she'd never relinquish her goals. No more than a baseball player would step up to home plate and anticipate a strikeout.

"Life would be empty." He'd set his mug on the porch and stood up to greet the new arrival. "Morning, Pete. How's that rash today?"

Gabe's former remark, "best not to have dreams," stuck in Annie's mind. What an odd thing for the doctor to say. Who—including Gabe Jones, who seemed to have everything—didn't have a dream to strive for?

Since the dessert had cooled, Annie decided to give the rhubarb pie to Mrs. Owens. There was enough fruit for at least one more pie, and Pastor liked his pies straight out of the oven. She struck off to deliver the dessert and pick up the widow's laundry. A couple of the community's married women took turns doing the new doctor's laundry, deeming the chore unfit for a single woman. Annie didn't mind. She got to see the new doctor every day, visit with him on the porch, share a few private moments. Her cheeks warmed at the thought of handling Gabe's personal effects, and yet some day some blessed woman would be doing exactly that. . . .

Who knew? Sometimes dreams had been known to come true.

Chapter 3

Daylight crested the horizon as Annie waited for Big'un to join her on the narrow porch. The cat sauntered out, and she closed the door, shielding the wicker basket containing a rhubarb pie. When she neared the saloon, her pace slackened. Something was afoot this morning at the Tired Monkey. The saloon did a slow business during daylight hours, and evenings weren't much better. When an occasional roundup camped nearby, the joint was busy, but otherwise, unless Freda let her husband out for a breath of fresh air, the bar was empty most days. Today there appeared to be something unusual going on. Loud music and whoops of male glee spilled through the swinging double doors.

She started off again at a hastened pace and headed in the pastor's direction, keeping an ear tuned to the bar activity that appeared to be getting louder. Mrs. Helprin's warnings about the decadent establishment echoed in her mind: *You stay far away from that tavern, Annie. It's not a fitting place for a lady to walk past.*

The warning was sound until the town built a ferry to carry folks across a wide stretch of White River. The admonishment was mute because the shortest way to reach the ferry from the Helprin house necessitated walking by the Tired Monkey. And when Pastor Sterling came to town, he chose to live across the muddy river and down the banks of Edgar's Cove, so the decision was out of the townsfolks' hands, unless they wanted to walk a half mile farther to catch the ferry.

Annie shifted the basket to her left hand and turned to encourage Big'un to pick up speed. At this rate, it would take an hour to cross the river, deliver the pie, and make it back to Dr. Gabe's office by eight thirty for the cat's daily exam. Annie caught back a puckish grin. She noticed she'd been smiling a lot the past few days, and she knew the reason why. She just couldn't grasp the effect Gabe had on her, or maybe she didn't want to acknowledge that she enjoyed the doctor's company too much.

When had she begun to look forward to the cat's appointments that seemed so senseless to her? Ordinarily she would protest the early morning chore, but instead she looked forward to the official visits and had no inclination to stop them—which meant they really must cease. She didn't have a romantic fantasy in her mind about Gabe Jones. She had plenty of time to marry and have a family of her very own. And truthfully? A town the size of Edgar's Cove wasn't exactly a breeding hole for eligible men. Just because the town had temporarily added one very attractive man was no reason for her to go all giggles.

She touched the ribbon in her hair. Why had she started tying back her hair with a red bow and making sure her overalls were fresh? Not a reason in the least. Other than Dr. Gabe, only two single men lived in the area: Horace Winslow, who had worn out three wives and at eighty-five was still clearly in the market for a fourth, and sixteen-year-old Teddy Mote, who lived across the road and down a piece. Annie's twenty-two years must look pretty old to him, even if she were interested in the tall, skinny teen with a gap between his two front teeth.

She glanced up when angry, feminine shrieks snatched her attention. Before, only male laughter dominated the rickety building that housed the men and the occasional woman who imbibed so early in the day. She couldn't imagine any lady living in Edgar's Cove cavorting in a saloon at this hour of the day.

Big'un caught up, and they approached the swelling ruckus. Annie had already made up her mind they would walk past the establishment as fast as possible and head for the ferry. Shepard ran that ferry seven days a week, and other than the brief time he took to enjoy a bit of fellowship with Annie's Keno group, he sat at his station until dark in case someone wanted to cross the river.

"Move it, Big'un," she whispered. In less than a minute they would be past whatever was taking place in the bar and safely on the path to the ferry.

Unfortunately, fifteen seconds shy of goal, the establishment's double front doors flew open, and two young, scantily dressed women tangled in a knot spilled out, skirts over their heads, white pantaloons flashing.

Gasping, Annie focused on the brawling women who were now throwing sucker punches at one another. The air turned blue with shouted oaths.

Annie's hand shot up to protect the basket containing the warm pie when the women rolled around on the ground, scratching and yanking hair. A handful of grisly looking men gathered in the bar doorway urging the combatants on.

"Atta girl, Laurie! Let her have it!"

"Upper cut, Carolyn! Use your upper cut!"

Big'un continued to plod on, seemingly unaware of his surroundings. When Laurie stood up and hurled herself at Carolyn in a cannon ball approach, the cat's sudden meows blistered the air. Carolyn caught the end of his tail and pinned the cat to the dusty street. Before Annie could set the pie aside and come to his rescue, Laurie was on her feet in a charging bull stance, racing toward Carolyn and a squealing Big'un who now blocked Annie's path. The pie and Annie were caught in the middle.

"No!" Annie screamed and tried to shield the carefully browned rhubarb treat, but Laurie was a sizeable opponent. The pie flew into the air when she slammed Annie sideways. Annie dropped to the ground and pie and crust spilled into the dirt.

The men roared with amusement, one going so far as to dart into the street and grab up what remained of the crusty treat. His hoggish smacks and disgusting pig grunts made Annie's stomach curl. She rolled to her side, trying to crawl away from the melee. When she passed Carolyn, she doubled her fist and smacked the woman's foot, freeing Big'un. The cat darted away, and Annie swiftly followed. The half-empty pie pan lay in the dirt and scuffle.

Gabe whirled when the office front door flew open. Annie, holding a frazzled-looking Big'un, stood dressed in clothing smeared with something sticky and pinkish. The young woman's overalls were filthy. His eyes focused on a red ribbon that sat askew on the top of her loose hair containing the same pinkish substance. "Annie?"

"Help," she said meekly.

Taking her arm, he drew her into the small office. "What happened?"

She drew a shaky breath. "Fight. Gigantic, nasty brawl at the saloon." She broke away and limped across the room and dropped into the chair. "It was a nightmare."

His gaze shifted to the cat who had the same strange light reddish-pink coating his face and paws. Blood? Too light for blood. He turned to check Annie.

"Check Big'un first. He was stepped on pretty hard."

"Can you slow down and make sense? Who stepped on whom?"

"Carolyn stepped on Big'un. Laurie knocked me off my feet and ruined the pie." She blinked back tears. "I think it was one of my better pies too."

Gabe reached for an astringent bottle and clean cloth and gently cleaned her wounds.

"What's this pinkest stuff?"

"Rhubarb."

He shook his head, tossed a cloth, and reached for another one. "I'm sure there's one whale of a story in there somewhere."

Drawing another deep breath, she told him about the encounter. Her eyes grew wide and expressive when she described the brawl. "I have honestly never witnessed anything like it. Two women rolling around in the dirt like hooligans! And the things the men shouted were. . .awful. I'm so thankful Pastor Sterling didn't witness the debacle. He would have fainted."

Gabe shook his head. "How did you get involved?"

"Just plain rotten luck." She winced when he touched the pad to a cut.

He finished cleaning the minor scratches and abrasions and then turned to Big'un. The cat looked pitiful with rhubarb smeared fur. Big'un blinked as if to say, "My life is miserable." After a cursory exam, the doc smiled. "No broken bones." He glanced at Annie. "He's using up his nine lives pretty recklessly."

"I'm afraid he was an innocent bystander." She gazed up at him with such confidence that guilt immediately struck him like a ball bat. She took everything he said as gospel. And he had misled her.

The past few days he'd been considering telling her the complete truth. That the past few days had been a joke, at least to him. When she'd brought Big'un in the day he was hit by the buggy, he'd had concerns about the pet but nothing major. The ruse to have her come back every morning was entirely a man's way of wanting to see a woman again. He wasn't a man to toy with a woman's emotions, but right now, seeing the glowing light of adoration in Annie's eyes, he realized his little joke had suddenly turned into a serious blunder. Not all women had a sense of humor, and while Annie's humor seemed to be intact, she was clearly a woman who did not appreciate ruses. At least not the kind he'd concocted. Yet his tongue refused to cooperate.

He changed the subject. "There was a ruckus at the saloon, you said?"

She nodded. "Two women wresting on the ground like bullies." She winced and touched the nail scratch on her forehead. "Poor Pastor Sterling's rhubarb pie."

"Pastor Sterling was there?"

"No, but his pie was." She sighed. "And I used the last of the rhubarb."

"Well, fall's approaching. You can make a pie from late summer fruit. I'm sure the pastor will understand, and you can make it up to him in the rhubarb department next spring." Gabe stepped to the small water basin and washed his hands.

"Oh well." She carefully eased off the exam table. "Big'un keeps life interesting." She turned to face Gabe. "I guess you'll want us both back in the morning?" Her tone held a hopeful note.

He reached for a hand towel. "I've been thinking. There's no longer any reason for you to bring the cat by every morning, and you're fine." He flashed a melting smile. "No need to put you out."

Her expectant expression froze. Recovering quickly, she touched the small of her back. "Oh dear."

He frowned. "Did I overlook something?"

"Well. . .it's nothing, really." She smiled weakly. "Just this tiny pain. . .slight, but pain nonetheless."

"Where?"

"Here." She touched the small of her back. "And here." Farther down her side. "Nothing, I'm sure. It's just a bit of discomfort."

"Really?" He helped her ease back on the table. "I'll have another look."

She maneuvered back to the table. His professional touch went over the areas he'd previously examined. "Nothing appears to be out of place. You might have a simple sprain."

"Oh? Is it serious?"

"No, but you'll have to take it easy for a few days. Cold compresses every few hours should help. I can give you some liniment to apply several times a day." He took her hand and helped her to a sitting position. "Should heal nicely in a few days."

"But I need to come back," she prompted.

"Not unless you feel that you're not making any progress."

Her smile faded. "You don't want to see Big'un anymore?" Her injured tone suggested that he was trying to brush her off.

Leaning on the edge of the exam table, he crossed his arms. "There's no medical need to see either one of you. With the exception that you and Big'un are going to be mighty sore for a while, you're both fine."

The light faded from her eyes, and the observation puzzled him. What do they say about lying? It takes two to cover one? As much as he would like, he wasn't misleading her now, but she appeared to take the truth as an unmistakable sign that his previous interest had waned. He leaned closer. "You're welcome to stop by and have coffee any time you like."

"No." She worked her way gently to her elbows and off the table. "I couldn't take up your time." She straightened and set her jaw in a determined line. "Thank you for all your help—and Big'un thanks you." She picked up the cat and cradled him in her arms. "What is the charge for today's service?"

"Nothing. I didn't do anything."

"Thank you. Have a good day, Doctor."

"Annie," he pursued softly. "I would like it very much if you would stop by and visit." He could see that he'd hurt her feelings. Had she guessed that all the early morning visits hadn't been required and merely played along because the occasions gave her joy too? He could only hope that was the case.

When the door closed behind her, he had a definite feeling that she wouldn't be coming around anymore.

"You can be honest with me, Big'un. What did I do to lose his interest?" Annie cradled the cat to her chest and limped to Mrs. Helprin's. Dry dust kicked up beneath her bare feet. Moisture hadn't fallen in weeks and the tiresome heat was a bother, but not as worrisome as why the doctor had so quickly lost interest in her. She hadn't mistaken the captivated look in his eye, and she surely wasn't fooled by the daily visits to his office. The baked offerings and beef swimming in potatoes and carrots hadn't bothered him. Fried chicken and noodles were always heartily welcomed, so what could she have done?

It was her weakness for going barefoot. She was too much of a tomboy for his tastes. He'd discovered that when she appeared shoeless at his office every morning. Tears brimmed her bottom lashes. Well, a man should love—or at least like a woman—for who she was, not who he'd like her to be. Too much fuss was made over footwear—unless there was snow. God made feet to walk on, not emphasize. She'd told the doctor right off she didn't wear shoes. Besides, what possible difference could her wearing shoes make to him? Other than he liked fancy women, the kind he knew in St. Louis. Successful, smart women who wore pretty dresses and stylish shoes.

Annie wasn't dumb, but no one would ever accuse her of being scholarly. Being scholarly would surely require wearing shoes, and to her knowledge there wasn't a single extra-smart person in Edgar's Cove. Some brighter than others, but no one had completed school except for one—and that was Annie Lawson. As long as the ferry ran, Mr. Helprin had accompanied her across the river and the buckboard ride to Flippin, where she attended a tiny one-room school with nine other boys and girls. Some mornings she and Whit left early to fish for an hour or so before the ferry left, if weather permitted. Those hours were some of the happiest memories of her life. Whit was stern—he made her bait her hook and clean her catches—but the lively twinkle in his lake-blue eyes held such love that Annie never felt deprived of anything.

Summer nights, they would sein minnows at the mouth of the river, their net filling with enough fish for a good fry, or they'd wade for crawdads, dragging a large net between them. Sometimes they would play a game. They'd pretend they were the twelve apostles the Bible spoke of, dragging in their loaded nets.

Or they would discuss baseball, one of Annie's favorite subjects—and yet another tomboy peculiarity. Mr. Helprin favored Excelsior of Chicago, while she knew every

Cincinnati Red Stocking by heart. As they worked the points with their net, they talked scores and how one player could out bat and outrun the other. Annie allowed that the Washington Nationals had been a team to contend with back when Arthur Gorman was their second baseman, but no one, absolutely no one was as bad, or as good as her Cincinnati Red Stockings. They could outrun, out bat, and out spit every one of Whit's silly ole' Excelsiors.

Annie sighed. The Red Stockings folded the same year Mr. Helprin died. At first it was too painful to listen to baseball with all the memories tied up with Whit, but she couldn't abandon her love of baseball forever. So last year she'd started following the St. Louis Brown Stockings, a new team that showed great promise. And she could name each and every one of the Brown Stockings, as well.

Her thoughts travelled back to her school days. Annie had graduated when she was fourteen. So she supposed she was the most educated person in the cove with the exception of Dr. Gabe.

She unlatched the gate and set Big'un on the ground. The cat gave himself a shake and fluffed up before he plodded toward the back porch. Undoubtedly his pride was more than a little bent today.

With a sigh, Annie glanced back in the town's direction. What had she done to lose the good doctor's interest? Or better yet, what could she do to regain Gabe Jones' attention?

Or better than that, why would she give a fig?

She let herself into the kitchen, fixed two big butter-and-blueberry jam sandwiches, and moved back to the porch, where she ate both of them.

Chapter 4

Fading summer days grew shorter and hotter in the cove. Annie kept busy with her usual schedule, now minus the daily morning visits to the doc. She had to admit she walked out of her way to avoid his office, and with every passing day she was forced to admit that she missed the appointments. Well over two weeks had passed since she'd sat on the office front porch and shared a cup of coffee with Gabe. Time hung on her hands. Saturday morning, she collected Mrs. Owen's laundry and dropped off Mr. Pierson's supper early before she wandered toward the ferry. The river conveyance was the common rope ferry that consisted of two heavy hemp cords stretched across the river opening to the opposite side. Shepard, with his mighty arms, pulled the wooden raft to the opposite side and then back by using the stretched rope.

The black man glanced up, his whittle knife in hand when she approached. The man was gifted with wood. He could take a twig and fashion it into a delightful flower for smaller children. "Good morning, Annie. You needing to go to the other side today?"

"No." She sat a cane pole and can of worms on the tip of the ferry bow. "Thought I'd do a little fishing, if you don't mind company."

"Mind?" He flashed a wide grin. "Always welcome your company, missy. Business been slower than cold molasses today."

"It's too hot to stay indoors." She settled on the bow, setting the can of worms beside her. Flies buzzed her head. "Thought I'd catch a batch of sun perch for Mrs. Watson."

"That so? Miz Helprin must be fixing' to come back real soon now."

"Not for a while. Her last letter said that her sister wasn't doing well, so she might decide to stay through fall."

He shook his head. "Real sorry to hear that. Her sister's younger than Miz Helprin, ain't she?"

"By several years." Annie threaded a hook with bait. "Doesn't matter. I can handle things here for as long as she needs. But she'll sure hate missing the area ball game." Flippin versus Edgar's Cove. The biggest event of the year. The cove always lost, but that didn't stop the excitement for the game that built all year long. "Ada loves baseball about as much as I do."

"That she does," Shepard agreed. "Sure been hoping we could find someone to replace ole Jimmy. He's not been looking real good lately."

"Really?" Annie sighed. "Well he is what—eighty-seven? He can barely throw a ball, and then there was that unfortunate incident with the mayor last year."

"Yeah, that was pitiful. Poor mayor was laid up for a spell."

"Jimmy can't throw hard, but when you take a ball straight to the noggin like the mayor did, there's bound to be consequences."

"Well. . ." Shepard paused and studied the carving. "Long as Miz Winslow makes it back by winter. This old ferry won't be running much during bad weather. The Mississippi has been known to freeze over."

"Honest?" She couldn't imagine the oddity—not sitting here, with the hot sun beating down her back. She'd seen small icy patches deep in the back coves during the latter part of January, but the whole river frozen over? Hard to conceive.

The older man chuckled. "Mary Watson sure does like her perch. I took her a batch last week, and nothing would do but I stay and have supper with her." He leaned back and continued with his project. "That woman can cook. Her cornbread makes you think you're in a different world."

Annie grinned. Shepard had a way of cheering her up, even when she was in a gloomy mood. She fished in the can of dirt and pulled out a second fat worm. "Men. All you think of is your stomachs."

"Well now I don't rightly think that's so. I think of lots of things."

"Like what."

"Like, what's on the other side of the ferry."

"You know what's there. Just a rutted road that leads to Flippin Barrens, where there's a general store, flour mill, and cotton gin. You've been down that road a hundred times in your life."

"I mean beyond Flippin. What's beyond there?"

"Beyond Flippin? I have no idea." She carefully threaded the second worm through the hook.

The older man chuckled. "Why do you always fish with two worms?"

"I like fat bait." They shared another moment of silence before she said, "I've never thought much about the world beyond the cove. Why would anyone want to live anywhere but here, where large oaks, persimmons, and cedars line the banks? And so peaceful—Shepard?"

"Ma'am?"

"How come you've never married?" He wasn't real old. His hair was completely white, but his arm muscles were thick as cord wood from pulling the ferry.

The tip of his knife shaved thin strips of bark. He didn't answer for the longest time, and Annie thought she might have gotten too personal. No one in the area knew much about Shepard. He ran the ferry and had made his home in a small shack along the banks for as long as she could remember. Folks said he was a loner. Annie always thought that he just looked lonely. Finally, he said, "I had a woman, once."

Annie glanced up. "What happened to her?"

He shrugged. "Just wasn't meant to be, little one."

"Did she leave you?"

A white smile flashed. "No, it was a mutual parting. She's a fine woman—made someone a fine wife. That man just wasn't me."

Annie paused. "I'm sorry."

His dark eyes fixed on her. "Me, too. I think we'd have been real good together."

Annie stood up and threw her line in the water. "Is she still around?"

"You ask a lot of questions for a young'un."

"I'm not so young. I'm sure everyone in Edgar's Cove considers me a spinster. I'll be twenty-three come January."

"Is that right. Twenty-three." He chuckled under his breath. "That old."

"How old are you?"

"Old enough to know you don't ask a person's age unless they volunteer it, but I don't mind giving mine. I'm forty-seven and right respecting of ladies that speak their minds."

Forty-seven. Nearly dead. But he looked healthy. Annie supposed she spoke her mind, but that wasn't anything new to Shepard. From the time she could toddle, she had visited the ferry, with Mr. Helprin chasing after her. Shepard was a lot younger then, but he was her friend. A loyal confidant. One with whom she could confide her deepest secrets and wistful dreams. He knew her about as well as anyone did in Edgar's Cove.

Horseflies buzzed the ferry bow. The sun beat down. Before long the leaves would begin to turn glorious reds, browns, coppers, and yellows. Annie longed for the mild afternoons and cooler nights when fog crept across the land and cradled the river with gentle fingers of mist.

"Shepard?"

"Yes'um?"

"Do you like the new doctor?"

"Well now, he's not rightly ours, yet."

"You know what I mean." It would be nice if Gabe decided to put down roots in Edgar's Cove but highly improbable. "I mean do you like him?"

"Seems like a fine young man. Why do you ask?"

She shrugged. He seemed more than fine to her. He seemed exceptional, but Shepard had a fine sense of people. He could say right off if they were good or bad.

"Do you like him?"

"Yes—I do. Very much."

Shepard's eyes fixed across the river. "Shore do wish I knew what lay beyond those banks." His tone held a bit of winsome longing. "Other than Flippin. Been to Flippin once, long time ago."

"Why don't you see for yourself?"

He shook his head. "No need. Just nice to think and imagine what the world's like outside of this cove."

"I hear it's big. Very big. Gabe told me about attending a real baseball game with his father last year—the St. Louis Brown Stockings."

"Which happens to be your favorite team."

"I adore the Brown Stockings. Anyway, Gabe said the air was so full of excitement that day that it was practically like breathing lightning—probably a couple of hundred people there." She glanced at Shepard. "You would have liked that."

"Yes. I've heard such stories, and I would surely enjoy seeing something like a real baseball game." He flashed a grin. "Like to see one with you, young'un. That would be a sight and sound to behold. The way your eyes light up and your mouth turns up at the corners when you talk about the players." His gaze grew distant as though he was sitting on wooden benches, right there in a ball field, watching professional players batting, running bases.

Once a month, Mrs. Winslow got her copy of the *Town Crier*, and Annie diligently followed the St. Louis Brown Stockings. They were a new team and made their fair share of mistakes, but she liked their fighting spirit.

Shepard's voice broke her thought pattern. "The doc hails from St. Louie. Did the good doctor get to see Ned Cuthbert play? I've heard it said that man can cover third base quick as a hummingbird. Did the doc mention who played the night he got to see them?"

"He did!" She'd been so impressed with the lineup that her head whirled when

Gabe had named the players. "Dutch Dehlman, Dickey Pearce, Joe Battin, Bill Hague, Tom Miller, George Washington Bradley, Ned Cuthbert, Jack Chapman, and Lip Pike. All of them starters that night."

"My my. You do know the game, and you have a fine memory."

She shrugged. "I love baseball. I wish I could see a real game someday."

"The men play baseball here in Edgar's Cove every fall. You see that."

"Oh flitter. That doesn't count. Most of the men are as old as Methuselah. Every last one can't get out of bed for a week afterwards, but Gabe said that the pro game was exciting." She realized she spoke with such enthusiasm that Shepard must think she was a ball fanatic, which, of course, she was. Everything Gabe said that morning offered a glimpse of a slice of life she never experienced.

"Uh-huh." Shepard held up the carved wood and blew off the shavings. "Sounds like someone and the good doctor get along real well."

"Actually, we're not friends." She fixed her eyes on her bobber lying listlessly in the water. "I thought we were, but apparently his attention has wandered elsewhere."

"You been taking Big-un by his office every morning?"

"I was, but not anymore. He said I didn't need to bother."

"That right?" Shepard shook his head. "Don't know why he'd say something like that. Seems I heard rumors about a nasty rhubarb pie accident a few days back."

Annie sighed. "Oh that. The doctor must think I don't have the sense God gave a goose. There was this fight between two women in front of the saloon—"

He nodded. "Heard all about it, several times. You dropped the rhubarb pie on the cat—"

"The pie was knocked out of my hand, and I accidentally spilt the contents on the cat, like anyone would that was confronted by two shameless women rolling around on the ground, pulling each other's hair out."

"I stand corrected." He flashed a long-suffering grin and inclined his head. "Something just got your bait."

By the beginning of the afternoon, Annie had produced a stringer of five perch and a small bass. Shepard shared his cheese and bread with her, and they ate lunch under a tall sycamore. A light breeze sprang up, and Annie found herself loitering, not yet ready to leave the fishing hole. The day had been so pleasant, but she should go and let Big'un out for his periodic outing.

"Is that Verdean coming down the hill?" Annie didn't know how Shepard would know, since he had a straw hat propped over his nose to shade his eyes.

Squinting, Annie watched the woman in a flowery dress coming toward the ferry, carrying a basket. "It's Verdean, all right."

"Can't imagine she'd need the ferry. She just crossed the river a couple weeks back."

The matronly figure made good time, waving now to draw attention. Her bonnet strings swung with the exertion. "Yoo-hoo!"

Shepard sat up and adjusted his hat. "Afternoon, Ms. Verdean. You needing to cross the river?"

Verdean shooed a fly. "Not today, Shepard. Thank you, though. I'm looking for Annie, and here she is!"

Annie stood up and brushed crumbs off her overalls. "Something you need, Verdean?"

"Not me, dear. There's something I wanted you to have. Lo and behold, when I went to the garden earlier I discovered my rhubarb was still putting off plants. Very unusual for this time of the year and especially since it's so dry, but I recalled you were taking a rhubarb pie to the pastor last week when you encountered trouble, so I said, 'Verdean, Annie needs that rhubarb more than you do—or more than your waistline does. You can just wait for the next crop.'" She giggled. "Anyway, I'm sure the pastor needs the sweet more than I do, so please make the reverend another pie. He so enjoys rhubarb anything." She extended the basket that she carried.

Annie knew the fact to be true. During the season, rhubarb jelly, pies, cupcakes, and relishes lined the small church entryway. Ten times more rhubarb than any one human could eat was afforded the pastor, but somehow Henry Sterling managed to get it all down. The man should be sprouting stalks. "Thank you, Verdean. I'm sure the pastor will be thrilled."

"Not a problem." Verdean released a whoosh. Removing a cloth from her basket, she dabbed her forehead. "While I have you, is there any truth to the rumor that Imogene Raines is going to resign her position?"

"Imogene resign?" Annie hadn't heard Imogene mention a word about the thought. Imogene would have to be carried out of the building kicking and screaming if she ever relinquished her positions of laying out the Keno cards and making coffee.

Verdean lifted a kohl brow. "Are you sure?"

"Positive. I'm certain that Imogene hasn't mentioned anything to me about leaving the position." If Verdean asked once, she'd asked Annie five times a year if there were any truth to Imogene giving up anything. The ninety-year-old killjoy would officially resign the day the elders carried her box to the small cemetery back of the church and not a moment sooner.

Verdean's features screwed into grim resignation. "That old heifer."

"Verdean!"

"Well. She's selfish—she should let someone else hand out cards or make coffee for a change."

Shepard cleared his throat. "Verdean, let me walk you back up the hill. It's a bit warm this afternoon, but I need a good stretch."

"Thank you, Shepard." The woman cast a frosty glance at Annie. "It's refreshing to see someone who cares about the elderly."

The ferry operator tucked the woman's arm safely into his side and carefully walked her up the hill. Shepard was such a good man. Whoever had walked away and left that man suffered the greater loss, Annie decided.

She studied the half-dozen stalks of rhubarb in the basket and shrugged. She might have lost Gabe's favor but she was becoming a professional pie baker.

Chapter 5

Gabe opened the door to the office an hour early. Business had been slow the past few days, and the hours crawled past. He'd been warned that Edgar's Cove was dead as a doornail most months, but the thought never bothered him unless he thought about the lifestyle he'd led before leaving medical school.

A doctor's life wasn't exactly sane: babies tended to come during the night, and someone always had a nick, scrape, or bruise to look after. There were the rare cases of an accident or heart failure, but in general doctoring kept him from thinking too much.

Don't let your thoughts go there, Gabe.

He wouldn't. He had gotten good at ignoring the past, pretending it never happened. He coiled his left hand into a fist and stared at the appendage. The sounds of cracking bats and the roar of the crowd filled his senses. The smell of sweat, dirt, the thunder of an expectant crowd. . .

Shaking the memory aside, he walked to his desk and sat down. No paperwork. Charts caught up. No patients for the past couple of days. He stared at the small woodstove and decided the extra heat for a pot of coffee wasn't worth the price of adding more warmth to the room.

Restless, he got up and opened the window to allow humid morning air to drift through. He'd tried keeping the building shut up tight to avoid the worst of the heat, but the ploy never worked. By mid-morning the office was an oven.

He stepped to the window. His gaze traveled Main Street, searching for a familiar figure. *Annie.* She had made herself scarce the last few days. He'd started to let himself feel the past couple of weeks—to allow a small patch of light into his old adversary. Gloom. Life hadn't turned out exactly as he'd planned. Most folks' had not. His mother's words came to him softly, "No use crying over spilt milk. God has a different plan for your life."

At the time, Gabe had resented her words, and those of everyone else who tried to pass the accident off as "God's will" or the standard, "Well, baseball wasn't meant for you. In time, you will look back and see why this happened."

For Gabe Jones, it was the end of the world. His world. The straw that broke the camel's back—every one of those senseless weasel words dug a deeper crater in his heart. Life had gone on. Dad got his wish for a son who had a dependable job. Doctoring was sacred. Every man in the Jones family followed suit except Gabe, who followed his heart and God-given talent.

A mirthless sigh escaped him. And where had his efforts gotten him? Filling in for a community no bigger than a speck on a map until the town could find a permanent doctor. An impossible goal. What person in his right mind would settle for a town the size of a ball field to set up a practice and hang a framed medical certificate that had cost an arm and leg to achieve?

He flexed his left fist, memories stirring, memories he didn't want to revisit. Ever. To the naked eye, his left hand looked fine. No one would ever guess that the hand couldn't squeeze a tomato, never mind a baseball. The feel of a left-hander's signature pitch. A knee-buckling curve that was practically unhittable for left-handed batters. The heart-pounding elation of striking out twelve batters in a row. The sweat-slick leather glove curved in the palm of the hand. . .

His gaze fell on the hard ball he kept on a shelf. A visual reminder of all he'd lost. Not very smart, but he kept it anyway. He walked over and picked up the ball, turning over the leather binding in his hand. The feel in his palm was like an old friend.

He stepped to the window and peered out on the street. Nothing was stirring. A couple of minutes later, he stood behind the building, hidden from public view. Rubbing the ball in his left hand, he savored the familiar feel. Should he? Just once. He wouldn't be accurate, but he'd bet that he could still hit the side of the shed that sat in back of the mercantile. He stood motionless, eye on the shed. He hadn't tried to throw for years. Never permitted himself even near a thread of his tattered dream.

Working his fingers, he loosened the covering, itching to try. He fixed his eyes on the shed, willing the effort. One throw. The roar of the crowd filled his head. The smells. The air of expectation heady in his brain. *One throw, Gabe.* Nobody's watching.

He reared back and threw. His hand stung like he'd touched a hot poker as the sound of shattering glass split the air.

Whirling, he raced back around the building and into the office and slammed the door.

Stupid dreams.

He sat and stared at the wall until he decided moping was not allowed. Maybe he'd take a walk. Stop by Annie's. . .

No, he would be gone shortly, and he didn't want to lead her on. He could easily fall for this winsome woman, but he wasn't ready to settle down. Or maybe he was. He left the office with no plan other than a walk to clear his head.

Annie kept an eye on the clock hanging above the kitchen table. Four-and-a-half minutes and the pastor's rhubarb pie would come out of the oven. Laying a hot pad aside, she stepped to the small mirror that hung over the washbowl and inspected her appearance. She'd taken special care this morning. A clean sprigged cotton dress—nothing fancy but more feminine than overalls. Her gaze strayed from the mirror to the dusty pair of shoes that sat next to the stove. She hadn't worn them since last winter and then only to church. She toyed with the idea of wearing them today.

Of course, Pastor Sterling didn't care if she wore shoes or not—no one in Edgar's Cove minded, but she might decide to take the shorter route to the ferry this morning, and that would mean that she would have to walk by the doctor's office. But then he most likely wouldn't notice if he was busy with a patient. She could walk past fast just so he wouldn't notice her. . .but if he happened to look out the window, she wanted to look her best, which she hadn't since they'd met.

"Oh fritter," she murmured. "Why do I care what the doctor thinks I look like?"

Because you like him. You like him a lot.

She stuck her tongue out at the image reflected in the glass. "What do you know?" She turned away and stepped back to the oven. One peek and she decided the pie could come out a couple of minutes early. The thin brown crust bubbled in the center with delightful aroma. Her thoughts strayed to her not-so-long-ago daily visits with the doctor. She missed his company. He was a good conversationalist, though she felt like she knew very little about him. Most men didn't blather on about their background, but she would have liked to know more about him. He knew everything there was to know about her. Maybe that was the problem: he knew *all* there was to know about her.

She carefully slid the pie onto the counter. This one was even prettier than the last. Pastor Sterling would be pleased. Now to get the offering safely to his house.

A moment later, she backed out of the screen door, gripping the basket containing the hot pie firmly in her hand.

Gabe stepped upon the Helprins' back porch. When he lifted his hand to knock, the door flew open and Annie, carrying a basket, plowed into him with enough force to knock him backward. The basket flew open, and she stumbled out of the doorway, knocking Gabe partially off the two concrete steps. She landed on top of him, hard. The hot pie tipped out of the basket, the perfectly browned crust popped open, and hot rhubarb seeped into Annie's hand when she reached to avert the disaster. Her screams filled the air when the blistering filling burnt the ends of her fingers. Big'un meandered out the open doorway, calmly switching his tail.

The couple struggled to regain footing. In a sea of arms and legs, she finally pushed away and sprang to her feet, wringing her scorched hands.

Gabe regained footing, reaching out to examine the injury. "You're hurt."

She jerked away, horrified he'd caught her in yet another embarrassing blunder. "No harm done, I tripped over the cat."

"You are not fine." He grabbed her hands and peered closely. "You have a bad burn." He grasped her shoulders and turned her toward the doorway. "Where do you keep your butter."

"Butter?" Annie wrung her hand. "You're hungry?"

"For the burn."

"Oh yes—the burn." Her mind whirled from his unexpected presence. Until this moment she had not realized exactly how much she'd missed seeing him. Her entire body managed to catch up with the tingle in her hand as he led her back into the house, fussing over the burn.

He paused and turned to meet her eyes. "I'm sorry, Annie. I shouldn't have stopped by, but when I saw your house I was reminded again of how I've missed our visits."

"I'm happy to see you too. I've missed our. . .coffee visits."

Her heart skipped a double beat when he shifted his gaze from the wound back to meet hers. True repentance shone in the beautiful depths of his eyes. He lifted her slight weight like a child and sat her on the countertop. She nodded toward the butter dish sitting on the table.

A moment later he applied the buttery ointment, his gaze still focused on her. "This is going to take a while to heal."

She nodded, forcing back tears. She had missed him so much. His touch, light and gentle, made her aware that she'd been foolish to try and ignore him. From the moment, he'd stepped into Edgar's Cove, she'd known that he was different—so unique from any man she had met. Catching back a sob, she grinned through a veil of tears. "I'm going to pray the next crop of rhubarb fails."

He made a face. "Perhaps Pastor Sterling would enjoy a nice apple pie."

"Whether he enjoys one or not, that's what he'll get." She winced when the sting deepened. "Thank goodness the pastor didn't know I was bringing a pie this morning."

"I would think the poor man has had his fill of rhubarb."

Annie had noted that Gabe attended church services every Sunday morning, and she was pleased. A godly man was at the top of her list of character traits she wanted in a husband. Twice he'd walked her home and shared lunch with her before they'd decided to avoid each other.

She met the doctor's gaze. "What are you doing here this morning?" Since they'd dodged each other so relentlessly, he was the last person she expected to see.

"Actually, I stopped by to apologize."

"For what?" she asked.

"I'm afraid that you misunderstood my intentions when I said it was no longer necessary to bring Big'un by the office." His smiled. "I didn't mean that you aren't welcome to visit any time."

An enormous rush of relief filled her. "Honest?"

"Honest." He leaned closer, and her breathing quickened. "You, Miss Lawson, are welcome to stop by any time." He bent and lightly kissed her lips.

Her heart was beating so hard she was afraid that he would see the steady *thump, thump* through her dress. She bit her lower lip and softly admitted, "I've missed seeing you."

He leaned in closer, so close she could smell his shaving soap. "Good, because the feeling is mutual, I assure you. And now that we have that settled, can I expect to see you more often?"

Nodding, she smiled. "You may."

Later Gabe washed the sticky pie mess off the porch while Annie changed into clean overalls. The dress would have to be laundered before Sunday. The sun rose higher as the two stepped off the porch steps. Gabe glanced at her. "It's a lovely morning. Would you like to walk for a while?"

Today was Wednesday—senior outing and then Keno. She glanced at the sun and noted it was still very early. The game didn't start until after lunch. "I would love to, thank you."

Side by side they strolled toward the placid river, noting morning wildlife scavenging for breakfast. When they approached the river, she reached for his hand. Without a word, he took hers, and they strolled along the banks. Breakfast smells of cooking bacon and coffee drifted from the stovepipes of still sleepy-looking households.

"I heard something about you the other day," he teased.

"Me? Who would be talking about me?"

"Shepard stopped by the office yesterday."

She paused. "Is he feeling badly?"

"No—nothing like that. He'd picked up a splinter he couldn't extract. He told me you're a baseball fan."

She flashed a wider grin. "Avid. What about you? Do you like the game?" Because if he did, that would make him just about perfect, which he was even if he deplored the game.

"Actually, I do. I'd hope to be a professional player when I was younger."

Her steps paused, and she turned to face him. "Seriously? You play baseball?"

He shook his head. "Not anymore, but I did then. Some folks thought I was pretty good at the game."

"What position?" Excitement filled her voice. If he said pitcher she would die. What if he'd been the likes of George Bradley?

"Pitcher."

Her knees buckled. He reached out to brace the fall. "Hey—whoa. Are you feeling lightheaded?"

"Giddy," she confessed. "I never once dreamt that I would ever get close to a pitcher, let alone actually know one." Pure admiration filled her voice—and the most delicious thrill she'd ever experienced. "Were you. . ." Dared she hope for a total miracle? "Did you play professionally? Were you as good as George Bradley?"

He chuckled. "No, never made it that far, but for a while there had been real hope." A distant look entered his eyes. "I was on a minor team for a couple of years, but dreams can die fast. One day I was helping a man build a front porch. I took my eye away from the board a moment—one brief glance, and severed the tendons in my left-hand thumb—"

She gasped.

"And that was the end of my dream."

She placed her hand on the small of his arm. "You *would* have been as good as Bradley. You and your family must have been crushed."

"I was, but Dad was relieved. Mom never said anything other than, 'Dreams often don't work out for a reason.'"

Annie bit back a negative response. What possible reason could God have had for ending such a promising career? "Oh Gabe. . ." All this time and he'd never mentioned anything about his former dream. "I assumed you wanted to be a doctor."

He offered a mirthless chuckle. "That was my father's dream, not mine."

"You didn't want to go into medicine?"

"I'd never given the subject a serious thought. I wanted to pitch, to feel the ball in my knuckles, hear the roar of the crowd. . . ." The couple started walking again, lost in silence.

Her dream was to one day see a professional ball game; his was to play baseball until his body would no longer allow. Annie couldn't imagine such a worthy dream shattered by the mere miss of a hammer head. Shattering a dream so quickly was senseless to her.

Silence lengthened until Annie realized the subject was still incredibly painful for Gabe to accept. Tension lines in his forehead increased, and she could hear defeat in his tone even when they paused to watch a turkey buzzard hawk dip down, pull a fish from the water, and soar into the heavens. Gabe made some offhand observation, but Annie knew that his mind was lost in the past.

She finally broke the silence. "All isn't lost. You'll set up practice in St. Louis, and you'll be able to see professional games during the summer."

"Maybe," he said.

Seeing a game and being a part of one was an entirely different matter. Annie wasn't about to try and convince him otherwise, but oh how her heart ached for this man. God intended for him to serve others with a gifted skill of medical knowledge. Two plans but only one destiny.

The sun lifted higher. The new day was fully birthed, and the lightness offered new hope. But Annie doubted that Gabe noticed. This day appeared to offer nothing more than painful memories.

And soon, Gabe would leave Edgar's Cove to serve a purpose he didn't choose.

For the first time in her life, Annie's faith was shaken. *Why God, have You taken so much from this man?*

Chapter 6

Gabe opened the office one morning and discovered that while he'd been distracted by a pretty girl by the name of Annie, hot summer days had evolved into mellow golden fall. The sky had turned a deep blue, and the smell of wood smoke in the air embraced Edgar's Cove's autumn splendor. Oaks, maples, and hickories now wore coats of varying colors. Walnuts and persimmons crunched underfoot.

He spotted Mayor Maynard Pulse, the closest thing Edgar's Cove claimed as a town decision-maker, set off at a fast pace toward the office. A brisk wind accentuated his pudgy features as he picked up speed. "Can I have a word, Doc?"

"Good-morning, Maynard. Are your sinuses acting up again?"

"Always," he admitted when he drew closer, "but that's not what brings me here today." He pushed past Gabe and stepped into the office, briskly rubbing his hands in front of the woodstove. "I have a bit of news to share. I received a most promising letter this morning."

"Oh?" Gabe stepped to his desk. "Has the mail come this month?"

"I think Alice just sorted it." Maynard reached into his coat pocket and waved a letter in the air. "Seems we finally have a candidate for town doc!"

It took a moment for the news to register. Gabe frowned. He had thought very little about St. Louis and the practice he'd planned to set up. He'd settled in Edgar's Cove like Big'un settled into a fat pillow for a nap.

"Now, it's just a bite, grant you, but there's an older fella in Kentucky who would like to live closer to kinfolk. He's got some clan over near Big Button, but he'll be closing his practice soon, and he's put out a feeler for this area." The smile faded from Maynard's reddish features. "We sure aren't in any hurry to see you leave, Doc. You've been good to this town, but everyone's agreed that it's not fair to keep you so long from your new practice in Saint Louie." He paused. "You are still planning on opening that practice?"

Was he? Doubts colored his mind. "I have a building reserved."

A grin appeared. "Just wanted to make sure. Of course, if you'd stay we wouldn't give this fella a thought, but seeing how it's only fair to consider your wishes, I'm going to invite him to come for a visit." He folded the letter and stuffed it in his plaid jacket. "That coffee smells good. Mind if I have a cup? The weather's got that nip in the air. Winter's coming on."

"No. . .help yourself to the coffee."

Winter in the cove. Cozy home fires, baked pies, fried chicken on Sunday. St. Louis, on the other hand, would have the finest restaurants, theatres, arts, entertainment.

And baseball on hot summer nights. He glanced around the small office, recalling minor injuries, coughs, sore throats, ague, scared children, and aging adults.

St. Louis would have the same maladies. Tall buildings and traffic jams would line the streets, while the cove could only boast of common folk and nature at its best.

Why had God brought him here, to this community that could only pay him a pittance and share baskets of garden produce and a stewing hen? Once his life held promise; now he was starting to question what he needed as he grew older. Only Annie, in her innocence and simplistic lifestyle, made sense to him. Annie who loved baseball and people. Quiet walks. Baseball. Holding hands while watching the sun set across the river.

For the past few weeks, memories had started fade, flashes of what he'd thought his life would be when he reached this age no longer hurt as much. Nothing made sense for so long, and now he'd ceased questioning God and railing at injustice. For the first time in a long time, he felt at peace in his body.

And now a potential new doctor was coming, and his world was about to change again.

Late that afternoon, Annie propped her bare foot on the examining table and sighed. "Stubbed it hard this time." A raw piece of skin dominated her big toe.

"If you'd wear—"

"Shoes"—she supplied the admonishment for Gabe for the hundredth time— "you wouldn't keep stubbing your toe."

"I'm glad to know that at least your hearing is good." Gabe doused a cloth with carbonic acid and set to work. "This makes twice this month—and the weather's turning cold. When do you put on shoes?"

"Not a moment sooner than I must."

He flicked her nose with the cloth, and she made a face. He paused, then bent and kissed her. She closed her eyes and pulled him back for a longer embrace. Lately touches and kisses came so easy—so welcomed. What would she do when he left the cove? She sensed that he was falling in love with her, but town gossip said a new man was coming to take Gabe's place. Annie carefully avoided asking Gabriel—as she now fondly called him during private times—if he really planned to leave. Other than her growing affection for this man, she had no right to ask his future plans. She knew them. He would continue on to St. Louis, and her life would never be the same.

Gabe and Annie turned when the door opened and one of the town's young women entered the office. She was holding a cloth to her mouth, choking back something.

Gabe finished with Annie and stepped to wash his hands in the small water basin.

"Mrs. Stovall?"

The young lady weakly nodded.

"Still feeling poorly?" The doc reached for a towel and dried off.

Issuing a pathetic groan, the woman promptly threw up on the floor.

An hour later, Susan Stoval and Doc Gabe sat on the office porch step. Late afternoon shadows deepened, covering the town in a mellow autumn glow. Gabe noticed that a sudden error occurred to Annie earlier when she bolted the room with her hand over her mouth.

Susan now sat on the porch calmly eating an apple. Gabe glanced at her. "How do you do that?"

She glanced up. "Do what?"

"Eat—after that sickness you just experienced?"

Shrugging, the girl devoured the apple. "Know what, Doc?"

"No. What?"

"Pregnancy always makes me hungry—and usually sick as a dog."

"I've noticed the trend in expectant mothers."

"Seriously. I know I've not been able to carry three others to term, but this time—this *time* I am blessed. I am sick almost day *and* night."

"You consider throwing up your socks every few hours a blessing."

"No, I consider throwing up my socks a gift." She patted her slight tummy mound that would soon grow fat as a watermelon. "I wasn't sick at all with the others."

Gabe chuckled. "Sorry, I can't make the connection."

"Of course, you can't." She pitched the apple core into a pile of leaves. "You're a man."

"In defense of men, I remind you that we do sympathize with women in your condition."

"Why?"

"Why? Well, there's always the risk of miscarriage at an early stage. Then, if the baby thrives there's often morning sickness, back aches, swollen feet, change of temperament—"

"Moody, unreasonable, paranoid, shrewish. I've heard all the complaints from Eddie, but he wants a baby as badly as I do." She leaned over and threw up the apple. When the spell passed, she straightened. "Do you have another apple?"

"Sorry. That was the last one." *Thank You, God.*

Sighing, Susan leaned back and studied the blue sky. "Sometimes we want something so badly that it ruins our lives when we don't get it. Each time I've lost a baby, I've railed and questioned God. Millions of women have babies every day. Why couldn't Eddie and I have just one?"

Why couldn't God have granted my dream to be a baseball player instead of a doctor? Why am I practicing in a cove in a tiny town? And starting to like it?

Susan sighed. "Just about the time I'd be railing and stewing and doing my best to make God the enemy, another pregnancy would come along. I'd get all excited, forgive God—even compliment Him that He had set things right. And then I'd wake up about eight to nine weeks into the pregnancy, and I'd have my monthly."

Gabe turned to look at her. "Did you accuse God of toying with you?"

"Goodness no. I'm saying God's timing isn't mine and Eddie's timing, but He's really good. Each one of those losses, in some way, made us stronger. More head-strong than ever to have a baby. And then one day I got to thinking. I don't run my life no more than I made the sky blue and the oceans rage. And He's not one of those catalogs you can send away for and order what you want, when you want it. Do you know they have this catalog out now—Montgomery Ward's—that you can order something and they'll send it to you by mail? But you can't order a tiny living soul. Only God can provide those. Well anyway, I told Eddie after every loss, maybe I'd been telling God how to run His business. Maybe, just maybe He knew all along what I needed and when I was gonna get it, and if I'd get out of His face and give Him room, He'd send me exactly what would make me happiest in life, in His time."

Gabe focused on her now quivering lips. "Are you going to throw up again?"

"Yes." She stood up, leaned over the railing, and heaved.

He averted his eyes. "You are truly blessed."

Wiping her hand across her mouth, she nodded. "I'd say. This time, I think He knows I've learned to trust His timing. This time, I'm pretty sure there's a real baby in there." She lovingly patted the small protruding bump.

Gabe got to his feet, stretching. "Well, Susan. I'd have to agree with at least one of your theories."

"Which one, Doc?"

"God is really good. This time, He's sent twins."

Gabe lingered on the office porch long after Susan left and he'd closed the office for the day. There was no rush to get to his room. Darkness came early now, only the overhead canopy of stars shedding faint light on the community. A figure made its way slowly down the empty street, lighting the three oil lanterns that hung on tall posts. When the oil was gone, the town would be dark. Shadowy. Dangerous, without light.

He knew what kept him here on the porch tonight. The slight stench of Susan's sickness reminded him of their talk. The woman's odd but sound theories about God and how she believed that He worked. God wasn't one of those new Montgomery Ward's catalogues. Gabe believed there was a plan for his life, but it was always his plan. Not His plan. Some would say he was going all religious now, pointing out that folks who believed in God believed in fairy tales. Gabe fully trusted that faith was not a fairy tale. For he certainly had never met the man or woman who invented the inner workings of a human body or hung a star or created first breath.

But he had met the Man who, no matter what Gabe wanted, had given him life, and if Gabe were to fully trust that this Man knew him like the back of His hand, it was the correct plan for his life. A specific, tailored map, guaranteed—if Gabe stayed out of it—to be the best course for his time on earth. No, he wasn't mad—resentful maybe—at God for taking the one thing that he loved with all his might away.

With what glorious reprieve had God replaced his dream? A dream so coveted that Gabe had lived his life never considering what he'd do or be when old age replaced youthful exuberance—when a bummed-up left fist couldn't squeeze properly. Here he was, approaching thirty, and he was temporarily living his life out in a community not much bigger than a good-sized gnat.

His gaze skimmed the empty streets. The smells of cooking suppers filled the air. The man lighting the town lamps, had this been his dream—was that God's big plan for him? He knew this man. He was married with six kids and had a handful of grandchildren who called him Papa. Was Papa living his dream? The times he'd been in the office, the man had seemed happy as a lark, praising his good health, his family, and his grandkids. He never seemed impressed with anything that lay beyond the placid shores of the White River. It would seem that all he wanted and needed in life was right here in Edgar's Cove. Gabe wondered if that man knew he was living the life planned for him?

Until lately, Gabe had never considered his wins, only his losses. Never home runs. Only outs. He was serving a community that he was growing to love, with a fetching barefoot woman who loved long talks and quiet summer-evening walks. With each passing day, he grew to love Annie more. His duties were light. He could fish when he wanted, have long talks with friends, and even grow rhubarb, if he wanted. He was in a place in life where he could plant seeds, sink roots, and even improve the quality of life for many. He glanced at his left hand and squeezed. That hand could still feel the silkiness of a woman, still a baby's cries, care for the ill, and pray with the ones who were about to depart this earth.

And he questioned God's judgment about a tattered ball.

Chapter 7

The following afternoon, a fancy-looking dude lugging a valise in both hands walked up from the ferry. The fiftyish-looking man looked and dressed citified. His long, aristocratic nose clearly defined an oval face. With the exception of one detectable silver streak in his dark hair and eyes the color of brackish water, he would be easily forgettable. No doubt, the visiting doctor. Stepping off the office porch, Gabe went to greet the newcomer.

"Have you a grievance against a buggy?" the man snapped. He set the valises down and gave them a swift kick.

When Gabe lifted a brow, the man said. "Those darn things nearly killed me! Haven't you someone who can carry my luggage?"

Burying a grin, Gabe said, "No sir. The cove carries its own belongings."

"My fancy-schmancy son makes those pieces of—" The air turned blue with language. No one used that sort of crass talk but Willis Sorrels when his bad tooth acted up.

"Insisted that I take them." The man went on. "Waste of good upholstery. I'd wager every one of my drawers have a hole in them!" Drawing a deep breath, he asked, "Where's the doctor's office?"

Gabe pointed. "Over there, but the doctor's standing in front of you."

"The devil you say!"

Gabe extended a hand. "Dr. Gabe Jones at your service. And if you'll permit me to hazard a wild guess, I would say that you are the recently retired doctor that wants to be closer to family?"

"I'm as close as I want," the man muttered. "But my kids think I'm getting old and helpless, so they want me 'handier.' " He reached out his left hand. "Harlon Simmons. Dr. Harlon Simmons."

"Doctor." The men shook hands.

Gabe reached for a satchel and received a swift whack on the hand. "Don't touch my things."

"Pardon?"

"I'm not an invalid, yet. I carry my personal effects." He jerked his waistcoat into place. "Where's the nearest boardinghouse?"

Gabe smothered a good laugh. The man was delusional. "The nearest boarding-house is located in Flippin. You'll stay with me."

You would have thought Gabe handed him a rattler. The doctor paused. His nose lifted, and his piercing gaze pursued Gabe from head to foot. "I do not stay with others. I require private quarters, thank you."

"If the town hires you, you'll have quarters. For now, I'm afraid we'll have to share."

The physician stiffened his back. "For the love of. . . Very well. It's apparent this will be a brief visit." He picked up the two satchels, and with the tip of his cane on Gabe's right shoulder, indicated for the doctor to proceed. Onlookers gathered and trailed Gabe and the stranger down the street. Gabe sensed that if the man made it overnight he'd be doing well.

"Number 6!" a crackly voice called.

Several in the church room marked off the number on a Keno card. "You'll have to speak up, Imogene!" Verdean shouted. "If you can't talk loud enough for everyone to hear, you have to quit!"

"Oh, hush up, Verdean." Imogene calmly placed the number back into the wire basket. "Everyone but you heard what I said perfectly."

Annie stepped to the open window to investigate the sudden commotion going on in the street. She spotted Gabe and an older man, followed by a small crowd of curiousity seekers, walking toward Gabe's office.

Clearing her throat, Annie announced to the gathered group, "Jewell? I'm putting you in charge of the game. I'm going to step out a minute."

Annie reached for a light shawl and left the game, welcome for the reprieve. Keno games were like running with bulls. Mean, ornery bulls.

She caught up with Gabe and smiled. "Hey."

"Hey." He paused and introduced the stranger. "Annie, this is Dr. Harlon Simmons."

She extended her hand. "Dr. Simmons. Welcome to Edgar's Cove."

The doctor's gaze dropped to Annie's feet. "Where are your shoes, woman?"

"I. . ." Annie glanced at Gabe. "I. . .don't wear shoes—leastways not in the summer."

"Don't wear shoes?" His harsh gaze pierced her. "Are you daft?"

Gabe reached to put an arm around Annie's shoulder. "She prefers going barefoot. Any law against that?"

"Other than the law of sanity?" The doctor shook his head. "None that I know of."

The entourage continued down the street until they came to the doctor's quarters. The crowd peeled away when Gabe ushered the doctor up the small flight of stairs.

"Good gravy, man! Is a person expected to climb Mount Everest every day?" The doctor puffed.

"If he lives here," Gabe said. He turned to take Annie's hand when she cleared the last step before he opened the door.

Harlon Simmons peered inside. "What's this? A rat hole?"

Over the next days, unusual words for a doctor were heard frequently in his office: "Unbelievable." "Despicable." "What are you, a whiny baby?" "Don't you ever wash your feet?" "Why come to me for a splinter? Dig it out yourself." "You have a bad headache. So what? So do I."

It seemed to Gabe he broke up more verbal spats than the visiting doctor treated illnesses.

By the time the third day rolled around, Gabe's nerves were on edge. When Annie stopped by the office with a large wicker basket and invited him to have lunch, he couldn't get out of the office fast enough.

"Lunch?" Harlon glanced up from the self-portrait he was drawing in ink. "What kind of slop can I expect today?"

"You're on your own today." Gabe flashed a grin and pulled on a light coat. Truth was, not a single woman in town had offered to provide the visiting doc his meal. Not one woman wanted her cooking spoken of in terms of *slop* and *an offense to the bowel*.

Fried chicken and apple pies no longer scented the small office. Those delightful days were gone.

"Am I ever glad you stopped by." Gabe stepped off the porch with Annie, and they started toward the water.

"Some little birdie told me that you might need a distraction today."

"Today?" He laughed. "Harlon Simmons would try Job's patience. Surely you don't think the town will hire him."

"Surely, I don't." She flashed another grin. "They're taking up money right now for a ticket back to where he came from, assuming you don't recommend him."

They walked in silence a bit. Crisp fall leaves lay in dying piles. Colors had started to fade ever so slightly. Soon, shifting seasons' winds would scatter the beautiful artistry across the river, and bare branches would step up to receive winter's howling winds.

Annie waved at Shepard when they passed the ferry and called out, "Lovely day!"

The ferry operator waved back. "Yes'm! Sure is!"

Soon they reached a secluded place that overlooked the river. Annie spread a checked cloth on the ground, and they sat down. "The new doctor. He really isn't right for Edgar's Cove, is he?"

Gabe shook his head. "Truthfully? I can't think of a town who'd want him."

"Gabe," she gently rebuked. She calmly set out the meal. Fried chicken, fresh baked bread, pickles, and beets. "You want to know something?"

"Sure." He leaned back, reaching for a blade of dying grass. He gently ran the stem beneath her nose, tickling her.

"I'm glad."

"You're glad. About what?"

"That Simmons isn't working out."

He feigned surprise. "Hasn't he been the model of patience and understanding to your friends and neighbors?"

"He's been like a popcorn husk caught under our tongues. We can't pick him out or worry him out."

Laughing out loud, Gabe tossed the blade of grass then sobered. "I have a confession."

"You? I can't imagine anything you'd have to confess about." She stuck a pickle into his mouth.

He sat up, gazing out on the river as he shifted the pickle to the corner of his mouth. "When I first came to Edgar's Cove, I didn't have to see Big'un every day. He was fine from the beginning."

Her hand paused, and she looked at him. "You lied to me?"

"I lied to you. At the time, I thought it was a harmless way of seeing you more often. So I lied and said that the cat needed close watching."

She set a bowl of beets on the cloth. "Well, Rumble Dementia is serious."

"There is no such thing as Rumble Dementia."

"Seriously? Well, one must watch a cat closely for the Whiskered Chill. You can't be too careful with that disease."

"The Whiskered Chill. I made that up too."

"You did?"

"All lies. Will you forgive me, Annie? I'm not a man prone to misleading anyone, and a day hasn't gone by when I haven't kicked myself for misleading you."

She paused to meet his gaze. "I will forgive you, if you'll answer me truthfully, now."

He crossed his heart. "I solemnly promise that I will never lie or try to mislead you again."

"Okay, you're forgiven, but do you seriously think I was stupid enough to believe the cat was in danger of anything? Especially those dreadful excuses of looming doom for Big'un? I swear I saw the cat laugh the morning when you ruled out Cat Scratch Fever."

He glanced at her with raised brow. "You saw through the deception?"

"Do I look daft? Of course I saw through the deception, but it's my turn to confess. I *wanted* to see you again."

His gaze softened. "You did?"

She leaned over and bit the other end of the sphere in the corner of his mouth and winked. "Completely," she managed around the pickle. Taking a bite, she wiped her mouth. "And you surely don't think I'm inept enough to stub my toe all these times I've needed your services?"

"You have been injuring yourself on purpose?"

"Our courtship has been rather painful, Doctor. I'm glad we're getting this out in the open."

Drawing her head closer, he kissed her long and hard. "You taste like pickle," he teased when their lips parted.

"Are you sure?" She wrapped her arms around his neck. "Perhaps your taster's off. Maybe you should try again. And again."

"Why, you shameless woman. I believe I will. I have a sudden hankering for pickles."

Food was forgotten in lieu of emotions long withheld.

Later, Annie packed the picnic remains and handed the basket to Gabe as they walked toward the ferry. "Take these to Harlon. He might be grouchy, but I'm sure a chicken sandwich will improve his attitude."

"You're very kind." Gabe accepted the basket but kept his arm around her as they walked to the bank.

"Harlon isn't going to work out for the town. So now we have to start over again."

"It's not my decision, but I fear I'll have a riot on my hands if I recommend the man to stay."

"Do you think he would?"

"I think in many ways, he's a lonely person looking for a purpose in life."

"You're being too kind. I think he is a crotchety old man with a despicable bedside manner."

"Maybe. Or maybe he's a man who hasn't found his place in life."

She glanced up. "You sound more like you're talking to yourself than about Harlon."

"You could be right."

He took her arm and steered her to the right where a weathered bench sat. The seat was put there for Mrs. Plaid who often tired out before she could purchase a needed item and then walk home.

Annie smiled her gratitude when Gabe dropped the picnic basket on the ground and sat down beside her. For a brief moment, the couple stared at the relatively quiet scene. Old man Steward dozed in the rocking chair in front of the barber shop. Edie Smith hurried down the street carrying a parcel wrapped in brown paper—no doubt she'd come from the tiny mercantile. The pleasant air held the faint scent of a tree line being burnt toward the end of town. As far as Annie was concerned, she could sit beside him forever. But a town like Edgar's Cove couldn't hold a man with Gabe's experience.

Annie turned to Gabe. "Since we've been confessing to each other, I want you to know that I've been thinking about what you told me about your injury and how it ended your baseball career. Funny how God works. If you had fulfilled your dream, we would never have met. You would never be here in Edgar's Cove."

She leaned back against the bench and focused on the view of the water. "Perhaps God does have a better plan for your life. What you are doing is so worthwhile, so important. You make a difference in people's lives."

He shrugged. "I was bitter for a long time, but if I couldn't please myself, I decided to please my dad, so I went to medical school. Lately God's been teaching me a bit about His plans and mine."

"You can't play ball at all?"

He lifted his fist. "Last time I threw a ball, I shattered a neighbor's window."

She sat up straight and sucked in her breath. "Did *you* break Mr. Moore's window!"

"I broke someone's window." He fished in his pocket and took out a bill. "Please give this to Mr. Moore and apologize for me. I was too embarrassed to knock on the door and explain."

She absently tucked the money away. "I'll think of something to tell him so he won't feel badly toward you."

"I would appreciate that."

A light slowly dawned inside her. Maybe Gabe wouldn't be an ace, but he would surely be better than Jimmy Denton. She slid a lowered lid look in Gabe's direction. Perhaps—just perhaps—this year the Lord had seen to work in a very mysterious, unimaginable way.

"Gabe—"

"No. Save your breath. I will not pitch for the annual ball game."

"How did you know what I was going to ask?"

"Lucky guess." He gave her a stern look. "I know how your mind works, and the upcoming ball game is all people can talk about."

"But—"

"But no. I mean it, Annie. I purposely haven't talked much about my previous occupation because I knew you would try to bolster my esteem by having me pitch in place of Jim Denton."

She sucked in a disappointed breath. "You knew about Jim and the game?"

He gave her a dubious look. "Everyone that comes into the office tells me about last year's game. Seems stuck in folk's brains."

"We lost 36–0. Edgar's Cove has never won a game against Flippin."

"Sounds like the team was never in the game."

"Very funny."

"And the cove would be in worse shape if I pitched." He reached for the picnic basket. "Unless I'm mistaken, I see Verdean sitting on the office front porch. I need to go."

Annie reluctantly stood up and trailed him into town, but the wheels in her mind churned. Gabe *could* pitch. Maybe not professionally, maybe not accurately, but she'd bet if he'd been good once, he'd still be good enough to pitch for Edgar's Cove.

Chapter 8

The end arrived swiftly for the potential new doctor.

"Lord almighty, woman! Your feet are the size of tug boats."

Gabe had turned to shoot a warning look at Harlon. The rather stout woman sitting on the examining table dabbed a hanky to her watery eyes. "You don't have to be so mean. I inherited my feet from my old Grannie Ruth."

"With feet this big, no wonder your bunion is the size of an onion." Harlon glanced up and grinned. "I'm a poet and don't know it. You've heard of Henry Wadsworth Longfellow?"

Gabe stepped to intervene. "Harlon, would you mind checking with the postmaster? I think I heard the Pony Express rider come through. I'll finish up with Mrs. Grant."

Harlon straightened, his eyes flashing umbrage. "I am perfectly capable of taking care of my patient. If you want the mail, you get it."

Gabe gave the patient a sympathetic eye and turned to leave. Harlon Simmons would be on the next ferry. The man was not only unacceptable for Edgar's Cove, but he made Gabe so mad he wanted to spit. It would be a cold day in a fiery furnace before he'd let this town suffer one more day with the likes of Harlon Simmons.

He left the office and stalked to the mercantile. A gust of wind followed him into the building. "Afternoon, Alice."

"Hi, Doc. Guess you saw the mail arrive." The woman stepped to a wire cage. "Expecting anything special?"

"No, just needed a breath of fresh air."

A grin lined her face. "Office a bit stuffy today?"

"Too stuffy. I plan to open the window when I go back."

Her eyes lit. "Seriously? You're not going to stick us with that pious old windbag?"

The tension broke, and Gabe chuckled. "The last thing this town needs is more wind."

"Not Harlon's kind of bluster, for sure." She stepped back to the window and handed him two catalogues and a letter. "Looks like you hit the jackpot today." When she continued to stare at him, he glanced up, raising a brow.

"Annie says you can pitch."

His heart sank. She would tell the whole town. "Used to pitch. Don't anymore."

"You know the whole cove's been praying that you'll reconsider."

"Reconsider what?" He was going to wring Annie's neck like a spring chicken! He'd clearly told her he couldn't grip a ball.

"Been praying about you. We figure the good Lord don't mind us asking for a decent pitcher. Game's tomorrow night, you know. You still have time to think about it."

Leaning closer to the cage, Gabe enunciated. "I don't pitch anymore. I can't." He held up his left hand. "Old injury."

She enunciated back. "You don't pitch professionally."

"I have never pitched professionally."

"Oh, you know what I mean. You were good enough for folks to think you had a future playing ball for a living."

Gabe shook his head. "Thanks for the mail, Alice."

"We don't need much," she continued as he turned and walked away. "Just someone who can get the ball close to the base. Jimmy hit the mayor in the head last year. He was in bed for a week with a corncussion."

"Concussion," Gabe corrected.

"That too," she said. "Anyways, the game's important to us, Doc. We got a real chance this year if you fill in. Are you sure you won't reconsider and help us out?"

"Quite certain, Alice. But thanks for the offer." He opened the door and exited the mercantile, wishing that he'd never told Annie about his old dream.

The thing had turned into a nightmare.

Gabe disposed of the unpleasant task of firing Dr. Simmons and paid for his fare out of Flippin. The last he saw of Harlon, the man was huffing his way down to the ferry, throwing fiery, derogatory remarks at all he passed. A few threw some back.

That night Gabe slept better than he had in years. Relief filled him. He didn't have to leave Edgar's Cove. He would fill in until another doctor could be found. He would lose a few month's rent on the office space in St. Louis, but the thought didn't bother him. He would not leave the cove until they had proper medical care.

The next morning, rain fell from a dark sky. He briefly thought about the town ball game but dismissed it. Nobody would be playing ball today.

Around noon, the sun popped out, and the day's heat started to build. There hadn't been one patient today. If he didn't know better, he'd think the town was shunning him. Trying to force him to the pitcher's mound. Well, the ploy wouldn't work. He'd called Jim Denton to the office yesterday and given him a head-to-toe physical. The gent was old, but his heart beat strong. He qualified to pitch.

Gabe cleaned the office from top to bottom. He was through by eight thirty.

He went outside to sit on the porch, aware that it was going to be a long day.

Around three thirty, the cove sprang to life. Men carrying bats and catcher's mitts made their way to the churchyard, accompanied by women and children lugging heavy wicker baskets. The smells of fried chicken and fresh baked pies wafted to the doctor who was still porch sitting. Even Shepard stopped by, offering a friendly wave. "Come join us, Doc!"

"No thanks, but good luck."

"This town needs more than luck, Doc. It needs an honest-to-goodness miracle!"

By four o'clock, Gabe closed and locked the office door. Unless there was an emergency, no one would be in need of his services today.

He later climbed the steps to his room, ate a cold supper from the remains of last night's fare, and settled down to read a medical journal. By now sounds of the annual baseball game filled the air.

The crack of bats. Cheers. Clapping. Groans.

Gabe glanced at the clock and noted the time. Five thirty. The game would be in the third or fourth inning in natural circumstances. Judging by what Annie had said, Edgar's Cove would be in the process of a merciless beating, lagging behind fifteen runs or more, and Jim Denton's arm would have given out two innings earlier.

The ball game is not your problem.

He turned a page and tried to concentrate. Fifteen more minutes passed before he tossed the book onto the small bed and got up to rummage through the small chest until he located what he wanted. It seemed that he would have to prove to Annie and the cove that he couldn't hit squat, but there was more than one way to win a ball game between amateurs.

And it would seem that Flippin had it coming to them.

He left the room, pulling on the garment before he slammed the door behind him.

Annie had kept a close eye on the ballfield entrance. Gabe would come. She knew he would come. The man she loved would never let her down—or the cove—no matter how loudly he declared that he didn't give a fig about baseball anymore.

She checked her pendant watch for the sixth time. Nearly six o'clock. She glanced at the scoreboard and noted Edgar's Cove wasn't doing so bad. Bottom of the third. Flippin was winning but only by 14–5. She'd seen worse. The earlier rain left a muddy field, and what would have been by now another merciless whooping was simply a pitiful performance by both teams.

"Stop looking for him and pay attention to the game," Shepard said. "He's not gonna show up." The two huddled together on the wood benches. Everyone in the cove but a couple of the oldest residents were in attendance. A light mist dampened jackets and shawls. Seems the weather couldn't make up its mind.

"He'll come," Annie murmured, huddling deeper into her wrap. "You watch. He might talk big and say that he doesn't care about the game, but he does." Annie's faith in the doctor only grew by the moment. She had fallen in love with this man, and once this game was over, she intended to think seriously about what to do about it. But first the cove had to get through this yearly torture.

Bottom of the fourth. Flippin managed a home run and two runs batted in before the umpire, Ray Burrows, called a slide into home plate "Out!" The Flippin player sprang to his feet, and the umpire, both team managers, and the player went head to head in the middle of the field. Fists shook. The Flippin manager walked in circles around Burrows, shouting, his face flushed a deep crimson.

Annie's eyes strayed to the field's entrance, and her heart missed a beat. Gabe stood in the light mist, eyes focused on the argument. How long had he been there? Her eyes focused on his clothing. He was wearing a ball shirt with the words *Minor League* sewn on the right sleeve. Relief filled her, but she averted her eyes to the game. Had he noticed her? She didn't think so. He was too absorbed in the verbal infield feud to notice her.

After a bit, the umpire turned and walked off, leaving the managers and player fuming. The crowd booed loudly.

"Get some specs, Ray!" a man shouted from the crowd.

"You're blind as a bat!" another called.

Ray Burrows turned and booed the hecklers. That's why the blacksmith had been the umpire for every Cove game since Annie was born. Insults rolled off him like water off a duck's back. She risked another glance at the gate and witnessed Gabe slam his glove to the ground. A grin slowly spread across her features. She'd never seen him so much as raise his voice, let alone throw something like a baseball glove. Obviously, he wasn't happy with the call.

If she wasn't mistaken, the Cove had just gained a new pitcher.

Excitement was palatable now as Gabe strode to the pitcher's mound. After a brief exchange with the Cove's manager, Ben Grison, Jimmy exited the field, and from all signs—throwing his ball glove in the air and giving a little jig—appeared to be relieved he was out of the sweat box.

"Well, gotta hand it to you, girl." Shepard turned to give Annie a wry grin. "How did you know he'd come?"

Her grin broke into a smug smile. "Sometimes a girl just knows these things, Shepard."

Gabe's warm-up period was worrisome. His left-handed fastball was still fast— just a bit off course. The first ball slammed into the rickety scoreboard and capsized it. The second ball zipped by the catcher, and part of the crowd scrambled onto the field. Some got up and moved.

Annie focused on Gabe, whispering under her breath, "Come on, sweetie, you can do this." The third ball sailed into the players' section and cleared the bench.

By the fourth ball, Gabe had gained some control. The balls came hard and fast, if not a bit inaccurate. He motioned to the umpire. The scoreboard was erected, and the game proceeded.

Annie noticed Gabe glance up in the benches and focus on her. She waved and lightly blew a kiss from the palm of her hand. "God bless you," she whispered.

He winked. Game on.

Maynard Pulse covered first. Young, skinny Ted Mote thumped his glove on second base. Horace Winslow covered third. Frank Otter planted his feet in left field; Pastor Sterling looked uneasy in center. Annie didn't recognize the man in right field. He must be new to the area.

"Let's play ball!" Ray called.

Annie had heard of wild pitchers. When a pitcher turned wild, even a seasoned player wasn't interested in being hit by a hard, fast ball, but Gabe's fast balls were beyond wild. The following pitches reminded her of popcorn kernels in hot grease. The balls fairly exploded somewhere near but never over home plate—a spot that very quickly was a place to be avoided by all cost.

Gabe drew back and threw the mighty misguided mortars like blistering darts. Flippin players stood so far back from home plate there wasn't much chance of connecting to the ball. A few brave stepped up, popped up, or caught the tip of the ball with the end of the bat.

By the bottom of the ninth inning, for the first time in history, a preteen boy high-stepped onto the field and hung the numbers 14–14. Tie.

The light mist had turned into a heavy sprinkle. Both teams' players were covered in mud. About ten minutes of light remained. Lightning flashes in the northwest outlined a sinister-looking cloud bank.

The Flippin manager called time out, and the two team managers met in the middle of the field.

Grison spoke first. "If we hurry, we can get this ended by the time the storm moves in."

The Flippin manager appeared to stall. "We still got plenty of time. My boys have never lost a game yet." He glared at Gabe. "Threw an ace in on us this year, eh?"

Grison shrugged. "Shucks. The doc claims he's real rusty."

The manager swore. "He's wilder than a march hare! Was he trying to hit my men?"

Grison stiffened. "Our pitcher never hit one man."

"If he had, he would have taken their heads off. He didn't get it over the plate once!"

Grison lifted a shoulder. "He didn't hit anybody."

Ray Burrow's voice interrupted. "Gentleman, we're burning daylight. Do we finish the game or call it a draw?"

Flippin's manager glanced up. "We've never lost a game to Edgar's Cove in our lives."

Burrows smiled. "Then play ball." He turned and started off when Flippin's manager cleared its throat. "Hold on!"

The umpire turned back. "Yes?"

Grison appeared to struggle with a decision. "It's likely going to rain us out. We'll reschedule."

Burrows glanced at the Flippin team. "Want to reschedule?"

The manager thought for a moment. "No. We're good. We need one more out."

Grison said, "It's getting dark. I say we reschedule."

Burrows nodded. "Might not be a bad idea. Hey Doc! You want to reschedule, give you time to polish up a little—didn't I hear that you once were headed for professional baseball?"

"That was a long time ago. Ray, but yeah. I had hoped that I was headed for bigger things."

A gust of wind from the approaching storm front left the men shielding their eyes from flying dust particles.

The visiting manager managed to say, "You're leaving for St. Louis soon, right Doc?"

"Well, I've been thinking about that. I'm considering sticking around here for a while." The pitcher glanced up to the bleachers, where he found a pair of familiar blue eyes riveted on him. "Kinda like the scenery, and I've grown fond of the cove." His gaze pivoted to Flippin. "I'll be around next year, God willing."

The manager's lips curled. "Smart aleck."

Gabe called back. "Flippin? That's 'Doctor' to you."

The man turned away. "Play ball!" He turned back to face Gabe. "We can whip your team any hour of the day or night."

The skies opened up and poured. Gabe's features turned sorry. "Oops."

The manager swore again. "We'll do a coin flip. Heads wins the game."

Ray Burrows shrugged. "You want to flip, Gabe?"

"Please—you do the honors, Ray."

The annual Edgar's Cove baseball game went down in the cove's history books. A tie was as good as first place. A plaque now resided in the small mercantile, hung next to the postal cage:

FLIPPIN VS EDGAR'S COVE 14–14 OCTOBER 3, 1876. WIN GOES TO EDGAR'S COVE. THERE ARE NO LOSERS WHEN ONE HAS HEART.

During the rainstorm, Annie had run onto the baseball field, straight into Gabe's waiting arms. Their mouths came together in an explosive show of recognized love. The crowd scattered and the downpour increased. Thunder and lightning splayed overhead. When the couple came up for breath, Annie whispered in Gabe's ear. "I *knew* you would come."

He kissed her nose, her chin. "Pretty sure of yourself, aren't you, little barefoot Annie Lawson?"

"Surer of you, Dr. Jones."

Their lips met again, and he whispered. "That's Gabe, to you, Annie."

"My sweet Gabe," she whispered. A driving rain drove them to seek shelter. Arm in arm they ran off the field. "Gabe?"

"Yeah?"

"Will you marry me? I know you have obligations in St. Louis, and admittedly Edgar's Cove is a far sight from the big city, but it's a nice. . . ."

"Yes."

Their footsteps paused. She met his gaze in the blinding downpour. "Yes, you know it's a far piece?"

"Yes, it's a far piece, and yes, I'll marry you."

Her eyes lit, and he reached to lay a finger across her lips. "We'll work out the details in a drier place. Annie Lawson, will you marry me?"

"Of course, I'll marry you. I just proposed."

"You did? I didn't catch that. Will you marry me?"

"You don't mind that I don't wear shoes and I'm not ladylike—not like the women you've known in the past?"

"Well, unlike the women I've known who do wear shoes and keep their hair all fussy-like, I am helplessly and head-over-heels in love with you."

She flashed a grin and drew his mouth back to hers, where she whispered, "That's good, because unlike any man I've met, I love you with all of my heart."

"Then we're in perfect agreement."

"Perfect," she said. Just the way God worked out His plan in her life.

Lori Copeland is a popular bestselling author of both historical and contemporary fiction. Her books have been nominated for the prestigious Christy Award, and she received two *Romantic Times* Lifetime Achievement Awards. Lori makes her home in Missouri with her husband, Lance, three sons, and ever growing family. Her hobbies include knitting prayer and friendship shawls and baking chocolate chip cookies.

The Castle
Made of Sand

by C J Dunham

Chapter 1

The sea glass began to glow blue, brown, green, and violet in the rising light of day.

Jennie lay on her bed, hugging her pillow, as her eyes, sandy with sleep, rested on the large pickle jar on the window ledge. It was filled with her treasures collected over the years, offered up by the sea. The pebble-like pieces of glass reminded her of the colors of the human eye, and almost as beautiful, but the action of the ocean had not only polished their rough edges but had also frosted the glass, dulling their once bright "vision."

These were fragments of human history. Someone's hands once held the bottle or dusted the lamp or placed flowers in the vase that was now nothing but remains, a teal shard here, an amber shard there. The clear fragments could have been the porthole of a ship that a sailor had once pressed his hand against as he longed for home. The green ones could have belonged to a piece of tableware that had been a wedding gift once upon a time.

The violet piece she stared at now could have belonged to a bottle of medicine that had kept a boy alive through a bout of fever. It had once been clear, but the mineral manganese that was added to glass to make it clear, ironically, when exposed to the sun, turned violet. So perhaps this boy's medicine had been kept on his window ledge while he lay in bed staring up at it, as she now stared at its last remaining piece. Or so she imagined. Which Jennie did with every waking breath.

But as the winter months progressed, the clouds that overcast the sky seemed to thicken so much that they half blinded the rising sun. Every morning since late January, Jennie watched for the sun to break out of its gray prison and radiate the contents of the jar in turquoise, teal, and navy blue; with brown, gold, and amber; with mint, jade, and emerald; and with the varying intensities of violet.

Ten more minutes passed, and she couldn't bear to lie still another second. Perhaps all the glass, like the once clear violet pieces, were darkening over time from exposure to light, and they would never again glow with the same vibrancy.

With a flourish, she threw back the covers in one billowing sweep. Blast Victoria's fame as the sunniest spot in all of British Columbia! It had become full of creeping shadows and dingy skies.

The blue heron that nested in the spruce outside her window croaked like a toad. A pair of swans honked as they flew by, as if sounding an alarm. Seagulls squawked from the nearby shore. It was a wonder she had slept through it all. She must have been in the throes of an exotic dream to be sure. Waking and forgetting every dream was like wine turning to water as soon as it touched the lips.

Slipping bare feet into a blue skirt made of calico, a fabric not as soft as muslin but not as coarse as canvas, proved her rank. She was neither rich nor poor, at least by her parents' standard. Of herself, society would say she was socially destitute because she was nineteen and still not married. But Jennie didn't care, she was free.

As Jennie had to do all the sewing in the house, it was she who'd made the skirt modern by trimming inches off the hem to imitate the style of the new rainy daisy skirts. Now that bicycling was the rage, hemlines had shortened to three-quarter length. The blouse once had leg-of-mutton sleeves, but she'd also pared them down and cut them off at the elbows. For all this, it wasn't enough, not for Jennie. She added what she called her gypsy scarf, a bright vermillion with a long dancing fringe, around her waist. To her collar she donned a yellow-orange necktie. If she had to be buttoned up to the throat, it would be with a splash of color.

Let the sky be overcast if it must, but she would not be downcast. Out of the tiny room she ran, on bare feet, out the back door of the little cottage and down the garden path.

She'd been born running, at least that was what her mother professed, usually in exasperation. The hydrangeas and peonies, the roses and the lilies and lilacs, were overgrowing their bounds, but rather than feeling guilty over her neglected duty (Mum couldn't see well enough to know the difference anyway) she let her fingers glide over the tops of the flowers, breaking their scents into the pine-scented air, and flew to the edge of the slope she had learned by heart, or foot as the case may be.

At seventeen, when the last of her friends had married, she swore she would defy age, and now at nearly twenty, she bounded with the zeal of childhood over the outcropping of smooth rocks and down the slope of soft beach grass to the shore. Curling toes into the sand, she swung out and around, dancing the part she had played in "The Dance of the Spanish Peasants" during the Queen Victoria Diamond Jubilee two years ago.

"La, da, da, da, dant . . ." She sang out the tune as she swayed and turned, dipped her feet this way and that, as she twisted her way to "her" dock.

Only fifteen blocks away stood the waking town of Victoria proper, Canada. Fort Victoria had only been erected maybe fifty years ago, but already there had sprung up what she was told was one of the prettiest towns in the world. Even as a girl she had needed no comparison to recognize the exquisite beauty of the island with its forested mountains rising in their majesty behind her, the pristine shoreline before her, and the emerald mist of pine trees lining it all.

Victoria Harbor was a mere five miles down the coast, and she could see a veritable forest of ship masts as they pricked the sky. Even so, this little alcove with its weathered dock had remained isolated except for the few residents, like herself, who ventured down the incline to visit.

No sentient being could be too vibrant in her estimation, but this past winter had taken its toll. Where was the Victoria she had always known? Why had the world become lackluster? Pervasive dinginess had settled on the island and refused to release its hold.

Well, it would have no hold on her. She flitted her skirt as she jumped driftwood in a ritual quest for abalone, shells, and sea glass along the wet sand. She stopped short when she spied a fishing trawler moored to the end of the dock. It was a weathered little vessel with white lettering spelling *Sand Crane* across the bow. The gunwale and pilothouse had once been white. No one was on board.

Scanning the coastline, Jennie spied a curious old gent whom she presumed to be the owner of the boat. He was an odd mix of a man. He wore the typical rubber boots, woolen pants, and cotton shirt of a seaman. But his white hair was long and tied back with a leather cord, and a shell-and-abalone necklace typical to the Native women swung from his neck as he knelt at the water's edge in the act of what appeared to be an Indian ritual. His sleeves were rolled high, exposing thick, sinewy arms. The knees of his pants were darkened from the lapping tide as he scooped water up to first wash his hands, and then his face, after which he stood and faced the dawn while reciting a prayer.

The colors of the sunrise were intensifying, and as he was a good distance down the shore, she chose to ignore him and trotted on toward her mark with sand flying up behind her. Bounding up onto the dock, feeling its boards creak beneath her feet, she drew in a great breath as if she could inhale the colors permeating the air.

Gulls swarmed a cluster of rocks offshore. Geese announced their flight as they passed overhead. The tires fastened to the side of the trawler formed a rubbery fender and squeaked as the tide nudged them up against the dock pilings. Flipping her skirt from side to side with the backs of her hands, Jennie waltzed down to the end of the weathered boards, humming a gay tune. Reaching the end, she sat with a poof of the skirt and dropped feet into the brisk salt water. Lying back, she mirrored her breathing with the motions of the tide swells as they rose up and down her calves. The colors of the sunrise at their zenith, she imagined the dark carmine and burnished gold were spreading over her like the most glorious scarf, unknown to even queens or fairies.

This was her ritual, and as unconventional as it was, it often ended with a prayer. Except today. Her legs had hardly adjusted to the cold of the water when something moved across the soles of her feet. Seaweed? But then it nudged her foot. Only one thing could do that, she thought: a sea snake!

Bolting upright, she jerked her feet up and looked down into the water. Through the transparent surface she could make out two black eyes staring up at her.

"What—?" she gasped, before realizing what those dark eyes belonged to—a baby seal! "Well, hello," she whispered, leaning her face down to the surface. It threw its nose up, splashing water. She laughed. "Where is your mother?" It threw its head up, mouth open. "Are you hungry?" The seal pup stared up with forlorn eyes. Jennie waited, watched, but there was no sign of a mother. Sealing was a booming industry here, and no doubt its mother had perished. She reached down into the water, and to her amazement the helpless sea creature let her stroke its nose. Its gleaming spotted skin, small white whiskers, and pleading black eyes were more than she could bear. "Wait here," she whispered, and tiptoed to the back of the boat where she found barrels full of fish in a solution of brine. Reaching in, she snatched up three by the tailfins and slipped back to the end of the dock.

"Bon appetit!" she said, and dropped one, then two fish into the seal's gaping mouth. By the third offering, the seal lunged up out of the water and took it from her hand. It swam a circle then barked for more. "Shhh, shhh. You want me to get caught? Go find some tasty live ones now," she whispered as she leaned down, noses almost touching. It would have taken less than a feather to knock her into the water. "I'll meet you here tomorrow morning. I promise. I have to go now. Mum needs my help. *I* have to work for my food."

The pup's gaze was irresistible. Jennie stuck both feet over the edge and swirled them in the water. The pup swam circles around her legs, rubbed its side along her ankles, and barked. She splashed it one last time. "Oscar," she dubbed. "You look like an Oscar. Tomorrow morning," she whispered, her face close to the water and its eyes, "I'll sneak you some more fish." She rubbed its chin and stood. It watched her walk away before disappearing into the depths.

The old fellow was walking back to the boat. He was tall and lean, and his hands revealed a strong man despite his age. The necklace was concealed beneath his shirt.

"A good morning to you," Jennie said as he approached. His beard was white and crusted with salt from dried ocean spray. How apropos, she thought, as he didn't reply or smile, just like a crusty old man.

Climbing up to the rocks, she paused to look out over the cove and saw the shine of Oscar's dark eyes peering up above the water farther out to sea. She waved to the pup. It barked as if in reply. That old curmudgeon could take a lesson or two from the seal, she thought, as he bent over his rigging. She turned one last circle, as if to wrap the dying colors of the sunrise around her one last time, and ran back to the cottage.

The screen door banged behind her. No sooner had Jennie stepped inside then she stopped in her tracks. Something was wrong.

Chapter 2

Thomas plowed up the plush staircase to the third floor of the opulent office building. He snarled at the gold plate on the eight-paneled mahogany door that read "Gallivan Shipping and Exports, Inc., Thomas Gallivan, Sr., President."

Thomas was a striking young man in a starched white shirt, soft gray linen vest and trousers, and matching spats over polished black shoes. Neither tall nor short, he had a pleasing frame and visage, and a dynamic smile when he wasn't fuming. His most remarkable feature was his eyes, a light gray that could change in color from blue to green, much like the moods of the sea. He kept his dark wavy hair a tad too long, his face clean-shaven; anything to set himself apart from the man he most despised—the one behind the door. Grabbing the gold knob, he broke into the office.

The president was dictating a letter to his secretary until she looked up with a start. Mr. Gallivan turned to see the source of the interruption. One look at Thomas and he threw his notes down on the large desk, also mahogany. If he wasn't impressive enough in Rothwell trousers, vest, and jacket, the barrel-chested man with close-cropped hair, long white sideburns, and a simmering glare in his dark eyes made him look every bit the business magnate as he stood before the broad windows that overlooked the San Francisco harbor—and his fleet of schooners steaming off into the open waters.

"What are you doing here?" he bellowed.

"I made it perfectly clear, Father." Thomas charged into the room. "I'm not going back."

"Your mother doted on you," his father snarled.

"Leave her out of this," Thomas yelled, every muscle in his chest tightening.

His father came around the desk at a charge. "You will continue your studies, and you will not step back in this town until you do!"

"What made you think I would ever want to work for you?"

"Whatever made you think I care what you want? Have you learned nothing? Life isn't about what you want. It's about duty. Family duty. And like your brothers, you will do yours."

"Except they wanted to do their duty. They always wanted the sea. I never wanted to run your legal affairs, have anything to do with you or this business. I graduated summa cum laude, and I did it for Mother. If I were you, I would get a refund on that tuition while you still can. I am not going to Harvard Law, I'm going to make my own way."

"At what?" his father roared, half with laughter. "You will be on that train in"— he yanked on the fob, pulling the watch out of the vest pocket—"three hours and twenty minutes, or you will be making your own way—on the streets." His father stormed over to him and continued his amplified verbal assault, gaining volume, almost spitting. "If you do not graduate the top of your class at law school, you will not have access to the manor or my bank account. You will not have your own valet, you will not have that Renault Voiturette, you will not have, in a word, a life!"

Thomas glared up at the imposing man, matching hot gaze for hot gaze in a long silence. At length he sighed, as if in compliance. "Fine. I'll be on that train," he said, and exited the room post haste. He could hear his father's voice continue his dictation with great satisfaction.

Chapter 3

"**M**um?" Jennie called out, sensing something was dreadfully wrong. "Papa?" There was no reply. The cottage was devoid of movement, voices, or the smell of sausage and eggs cooking on the gas stove. This was so uncharacteristic of Mum that it was alarming. And where was Papa?

The darkness that pervaded the small dwelling became disorienting. Jennie ran her fingers along the wainscot as she moved down the hall, as if a carefree gesture, when in fact it was to steady herself.

Over the past winter the house had become almost unbearable, as if the gloominess had seeped in through the cracks and corners. Her mother scolded her for wasting candles during the day, but she'd felt desperate for a light to focus on. It was just her luck that the ensuing summer had been unusually overcast as well.

"Mum? Pa? Where are you?"

"Here," returned a soft alto voice from the kitchen.

"Mum?" Jennie said again as she stepped through the doorway, shocked to see her mother just sitting at the wooden table, no bowls of flour for the day's bread and biscuits, no plums or currants for jam, though she'd had Jennie pick them for her yesterday. Even though Martha Farrow had progressively lost 70 percent of her vision, she loved to cook. The worse her vision became, the more time she'd spend in the kitchen, until she was there from dawn to dusk cooking and baking. And so, Jennie spent afternoons taking the abundance of loaves and baskets of biscuits to neighbors and poor members of the congregation.

"No deliveries today, then?" Jennie asked with a careful tone, coming slowly into the shadowy kitchen. "I woke myself today," she offered, hoping for an explanation of her mum's peculiar behavior. Mum only offered a weak smile. "Did Papa leave already?"

"I'm not feeling well today, Jen. Your father had bread and jam. I sent him off early." Even ill, which was rare, her mother didn't like to be fussed over. Her parents exemplified the two *P* words Jennie despised: *practical* and *pragmatic*.

"I'll make you some tea with milk."

"We're out of milk." Her mother sat with her hands buried between her legs in a deep fold of her dress.

"I'll ride into town and get some. I'll do a delivery to you for a change." Jennie smiled her reply.

"Yes." Her mother's eyes brightened. "I would like that."

"At last! I get to do something for you! I'll be back within the hour to put you to bed with tea. I'll make bread and fix eggs." As she turned to leave, her bare foot landed in a cold puddle of water. Had she tracked it in? No, her feet were dry when she'd entered. Looking down, squinting, she saw water dripping from the tray under the icebox. Jennie couldn't remember a time when it had overflowed; Mum always emptied it first thing every morning. "I'll empty the ice tray," she said, and was concerned when her mother made no response. She lightly touched her mother's brow. No fever. Mum took her hand and patted it.

"I'm fine. I'll empty it." With an affectionate shove, she quoted Jennie, saying, "Go fly on the wind. Perhaps today the sun will be so bright it will break open the sky." She motioned to the lump under the hand towel. "Take the leftover bread to Rachel Lu. Tell her I'm sorry, it's all I have."

"And when I get back—"

"You'll do your chores." Her mother cut her off. "And trim the garden for a change—I can smell the weeds overtaking the flowers—and play your songs ten times each."

"You mean your songs," Jennie complained.

"No, I mean your songs. Those ragtime pieces may be fun, but it's the hymns that will give you strength." Hymns were synonymous with scripture for Mum. In fact, they were psalms, prayers set to poetry and music. "And put your shoes on."

"Mum!"

"Don't 'Mum' me, child. You know what your father says."

Jennie grabbed her slippers and flew out the door, barefoot. "I have my shoes!" she called back, waving them over her head. She dropped them, with the bundled bread, into the basket of the bicycle, then hopped on the seat and took off for the road. Glancing back, she could see the dark outline of her mother through the kitchen window, head bowed on forearms on the table. Perhaps Mum hadn't slept well last night, that was all.

A recent heavy rain had left wagon ruts in the dirt road, but for some reason Jennie couldn't see them, and they caught at her wheels, nearly throwing her off balance. Feeling clumsy, as if she were on a ridiculous velocipede, she dismissed it as "Just a lark." Life was too grand to be bothered with niggly details.

Choosing the center of the road instead, where there'd be no ruts, she rode so fast the pedals almost got away from her. Down the hill, steep and rough, she threw her arms up in the air to "fly on the wind." The bike hit a bump, and she grabbed the handlebars just in time to keep the bike upright and laughed merrily.

She rode past James Bay and its flotilla of yachts and clubhouses, past charming driveways and the large homes, some of them manors. On she sped, thrilled by the rush of wind and color as morning sun sparkled on the water and made the wavelets prance. On through the neighborhoods, until she shot out onto Government Street and the world of Victoria Harbor opened up in a breathtaking panorama.

On the eastern side, a landlocked harbor full of unfurling sails or billowing steam from boats of every size. Ferries, schooners, skiffs, and even tourists in canoes, rippled across the glittering water. At fisherman's wharf, people were already buying and selling cod, salmon, haddock, crabs, lobsters, or dog fish for oil. Natives and local artisans sold woodcarvings and paintings along the waterfront. Perhaps this was where the ponytailed fisherman got his Indian necklace? But why a woman's? Such a curiosity, but no time to muse on it. Jennie thrust the pedals down with her weight and shot out along the wide road full of horse-drawn wagons and carriages, pedestrians, other bicyclists, and a double-decker bus.

On she flew past the brand-spanking new parliament building. Up on the newly seeded lawn, it sat like a grumpy old barrister; solid, its gaze fixed out over the harbor, the ocean, and beyond to British Columbia over which it regulated all legal affairs of state. It should have been romantic, considering it was built in the Romanesque style with thirty copper domes. Perhaps once the copper turned a lovely shade of green it would look more inviting, but the large limestone blocks made it appear too permanent, too stoic, too imposing for Jennie's taste, except at night when it was lit up with electric bulbs. That was spectacular, when she got to see its profile beaming white and gold against the black of night. But her parents rarely let her out alone at night, and they were too fuddy-duddy to go out with her.

Pulling on the handlebars, turning her back to the water scene, she rode up the hill to the very top, past the shops and offices, past the streetcars, up to where she could get the grandest view of all—of Craigdarroch Castle. It wasn't meant to be a castle, but that's what the locals called the newly erected and enormous mansion complete with its balconies and thrusting turrets. There, the Dunsmuirs, the coal barons and multi-millionaires who owned most of the island, lived atop that lush green hill. A few pretty houses dotted the base like ribbon roses in the hem of a green skirt.

Daydreams are free and private, and as Jennie stood over the cycle, one foot on the high pedal, the other on the ground, she imagined a secret Dunsmuir son was looking out one of those high windows at her, and thinking how extraordinary she looked in her fabulous scarf. Yes, it was childish, she knew, but hadn't she vowed to never grow up? And how could any flesh-and-blood girl not secretly revel in the idea of her own personal fairytale? Ah, to have but a peek inside, to walk those splendid halls—in bare feet, of course!

She'd overheard so-and-so from church whisper about how Jennie Farrow was over-indulged by her parents, how she'd measure up to nothing if she didn't marry, or at least go to college to be a nurse or teacher, something. "She flits around like a butterfly, wasting away her days," one said, and Jennie didn't care. "I want to be free," she told her mother once. Her mother, unable to tie her daughter down, bit back, "Your father and I had you late. What are you going to do when we're gone?" She had rebuffed her mother by saying, "I'll inherit your house and have a garden and chickens. Until then, I want to live, Mum!"

And so, Jennie did live, relishing life. But as she gazed up at the castle, something strange happened. It lost its sharp edges, the windows their bright reflections. Was a fog settling over Dunsmuir Hill? But the sun was shining. Blinking fast, she turned away, deciding it was the glare from the sun. On she rode to Chinatown, making a wish for her own castle as she glided under the ornate Chinese arch and on to deliver bread to Mrs. Lu.

Once home, Jennie found her mother sitting in the chair beside the piano. "All right, Mum." Jennie sighed and made the cup of tea with milk, which she handed to her waiting mum. Taking her place at the piano, she squinted to sight-read "Maple Leaf Rag."

"No." Martha Farrow's tone was flat.

"Mum," Jennie turned to plead, "Papa just bought it for me. It's all the rage, and I haven't played it through once yet." Her mother's expectant silence elicited another sigh. "Fine. Which one?"

" 'Tarry with Me'," came the reply, followed by a sip of tea. "And sing it for me, will you, Jen?"

Jennie complied, playing and singing the music by heart.

"Now the shadows slowly lengthen,

Soon the evening time will come;
With Thy grace, O Savior, strengthen,
By Thy help I would go home.
Tarry with me, O my Savior,
Lift the veil of mortal night;
Let the fields of verdant glory
Burst upon my eager sight."

Chapter 4

Thomas stood on the top marble step of the mausoleum, his hand pressed against the ornate wooden door. It had a small glass window too high to peer through and made it feel as if his mother was all the more out of reach.

The marble structure was covered with reliefs of cherubs and garlands to convey a pretense of husbandly love, when in truth, it was erected not for Lucretia Gallivan, but to boast of the new family cemetery, her body being the first laid to rest within its cold, stone walls.

Thomas placed a single yellow rose, his mother's favorite flower, in the small ceramic vase attached to the wall. "I have to leave, Mom," he whispered against the teakwood. "There's only one place left for me, and that's near you."

A baggage boy helped Thomas transport his luggage and trunk to the train. A furtive glance over his shoulder revealed the otherwise discreet and watchful eyes of one of his father's security agents ensuring the heir did in fact board the train bound for Kansas City, with assumed continuation to Massachusetts.

Sporting a red-striped Salazar Vest and matching trousers, Thomas boarded the train and took his seat in the first-class carriage. He conspicuously sat next to the window, where he lounged back into the wide cushioned chair that would have blended into any manor sitting room. Tasseled drapery was tied back above his shoulder, and instead of drawing it shut, he leaned his cheek against the glass and pretended to close his eyes. Looking through his lashes, he saw the steadfast eyes of the agent that remained on target—him—until the train pulled away from the San Francisco station.

Thomas didn't believe in Poseidon, or any other god of the deep, but the sea did seem to have a mind of its own.

He had switched trains at Salt Lake City and changed his connection to

Vancouver, where he boarded a Hudson Bay Company ferry at Coal Harbour. The *Lucky Lucy* was a sternwheel paddleboat, taking on nine other passengers for what should have been a five-hour sea journey to Victoria Harbour. But the farther the boat tacked a route across the Strait of Georgia, the worse the gale became. The black clouds amassed overhead and black water swelled beneath, and the puny boat seemed to be crushed between the two. Winds blew on the nose from the Southwest with gusts up to what he guessed were over sixty knots. The waves were fifteen feet high and closely packed, sending spray up over the second deck with the force of a blowhole.

Why wasn't the captain taking them back to the mainland? There was no sign of a break in the storm ahead, and the ferry wouldn't take much more of this punishment. The upper deck served as a cover for the passengers on the main deck, but the winds blew waves sideways into a pelting spray that doused them over the open rails. Soaked to the skin, Thomas ran up the steps leading to the top deck and the pilothouse.

He knew they were in trouble when the waves slammed this upper deck, the foam like white paws swiping his ankles. It took his feet out from under him and he fell, sliding as the boat heaved sideways at a forty-five-degree tilt. He hit the metal rail and grabbed a slippery bar, all but washed overboard.

One more of those coupled with a sixty-knot gust and the boat would capsize. In the sting of the spray, trying to shield his eyes with his hand, he managed to see the dark form of the captain through the glass window of the pilothouse—see his arm rise as he took a long draught from a bottle before throwing it down and swaying backward. The captain was drunk.

What could Thomas do? Commandeer the helm? He had heard sea talk all his life, and had gone out many times on the yacht, but he was no sailor. Instead, in a sliding crawl, he let the tip of the boat wash him back to the stairs.

On the steps, he was met by a crewman with blackened face and hands as he ran up from the boiler room. "We've got to turn around!" Thomas yelled against the gale.

"Engines are at max. We're running out of dry coal!" the man yelled in reply. "There's a leak in the hold! I'm going to tell the cap'n!"

At that moment Thomas saw another wave rise, and in its hollow, a tree. Hurling himself down the remaining steps, he let the momentum of the fall slide him across the wet boards of the passenger deck. The shouts of the men were lost in the screams of the wind and women. His feet slammed into the locker that held the life vests. The wave crested the upper deck, followed by the sound of the missile. The uprooted tree, hurled from one of the small islands in the strait, exploded through the hull. Its pointed top branches shot out the starboard side, while its snarled mass of roots landed with a crash in the portside. The black wooden tentacles looked like a monster from the depths.

While men yelled and women screamed, Thomas threw open the locker and grabbed the life vests made of blocks of cork sewn to canvas and shoved one after another into the arms of the passengers as he shouted, "We're going down! We're going down!"

There was a hope that the massive roots weighing down the portside would stabilize the craft in the up swells. But the drunk captain decided that moment to turn the ferry around. Before making a complete turn, another wave heaved the starboard side up, and the mass of roots swung down like a pendulum and capsized the ferry.

Chapter 5

Morning twilight came with a great draw of breath. Jennie sat up out of sleep with an inrush of anticipation. But of what? Something serendipitous was about to happen, she could feel it like the rise of hair on the neck just before a strike of lightning.

She blinked at the jar of sea gems. They were blurry, but it only was natural, she told herself, as her eyes were still adjusting to the gloaming. She bounded out of bed and slipped on the brown skirt. Buttoning up the shirtwaist, the final touches to the outfit came with a bright-red-and-yellow needlepoint belt and a red ribbon around the collar. Barefooted, as usual, she slipped out of the house before her parents awoke. Mum continued to sleep past dawn and baked less. There was no sign of illness, but she wasn't herself. Jennie couldn't cope with trauma in any form, and so she refused to acknowledge what should have been obvious. It was as if she'd developed two different brains. One for her inner world where everything she imagined was possible and another for the outer world fraught with bothersome strictures. The latter she pushed aside like a box shoved under a bed. Even as she assumed more chores and spent the afternoons playing the piano for her mother, her thoughts were prancing elsewhere.

The days may have now belonged to chores, but the dawn was still hers. It had been two weeks since Oscar first introduced his wet nose to the sole of her foot. After that first morning she'd left a slice of bread for every fish she swiped from the fisherman as he did his morning ritual. By the third day he confronted her.

"Leavin' bread don't make it any less stealin'. Takin' a man's livin' without ask'n' is the worst kind o' theft." His voice was gravelly from disuse, and his tall form intimidating. Jennie might not have returned the next morning if not for Oscar, and when she did, she discovered five fish waiting on the end of the pier. The following day she gave the seaman an entire loaf she'd made herself, which earned a crooked smile. The next day she knelt beside him at the water's edge and summoned the courage to ask him the meaning of his daily ritual.

"Songhees elder taught me," he said. "If I want to connect with the Creator, I should come to the water every dawn, wash my hands like so, then my face. I stand and face the sunrise and recite the things I be grateful for."

"Are you an Indian?" she asked dubiously. No, he said, he was Croatian, a Simun Pavich, born in San Francisco. When Jennie pried and asked about the necklace, he became a silent curmudgeon once more, walked to the boat, and sailed off for the wharf without so much as a farewell.

Today she ran to get to the bank early so she could perform the ritual alone. There had been a gale the night before, and the sand was still dark and wet and refreshingly cold beneath her feet.

She knelt at the water's edge, letting the sea soak into her skirt. She reached into the water and cleaned her hands and face. Then she stood and faced east to greet the sun as it peered over the horizon. "Creator and Father, I am grateful for my bicycle and sea glass. I am grateful for my Mum though she tasks me with chores I loathe. I am grateful for my Papa though he is a very, very quiet man. I am grateful for the strange fisherman, and especially for Oscar."

Jennie waltzed along the water's edge, letting the tide wash over her ankles, feeling the sand draining out from under her feet. Neither Oscar nor the curmudgeon came as the sun rose, and she found herself fretting over them. At length, the *Sand Crane* came into view, the propeller growling against the tide. Sloshing water, it steered up against the dock, where the old man threw the mooring line over the piling. She bounded up onto the dock with a cheery, "Good morning, sir! How was fishing?"

He grunted, a pipe in his mouth today, and nodded toward the barrels. She saw that they were only half full.

"Happy day for those fish," she chimed, but he only returned a frown. "I meant no disrespect. Not now, not yesterday. I'm sorry I asked about the necklace. I didn't know it reminded you of some great sorrow." He grunted as he pulled on a massive rope that must have weighed more than she did. "I've wondered why you dock here instead of the wharf. I figured it was to save a dock fee, or maybe for the quiet."

He regarded her with a raised bushy white eyebrow. "Yo' shor is a tonic to yo'self."

"My mother used to listen to my fits of loquaciousness, but of late she's been under the melancholy and has me playing on the piano the same songs over and over and over again, forcing me to memorize them, and now recipes. She's fallen into a quiet state, so I don't talk to her much, giving her thoughts room to breathe."

"Maybe yo' need to take a breath once in a while. Yo' be spoutin' off like a humpback what's sounded too long."

"I'm sorry. I can't help it. Oscar hasn't come yet, and you're low on fish even if he does?"

" 'Twas a storm last night, a boat-eater. Lost a ferry. Cap'n and crew unaccounted for. Nine passengers found with life vests. One still missin'. A sorry night for sure. You had a good night's rest, clear sky today, so what you frettin' over?"

"I don't know what you mean. It's dim as dusk."

He reached up from the boat and grabbed her hand. "Open it." She did. "Don't you feel that? The heat of the sun?"

She jerked free and put both hands behind her back. "Of course I do." He harrumphed and returned to untangling the massive line. "Maybe Oscar got caught in the storm?" The old man seemed to ignore her as he wound the rope into a neat pile. Jennie turned and trotted to the end of the dock, searching the water.

"I see him!" She bounced on her toes as she called out to the pup. "He has something in his mouth," she exclaimed as Oscar swam near. "Have you brought a gift from the sea?" She took the shattered piece of wood from his mouth. "Oh, dear, it looks like flotsam from a wreck."

The old man shot up straight as a rod. "What have ye there?"

Jennie showed it to him. "There's a carving of a fish. It's painted green."

The fisherman all but grabbed it from her. "Let me see that!" Jennie would have expressed indignation had he not been supplying Oscar with free fish. "This is from Jerome's boat," he said, tapping it with the stem of his pipe.

"Maybe Oscar got it from the site of the wreck," Jennie offered.

"Twenty boats been scour'n the sea. Nowheres else to look."

"What if Oscar can lead us to it?"

"It's a seal, not a dog!"

"Dogs can smell on land. Who says seals can't smell in the water? I'm going to try." Jennie leaned down and helped herself to a fish from the barrel. The old man grunted. "You want this?" She dangled the dead creature over the seal. Oscar leaped up and took it out of her hand with one gulp. "Let me have that," she said to the man, taking the piece of wood and another fish. Showing them to Oscar, she coaxed, "You want the fish?" She waggled it up where he couldn't reach. "Take me here." She pointed to the board. "Give me more of these."

To both her and the fisherman's surprise, the seal barked, as if in reply, and swam out into the bay. "I'll be a cross-eyed mackerel!" the man exclaimed, and yanked off the mooring rope.

"Wait!" Jennie exclaimed. "I have to go with you!" and without so much as a nod of approval she jumped down into the boat. At intervals, they threw a fish out to the

The Castle Made of Sand

seal. Oscar had grown more than she realized and was as fast as any seal, dipping under and skating over the surface of the water. The boat followed the selkie, for now Jennie was certain that's what Oscar must be. He led them to an islet that was no more than a collection of rocks. There were hundreds of these dotted throughout the Georgia Strait. Here, piles of flotsam lapped against the hollow spaces between the rocks, but no sign of life. The fisherman's shoulders sagged, reducing his height by inches under the weight of the disappointment.

"A seal ain't no huntin' dog," he growled, turning the helm about.

"Wait!" Jennie shouted from the prow, pointing to the seal as he leaped up on one of the jutting rocks and waddled on flippers to a hidden crevice. He threw his head back and barked. "There! There!"

The boat heaved to the side, Simun bringing it around, and she spied the form of a man wedged between two boulders, his arms a tangle around a sprouting pine tree.

The fisherman rowed out to the man. "He's alive!" Back at the boat, as Simun lowered the limp form over the gunwale, Jennie eased the victim's head and shoulders down onto the pile of nets. He was younger than she expected, about her age. Wet clothes clung to his ghost-white skin; his lips were blue. Through his ripped shirt she saw a terrible gash across his chest. There was very little blood, and whether the wound had coagulated or hypothermia was preventing circulation, she didn't know. He needed immediate medical attention either way. Wrapping him in a wool blanket, she propped his head on her lap. There was something about him, something different from anyone she'd ever met. You're a fool, Jennie Farrow, she chided herself. What she saw was a half-dead man whose life depended on them getting him back to the island fast as a spring tide. That's all.

Chapter 6

Momentary consciousness came like cracks in a doorway. For a fleeting moment he saw an angel with a golden halo glowing around her face as she read to him from *Alice in Wonderland* and then pausing to tell him how, as a girl, she'd once sewn buttons and ribbons onto hats and collars for a Mad Hatter tea party with her friends.

Another time, it was the sound of a piano that stirred his faculties. Playing ragtime. It would be grand if angels played ragtime in the celestial realm, but with so many mistakes? Disharmonic chords squawked like a gull in his ear. Well, whoever said angels don't need practice?

"Miss Farrow," a woman's mild voice softly snapped. "Please. Patients are resting. You promised something soft."

"I was playing with the soft pedal."

"A hymn, a hymn, if you please."

Light flashed off a silver cross that swung from the veiled neck of the black-robed figure as she leaned to place a hymn book on the piano.

"No need," the young woman sighed. "I already have dozens thoroughly rehearsed."

The sunlight shone through the window on her hair, and he was sure she had a halo. Or were there gold strands in the brown hair? Dreaming, he thought, this must be a dream.

She began playing a hymn his mother often sang, "Abide with Me." Even half conscious, his vocal cords recalled the melody, and they began to vibrate to the tune. The piano stopped. With a slow blink against the glaring light of day, he saw her body whirl around on the bench, hair swinging out around narrow shoulders, and he glimpsed a face that would be embedded in his mind even in sleep.

"Nurse!" the young woman shouted.

"Shhhh!" returned a reprimand.

"No, he's awake!"

The last thing he saw were two faces leaning into his, one with a black head-dress, the other with the most wild and vibrant eyes he'd ever seen.

The mental haze parted a third time as a pillow was being fluffed behind his head. Was it time to wake for school? "Mother?" he murmured.

"Hardly," returned a sassy voice, "or else I gave birth to you when I was four. That would qualify me for the circus."

"Wh—what?" All went black.

There was a poof as a second pillow was propped under his head, raising it up.

"You need to eat something or you'll waste away like a beetle on its back. Here, I have some soup." A warm piece of metal was placed between his lips, and simmering broth poured into his mouth. This repeated several times until he reached up and caught her hand, spilling the broth on his bare chest, waking him further.

"Wh—what? Where. . .where am I? Who are you?"

She all but dropped the bowl on the metal nightstand and leaned nearer. She smelled like flowers as she reached over and lifted hair from his brow.

"Is that better? Can you see me?"

Her voice. . .had he heard it before? Did he know her? "Who are you?"

"You're at St. Joseph's Hospital in Victoria. Your ferry went down in a storm. Oscar rescued you, and now you are safe."

"Oscar?"

"He's a seal pup, though after all the fish I've given him, he looks more like a miniature walrus."

"Walrus?" he groaned. "I'm. . .dreaming."

"No, no, no! Don't do that!"

A small hand patted his face, but he couldn't feel her skin. Was his cheek numb? Covered with scars? He heard himself groan.

"Come back! You've been unconscious for three days. You have to eat or they will put a tube down your throat."

"What?" His eyes opened.

"Ah, that's better. Hello." Her smile was whimsical with a dimple on the left side. He reached up and touched it, and it deepened as she smiled into his finger. Why did he do that? Who was she?

"The staff is shorthanded. I've been looking after you every afternoon, after I feed my fat seal and make my deliveries. Sister B. asked me to try and feed you some broth."

"Who—" He blinked hard, rubbed his eyes with a weak hand. "Who are you?"

"Jennie Farrow. Pleased to make your acquaintance."

"Jena?"

"Jennie."

"Jena Farrow?"

"I can be Jena, if you like. The big question is, who are you? You're the mysterious stranger here. They wanted to call you Sixteen, your chart number. I protested that you don't look anything like a Sixteen, but nuns can be so unimaginative. I wanted to call you Ulysses, which is the Roman name for Odysseus who survived great trials at sea, but the sisters would have none of it. I tried to tell them that Ulysses was also an American war hero, but noses were still turned up against it."

"So," she said with a new breath and a pause, "can you break the spell of the Unknown Man and tell us your name? Please say it isn't Sixteen!"

His thoughts stammered inside a reeling head. She leaned her elbows on her knees and said in a sympathetic tone, "You do have a name, don't you?"

"Eh, yes, yes, of course I do." He struggled to sit up until she shoved another pillow behind his back for support.

"Are you in shock?" she asked.

"I—I don't know. I don't know anything. Where I am? How did I get here? Don't know my name."

"A teacher once told me that when taking a test, write down the first answer that pops into your mind, it's usually the right one. So, what is the first thing that pops into your mind when I say, 'What is your name?'"

"Gavin."

"Gavin?" Her eyebrows rose in approval, and he noted that even their shape was delicate and whimsical. He was entranced by every part of this beautiful stranger. She was unlike any woman he'd ever met, or was that only because he couldn't remember who in his life he had ever met?

"Gavin," he said with a chuckle of relief. "Yes, that sounds right."

"Last name?"

He shook his head.

"No matter. Gavin is a great start and fits you perfectly. I must say, now that you're awake, I can see that you're nothing of the Ulysses sort. You look just like a Gavin. I should have guessed!"

He could feel his lips slide into a deep smile, and it felt like it had been a great while since they had formed anything close to an upward slant. The left cheek ached from the pressure. He touched it, felt the beginnings of a beard.

"Careful, you've a nice collection of bruises. You were discovered on the rocks.

You also have a splendid gash on your chest. It's deemed a miracle by the staff that you don't have a single broken bone, that you survived the ordeal at all. The consensus is that God has spared you for a great purpose." She leaned forward with a wink. "No pressure."

Glancing down, he saw the bandage across his chest, felt the crinkle of stitches as he moved his arm to touch it. What had happened to him?

He managed to swallow spoonfuls of soup before a wave of fatigue overtook him and the blackness enveloped him once again.

Chapter 7

I am Jena now!" she announced as she trotted through the front door of the cottage. Mum was making bread and cookies. "Mum! You're baking again. You feel better, at last?"

"Yes. I only needed my Jen to sing me to health. And whatever do you mean by Jena?"

"The young man at the hospital woke today. He kept calling me Jena."

"The only man who'll be changing your name will be your husband."

"Hope should be your middle name."

Her mum put up her flour-covered hand; it hovered a moment before honing in on Jennie's cheek. "I pray every day that my child will not be left alone in the world, no matter how free she pretends to be."

No retort came to Jennie's lips, instead a warning entered with a burning sensation that seemed to say, *Brace yourself.* Shaking it off, she instead clasped her hand over her mum's, pressing it to her face. "I shall never be alone for I shall always be with you." Now she drew the flour-crusted hand down with a pat. "But if changing my surname is a prerequisite to matrimony, then I'm sorry to say I shan't be marrying this mysterious young man, even though he is over-the-moon with good looks and charm, because, as of now, he hasn't a last name. I suppose I could be Mrs. Jena Blank!" She gave a theatrical sigh. "The poor fellow can't remember a thing."

"Anything?" Mum went back to kneading the large bowl of dough.

"Not a whit. Doctor says it will come back to him in time. What he needs is fresh air and familiar surroundings to spring his memories."

"Poor boy. How terrible! No sign of family yet? No one's come looking for him?"

"Not a one. The Chief Constable put the word out as far as Vancouver, but there's been no missing persons reported anywhere. I think he's an orphan like Oscar." She pinched some dough and dropped it into her mouth.

"Oh, you're the orphan magnet now, are you? And get your fingers out of my batter!"

"I don't think you're half as blind as you say you are." Her mum's expression fell. "Oh, Mum, I'm sorry."

"Get along with you. Finish trimming the garden so you can have your orphan boy here for tea and biscuits. Goodness knows he needs a hand up. Where will he stay?"

"The sisters will feed him and give him a cot forever if need be. It's what they do."

"Jennie," she chastised with a punch into the dough.

"I'm quoting Sister B., Mum."

"Respect your elders, child!"

Jennie sighed and pinched off another piece of dough. "Sister Bernadette. Hey, can I take some biscuits to Simun tomorrow morning?"

"Your father and I are concerned about your meeting him down there."

"He gives me free fish for Oscar. A pup-lover can't be bad, and he saved Gavin's life."

"Who?"

"That's the castaway's name."

"You mean the patient's?"

"Patient sounds so bland, don't you think?" Her mother sighed, as usual, and Jennie carried on. "Simun is a Croatian from San Francisco who came here when he was my age. He hired onto a schooner that transported prospectors during the Fraser gold rush, ended up marrying a Songhees woman who taught him Christianity. How wild a twist is that? That's all he'll say. I think she died a long time ago and he's never recovered. He wears her shell necklace. It's awfully romantic, don't you think?"

"Romantic? It's tragic is what it is."

"I know, but how ethereal to find true love. It would be like Romeo and Juliet except he's still alive."

"A loon dropped its egg into a duck nest, and the ducks still don't know what to make of the strange bird that hatched." That was what her mum often said whenever she thought Jennie was being ridiculous. But to Jennie, she was being perfectly sensibile.

Jennie kissed her mum's powdery cheek, tasting flour. "I know that loons are your favorite."

"Yes, they are."

"I do feel like a bird flying with its feet dragging the ground. I need to ride my bike. I feel so full of—I don't know what. It's like all the colors have come alive around me even though the sky is gray as lead."

Her mum walked to the window and put her hand out. Sunlight streamed onto the palm. Was she trying to feel the colors Jen so thoughtlessly bragged about? Jennie bit her lip with regret, wishing she'd learn to think before opening her mouth.

Her mother made a fist, and Jennie assumed it a poetic gesture of grabbing the light. "Go, Jen girl. Go ride your bike for as long as you can."

Chapter 8

After a week of confinement, Gavin was set free.

Jena had come to St. Joseph's every afternoon and been the light of his empty days in the hospital. She brought fresh biscuits, bread, and fruit for picnics on the sun porch, so he'd have at least a view of Humboldt Street. As fascinated as he should have been with the view, like a babe opening his eyes on the world for the first time, he found he could hardly take his eyes off of her.

She had serenaded him with hymns, the only songs allowed, on the piano that she had rolled to his bedside from the convalescence room. He imagined that the nuns had protested, but this girl had such a carefree yet quirky willful way about her, it was impossible to say no to her.

As no one had come forth to claim him, and he had no money to pay for services rendered, he was asked to give up his bed. Dr. Trimble had assessed his wounds, removed the bandages and stitches from his head and chest, and ascertained that all that could be done for their "Mr. Gavin" was fresh air and mild activities to rejuvenate the senses.

The sisters, however, had no intention of turning Gavin out onto the street. He was given a cot in a storage room and a generous offering of nightly meals until he could find his way into a new life.

He was sitting at the piano trying to pluck out a vague tune, and failing, when Jena popped into the room. No longer in hospital clothes, he was wearing a deep-blue work shirt and black trousers, both a bit oversized and clearly something the sisters rummaged up for him.

"You remember something?"

He sighed. "It's as if my fingers should know what to do, but they just bumble about like a drunken soldier. My feet too, as if I should know where to go, but don't. I'm useless, Jena."

"They just need a nudge in the right direction. Here." She sat down beside him, placed her hands over his, and as her fingers tapped his, he pressed the keys, playing a choppy version of "Angels We Have Heard on High."

"You hold your hands at the keys like a pianist. I bet you played and that it'll all come back to you at once." She smiled at him and then took him by the hand, pulling him up to his feet and out the front door. Even there she didn't release his hand. It was a gesture of acceptance, but was that all?

Gavin shielded his eyes from the white glare of the sun, a welcome change from the white walls, and he inhaled the scent of pine, replacing the permeating smell of antiseptics.

"Seeing as you're dressed today for an outing," she said with her typical whimsy, "I thought we'd take a streetcar to my father's shop."

Gavin wanted to lean halfway out of the vehicle as it glided down the street, bell clanging, but his chest wound didn't allow for strenuous arm movements. Instead, he sat beside the girl of his dreams, literally, as it was her voice he'd heard reading to him as he slept. She amazed him, intrigued him, and was beginning to bewitch him.

At the optical shop, Gavin stopped and stared, trying to take it all in, the rows of eyeglasses on the walls, the optical equipment and charts. The jewelry counters and displays, the clocks on shelves, did little to pique his interest. Instead, he was bowled over with a sudden insatiable desire to learn about this optical aspect of medicine.

He was introduced to Peter Farrow, Jena's father. He was soft spoken, congenial, the epitome of a proper English gent. Gavin found it difficult to believe this man could be Jena's father. He'd expected a large and robust fellow who'd as soon slap him on the back as shake his hand.

Gavin was more keenly interested in Mr. Farrow's mind than anything else once they began to converse about his occupation.

"My only intention was to open an optical office when we came in seventy-eight, a year before Jennie was born," Mr. Farrow explained. "During the gold rush we had upwards to ten thousand people come through here. Once it died down, I found I had to supplement my business, thus the jewelry and clock repair. I am an optician first and foremost, a doctor of the human eye. I find nothing more beautiful on this planet, not even jewels. Here." Mr. Farrow took a large tome from a collection on the back shelf and opened it to diagrams of the eye. "The iris is as complex in symmetry as it is beautiful in appearance."

"This is fascinating, sir. If I help around the office, sweeping, cleaning, anything you need, may I spend some mornings studying your books?"

Mr. Farrow grabbed Gavin's shoulder in what was surprisingly almost a slap. "My young man, you are welcome anytime, no need to clean. I'll be happy to answer any questions you may have. I was tutored by a Doctor Lundsworth in Canada, a great mind. I would be honored to impart any knowledge you may seek."

That night, Gavin was restless on his cot in the hospital, his mind reeling over the diagrams and equipment and lenses in Mr. Farrow's office. Did this have something to do with his past? Was his father a doctor?

Jena took him out on constitutionals through the streets of Victoria, trying unsuccessfully to trigger a memory. Instead, he made new memories of the two of them together, eating a new cookie called Fig Newtons, drinking sodas, and walking the wharf and Government Street. Especially sweet were his new memories of riding on the top of a double-decker bus and watching the glints of gold in Jena's hair as she laughed in the wind with that spectacular laugh she possessed. Over the ensuing months, he felt like a dumb brute, so he divided his mornings between the optician's office and the library, where he read some of Jena's favorite books so he would have something to converse with her about.

He read all of Mr. Farrow's volumes and found that he could recall complete passages. Mr. Farrow said he had a photographic memory. So why couldn't he recall his own life? Did he not have one? Was he a vagabond? Had he stowed away on that ferry? Did he have no family, or did they not want him? He was torn between fear of discovery and fear of never knowing who he was.

But this frustration dimmed quickly with each passing day that he spent with Jena. All Gavin could think about was becoming an optician like her father so he could support a wife—Jena. Mr. Farrow intimated that he wanted someone to take his place when he retired in a few years, and Gavin was given the opportunity to be tutored for free under one whom he esteemed to have a great and unappreciated mind.

One morning Jena had promised a great surprise. He had to leave the hospital before dawn and meet her at the wharf. There he found her and an imposing old man waiting for him on a fishing boat. With them, he sailed to a small cove, where Jena taught him a Songhees ritual prayer of washing at the water's edge and then facing the rising sun to offer a prayer of gratitude. Jena thanked the Father for Gavin, and he peeked, watched the slight flutter of her closed lids, the graceful movements of her lips, before he offered a silent prayer of thanks for her. Was this his first prayer?

Afterward, he followed Jena onto the dock, where he met his rescuer, a half-grown seal that hovered just under the surface, eyeing him.

"Come, Oscar," Jena said as she leaned over and splashed the water. The seal rubbed its nose up against her palm. Dipping her bare feet in the water, she began playing with the pup as it swam circles around her and then leaped up through the transparent surface with a throaty bark.

Simun threw five fish out of the boat. The glittering scales smacked the boards beside Gavin. "Go on," Jena said, "he won't bite." Gavin threw the fish to the seal, laughing as the pup-eyed creature splashed its nose at him, begging for more.

"How do I thank you, Oscar?" The seal barked. "Ah, more fish?" In response, Simun threw two more with a grunt and returned to swabbing his deck.

Back on the beach, side by side, Gavin walked barefoot in the sand with Jena. His heart raced as he got the courage to hold her hand. She not only accepted his hand, she entwined her fingers with his and pulled him into a run.

"Come, look!" she said, pulling him to a pile of driftwood. Resting on top was a jar full of polished bits of glass. "I found them here on my beach. Have you ever searched for treasures?"

He felt like a fool when all he could do was shrug.

"I used to build sandcastles here when I was a girl. I was never very good at it. They didn't look anything like what I envisioned, nothing like the one up on the hill."

"Ah, the Craigdarroch structure?"

"I have daydreams of what it must look like inside."

"I wouldn't know anything about that, but I can build a castle just for you." He had Jena retrieve cups and bowls and a mixing spoon from her kitchen, and to his amazement, his hands intuitively sculpted a castle three-feet high with turrets and battlements, a moat and drawbridge, and created stained-glass windows using sea glass.

"By ginger! I've never seen anything so spectacular!"

"I used to build them for my youngest brother when we played knights and war games with his figurines. . ." Gavin's voice trailed off as soon as he comprehended the words that had just issued from his mouth.

"You have brothers?" Jena said, her brows arching.

"I—I don't know. I don't know why I said that."

"It's a start." But rather than appearing excited at a possible recollection, she seemed worried.

"What is it? What's wrong?"

"Nothing." She shook her head with a shrug as they sat half reclined beside the castle.

"Something's troubling you. Did I say something wrong?"

"Of course not. You're always perfect," she teased, but the look in her eyes said otherwise.

"Are you afraid I'll remember my past life and. . ." His voice trailed off again, afraid to vocalize the last word.

"Leave?" She dug her toes into the sand, hugged her knees, and looked off at the watery horizon. "Will you?"

"No." He rolled onto his knees and lifted a strand of fallen hair from her face. "Jena, no."

"What if I don't belong in your life?" She took his hand and caressed his ring finger. "What if you lost a ring in the storm?"

He turned her face toward him. "Jena, I would remember that, I'm sure of it."

"Gavin, you don't know what will happen when your memory comes back."

"Then I won't remember, ever, not if it means losing you."

She looked down, biting her lip. After a painfully long silence, feeling clumsy all over again, not knowing what to say, he just stared into her face, as if he might find the words there. All he could think to say was a diversion. He raised his hand and touched the space in her left eyebrow.

"What is this?"

"I pulled a skillet down off the stove when I was three. That's where it hit me. It burned the skin. The scar left but the gap remained. Mum has always said I'm too curious for my own good." She stood and dusted the sand off her blue skirt. He jumped up beside her.

"Jena, I'm not going to hurt you. I would do anything but hurt you, anything for you."

"I'm scared," she said, and her eyes showed it. "I don't like being scared."

"Please, Jena, I swear nothing will come between us. Your father is training me; he wants me to take over his office in a few years. I'm going to find a night job to earn money so I can." His throat constricted, taking the words with it. In that moment he realized that he was scared too, of losing her; it overcame his sensibilities, and the next thing he knew he was kissing her. The shock of feeling her lips on his sent his hands up, cupping her face. His mind reeled. He expected any second for her to break his hold, run away, and leave him alone on the beach. But she didn't. She leaned into him with a deep intake of breath; her hands came around his neck, her fingers into his hair. His arm locked around her waist and lifted her up as the kiss deepened.

The fear of the other's reaction overtook them both at the same time and they parted, but only a few inches, looking into the other's eyes for approval. And then they laughed simultaneously, laughed with the thrill of the discovery they saw in each other's eyes.

"You are so beautiful," he gasped as he stroked her hair. "I wanted to tell you that the day I woke up. I've been aching to say those words ever since."

"But you can't. You can't say them." She pressed her fingers over his lips. "Not until you remember. Not until I'm no longer the only woman you know."

He pulled her hand down. "Are you going to send me away?"

"No!" She drew her arms around his shoulders as if she were the one drowning now. "I love you, Gavin. But I'm scared that won't be enough."

He chuckled in her ear. "You, not enough?" He tightened his arms around her waist. "You'll see. Nothing's going to change. Nothing's going to come between us."

He carried the jar of the remaining sea glass up the hill, following Jena's lead. There he found an erratically groomed flower garden with a small table topped with a lace cloth, a tea set, and a glass plate of frosted teacakes.

"Is this where you had your Mad Hatter tea party?" he asked.

"You remember that?" She was delightfully surprised.

"I remember everything you've said to me. It's all I remember. This"—he gestured to the table with his eyes—"is a lovely surprise. It is with great honor that I accept your invitation, Alice." He bowed. She laughed.

They sat at the table under the willow tree for hours. She drilled him with questions about his favorite colors, and would he like painting or sports? "I suppose I don't care what I do so long as it's with you. I've been talking to the locals," he said, taking her hand over the table. "They say that Beacon Hill Park is a must for a beau to take his girl. Could I prevail upon you to join me for a picnic there tomorrow?"

"You are a bit of a Mad Hatter, aren't you? Full of surprises. It would be my honor to join you, sir. But our day isn't done. My mum has invited you to join us for dinner again."

"Your mum is swell. Sometimes she feels like my own."

"She said it's the least she can do after you whitewashed the fence."

The Farrow home had become like his own, and the meals always splendid, but all he had to compare them with was the hospital food. Even so, they were delicious. Peter Farrow praised Gavin to his wife, and he and Peter got into yet another involved discussion on the field of optometry. Tonight it was on optic nerve connections and how they played into man's world perceptions. When dessert was served—freshly baked cinnamon rolls—Mrs. Farrow insisted on a change of topic. "I'm sorry you as yet have not regained your memory, but I wonder if you have formed any views on religion?"

The image of a church interior popped into Gavin's mind. In a flash he saw himself as a boy sitting beside a beautiful woman, poised, elegant, with a white-gloved hand holding his. She smiled down at him with tender eyes and a pleasant yet sad smile on her lips. Stained-glass windows cast a colorful halo around her high-top bun, and he had thought she looked like an angel. An insatiable longing for her swept over him, and he grabbed the sides of his chair to steady himself.

"Gavin?" Peter asked, seeing his discomfiture.

"Fatigue," Gavin lied. "I have momentary lapses. Excuse me, Mrs. Farrow. To answer your question, my mind can't form doctrines, but I believe there is a God and that He saved me to fulfill a special purpose." He smiled at Jena, who returned it with a knowing gleam in her eye. "More than this, I am an empty slate. I have enjoyed your church meetings immensely."

"I think it is my daughter's company you have enjoyed immensely," Mrs. Farrow retorted with a sly smile.

After dinner, at the prearranged time of nine o'clock, Simun returned to the cove to take Gavin back to the harbor. Jena came with him. They sat on a locker with their feet on a coil of rope, the damp tasting of brine, the moon riding across the dark water as if in greeting, the stars filling the sky.

After ascending the seawall steps, Jena laid her hands on Gavin's forearm and they walked along Government Street on their way to St. Joseph's. The Parliament Building was neo-baroque in design, though how he knew that he didn't know. It had thirty-three copper domes, and the profile was lit up in electric lights against the backdrop of night. "It looks like something out of a World's Exposition," he remarked.

"It is enchanting. The lights aren't as bright as usual. They are quite dim tonight."

"Dim?" he said, confused, for the white of each light seemed to puncture the night.

"Makes me wonder how they change them out. I wish you could have seen them at their brightest. It looked like stars had landed on the roofs."

"Indeed," Gavin replied, unsure what she meant. Perhaps there had been more lights before? "I dread the very notion, but the gentleman in me feels that I must escort you back to the boat." With that she sighed and leaned against his arm as they turned back.

"I wish this moment would never end."

"Would it be scandalous if I sealed it with a kiss?"

She turned her face up to his, and it was breathtaking to look down into her eyes that glistened with the reflection of the lights. He held his breath, as if that could hold back time in its place, and he leaned down and placed a soft kiss on her lips.

Chapter 9

"S he should know, Martha."

It was Papa's voice that woke her the next morning. It came from the entryway. Was he leaving already? Jennie sprang out of bed and rushed toward the front of the house, but stopped when she saw the dark figures of her parents silhouetted in the opened doorway. It was still twilight. Papa was leaving early. "She can't know," Mum whispered with words as rigid as tin and as likely to fold. "It'll take the heart right out of her. Peter, we can't, we mustn't tell her."

Papa kissed her on the forehead and squeezed her arms. Mum clung to him, holding the lapels of his coat. Jennie had never seen them like this. On the one hand, it was a window into how much they loved each other, as it was rare they openly displayed affection. On the other hand, what was this crisis that nearly folded Mum in half? And made Papa so tense? There was a wet spot on his face, and Jennie looked away, pretending she hadn't seen a tear.

Apprehension locked arms around Jennie. There was a fear, unnamed and unspoken in her heart. She never allowed it to surface, for nothing, nothing would rob her of her free spirit. Like the loons and cranes and gulls that flew on the air, soaring in the updrafts, she would fly above all this worldly trouble, even if it meant pretending it didn't exist.

Avoiding anything but superficial conversation with Mum was easy this morning as she was in a quiet way, which was surprising, as it was Christmas Eve. Mum always talked about her favorite "ghosts" of Christmas past, what she called those memories, as she made her traditional Christmas cookies for the neighbors.

Jennie bounded down the hill to give Simun fresh biscuits and hot cross buns, and an invitation to Christmas dinner. He answered with a rather shy smile, which meant yes, and gave her fish, which she trailed back and forth over the water, making Oscar work for his food. She splashed her feet like a propeller in the water, laughing as the seal swam circles around them, and then, when her feet came to rest, he put his chin on the tops of them and looked up at her with his pathetically adorable eyes before swimming off.

Jennie returned to the house and played Christmas hymns, now by heart, on the piano for Mum without being asked, in the hopes of bringing cheer, then took off with the day's deliveries and to the optician shop, where Papa now paid Gavin as an assistant. She was certain Gavin would propose to her as soon as he saved up for a place—or maybe on Christmas morning?

It was a chilly December morning. She had to wear shoes and her orange pull-over sweater, but she didn't feel the nip, anticipating the gayest of holiday celebrations tomorrow with both Gavin and Simun. Today, Jennie not only "flew" on the cycle, she was entirely airborne over the potholes and ruts.

When she shot under the red Chinese gate of Chinatown, Jennie made her wish, as selfish as it was, for Gavin to never get his memory back. After Mrs. Lu's delivery, she pumped like a mad woman to Mrs. Crawford's at the end of Dunford Street, not taking the time to warm up inside her house and chat. Instead, she flew off on her bike to Mrs. Smith's. After all her deliveries were made, she shot down the hill with enough speed to break the brakes, but the bicycle still stopped on command outside the hospital.

Were her feet touching the steps? As she waltzed through the entrance pavilion with its large columns supporting the second-floor balustrade, it felt as if she were floating. Through the entrance doors and their beveled glass she trotted. She was going to invite Gavin to a race on the beach and then to go out fishing with Simun—surely Papa would let him off early today as it was Christmas Eve? She ignored the nun who chided, "Miss Farrow!" when Jena nearly knocked her over.

Down the hall, she rushed to the storage room door and knocked, both hoping she wasn't waking him and not caring if she did. There was no answer. She knocked again and whispered through the keyhole, "Gavin? Aren't you awake yet?"

"Miss Farrow." The same nun approached, her voice not so reproving this time.

"It's shameful, I know," Jennie confessed, "but I love him, and I simply can't wait another second to see him." She was sure the nun would castigate her for that one, but she received a very different reply.

"Miss Farrow, our Mr. Gavin is no longer with us."

"What—what do you mean? No longer with you?"

"He left early this morning."

"Where did he go?"

"To the castle."

Jennie's spirit felt tangible, as if it had just leaped up into her chest. "Is he trying to surprise me?" Why would Gavin go to the castles they built on the cove? Did he want her to meet him there? Was he about to propose to her today?

"I do not believe so, Miss Farrow. Our Mr. Gavin is actually Thomas Gallivan."

"What? What do you mean?" It felt as if the words sifted through her consciousness like sand through her fingers, all of them escaping her as the nun continued.

"It would appear that he is from a very wealthy family in San Francisco. A write-up about the shipwreck appeared in a Vancouver paper, and that was a lead that alerted his family to his whereabouts. They sent a telegram requesting friends of the family, the Dunsmuirs, to take him in until a reunion can be arranged."

"The Dunsmuirs?" Jennie's voice choked, as if filled with sand. "Gavin is gone?"

"Yes, Miss Farrow. Though he looked none too happy to leave. I'm sure a convalescence up at Craigdarroch will afford him much needed rest and the attention we could not give him. His father's personal doctor seemed to believe that his condition is far more severe than we'd supposed."

"They took him away? And he went with them?"

"Yes. You will not find him here any longer. You were a bright spot in his life. I'm sure he will never forget the debt he owes you. His gratitude will follow you all the days of your life, and my respect with it."

"Gratitude?" Jennie's voice failed her, and it came out as a rasp. There were no imaginary wings to take her away from this, no avoiding the pain that drove itself like a knife into her chest. Gavin was rich. He was inside the castle she could only regard wistfully from a distance. Now his memories would come back, and she felt in her heart that he never would.

The nun was speaking, but the pain garbled her words in Jennie's head, and she turned and walked listlessly out of the hospital.

The jar of sea glass sat on the window ledge. The sun had darkened them even more. They no longer glowed.

It was with reluctance that Jennie opened her eyes to another day. She had to pull out of this, but didn't know how. Gavin surely had his memories back, but she wished she could be rid of hers—of the memories of the too-short months they had spent together.

It had been a week now since Gavin disappeared from the hospital. Christmas Day had come and gone without word from him. If he meant a word he had said to her, if his promise that nothing would come between them had been true, he'd had seven days to prove it. But he'd not deigned to send a letter, not even a note. Nothing. He had gone back to his life, and now she was paralyzed, unable to return to hers.

"Fool, fool, fool!" she hissed at herself. In an impulsive sweep, she threw back the covers, got out of bed, put on the brown skirt, and tied the scarf around the waist. She tied the ribbon up in her hair and marched out of the room, pretending she could be carefree as before. But her bare feet felt cold and heavy. Still she trudged on through the cottage and out the back door. She made herself bound to the outcropping, ignoring the nip of the chill breeze on her toes, and slid down through the beach grass to the shore.

Simun wasn't there. Only a small pile of fish at the end of the dock, one acting as an anchor to a note that read,

Gon to Vancuver fer samon n crab. Back in a week. Seen yer seal out by Whale Rock with other seals. He do no need your fish no more. He catch n his own jest fine. Here is a few salted ones. They will keep. Wash off for feeding Oscar. Pray for me—Simun Pavich.

So, Oscar didn't need her anymore either? She waited at the dock, but he didn't come. Maybe he only came for the fish and was smart enough to figure out that no boat meant no food.

"Well, dash it all, I don't need you, either." She dragged her feet back to the shore, ignoring the burn of the cold. Winter had been mild thus far, but even so, all she wanted was to go back to bed, to curl up like a pathetic little hedgehog and never come out. But Simun told her to pray for him, so she knelt at the shoreline and scooped the water up in the palms of her hands. Memory can be a cruel companion, and it brought the phantom image of Gavin kneeling beside her, scooping water. For the first time that she could remember, Jennie began to cry. As she washed her face with salt water, saline fluid poured from her own eyes, and she wished she could give herself to the ocean. Now the repressed fears surfaced all at once. "Father, I don't want Mum to go blind. Please, don't take her sight. Please don't leave me alone. Abide with me, 'Tis morning tide. The days have come and now he's gone. Oh, Savior, stay this day with me, behold, 'Tis morning tide."

Twenty years old, all her friends married and living their own separate lives, all too busy for Jennie, and she had pretended that she didn't care. But she had, and she did. Her mum's greatest fear for her was also her own: that she would end up alone.

She stood, faced the sunrise, and said, "Thank you for Gavin. At least now I have known what it is to feel loved. Give him happiness. I pray for Simun. Bring him back to safe harbor."

Back in the house, Jennie put on an apron and stood next to her mum and began plowing her hands through the flour and water, turning the mix into dough. Her mum sensed that Jennie was crying softly, tears falling into the dough, but she said nothing, and for that Jennie was grateful.

Another day went by, and still Jennie had forgotten how to "fly." Tomorrow was New Year's Day, and it was as far from the year she'd hoped it would be as the day is from night. Today, she rode like everyone else, pumping against gravity, making deliveries in silence. When she returned to the cottage, there was a Packard motor car waiting at the side of the road. It was shiny black with a cushioned carriage seat and huge wheels. Her heart raced at a hummingbird's pace. Gavin? But as she drew nearer, she saw only one man in the vehicle, a driver wearing a suit and white gloves.

What was he doing here? How dare he park here and stir up an ocean of false hopes? The chauffeur got out, adjusted his cap, and turned to walk up to her cottage door.

"If you want directions, it's no use asking there," Jennie called. "I ride all over Victoria. It's me you'll be wanting to ask."

"Good afternoon, miss. I'm not looking for directions, I'm looking for a person. I've been sent to collect a Jena Farrow."

Chapter 10

Gavin lay under a crewel embroidered bedcover. As when he was rescued from the sea, he once again lay in and out of a stupor.

The room was painted a hunter's green. There was a fireplace, a window with striped damask drapes, a man in a tweed suit sitting in the corner reading a paper, and an older man reposed in a bedside chair.

No sooner would the blurs gain definition than the older gentlemen, who often took his pulse, would push a pill into Gavin's mouth and chase it with a large gulp of water from a glass. He had to either swallow or choke. The doctor would reassure him, tell Gavin he would be in the comfort of his own home soon, before he lapsed back into a drugged sleep.

After several days he was permitted to remain awake long enough to take meals. The doctor told him that he had been in a yachting accident while he was on vacation. He had lost his memory and was suffering from delusions, but after a week of rest he would be fit to return home to convalesce there.

Gavin's first breath was always breathed with one word on his lips, "Jena?" Repeatedly he was told that there was no Jena. "Where am I?" he asked on the third day.

"You are a guest at Craigdarroch Castle in Victoria," the doctor said. "You are friends with Alex Dunsmuir. You've visited here several times over the past ten years. They have taken you in until you can be transported home. We suspect you were coming to visit them when you went overboard."

By the fifth day, Gavin's fogged brain was able to piece together his situation. He refused in his heart to abandon the face of Jena, to cast her off as a delusion. But it was true that he had lost his memory, and without it he couldn't be sure what was or wasn't true. His father must be real, for he was the one who sent the doctor. The Dunsmuirs were flesh and blood, for he saw them as they peered in to greet him when allowed. But there was no Jena. Could she have only been a vivid dream?

Gavin was told that the man in the corner was also from San Francisco, sent by his father to oversee Thomas's safe return. Gavin had stopped arguing about his name, for it only fueled the fire of "proof" of his deluded state. On the seventh day, Gavin woke only hours before his departure for the States. The doctor was in the hallway conversing with the Dunsmuir family, and his father's agent, as he was called, was asleep in the chair when the maid brought lunch in on a tray.

"Miss," Gavin whispered as he pulled her nearer, "will you do something for me? I am Thomas Gallivan, a very important man. Have the chauffeur drive to 57 Granite Creek Road and collect a Miss Jena Farrow and bring her here at once. It is imperative, you understand? Go straight to the garage; don't speak to anyone before you give him the message."

The maid's head trembled a nod, all but overtaken with nerves by the urgent assignment from the wealthy heir. She skittered out the door, and Gavin could hear her feet trotting rapid-fire down the stairs. Please, Jena, please be real, he said to himself as he dropped his pounding head back into the pillow.

The doctor returned a few minutes later, announcing, "Dear boy, you are fit for travel! We have sent someone to bring the auto around and take you to the yacht." A different maid entered, as if on cue, with a pair of brown linen trousers and a white silk shirt draped over her arm, a pair of brown leather shoes in hand.

"I need a few hours," Gavin gasped, holding his temple. "Fierce headache."

"My boy, it is only a few minutes to the harbor, and you will find the yacht a luxury equal to this. In fact, the bedroom was furnished by you, the mattress one of your choosing. I think you will find the sea air and tranquil ride most beneficial."

"I'd rather stay," Gavin asserted.

"This is not your castle, my good boy. It's not your choice. If asked to leave, then you must leave."

Gavin assumed that if he didn't dress himself the brute in the corner would do it for him. The clothes did feel familiar against his skin. He deliberately inched out of the room as if too stiff and sore to move any faster, praying the chauffeur would return soon. If the car was empty, then Gavin would know, and a part of him would die inside.

It was a mystery what became of the car and driver, so while the staff scurried to learn their whereabouts, Gavin was placed in the drawing room, in a chair beside the large windows. He watched with bittersweet anticipation. And then at last, the motor car pulled up the drive. It veered out of view around the backside of the castle before pulling to a stop below Gavin's window a few moments later.

Except for the driver, it was empty. It felt as if his heart collapsed in on itself, and he dropped back into the chair in despair. "Jena," he whispered, wondering how the human mind could invent such a woman, could conjure up such lifelike detail that he had thought were memories. Perhaps the mind can't exist in a vacuum, and with the absence of all memory, it had conjured its own.

Chapter 11

Everything seemed to swirl inside Jennie—her thoughts, her stomach, her doubts, as the Packard pulled up through the stone pillar gates. Would her fear be realized, that once Gavin's memories were restored so would a past life and personality? Of all the dumb luck, he had to be wealthy!

Why had he sent a motor carriage for her instead of coming himself? He was perfectly capable. It seemed evident that he had "summoned" her for some cordial apology, a trite little thank-you for her kindness during recovery and then a polite adieu. How could she bear it? She couldn't bear it! She shouldn't have come!

The butler appeared from a side door and waved the driver to the back of the castle. Jennie was all but ordered out of the auto, and a stiff finger pointed at the small door. So, she wasn't good enough for admittance through the front door?

"Since when do we pick up the help? And in the family car?" she heard the butler hiss at the driver. Confused, she ran down a narrow staircase and ended up in the servants' quarters in the basement. The head housekeeper told her to put on a black dress.

"I was summoned to Gavin, I mean Thomas Gallivan," Jennie protested.

"At least you're early. Here, put this on. You'll go with Bertie to clean his room. Mr. Gallivan is leaving."

It was more than evident that she'd been mistaken for the help. Pride burned Jennie's face, but the longing to see Gavin, even if only one last time, drove her to do as bidden.

Now the world around her seemed to whirl as a maid escorted her up another set of stairs while throwing a white apron with ruffles on over Jennie's dress and tugging a white cap on her head.

Jennie had been eleven years old when the castle was completed. As the stone walls went up, she'd longed to see the interior, daydreamed of walking its halls. Now the great structure consumed her. Instead of being enchanted, she was overcome with intimidation.

There was wood everywhere. The floorboards, the paneled walls and ceiling, and the massive stairs made the interior not charming, but heavy. A huge baronial fireplace in the main hall could have swallowed her whole. Peering through another doorway, her gaze was met by a long room, its ceiling covered in museum-quality murals, its furnishings gilded. A man, a Dunsmuir, she assumed, in a smart linen suit, stood with his back to her as he looked out the window.

"Come on!" urged Bertie with a tug on Jennie's arm that pulled her away. "It's almost New Year's," she whispered as she all but pushed Jennie up the broad and carpeted staircase, "and we want to get our work done so's we can get off to family."

Picking up the morbid hem, Jennie ran up the remaining flight. In the guest room, painted a rich hunter's green, her eyes cared little for the opulent details. All she wanted was to see Gavin, but the bed was empty.

"Where is he?" Jennie half wailed.

"He's gone, if that's what you're worried about. They've taken him away."

"They? What do you mean 'taken'?"

"Poor sot ain't right in the head. I brought his breakfast tray up once, and he was right out of it, drooling, mumbling 'Jena' over and over. The doctor was right troubled about it. Said this couldn't be allowed to go on. So, I reckon they've taken him back to San Francisco for better treatment." The maid ripped off the sheets. "Don't just stand there, get cleanin' up. Take the tray to the kitchen."

"Gavin," Jennie gasped. It must have been him in the drawing room!

Jennie grabbed the tray as an excuse to bolt from the room. She ran back down the stairs and to the drawing room, tray in hand, the silverware jiggling so hard the clanking of metal on metal could have awakened the dead. The cup that had been turned upside down had rocked over on its side, revealing partially dissolved pills. She froze in place like one of the statues in the hall: Gavin was being drugged. He was trying to hide the pills. Was the doctor sedating him? Why? That's why he'd not come or written!

The castle seemed deserted, but it was so enormous, four levels high, it could hold a crowd upstairs and appear ghostly down here. Jennie bolted unseen to the drawing room, but once inside, after scanning the length of it, saw no sign of Gavin. But through the window she could see the chauffeur's hat bobbing just above the ledge. Dropping the tray with a crash and a clatter, she ran for the window. The driver was opening the door for Gavin, and the doctor stood behind his patient, hand on the shoulder, as if to guide him down into the car.

Jennie unlocked the large pane of glass and pushed it open, shouting, "Gavin! Gavin!" He looked through the window of the auto, squinting up at her. The doctor waved a dismissive hand in her direction, and she heard him say, "Just a maid airing out the room. Don't give in to these delusions. They are typical of head injuries."

Before she could pull off the cap and jump through the window, and she would have had she time, the door was closed. But as the doctor walked around to his side of the motor carriage, Jennie spied a piano nearby. She sat down and began playing "Abide with Me 'Tis Eventide," hitting the keys as hard as her fingers could bear. But when she sprang back up, fully expecting Gavin to be stepping out of the motor car and running back into the manor, she saw instead the car speeding down the driveway.

She ran outside and raced down the drive after the car, but it was already gone. If only she'd ridden her bicycle! "Gavin," she choked. Clouds seemed to blacken in the now crushing vault of the sky. She would have run after the car, but she knew enough about the harbor activity to know that these great yachts had skipper and crew ready at a moment's notice to sail off. Gavin would be in the open water before she could set foot on the wharf. And she crumpled, right there, on the spot, in the middle of the drive.

It might have been a minute or an hour, Jennie couldn't tell. All the world turned to shadow and blur as she wept. She became paralyzed by pain and loss, by guilt and self-incrimination. If only she had come sooner! If only she had known!

"Are you all right?" A soft and elegant voice came up behind her. Looking over her shoulder, Jennie saw a beautiful woman of maybe thirty, sporting a tennis outfit, with a racket in hand. "Oh, dear, has Mother been harsh again? You mustn't let her have her way with you. All the strife between her and the boys is giving her ill spirits. Come." The woman coaxed Jennie to her feet.

"No, you don't understand."

"No, I don't. I was playing lawn tennis when it all must have happened." She called out to her tennis partners about to enter the castle through the main doors, "Go on! I'll be in soon! Pack for the voyage!" And then turned her attention back on Jennie. "Come inside and tell me what happened."

To Jennie's astonishment, the woman, called Effie, a Dunsmuir no less, brought Jennie up to her bedroom and closed the door. She was very gay and energetic. Jennie immediately began to plead with her and told her the entire story about Gavin.

"Oh, jiminy!" she exclaimed. "This is the stuff of novels! I don't know if you're mad or not, but you're certainly clever. You know he hasn't died, just relocated. Go to San Francisco. If what you say is true, then go after him, girl! But you can't go looking like that."

Effie dressed Jennie in a gorgeous pearl-studded dress with matching high-heeled shoes. As Jennie slipped them on, she recalled the tailored suit she'd seen Gavin wearing in the drawing room. She hadn't even recognized him because of it. As she looked at herself in the oval stand-up mirror, she no longer recognized herself. Gavin was a wealthy man, as rich, she supposed, as the Dunsmuirs. Did he likewise live in such an estate? She couldn't imagine living inside what was no longer an enchanting castle but a monstrosity of empty spaces full of distant echoes. Instead of sand beneath her toes and an arching sky above, pearl-studded shoes pinched her toes and stone walls boxed her in. Was this how Cinderella felt after she married the prince? The fairy tale ended when real life began, and Jennie found herself standing outside the bounds of her imagination, and it was frightening. What was to become of her? Would she end up spending her life alone in an empty cottage with the memory of a castle made of sand to haunt her all her days? What if she managed to find Gavin? Could she spend her life in this confinement?

And then she knew: she loved him. Looking down at the splendidly beautiful and splendidly awful shoes, she knew that she would sacrifice herself and all she had once loved to be with him again.

"Just so you know," Effie said as she pulled the scarf out of her hair, "my friends and I are taking the yacht to San Francisco for New Year's. The entire town turns into a wild, thrilling fete, a citywide soiree of unthinkable fun. I could smuggle you aboard. My own little stowaway," she said with a wink.

"Do you know where Gavin, I mean Thomas, lives?"

"I do indeed, though I've never been there. He and my brother Alex, who lives in San Francisco, were great chums. Both rather sullen fellows, hardly a party when you put them together." She sat on the side of the bed and crossed her legs, her movements like loose hinges.

"Why are you doing this for me? You're—rich."

"Listen, pet, we weren't always rich. My older sisters married common men, live rather common lives. I'll put my money on the common girl getting the rich man, even if the odds are stacked five miles high against her."

Jenny had never stepped foot off the island, had only watched the great ships sail away out of the harbor. Could Effie be trusted? Could she stoop to being a stowaway? All these doubts and fears were overridden by the final question: What if she never saw Gavin again?

Chapter 12

It turned out that the sisters at St. Joseph told the doctor that Gavin had stayed at the hospital during his entire visit, which he had, in the closet most of the time. So naturally, the doctor assumed that all Gavin's talk of a seal and a fisherman and a barefoot girl on the beach had been a delusion. Did the doctor actually fear Gavin would run off after an imaginary girl, that he was a danger to himself? The sedation smacked of someone else's hand, and Gavin needed no memory boost to know that this doctor was on the payroll of a very rich man whom he was told was his father.

The pills were no longer administered during the voyage, but once he had come fully to his senses, he was trapped on a boat in the middle of the ocean. In a day, the yacht moored at a private dock at the foot of a cliff upon which sat a mansion of no meager size. This was home? His heart ached with a vivid and real pain as he longed for a small cove and a pretty little cottage.

His escorts breathed on his back as he walked up the wooden steps to the estate, but upon arriving at the top, he spied a small family cemetery. As if there were pulleys on his feet, he was inextricably drawn to it, to a tall marble mausoleum. "Open it!" Gavin ordered, his commanding voice startling himself. To his surprise, the agent moved promptly to obey and the doctor equivocated. Gavin instantly recognized that he was on his turf, that he was the son of an important man.

"Mr. Gallivan," the doctor said in a shockingly obsequious tone, "I do not think this is wise."

"Do you want me to remember or not, man?" Gavin retorted, and now his tone dismayed him. What had come over him? As soon as he set foot on these lush grounds he felt he had turned into a different person, a solemn and irritable man.

The groundskeeper appeared post haste and unlocked the thick door. "Leave me," Gavin ordered, and once again, to his surprise, the three men obeyed. Gavin closed the door behind him, the chamber illuminated by a stained-glass window of an angel. As he entered the suspended shaft of light, it seemed as if he'd stepped into a time capsule. The instant his eyes locked onto the name engraved into the granite plaque over the funerary recess, he broke and fell to his knees. "Mother," his voice wept. And he remembered. Everything. It came in a rush, as if the very organ of his heart broke and hot emotion flooded his chest. Hands on the cold floor, head bowed nearly to the floor, pent-up tears from the past years broke from his eyes and he wept. Caving, holding his head, he prayed, perhaps his first real prayer.

The only gentle influence in his life, the only one from whom he felt love, had been taken from him. Illness had ravaged her delicate frame, but Thomas believed she had died from the neglect and abuses of a cold-hearted husband. He had not always been that way, she told him once, and as she reminisced, she had smiled. Sun had highlighted wavy blond hair, and he, a mere boy, saw her eyes light up with memory of the man his father had once been, and in that moment, she had looked like an angel.

What his father had been, Gavin didn't know, but his insatiable greed to build an empire had consumed him and turned his soul black. To Gavin's complete astonishment, for the first time in his life he felt pity for his father. And then, for the first time since his mother's death, he felt her nearness, even her arms wrapping him from behind, like gossamer threads of a sheer veil enfolding him.

There came a draft, and with it came words he felt more than he heard. "We will be together soon, but you need to be with Jena now."

What had ruined his happiness to this point? His father's control over him, dictating his course and future. Thomas had finally bucked all of it, his father, this life. That's why he had been on a boat, a ferry, and nearly drowned. Thomas, no, Gavin rose, slowly, hands fisted in determination, until he stood on a solid spine, drawing all of his height up in decision.

A Rolls Royce was pulling up the driveway as Gavin rounded the mansion, his escorts not far behind, having hovered in the shadow of the willow tree until he had emerged. Out of the auto, gleaming black as polished obsidian, stepped Thomas Gallivan, Sr. He too rose to full height when he saw Gavin approaching, his face stern as an admiral staring into battle. As Gavin closed the distance, his father's expression softened, and it appeared a strain to do so.

"Thomas! Son! I can't tell you how I've—"

"Don't bother." Gavin cut him off as he walked up to his father. "I remember. I remember our last encounter. I remember the veiled threats. I'm done, Father. I think I can at last forgive you for more than Mother's death, even for the bitter life you gave her. No more your sword of Damocles you've held over my head. I'll cut the thread, I'll let it fall, fall between us. I have but one thing to say to you: disinherit me. I want none of this. I'll have none of this."

With that, Gavin walked around his father, then stopped, turned, and announced, "And my name is Gavin." On he walked down the white brickwork drive, down between rows of birds of paradise and sculpted shrubbery. His father blasted curses after him.

"If you step foot off this property, you will never come back. Ever. I'm warning you, Thomas! Not a penny! There will be no forgiveness!"

At the end of the drive, flanked by statues of griffins with claws in the air, Thomas took his final step off of the estate, and Gavin never looked back. He had but one goal, and that was to return to Jena.

It was sunset, December 31, 1899. In a matter of hours it would be a new century, and for him, a new life. He drew a great breath, feeling free for the first time in his life. But without any money, how would he cross these waters to the island he now called home? Would the once prestigious Thomas Gallivan, Jr. stoop to become a stowaway?

Chapter 13

When Effie Dunsmuir had suggested Jennie stowaway on their yacht, it wasn't a metaphor or a joke. Joan Dunsmuir, the wealthiest matriarch in Western Canada, was among the party, and she would have thrown Jennie off the boat at the first sighting.

Effie, who thought this a game, hid Jennie in the hold, accessible only via a hatch. Here, Jennie huddled in a heap of life vests and tackle, listening to the thunderous echo of waves as the vessel sailed over a choppy sea. She had hours to stare at the gorgeous shoes, her feet feeling colder than if she were barefooted.

What am I doing? she asked herself over and over again. *I don't fit in this world any more than these shoes fit my feet.* What was she going to do? Walk up to Gavin's estate and just knock on the door? Would this dress get her past the butler? Would Gavin be able, or even willing now, to come down his marble or gilded staircase to see her?

But that could be the least of her problems. Jennie lived for the day; freedom meant footloose and carefree. When a way presented itself to be whisked off to San Francisco after Gavin, she had seized it without thought of a means to return. And then after she had been stuffed into this hold, Effie informed her that plans had been changed. After New Year's in the Bay, they would sail to the new town of Dunsmuir, California, to see the fountain Alex had built in the square. Jennie would have to find a more "aboveboard" way back to the island, and she had no money.

If the Gallivan estate closed its doors on her, what was she to do? Through the floorboards of the upper deck, she could hear the gaiety above. A small band played ragtime tunes. Peals of laughter broke out over the music like waves against rocks. The sound stung like saltwater in the face. There, in the emptiness of the hold, feeling deserted by all her friends, the scripture her mum made her repeat so oft from John chapter sixteen came to her, "Behold, the hour cometh, yea, is now come, that ye shall be scattered, every man to his own, and shall leave me alone: and yet I am not alone, because the Father is with me."

There, in what felt like the darkest corner in all the earth, Jennie began to softly sing, "Abide with Me 'Tis Eventide."

"Psst! Pssssssst!"

Jennie woke. She must have fallen asleep on the coil of rope, her bare forearms scratched up by the prickly twine. Looking up, she saw Effie ducking her head down into the hold. "Hurry! This is your chance! Everyone just left and the pilot is in his cabin. Wait a minute after I leave and then creep off the ship, but make sure no one sees you. Good luck and happy New Year. In the event I lose my bet, I'll leave some money for you at the front desk of the Grand Hotel. It will be his loss, I assure you, for I think you're a great gal for braving all this." Her wink was punctuated by the drop of the hatch.

Jennie made it off the yacht unseen, but it was nightfall, and though there seemed to be no clouds in the sky, she couldn't make out a single star or even the moon. The wharf and the streets all around were lit up, so perhaps they dimmed the celestial lights?

The high heels of her shoes kept sticking in between the gaps in the dock, and she could barely make her way to the boardwalk. To her alarm, a fog began to settle, enveloping everything, and on a clear night? It was a warm one considering it was winter. It couldn't have been chillier than sixty degrees. At this rate she'd never find Gavin's estate. What if he wasn't even there? What if he was out celebrating with an entourage of friends and glamorous women? What if she ran into him and he pretended to not remember her?

Climbing the steep hill—who in their right mind would build streets on such dangerous inclines?—Jennie became lost. "Excuse me, could you tell me where—?" she tried to ask people as they passed, but by the time she sensed someone beside her, that person had passed before the sentence was finalized on the air. This was when the denial began to be stripped away. Truth became all-seeing eyes that stared her in the face: she was going blind. There was no fog, just as there had been no overcast sky the winter through. The growing shadows weren't an anomaly of nature, but dimming in her eyes over the past year.

"No," trembled from her lips. As she stumbled against a brick wall, it was followed by the unanswered plea, "Gavin." How could she find him like this? How could he want her like this? He had fallen in love with a laughing sprite, a lively girl full of life—and sight.

"No, please, no." She spoke as if to the brick in front of her face, but in her heart it was directed to the only Being who could hear her. "Please, see me!" she choked as she stared with eyes wide open, so wide the lids began to ache, but all that she could see now was absolute darkness. It was as if she'd fallen into a pit. There had to be a way out! She blinked, and blinked, and blinked again, harder each time. She rubbed her eyes, squinted fiercely, defiantly. Nothing. All she could see was. . .nothing!

Turning, pressing her back against the damp bricks, she heard the clanging of multiple streetcars. One whizzed by in front of her. Sounds became acute, loud. Doors banged shut, laughter rose from gathering voices, filling the streets.

Tin horns were a high-pitched treble to the percussion bass of cowbells, all overpowering in the babble of the streets. From another sector of the city she could hear the shrill sound of squeaking pipes.

"Stop it! Please, stop!" she yelled, but amidst the commotion it was as if her voice only reverberated in her head, as if spoken under water. Disoriented, she stumbled along streets, being literally carried at times by the ebb of human bodies until she could find refuge in doorways. *Oh, Savior, stay this night with me, behold 'tis eventide*, rang through her mind even as a church bell rang out overhead. A church bell? A church!

Pawing at the walls, she groped her way up the steps, where she sat, panting, crying, her palms sore. But amidst the din, her ears seemed to sharpen, and she heard sobs up above her. Scooting up three more steps, she begged, "Please, can you help me?"

"Leave me alone!" It was the voice of a girl, about her age.

"Please!" Jennie begged, and then, for a moment, her heart softened. She closed her eyes to stop "seeing" inky blackness, to retreat into the world inside her mind, and tried to imagine the girl. "Why are you crying? Are you lost?"

It took several attempts, but at length the girl calmed and told Jennie that her pa had come down with the dreaded polio. He had been unable to work for a year and now was on the brink of death. She had come to ask God for a miracle. "My ma is working herself to the bone, but it's not enough. My last pair of shoes have fallen apart. God doesn't care, not about us!" She sniffed back angry tears. "I prayed and prayed, and I waited. Nothing. He doesn't care. No one in the world cares. Listen to them!"

"I used to believe in serendipity," Jennie said. "But now I wonder if the little surprises that come just when we need them are more than that. I have to believe it. Maybe I was meant to find you? Maybe you can help me?"

"How can I? I got nothin'. I can't even get work looking like this, in these rags."

Jennie grabbed her arms in aggravated fear. This girl wouldn't help her. No one would! There was nothing more terrifying than being lost in a strange city, far from home, and blind. The girl sniffled, on the verge of another bout of despair, and a strange thought came to Jennie. "What if I was meant to find you?"

"What can you do? Cure my pa?"

"You want to trade clothes?"

"What do you mean?"

"I bet if you wore this dress and these shoes, did your hair nice, you could get hired as a waitress or a nanny. Or maybe you could sell them and buy a pretty skirt and blouse and sensible shoes? Maybe He does hear you, and sent me to help?" Jennie nearly choked on her personal horror—she couldn't comprehend blindness even as it was happening to her. She'd rather die than be blind! But something sweet stirred below the pain, and she had a nearly overwhelming need to give this girl her clothes. "Truly, I won't need these," she said as she took off the shoes, fully aware that she needed shoes now more than ever. She didn't allow herself to contemplate the injuries she could sustain as she heard bottles being broken in the street as citizens were already getting drunk.

Jennie followed the girl into an alley where they could hide behind crates to switch clothes. Pride kept her from letting on that she was blind, and in that instant Jennie realized her mum had done the same, only not out of pride, but compassion. Only now did Jennie let herself acknowledge what she'd only half-seen that morning when she sensed everything was wrong, when Mum had been sitting, just sitting at the kitchen table: it was the morning Mum had gone completely blind. *She mustn't know,* Mum had told Pa in the doorway. *It'll take the heart right out of her.* What if her mum had been talking about herself that day, about her blindness? And then the truth glared into her soul with the next thought: What if Mum had realized that Jennie had inherited this eye disease that had no name? That's why she made Jenny memorize songs and recipes—she knew Jennie soon wouldn't be able read the music or the words. "Oh, Mum," she gasped with the realization.

Having traded clothes, Jennie could smell the odors of the girl's life on the fabric—candle smoke, which meant she had sat over a tiny flame in an effort to get warm or to work at mending; potato peels and flour, which may have been her family's only source of food; coal, which meant she had to stoke the stove. It was as if the weight of the girl's life had come down on her, and it came as a blessing in that it was a momentary distraction from Jennie's own horror that threatened to engulf her.

"Please, help me," Jennie begged, putting out a hand. Should she ask to be guided to the Grand Hotel? What if Effie had changed her mind or forgotten to leave money? Money could pay for a streetcar, but how would she find the one to take her back to the wharf and then get on it? Once at the docks, how would she find a ship to take her home when just walking seemed a task too difficult to bear?

If she could just get back to the yacht, Effie would help her, she was sure of it, if only to direct Jennie to the right boat and maybe loan her the money for the ticket. "Will you guide me to the wharf?" she finally articulated. There was no answer, but the girl moved. She must have nodded. Jennie's hand lunged out and gratefully found the girl's shoulder. The tiny pearls under her fingers reminded her why she had come, how she had hoped this dress would gain her admittance into Gavin's world. Now there was no hope; she'd never find him now. He was gone. Lost to her. She sobbed quietly as she was drawn across the street, sorrow mingling with the terror of sightlessness.

Jennie was led into the living stream of bodies that had flooded the city. The onset of howling, hooting, and pandemonium signaled the imminent countdown as she was led down a steep hill. A streetcar stopped nearby, passengers flooded the sidewalk, the bumping tore Jennie's hand away, and in a matter of seconds, she was alone in the crush. She opened her mouth to call out, but realized she didn't know the girl's name. As Jennie was rammed from side to side, Christmas boughs thrashed her face from revelers waving them in the air. She reached out to feel for a wall, a doorway, anything to press against for refuge, but all she felt were shirts and waving arms. "Stop, please!" she yelled against the jostle of bodies, to no avail. Her puny voice could hardly be heard amidst the sudden shouts of every human voice as church bells throughout the city clanged out the arrival of the New Year. Fireworks exploded overhead, taps played out on bugles. She pressed her hands against her ears, but the very air around her reverberated like a drum. It was officially the new century.

This wasn't happening, this wasn't happening! She was caught in a nightmare. Or had she, like Gavin, been knocked unconscious? Was she still in the bowels of the boat caught in a Poe-like terror? In a mania, Jennie began pushing and flailing to get free of the press of bodies. Shoving from side to side, she stumbled over shoes and boots, crying out in pain as her bare foot stepped on a lit cigar that burned what felt like a hole through the instep. Soon after, the other foot found a piece of glass. In reflex, nearly falling over, she plucked it out and there followed a soft stream of blood. Shock numbed her vocal cords as she pawed her way down the street with no objective in mind except to get free of the suffocation of bodies.

At the bottom of the hill, she fell forward onto damp wood that smelled of brine and algae. It was as if she had been spat out of a great mouth onto the boardwalk. From here, she was able to find the railing. "Effie!" she cried out. "Effie! It's Jennie! I need help! Effie, it's Jennie!"

The boards beneath her feet began to vibrate as a stampede of squealing partiers ran toward her. Jennie hung on for dear life, but the force of their bodies, evidently blind with drink, rammed into her, sending her sprawling through an opening in the railing. Her body and face slammed down against wet boards, splashing saltwater into her eyes. She grabbed her face as she rolled onto her back, crying from the pain.

"Help me! Someone help me!" she wailed with all the force in her lungs. But no one came. Staggering up onto her feet, she was turned around. Which way was the boardwalk? "Effie, it's Jennie!" she cried out, though it all seemed in vain amid the tumult that threatened to drown her. "Help me!" she shouted repeatedly as she walked on the sides of her feet. Waving her hands in front of her, desperate to find purchase, all she felt was air. Mist congealed on her face, falling as salty tears, mingling with her tears, as she pled for her Father to see her, to please see her! But her next step took her off the end of what she now realized had been a dock, and she fell, hitting the water face-first.

Arms flailing, she choked on seawater as she tried to grab hold of something, anything! The skirt was wool, and as it soaked up water it became three times its weight. She might as well as have been tied to an anchor, and she was pulled under.

Chapter 14

Was it dishonest? He wasn't sure, but Gavin used his account at the Grand Hotel one last time to send a telegram. He turned from the counter to take a final glance at the opulence and found that there wasn't a shred of remorse, only relief in leaving all this behind. As he walked toward the glass doors, he nearly ran into a young woman.

"Effie!" he exclaimed, recognizing her at once. It was another moment of victory in that he remembered yet another face.

"Thomas?" she exclaimed, and her eyes sparkled. There had always been something very special, very bright about Effie. "What are you doing here? I thought you would be at the hospital!"

"I don't need a hospital. I am perfectly fine when I'm not being drugged. I recall I was at Craigdarroch?"

"You were indeed, though we hardly got as much as a peek at you. Did you know a girl named Jennie came to see you? She had such a story to tell!"

"She was there? I knew it! Effie, I have to go back. I have a boat coming but nowhere to stay."

"You? Nowhere to stay? Don't be preposterous."

"My father's cut me off."

"Thomas! How dreadful!"

"Far from it. I'm finally free of the man."

"Well, Jennie's looking for you. I gave her a lift on the yacht. Where she could be in all this, I don't know. I gave her my pearl-studded dress, the one I wore at the races last year, you remember? Anyway, I thought it might help the poor thing gain admittance into your estate. Goodness knows, she would have been turned out in that maid's uniform, or put to work!"

"Effie," Gavin interrupted, his muscles tensing at the thought of Jena out alone in the chaos, "where is she now?"

"How should I know? Oh, don't look at me like that! I told her I would leave money for her here, in the event she didn't find you or you turned her out."

Gavin grabbed Effie by the shoulders. "Has she picked up the money?"

"I only just got here from dinner at the Fat Herring. Astoundingly good food for the name. Here." She opened her beaded purse and handed him a clip of folded bills. "Why don't you give this to her when you see her? And Thomas"—she looked him in the eye—"call on me if you get down on your luck. We're still friends," she said with a wink, "regardless of the abominable pranks you once played on me."

"I'll make this up to you, Effie!" Gavin said. He planted a kiss on her cheek and ran out the door.

Knowing that Jena hadn't picked up the money eliminated the possibility that she had taken a cab or a streetcar to his father's estate, or anywhere beyond walking distance, for that matter. On foot, and in this crowd, she couldn't have gotten far from the wharf. It only made sense that she would have come this direction, toward the hotel for the promised money. What was she thinking? Coming to San Francisco alone? Her parents must be out of their minds with worry. But the mental reprimand was swallowed up in the overpowering relief that Jena had come for him.

Gavin was a dashing figure in his suit and leather shoes as he jumped around bodies and zigged and zagged through the clumps of celebrators. It was hours into the night when he managed to work his way down toward the docks under lamplights. Discouraged, racking his brain for where she could be, he felt a desperation come over him, an urgency to find her.

"But where is she?" he whispered under his breath, and it was more than a mere exclamation. It was then he saw the bobbing figure in a pearl-studded dress. "Hey! Wait!" he called, waving his hand above his head. "Wait! Jena!" he shouted, and pushed and shoved his way through until he grabbed the figure from behind and whirled her around, fully intending to plant a kiss on her lips. But the face that greeted him with mouth and eyes wide open was not Jena.

"Who are you?"

"Who are you, I should be askin'. Keep your hands off me!" It was only a girl of maybe fifteen. The dress and shoes were a size too big, a near fit but loose enough to reveal her age.

"Where did you get that dress?"

"That's none of your business, mister."

"Look, I have to find the woman who gave it to you. Please! Where is she?"

"Darned if I know. She gave me this dress, you know. I didn't steal it off her body! She traded me. They're a gift, and you can't have 'em even if you could take 'em."

"Listen, miss, all I want from you is to tell me where she is."

"I was showin' her the way to the docks, but the crowds separated us. It was real strange-like, the way she held onto my shoulder to follow me, as if she were walking blind."

Gavin's eyes spread with realization and fear. Surely not? But her mother was blind, of that he was sure, for when he'd had meals with them he'd seen how her eyes never followed any movement or responded to light. Jena had complained multiple times at how dark the sky looked, even when it was sunny. He had assumed it was because her personality could never get enough brightness, color, or vitality. But then it dawned on him, the chapter on genetic eye diseases he'd read in her father's book.

"Here." He shoved a bill in the girl's hand. Her eyes lit up like it was Christmas Day. "Tell me where you last saw her."

Gavin ran sideways through the press of bodies to squeeze past the multitudes now filling the streets. Streetcars couldn't even pass; all traffic was on foot. "Jena! Jena!" he shouted in every direction, scanning every face. It seemed hopeless when the bells tolled the New Year, and horns and bells and voices rang out. Confetti flew like multicolored insects in the lamplight. Fireworks popped overhead, turning the sky an electric white and blue, raining sparks. He ran past a church, its doors wide open, perhaps eager to receive all the sinners from the night. He heard the preacher booming out a sermon.

"Excuse me, excuse me, please," he said as he pushed his way down the street. When he made it to the boardwalk, even through all the commotion, he heard a woman call out for Effie. He looked in the direction of the sound, but it was difficult to hone in on its location.

Again, came the voice, shouting for Effie, and then, "It's me, Jennie!" Jena! Gavin pulled lovers apart, grabbed at arms and yanked, to tear free of the knot of citizens. One last time he heard Jena calling, but as he scanned the boardwalk, there was no sign of her.

"Jena! Jena!" he called, cupping his hands at his mouth. He strained, listened, and then he heard a splash at the end of the dock. "Jena!" Was that her? If he had not suspected that she had lost her eyesight, he would have assumed it was the splash of a seal or a large sturgeon. He ran down the dock, peeling off his coat and casting it behind him. He stood at the end, scanning the water. There was no sign of her, of anyone, of any movement. "Jena!" He whirled, looked around. No one, yet he had heard her voice. Turning, he dove into the water.

There was a reason he had never taken to the sea as his brothers had. He was a weak swimmer, but he could dive and he could hold his breath, which he did, but even with eyes wide open against the burning saltwater, he could see nothing in the dark abyss of the bay. He began to swim from side to side, feeling for her in the water, when a thought entered his mind with force: Jena had traded clothes with a girl whose dialect gave her away as a member of the poorer class, and as such would have worn a heavy broadcloth skirt. If Jena was wearing it now, the weight of it would drag her down.

Jumping up out of the water, Gavin got back on the dock, where he took a tremendous breath and dove straight down with all the power in his legs. Deeper and deeper he swam. She could be anywhere! He continued to swim with wide strokes, feeling in every direction for her. At last he felt fabric brush his fingertips. Lunging in that direction, he reached out and felt a leg. Grabbing it, pulling the body in close to him, he swam for the surface with great arm strokes. Once his, and then her face, broke the surface, his lungs inhaled to relieve the excruciating burn. But hers did not. She remained limp in his arms, white as the ghost she was becoming, or already was.

Chapter 15

Her eyes opened, expecting to see the jar of sea glass radiating on the window ledge from the dawning light. But all that greeted her was this maddening, all-consuming darkness. She bolted up, crying out, "Mum!" Arms enfolded her, held on to her as if to precious cargo.

"I'm here, Jen girl, I'm here. You're safe." A familiar hand stroked Jennie's dry hair. "You're home and you're safe."

"Mum! I can't see! I can't see anything!"

Her mother began to rock her as she sat beside her on the bed. "I know, I know, dear child, I know."

"Mum." Jennie tightened her grip on her mum. "It's you too, isn't it? Even when I could see, I was too blind to see. I'm sorry, I'm sorry, Mum." Jennie wept as she in turn rocked her mum.

As terrifying as it was to be blind, the comfort she felt from her mother's embrace calmed her, and she learned to close her eyes when it became unbearable and to retreat into her imagination where every scene was vibrant and full of color.

Gradually, she got out of bed. Her papa had sewn a different kind of button on the hem of each of her clothes, and with his help, she learned to differentiate the colors. In a fit of angry despair, she hurled the gypsy scarf out the window, and the jar of sea glass with it.

Her mother counted steps with her from room to room. She already knew the way by "foot" to the beach, but couldn't bear to go down to it, her heart broken over the loss of Gavin. She couldn't even go down to take bread to Simun, even after her parents told her that Gavin had saved her and had sent for the fisherman to bring her back.

"Where is Gavin now?" she asked.

Mum stroked her hair, twisting the strands as if practicing to weave it for her in the future. "You fell into the water. It was a miracle that Gavin found you, brought you back to us. He sat with you on the boat, kept you bundled and warm, all the way back, he said. But he had something to do while you slept."

"It's been a week, Mum."

"I know. But we must count our blessings, and we are blessed that we had him in our lives and that he brought you back to us."

It was several days later when Jennie sat at the piano. She couldn't bring herself to play the hymns she knew by heart, the ones she had played for Gavin in the hospital. The memories should have been bittersweet, but they were just bitter. She couldn't feel free again, much less carefree. The Jennie she had been was gone, and a sullen girl had taken her place. For the life of her she couldn't smile. What kind of a life would she have now? "We had you late in life," her mother had said, reminding her that they would pass on many years before Jennie, and she would not only be alone in this cottage, she would be alone in the dark. It was more than she could bear, and she felt that she wanted to die as her fingers lay limp over the keys, her ragtime piece she never learned propped up, she knew, in front of her face, but she couldn't see the sheet of music now to learn it. She never would.

Someone came up behind her. It was a man, she could tell by smell though she wasn't sure just how. "Papa?" she asked. Why was he home in the middle of the day? There was no answer but a breath next to her ear and then hands sliding down her arms, fingers spreading out over her fingers. Her heart beat at a hummingbird's pace. Dared she hope? But it was him! She knew it, not by sight, but by a deeper sense she never before knew existed.

"Gavin?" Her voice trembled.

"You can play it."

She couldn't speak for a moment, every force of will in her body trying to turn her around, to reach up and hold him, to bury her face in his shoulder. But pride won out. Why was he here? To say goodbye to the blind girl? To absolve his conscience?

"Gavin," she choked, then drew a steadying breath. "No, I can't. I can't see. I can't see anything!"

"But you can feel." He pressed down on one finger, then another. Note by note, his fingers over hers, together they played a very slow version of the first line of the piece. He could play, that's what his fingers were trying to remember that day in the hospital.

She could contain herself no longer and whirled around on the bench and grabbed him, held onto him, choking on tears as she buried her face in his chest. He knelt down and drew her into his arms, picked her up, and carried her outside.

"I thought I'd never see you again," she said into his neck and then choked a sardonic laugh at the irony of her own words.

The Castle Made of Sand

"Jena Farrow, you always knew you'd see me again." He kissed her hair. "You came for me. My angel twice over."

"Gavin, I'm not the same woman you fell in love with."

"You are exactly the woman I fell in love with." He was carrying her through the front yard.

"Where are you taking me?"

He didn't answer. Instead, he placed her onto a bicycle seat. She covered her face to hold back the tears then said through her fingers, "What are you doing? I'll never ride again!"

"Not true. You'll never ride again—by yourself."

She heard the *ching-ching* of a bicycle bell, but she couldn't feel one on her handlebars. There was also no basket. This wasn't her bike. "What is this?" she asked.

"It's a bicycle built for two. Put your feet up on the pedals, I've got you." She lifted her feet. The bike didn't fall over. Her bare feet felt for the pedals, found them, and then she grabbed the handlebars. "Ready?" he asked. She nodded, a laugh of anticipation slipping out. She clapped her hand over her mouth, as if that would also hold back the tears. It didn't. The nightmare was starting to turn into a dream, one she dared not believe in, and yet she was mounted on top of a bicycle again.

She heard his foot as he kicked off, and then a surge went through her stomach as the bike launched forward. A squeal rang from her mouth as she was sped forward, the moment more thrilling than ever before.

"Pedal!" he ordered. "I'm not your chauffeur!" And he laughed. Oh, the sound of it, penetrating more than her ears! The sound of his voice that struck chords in her bosom she never knew she had! It was another sensation she'd never known before. She pedaled faster and faster; felt the momentum pick up until her hair flew out behind her, followed by her arms as she flew down the hill in a rush of such joy she couldn't contain it; and laughed until her ribs hurt.

They returned, and she felt glum once more. "Do I have to return home?"

"You will always be going home, I hope." He paused as he lifted her up off the bicycle. "With me."

Her heart hammered out the words, "What do you mean?"

"Take my hand." Why did he ask? He took it anyway and guided her down a path.

"Wait, this isn't my cottage. It's back behind us."

"Yes, it is."

"Where, what is this?"

"You gave me the vision and courage to free myself from my father. But doing so left me a destitute man. I came to the island in the first place to find my mother's family. She grew up here. I had been cut off from them after she died. It took me a week, but I've located them and can't wait for them to meet you. They love you already!

"I'm still working for your father, and I'd thought perhaps the nuns would let me sleep in that closet, or Simun on his boat, until I could afford a place of my own and gradually save up enough to buy us a home, if you'd have me. But your father, he offered to co-sign a loan for our own cottage. I hope I wasn't presumptuous, but I thought you'd want to be near your mother, and of course the cove."

"But this is the derelict house!" No one had lived here for ages. Where were all the weeds? Though she couldn't see them, she understood how her mum had known Jennie had not trimmed the garden: now Jennie not only smelled everything, a whole new world of scent, she recognized the lack of it.

"Not anymore." He took her up to the doorstep. "Here, reach up." He took her hands and ran them over the top arch. She felt the smooth shapes she knew so well.

"It's your sea glass. I hope you don't mind, but when you threw them out your window, I assumed they were mine for the taking. I cemented the sand from our cove over the doorway and made a mosaic with the glass. So this can be our castle made of sand, one that won't wash away. It will be ours for the rest of our lives." He placed his lips over hers, not in a kiss, not yet, but with a smile that encouraged her lips to form the same. He put his arms around her waist and drew her up into his arms. His scent was unique and intoxicating. The feel of his skin, of his hair, it was vibrant.

"Jena Farrow, will you marry me?"

She began to cry so hard she almost couldn't speak, "Yes! Yes, Gavin!"

He sealed the proposal with a kiss then swept her up off her feet and ran with her next door to her cottage, to tell her parents. Only then did she realize that he loved them like his own.

"There's one more surprise I have to reveal," he said. He took her hand and they ran to the cove. Simun was there with his boat, and the crusty old fisherman planted a kiss on her forehead then gave her a basket of fish.

"A whole basket?" she said. "How much does Oscar eat?"

"That's the rub," Gavin said. "Here, drop your feet into the water."

She did. The brine stung the still-healing cut and the burn, but she forgot the pain when she felt Oscar's nose rub along her feet, once, twice, three times. "Oh, Oscar, I've missed you too!" But then there were three, then four noses that rubbed along her feet and ankles all at once. With a shriek she pulled her feet out, only to hear Oscar bark, followed by three other tiny barks. "What, what is this?"

"There is one serious mistake you've made, Jena Farrow," Gavin said.

"What?"

"Oscar is a girl. She's had pups."

"Heavens have mercy!" she exclaimed. "No wonder he was so fat!"

"You may not be a selkie," Gavin said, "but you're as close as they come. The seals all love you." He sat behind her and held her as she threw out fish and heard the sound of the seals jumping up to catch them. She splashed her feet as a veritable herd swam around her feet. It was only the beginning of the family she would eventually have with Gavin, inside their own little "castle," built not of stone but of wood. . .and a mosaic arch of sand.

CJ Dunham is an author, presenter, and storyteller. She has performed across the country, given creative writing presentations, has published a fully-illustrated children's book, and her work has appeared in national magazines. A mother of five and grandmother of thirteen, Dunham enjoys cycling and pretending she can paint. Learn more at authorcjdunham.com and @CJDunham1.

A Teacher's Heart

by Cynthia Hickey

To my family: You are cherished

Then Peter came to Jesus and asked, "Lord, how many times shall I forgive my brother or sister who sins against me? Up to seven times?" Jesus answered, "I tell you, not seven times, but seventy-seven times."
MATTHEW 18:21–22 NIV

Chapter 1

Mary Jo Stevens stared at the rickety wagon in front of her. There was only one spot to sit next to the driver, and Mama Aida would need it. The back didn't have much more room, loaded down with crates of school supplies donated by the church.

"Climb on up, Mary Jo." Mama Aida climbed onto the seat. "Hop on back. We've got to get a move on. Dark is coming, and it's a ways up the mountain to our new home."

With a sigh, Mary Jo did as her mother-in-law said and perched on the back of the flatbed. The driver clucked to the horses and sent them jolting ahead. Mary Jo promptly slid off the back and ended up in a pile of rocks and leaves.

"Wait!" She ran to keep up, dragging her satchel.

The wagon continued without her. Darkness fell early in the mountains.

She stared for a moment, mouth gaping, then clutched the handle of her satchel tighter and began the long trek to her new home as the night deepened around her. She had no hope the wagon would turn around and fetch her. The road ahead wasn't wide enough. Why hadn't they sent someone with an automobile?

A horn sounded behind her.

Mary Jo screamed and leaped into the ditch. Ask and you shall receive. Hadn't she just wished for an automobile? Yes, but not for one to almost run her over.

Something screamed in the trees behind her. Mary Jo dashed for the truck. "Someone's in there. They're injured."

"No, ma'am, I reckon that's a cougar. You might want to climb in here." The passenger door opened.

A cougar? She couldn't get in the truck fast enough. Only then did she realize she'd left her satchel in the ditch. It held almost all of her earthly belongings. "My bag."

"I'll get it." A man, so handsome Mary Jo forgot about her fear, grinned at her. Blue eyes twinkled under inky black hair. A cleft deepened in his chin.

"But. . .the cougar."

"It won't harm me. Just stay in the truck." He rushed to fetch her bag, returning without harm. He closed his door, shutting off the dome light. "I'm William Wright. Folks call me Bill."

"Mary Jo Stevens. The new teacher." She held out her hand.

He returned the shake. "I'm a demonstration agent for the Arkansas Welfare Department. I'm here to help the people of this hollow live better lives."

"It seems we share a common goal."

"I guess we do." He pressed the gas and took them bouncing down the dirt road. "Why are you wandering out here alone?"

"I fell off the wagon. My mother-in-law and the driver probably haven't noticed I'm gone." An idea that rankled. Mama Aida would be babbling on about whatever interested her that day and most likely wouldn't look back once.

"We'll catch up to them with little trouble, I'm guessing." He cut her a sideways glance. "You're married?"

"Widowed, going on five years now." The pain had lessened after Frank's death. "Mama Aida had nowhere to go but to stay with me."

"That's kind of you."

"We get along well, thankfully." She stared out the window at the darkness. She was grateful. Mama Aida had claimed her as daughter from the moment she'd met Frank at the age of fifteen. They'd had two wonderful years of marriage together, until he died in a logging accident.

"There they are." Bill motioned ahead, the truck's lights illuminating a wagon. "Do you want me to drop you off?"

"No, thank you. There's no room for me." She waved as they squeezed past, tree branches scraping the side of the truck.

Mama Aida's mouth dropped open before she spoke words Mary Jo couldn't hear over the rattle of the truck. "Oh, I'll hear about it when I get home. She'll want to know all about the stranger who drove me home. You aren't a serial killer, are you?"

Bill laughed. "Nothing as exciting as that. Maybe you'll be able to help me once you know your students' families better."

"With what?" She turned sideways to face him.

"Well, I teach men how to build sturdy, inexpensive farm homes, using stones and concrete so they last longer."

"Not a lot of concrete out here."

"I also teach the women how to make furniture and tick mattresses. How to grow and sell products from their gardens and kitchens. I form better baby clubs for women to learn how to care for their children."

"So, you butt into people's business." She narrowed her eyes.

"No. I help them." He glanced at her and then back to the road.

"The people up here are proud." She crossed her arms. "They won't take to a city boy coming in and telling them how things are done. I bet you have all kinds of ideas on how I should run my classroom too."

"I have some brochures, yes." He cut her a sideways glance.

"That's my house, I think." She peered through the window, searching for the schoolhouse. Yes, there it was. That meant the tiny house next to it belonged to her and Mama Aida. "Thank you so much for the lift." She climbed out and then stood at the window. "Mr. Wright. You'll need to proceed slowly with these people. Respect their way of life. Tiptoe around them until they trust you."

"Are you from here?"

"Yes. I grew up here until moving to the valley, where I went to college." She grinned. "It's good to be home." She slapped the side of his truck and turned to welcome the arriving wagon.

The lovely strawberry-blond teacher might think him a meddling city boy, but Bill intended to help these people. He'd stay in Pilgrim's Hollow until his job was finished.

He shifted the truck back into gear and drove away in search of his own rented house. The welfare department paid him to help people, and that's what he intended to do.

He found his small, one-room house behind the general store and carried his bags inside. It wasn't fancy, but it was clean, consisting of a small kitchen area, a single bed, a table with two chairs, and a wood-burning stove. He'd be comfortable enough during his stay.

He hung his few shirts in the armoire. Folded his trousers and set them in the bureau drawer, then toed off his boots.

It bothered that Mrs. Stevens passed judgment. Raised by a single mother, living on one meal a day because of poor living conditions, had made Bill jump at the chance to work for the welfare department. Cleanliness, education, and information was usually all it took to help those still living in backward ways.

He sighed and lay on the hard mattress. He stared at the ceiling. God had brought him to Pilgrim's Hollow, God would set his path.

The sun streamed through the thin, gauzy curtain on the window, jolting him awake. What would the people think if he crawled out of bed after most of them were already working their fields?

He quickly splashed water on his face from a basin on the sideboard, slicked back his hair, and then dressed. Grabbing his briefcase with his brochures, he headed outside. Turning left, he walked to the five buildings that made up downtown.

A general store, which also sported a shiny gas pump. A drugstore, complete with soda fountain. A church, a schoolhouse, and a feed store. If he could get the businesses to allow him to leave his brochures, it would generate interest when customers came in.

He chose the general store first. A bell jingled over the door as he entered. The aroma of pickles, yeast, and candy greeted him. With a smile, he approached the glass-fronted counter. "Good morning. I'm Bill Wright with the Arkansas Welfare Department. I'm wondering if you would be so kind as to let me leave these brochures on the counter for your customers?"

"You're from where?" The portly man frowned. "You want to leave what? We aren't partial to propaganda."

"No, sir, this is full of ways to enrich your life. I'll be holding an informative meeting at the church on Sunday afternoon. I hope to see you there." Bill set a handful of the shiny pamphlets on the counter.

The bell jingled, announcing the arrival of a customer. Bill turned with a smile, prepared to greet the person. "Mrs. Stevens."

She nodded. "He's all right, Mr. Wilson. New to town." She slapped a piece of paper on the counter. "Mama Aida is insistent she get this list filled."

"I'll get right on it, Mary Jo." He studied Bill for another few seconds then turned to his work.

Mrs. Stevens reached for a brochure and opened it. "Nicely put together."

"Thank you." Bill leaned against the counter. "Thank you also for opening a prospective door with the store owner."

She shrugged. "I can't judge you until I've seen your approach. Leaving brochures isn't forcing your opinion on anyone."

He sighed and stepped back as Mr. Wilson brought her the order. "I hope to see you at the meeting on Monday afternoon after school."

She nodded, her hazel eyes sparkling. "I'm looking forward to it."

He bet she was. Clutching his briefcase, he headed for the drugstore. The young woman behind the counter was much friendlier than Mr. Wilson. She cupped her chin and leaned her elbows on the counter. "You're new."

"Yes, ma'am, I am. I'd like to—"

"Don't call me *ma'am*." She pouted. "I'm Daisy."

"Bill. I'd like to—"

She straightened as someone else entered. "Good morning, Preacher Dean."

"Good morning, Daisy. Mrs. Malcolm asked me to pick up her prescription." He held out his hand to Bill. "Dean Robertson, pastor of this flock."

Bill introduced himself and repeated the spiel he'd given to Mr. Wilson. "I'm looking forward to meeting these fine people."

"They won't be accommodating at first, but you'll win them over." He took the brochures from Bill's hand and laid them on the counter. "Daisy, make sure you pass these out, will you?"

"Sure thing, Preacher." She winked.

He laughed and wagged a finger at her. "Naughty girl. No flirting. I'm much too old for you." He clapped Bill on the shoulder. "Watch out for that one."

Bill glanced out the window as Mary Jo strolled by. "What about that one?"

"Lovely, respectable, and a lover of this hollow." His eyes softened. "Everyone loves Mary Jo."

Including the pastor, unless Bill was mistaken.

"If you can get her on your side, the others will follow."

Bill nodded. He intended to do just that, if Mrs. Stevens would allow it.

Chapter 2

Mary Jo studied the list of test scores in her hand. One stood out, high even for city standards. "Daisy, would you please approach my desk? The rest of you may continue silent reading."

Sounds of "Ooh, you're in trouble" sang through the room. Mary Jo smiled to ease the obvious discomfort of her oldest student. She motioned to a nearby chair.

"Have you thought of what you'd like to do with your future? You're too old for this school, and I must confess, it's a puzzle as to why you come every day."

Daisy picked at the cuticle of her thumb. "I like learning. I want to go to college, but I'd need shoes and a nice dress to wear for the orientation. I missed a lot of school recently when I went to help my ailing aunt." She peered up from lowered lashes. "I'd also need a reference."

Mary Jo leaned back in her chair. It wasn't uncommon for students in the hollow to not have shoes. Many only received a pair in the winter, and a used pair at that. The fact that Daisy wanted to go to college warmed Mary Jo's heart. She peered at the girl's feet. "I'll lend you a dress and my shoes. We look to be about the same size."

"Would you really?" Daisy clapped her hands. "That's grand." Her smile faded. "I would need a bus ticket. Perhaps I could work here, after school, cleaning?"

"Don't you have a job at the drugstore?"

"Yes, but I'll need spending money while I'm in Little Rock." The girl pouted.

Sighing, Mary Jo nodded. "I can help with that too. But, remember. . .I need these things back, especially my shoes. Come by the house later and collect your things."

Daisy leaped to her feet. "I'll go reserve my seat on the bus. I can do that from the general store." With those words, she was gone, her bare feet slapping the wooden planks of the floor.

Later that day, Mary Jo headed to the general store to pay for the ticket, dismayed to discover the girl was leaving on the morning's bus. "So soon?"

Mr. Wilson shrugged. "It only comes once a week. A person has to get on when they can."

"I understand." Mary Jo paid for the ticket and headed home.

Daisy stood from her seat on the steps. "I'm here, Mrs. Stevens."

"I see that. Isn't Mama Aida home?"

"I didn't knock."

The girl might be smart, but she didn't always think clearly. Mary Jo smiled. Weren't we all like that? "Come on in. I'll fetch the dress." She motioned for Daisy to have a seat on the sofa then headed to her room.

She only had two nice dresses for church and hated to lend one of them, but she did own three skirts and several blouses. She pulled down a brown pleated skirt and pale-yellow blouse. These would make Daisy look like the flower she was named after. Mary Jo toed off her shoes and padded to the living room. Using the back of a used envelope, she scribbled down her address.

"Here you go. I've enclosed a bit of money to pay for the postage in returning these items." She gave the girl a hug. "I wish you all the luck and will be praying for you."

"You're the best teacher ever!" Daisy returned her hug and dashed out the door.

Mama Aida, leaning against the door jamb, sipped from her mug of coffee and then said, "Your kind heart is going to be your demise. That girl is as loose as the shingles on this house." Her gaze flicked to Mary Jo's bare feet. "You won't see her or your shoes again."

"Of course, I will. No kindness ever goes unpaid." Mary Jo smiled. "Speaking of shoes, I'll need to borrow yours during school days."

"My feet are smaller than yours. You'll stretch them out."

Mary Jo raised her eyebrows. Surely, the woman she supported wouldn't deny such a simple request.

"What about church?" Mama Aida's eyes widened.

"It isn't as if I've not gone barefoot before."

Mama Aida huffed. "Fine, but don't come crying to me when you get bleeding blisters."

"I won't. Thank you. May I borrow them now? I'm supposed to meet Mr. Wright in the Sunday school rooms. He's doing a demonstration on cleanliness and requires my assistance."

A few minutes later, Mary Jo hobbled down the road proudly dubbed Main Street. Pastor Dean joined her.

"Something wrong with your feet?" Concern flickered across his face.

"Not a thing." She forced a smile. "Are you attending the demonstration?"

"Wouldn't miss it. I wholly plan on supporting our Mr. Wright." He smiled and crooked his arm toward her. "I truly believe he can help our community."

"If people will let him." She leaned heavily on his arm, slipping free when they stepped into the church.

Mr. Wright looked surprised but then grinned. "Exciting, isn't it? Ten women have arrived. I had hoped for more, but this is a wonderful beginning."

"It is." Mary Jo was surprised that many had come. Most likely it was curiosity that lured them in.

"Please join me at the front of the room, Mrs. Stevens." Mr. Wright held the door open for her.

"Please, call me Mary Jo. Otherwise, I feel as if you're one of my students." She limped to the front, Mr. Wright following.

"Then I insist you return the favor by calling me Bill. You must not have heard me when I found you on the side of the road."

She chuckled. "My apologies." She took her place behind a table and casually slipped her heels from the shoes. Mama Aida would kill her if she broke down the backs, but her feet couldn't take the pinching and rubbing another second. She yanked her attention from her feet to Bill who faced the group of women and spoke.

"Cleaning your hands after tending to your livestock, working the garden, or changing a soiled or wet diaper is essential in helping to prevent the spread of germs. A good strong soap and hot water are the best tools for achieving this. Your hands please." He held out his hand for Mary Jo to place hers in his.

Her eyes widened as she did. "Oh."

Standing behind her, he dunked her hands into a pan of water and rubbed them together. "Now a generous lathering of soap, like this." He rubbed her hands across the bar, creating a good lather. "Make sure to get the soap under your fingernails."

She couldn't breathe. He smelled like soap and a pine-scented aftershave. The thought that she should step out of his arms occurred to her, but she couldn't bring herself to move. Why hadn't she noticed before how strong his arms were?

Mary Jo's hair smelled of chalk and sunshine. He'd acted impulsively by stepping behind her, but once there couldn't withdraw without it appearing more improper than it already was.

Pastor Dean frowned from the back of the room. Because of the improperness? Or because he was Mary Jo's beau? Surprise had slapped Bill in the face when he'd seen her enter the church on his arm. What a fool he was. Bill had just met the lovely teacher. Of course someone as pretty as her would already have someone in her life.

He stepped back, feeling as if he'd just let go of the most wonderful thing in his life. "Any questions?" He scanned the group of serious-faced women.

"I got one," said a woman from the front row. "I'd like to know how you expect us to get all this soap you want us to use. It's too expensive to buy and takes a good amount of time to make."

Bill was prepared for this question. "But calling in the doctor is more expensive than the soap and preventable illness results in days in bed."

The woman shook her head. "Nope. We give the doctor eggs or butter."

Bill sighed as the other women nodded their agreements. "Just please consider the lesson I've taught you. Cleanliness really does make a difference."

Mary Jo raised her hand. "Ladies, it really didn't take a lot of soap." She held up the bar. "Yes, you'll use more if you have children, but look how soapy the water still is. One basin of soapy water will last you all day."

Murmurs spread through the women. It seemed they would listen to Mary Jo, when they wouldn't consider his words. He needed to make sure she attended every lesson and agreed with him, or he'd never get through to the community.

After the women filed out, Bill turned to Mary Jo. "Thank you for standing up for my idea."

"I agree that cleanliness is good." She fiddled with something under the table. Wincing, she joined him on the other side.

"May I walk you home? I have something I'd like to discuss."

She glanced at Pastor Dean then nodded. "I'll let him know and meet you out front."

Bill nodded at the pastor on his way out and then waited in the growing darkness for Mary Jo. He'd almost given up on her joining him when he heard her voice.

"I'll see you tomorrow, Dean." She patted the man's arm then smiled at Bill. The night wasn't as dark anymore.

Since it seemed even more apparent that the pastor was courting Mary Jo, Bill didn't offer his arm. Instead, they strolled side by side toward her house, behind the school. Mary Jo limped beside him. It almost seemed as if she tried not to bend her foot as she walked. Bill glanced down at her serviceable shoes. The left one sported a scuff mark that looked like the state of Texas. He supposed a teacher did spend a lot of time on her feet. They were bound to be tired at the end of a long day.

"I'm wondering, hoping, actually, that you'll help me with my work," he said.

She glanced up. "How?"

"These people listen to you. You're one of them. Several of those women will now wash their hands before touching food because you agreed with me." So strong was his desire to take hold of her hand that he shoved his into his pockets. "Harvest time is coming. I'd like to show them how to safely pack their food and transport it down the mountain to sell."

She frowned. "They eat what they grow, Bill. Rarely does anyone have anything to spare. If they do, they give it to those in need, or to the preacher, or to the teacher. Those with little to no income."

"What about the baby clubs?"

"If you can somehow convince them you aren't trying to tell them how to live their lives, it might work." She stopped at the stairs to her porch, climbed to the second step, and turned, coming into eye contact with him. Her eyes glittered in the light of a full moon. "I'll help you where I can and try to prevent you from alienating anyone."

He placed a hand on the railing and stared into her face. "I heard what you did for Daisy. You've a kind heart, Mary Jo."

She ducked her head. "It's what anyone would have done."

"No, not anyone." He glanced at her feet. "Not everyone around here has a pair to spare." He grinned and headed toward his own home, whistling. Before he turned from the street, he glanced back to see Mary Jo, still standing on the porch, as if watching him walk away.

His heart jumped. Maybe things weren't solid with her and the pastor. He and Mary Jo were on their way to becoming friends, but maybe, in time, they could be something more. He resumed his whistling and walked up the small dirt path to his door.

A box lay on the stoop. He unlocked his front door and carried the heavy box inside. Using a knife, he cut open the flap. A new bar of soap—and a sleeping infant—wrapped in a dirty blanket, lay inside.

Heart pounding, he lifted out the baby, dashed out his door, and raced back to Mary Jo's. She and her mother sat on the front porch. "I need you," he said, thrusting the baby into Mary Jo's arms.

It promptly opened its mouth and wailed.

"What in the world?" Mary Jo stood, eyes wide.

"Someone left the. . .baby. . .on my stoop." He tried to regulate his breathing. "And a bar of soap. I don't think they listened to me at all."

"Oh, they listened," the older woman said. "They thought you the best candidate for taking care of this child, you being so clean and wise and all."

"Please say you can help me," he said, still looking at Mary Jo. "I can't take care of a baby."

"First thing is to contact the authorities." She cradled the infant. "We'll watch over the precious thing until then."

"Silly." Mama Aida clumped into the house.

Bill glanced at her shoes as she left them. The left one bore the same scuff as the pair Mary Jo had worn. In exactly the same spot.

Mary Jo sighed and padded on bare feet into the house. She paused before closing the door. "Don't worry, Bill. Everything works out."

Chapter 3

The next morning, Mary Jo cradled the infant and stared into the sheriff's face. "Did you just say I'd have to keep the baby?"

He removed his hat and nodded. "Just until a more permanent home is found."

"I work, Sheriff. I spend my days at school, teaching these children. How am I supposed to care for a baby?"

He glanced over her shoulder at Mama Aida.

"Oh, no." Mama Aida shook her head. "I'm much too old. Give the poor child to that meddling newcomer. It was given to him."

"*She*, Mama Aida. She was given to Bill." Mary Jo patted the baby's back. The poor thing couldn't be more than a few weeks old. "She needs more than I can give her."

The sheriff shook his head. "You're all she has. Maybe the mama will come forward."

"I reckon I won't give the child to her." Mary Jo frowned. "Any woman who would give up her baby doesn't deserve to have it back."

"Oh. I almost forgot." He dug into his breast pocket and handed her a letter. "I offered to bring you your mail. Have a nice day." With those words, he left Mary Jo feeling horribly inadequate.

She handed the baby to Mama Aida, who despite her grumbling, cooed and spoke baby talk. Mary Jo sat on the empty rocker and opened the letter.

Mrs. Stevens, I reckon I can't bring you back your shoes and clothes. I've got a job and a fiancé. We're headed to Memphis. Thanks again. Daisy.

Could the day possibly get any worse? She'd had to wear Mama Aida's shoes for a little more than a day, and it felt as if blisters and cramped toes might become a permanent thing.

Mary Jo had tried to be understanding as the days went by, but enough was enough. She needed her shoes. "How much money is in the cookie jar?"

"Less than a dollar."

She stared at her mother-in-law. "What on earth have you been spending my paychecks on?"

"Food. I made you that new dress." Confusion flickered in her eyes. "What's got your undies wadded up?"

"Daisy isn't coming back or returning my things. I need money for shoes."

"Then have Bill pay you for your help." She kissed the baby on the forehead and handed her back to Mary Jo. "You might want to name her, now that you're a mama and all." She smiled and entered the house.

A mother? Oh, no. Mary Jo headed at a brisk pace to Bill's tiny house. "I cannot care for her," she said, the moment he answered the door. "I have a job, and soon she'll be too big for me to take to the schoolhouse. Mama Aida refuses to babysit. You must take her." Her heart lurched at the words. She gazed down at the precious face. What a difference a week could make in how someone's feelings could change from annoyance to love.

"I'm a bachelor. I can't take care of an infant." He took a step back.

"You could use her as a demonstration."

"Having you bring her with you is the same."

"Look William Wright. I've had a bad day. . ." Week, month. "I don't need an argument from you."

"I'm not arguing. I'm being the voice of reason." He crossed his arms.

"Thank you for your help. You may do the demonstration alone tonight. I have lessons to prepare for." She stormed away.

"See you at church," he called after her.

Instead of going home, Mary Jo carried. . .Rose. Yes, that would be her name. At least until a home was found for her. She carried Rose to a log by the stream and held the sleeping infant while she listened to the babbling of the brook.

Her thoughts drifted to Daisy's deception. How many times must one woman forgive? She glanced toward heaven. "I really can't take any more burden, Lord. No shoes, a baby, what's next?" she whispered, almost afraid to know the answer. "I'm tired, I have no money, and I have no shoes. I think I might just be in need of a miracle."

Rose started to squirm and fuss, signaling it was time for her to eat. "See, little one? I don't even have the sense to bring along a bottle. Will you be all right with a bottle? Don't you need your mama's milk?"

Rose blinked up at her and waved a tiny fist.

"You sure are cute." Mary Jo stood and headed home. Life might be hard, but she had to remember that it always worked out.

She stepped into the street leading home and stopped at the sight of an outhouse engulfed in flames.

"It was an accident," Mama Aida yelled. "I set a lantern down inside and promptly forgot about it when I went inside to prepare dinner."

Tears sprang to Mary Jo's eyes. She never should have asked what's next.

Bill sprinted alongside several other men until he reached the source of the fire. His eyes widened at the sight of a flaming outhouse. He laughed. That was a sight he'd never seen before.

His smile faded as he glanced over at Mary Jo. Tears streamed down her lovely face.

She looked his way then wiped her tears on a corner of the baby's blanket. "What on this green earth is so funny?"

"Nothing?"

Sparks practically shot from her hazel eyes. "Go ahead and laugh, but Rose needs a bottle." She whirled and stormed toward the house.

The pastor caught up with her and walked her inside, leaving Bill feeling every bit a dunce. He grabbed a bucket. He might as well make himself useful.

"We're going to need volunteers to rebuild this outhouse," someone shouted. "Any takers?"

"I'll do it." Bill was good with his hands and could make it something different from everyone else's. After all, didn't the community's teacher deserve something nice?

It took him his entire Saturday. The pastor left hours ago, and there had been no sign of Mary Jo. Bill put the final nail into the door and stepped back to appraise his handiwork. Pretty good. He'd been told many times he had a skill with wood.

"What in tarnation is that?" Mary Jo stood next to him, hands on her slender hips.

"Your new outhouse."

"This isn't Japan, Bill. We don't need pagoda roofs and carvings of cherry trees."

"You don't like it?"

"It's much too beautiful for an outhouse." The corner of her lips twitched.

"Is the red roof too much?" He smiled with her.

"A bit."

"I sometimes tend to get carried away." Her giggle made his day brighter.

"I've noticed." She faced him. "I'm sorry for my behavior earlier. I will be at your demonstration with Rose."

"Demonstration!" He whirled and raced home. He needed to gather up the supplies needed for the very first baby club. Twenty young mothers had signed up, and he didn't want to let a single one of them down.

He smiled as Mary Jo entered the church later that evening, and he ignored the presence of Preacher Dean by her side. Bill had subtlety asked around and no one could tell him with any certainty whether the two were courting or not. In Bill's mind, that meant Mary Jo was free to accept his attention if she wished.

She wasn't limping as she made her way down the aisle carrying Rose. Bill glanced at her feet. Ah, she'd chosen to go barefoot. How could he offer her the needed funds to replace the shoes Daisy had kept?

"I've brought Rose," she said, setting the basket holding the baby down on a table. "Be careful, Bill. These women have been doing things the same way for years. They may not take kindly to being told they're bathing their children wrong."

"That isn't all we'll be covering." He sighed and set a white piece of flannel next to Rose.

"I'm not trying to be mean, Bill. I want you to know what to expect." She lifted Rose.

"I do. This isn't the first town I've been in. I'll do my job here then move on to the next." He pulled a metal basin from under the table, noting the blisters on her feet. They looked painful.

Straightening, he asked, "You work hard helping me. Let me pay you for your time. You have Rose to care for now."

She narrowed your eyes. "I don't need your charity, Bill. I also know that my position is often voluntary. I'm not stupid. I know what your job entails."

"I meant no offense. I only want to help with Rose, and contributing financially is the best help I can give."

She tilted her head. "How much?"

"Fifty cents a session." He almost told her that would purchase a pair of shoes in a month's time, but thought it wise to hold his tongue.

"That will be perfect. I need some flannel to make nightgowns for Rose."

He shrugged. So, she'd still use the money for someone other than herself. He'd have to come up with another idea. It didn't do for the teacher to walk around barefoot, or permanently injure her feet by wearing shoes that were too small.

Her face reddened as she caught him looking, and she went to greet the arriving women. She warned him against overstepping boundaries with the others when, in fact, Bill was in danger of overstepping boundaries with her.

"You have no idea who might have left the baby?" a mother holding twins asked her.

"Not a clue." Mary Jo shook her head. "I've asked everyone."

"Well, that Daisy did leave for a good while."

Other women nodded their heads in agreement.

"I'd bet my little ones' nappies that the baby is hers."

"But she's in Little Rock," Bill interrupted.

"No," Mary Jo said, "her letter said she's moving to Memphis."

Bill sucked in his cheek. It was quite possible Daisy's parents had left the baby on his stoop. He'd pay them a visit tomorrow. If they had left Rose, he'd insist they take the child back or send her to an orphanage. Mary Jo was in no condition to take in a newborn, and he sure wasn't.

He clapped his hands to get everyone's attention. "Please take your seats. We have a lot to cover tonight. I'd like for each of you to get a hands-on chance to practice my teachings."

When everyone had gone through and washed their infants, Bill keeping the water fairly clean in between children, by running back and forth to the pump and stove, a woman laughed. "Little Lucy is clean for another month. If you think I have time to run back and forth like you have, mister, you're sorely mistaken."

"That's right. A little dirt never hurt anyone," another said. "Besides, how dirty can a baby get anyway?"

"Most of you have dirt floors. They get quite dirty." He stared at the faces looking back at him. Several needed a good cleaning of their own. He glanced at Mary Jo for help.

She smiled. "Ladies, Mr. Wright is blessing us by sharing his knowledge. We don't expect you to do everything he is showing you, but if you can bring it upon yourselves to use a few, you'll see a positive impact on your families. Will you have to work harder? Yes, but nothing good comes easy."

She flashed Bill a grin that almost stopped his heart with its brilliance. Then, Preacher Dean stepped forward to offer to walk her home, and the light dimmed.

Chapter 4

It makes sense, Mary Jo." Dean leaned on one elbow on the quilt and reached for a fried chicken leg. "We're both from here. We both want what's best for the community. Now that you have the baby. . .well, marriage seems like a win-win situation to me."

Mary Jo stared over his shoulder to where the afternoon sun sparkled on the lake's surface. While his words made sense, he'd not said one thing about love. Good marriages had been based on friendship before. She returned her attention to the man peering up at her. "May I have time to consider your offer?"

"You make it sound like a business proposition."

"No more than your proposal." She glanced up to see Bill stroll by the lake. He flicked a look toward them, nodded, and continued on his way. Mary Jo couldn't help but wonder whether she would have accepted Dean's proposal easier before Bill picked her up from the side of the road.

"I'm able to confirm that Daisy is indeed Rose's biological mother. In fact, her mother told me Daisy is sending you a letter, saying she wants you appointed as guardian. It seems she went off for a while right before we got here and had that little girl. The aunt she left her with couldn't care for the baby anymore so here she is."

"Then why was the baby placed on Bill's stoop?"

He shrugged. "The widow Mason said it was in retaliation for Bill's high-handed soap ideas."

Anger rolled through Mary Jo like waves on the lake during a storm. "This poor baby is being used as a pawn." One more reason for her to throttle Daisy if she ever saw her again.

"Careful not to judge." Dean wiped his hands on a napkin then stood and held his hand out to her. She gripped it and allowed him to pull her to her feet. "We don't know what is going on with Daisy."

"She may be book smart, but the girl has no common sense." Mary Jo stared at her bare feet. The bottoms were becoming as calloused as a child's who ran barefoot every day.

"Let me buy you a pair of shoes."

"I'm fine." She helped fold up the picnic quilt. "Rose and Mama Aida come first."

"You're a good woman, Mary Jo. You'll make a fine preacher's wife."

Her eyes widened. No, she wouldn't. Her feet hurt, and she now had an infant to care for. She carried a lot of resentment in her heart. A good woman would forgive and forget. With Mary Jo, it was a daily struggle.

"Thank you." She grabbed the basket holding the baby and set off for home. "You sure are a good baby, Rose. You slept right through lunch. Your mama doesn't know what she's missing." She smiled into the basket, marveling at the perfection and beauty of the sleeping baby.

A sharp pain jolted through her heel. She hobbled over to a large rock, sat down, and pulled out a deep thorn. Tears welled and ran down her cheeks. Not that her foot hurt enough to make her cry, but that an act of kindness toward a student had resulted in such difficult circumstances. Weren't good deeds meant to mean something?

Rose, past her mealtime, opened her mouth and wailed, joining her cries to Mary Jo's.

"What's wrong here?"

Mary Jo opened her eyes to see Bill kneeling in front of her. "Nothing." She covered her face with her hands. "I'm indulging in a small pity party. I'll be right as rain in a few minutes."

"Your foot is bleeding."

"I know. Hence the pity party." She opened her eyes as he took her foot in his hands.

He rested it on his thigh and pulled a crisp white handkerchief from his pocket. Forget the pain in her heel. Her ankle heated where his hand was. Mary Jo tried to pull away, only to have his grip tighten.

"Hold still. I don't have any water, but this will at least keep it from getting any dirtier." He grinned. "Shall I carry you on my back?"

"Absolutely not!"

"Very well." He handed her the basket of screaming baby. Before she could stop him, he scooped her and basket into his arms and headed for her house.

She couldn't breathe, much less speak. His long strides made short work of the walk, and he set her on the steps much too soon. She stared into his eyes. Mercy, the man was handsome. Kind too. Mary Jo should have said yes to Dean's proposal and rid her head of silly notions regarding Bill. The man had made it quite clear he planned to move on when his job was done. "Uh. . .thank you."

His grin widened as he rested his foot on the lowest step. "Any time. It was my pleasure, completely."

The flirt. She smiled back. "I'd best get Rose fed." She took the baby from the basket but didn't move inside. Rose's cries stopped.

"Yes, you'd better."

What was wrong with her? Why couldn't she move?

"For Pete's sake." Mama Aida stepped outside and took Rose. "Don't make the baby suffer so the two of you can ogle each other. Come on in for some lemonade and cookies, Mr. Wright."

"Bill," Mary Jo said softly.

Mama Aida thunked her in the back of the head. "Wake up." She went in the house, letting the screen door slam shut behind her.

The thunk did indeed wake Mary Jo from her stupor. Her foot regained its throbbing; her face heated. Still, she stood there like a ninny.

"I heard something about lemonade?"

"Oh, yes." She whirled and opened the door. "Please go on in to the kitchen. I'll clean up my foot and join you in a few minutes." She limped as fast as possible to her room. After washing her foot in the basin and wrapping a clean bandage around it, she put on her oldest sock and went to join Bill.

While carrying Mary Jo, Bill had been fascinated by how wonderful she felt. As if his arms were made to hold her. He bit into a fresh chocolate-chip cookie.

"Oh, good, you helped yourself." Mary Jo limped to the table and sat down next to him. She reached for the pitcher.

"Let me." He took the pitcher and poured her a glass of milk.

"Thank you. I'm sorry you came upon me in such a silly state." Her shoulders slumped. "Everything just crashed down on me."

He put his hand over hers. "You've taken on a lot right now. You're a good person, Mary Jo."

Her face darkened. "Please don't say that. I had a moment of weakness." She got to her feet and slapped her palms on the table. "If you could read my mind, you'd take those words back." She left him sitting alone at the table.

Refusing to let her behavior ruin his day or change his opinion of her, Bill finished his cookie and let himself out. Soon, he knocked at the parsonage.

Pastor Dean opened the door and shook his hand. "Bill, what can I do for you?"

"I'm wondering whether or not the church has some clothing donations I can dig through."

"Needing something in particular?" He closed the door and led Bill to a door in the back of the church. "There's a closet here, where the women put such things. I doubt we have much, it being the Depression."

"Thank you." Bill took his time digging through the box, until the other man got bored and left him alone. He'd spotted what he wanted seconds upon glancing inside. He pulled a pair of women's oxfords from the box and measured them with his hands. Perfect. He'd have to repair the holes in the sole, but a certain, kind-hearted school teacher was going to have a pair of shoes.

"Are you finished?" Dean looked into the room.

"Yep." Bill wrapped the shoes in an old coat. "Thank you." He rushed past the man. Not being sure how Mary Jo would react to the gift, he didn't want her to have any warning.

Back at his cottage, he turned on the one bulb hanging from the ceiling and studied the barely there sole on the shoes. He needed leather. Leaning back in his chair, he contemplated his briefcase. It had a compartment inside that wasn't needed. It would work.

He traced the shoes onto the leather divider from the case, making the new soles a fraction smaller, and slipped them into the old shoes. They weren't fancy or new, but they would protect her feet.

Once night fell, he headed back to her place and set the shoes next to the front door. He slipped a note inside that read "For the teacher." Proud of his accomplishment, he strolled home, whistling a jaunty tune.

The next morning, he found a note, along with the shoes, that read, "If you want to leave anonymous charity, which I will not accept, then you shouldn't whistle the same tune you whistle every night as you walk away."

Laughing, Bill carried the shoes and the note inside. He'd find another way to get them to her. He set them on the table, sat down, and folded his arms behind his head. Perhaps he could have one of her students give them to her as a gift. Surely, she wouldn't deny a child.

The moment he heard laughter at the schoolhouse, he risked being taken as a predator and waved a boy over to the side of the building. "Here's a coin if you give these shoes to Mrs. Stevens. Say they're from you and it means a lot to you that she take them. Can you do that?"

The boy nodded, took the coin and the shoes, and raced toward the front of the building. Bill peered around the corner in time to see the child toss the shoes through the open door and shout that a man sent them for Mrs. Stevens.

Bill closed his eyes and groaned.

"Mr. Wright."

He opened them to see Mary Jo, surrounded by at least twenty children of varying ages, glaring at him. Dangling from her fingers were the shoes.

"I appreciate the gesture, I really do. But I am sure there are people in this hollow that need your attention more." She held out the offending objects.

"Mrs. Stevens." He copied her stance and crossed his arms. Two could play this game. "I'm in Pilgrim Hollow to help people. You are a member of this community, hence I am perfectly justified to help you."

She closed her eyes and exhaled heavily. Bill got a strong impression she may have been counting to ten. She opened her eyes and squared her shoulders. "Look at my students, Mr. Wright."

He did. Not one of them wore shoes. Not. A. Single. One. "If I remedy this, will you accept the shoes?"

"Yes." She gave a thin-lipped smile. "Work your magic, Mr. Wright." She dropped the shoes and, like a mother hen, shooed her little chicks into the building.

Bill had no idea how he was going to find twenty pairs of shoes in various sizes. He dashed after Mary Jo. "Tracings, please." He gave a wave through the open door.

She glanced up with wide eyes then nodded.

Bill rubbed his hands together. He had some letters to write.

Chapter 5

I t's time to go, Mama Aida." Mary Jo gently swayed, with Rose clutched against her. One of the families in the hollow had lost their home to a fire a few days ago, and Bill was taking this opportunity to show them how to build a sturdier house. The women were bringing the food and sewing a quilt.

"I don't think there's a thing that Bill Wright doesn't know how to do." Mama Aida stepped from her room and took Rose. "Taking care of babies, being clean, now building a house. What else does he have up his sleeve?"

"Furniture and mattresses, to name a couple." Mary Jo grabbed the basket of fresh-baked biscuits and beans.

"He's going to make a right fine husband someday. Are you looking to get hitched again?"

Mary Jo rolled her eyes. "Not anytime soon." *Oh, please don't have any idea that Dean prop—*

"Well, I heard that a certain preacher asked you." Mama Aida grinned over Rose's head. "What did you tell him?"

"That I needed to think about it." She'd be talking to Dean about the inappropriateness of spreading such things among the people.

"Because of Bill, right?" Her eyes twinkled. "I bet you would have said yes in a minute, if that man hadn't arrived in this hollow. You've been a widow for five years. My boy would want you to love again."

Which was true. Her husband had made her promise him on his deathbed that she would move on with her life. Well, life seemed to be sweeping her along in its wake. "We need to start walking or we'll be late." Mary Jo shoved open the front door to the sight of Bill's truck idling outside.

"Thought you might like a ride," he yelled through the open window.

"Yep," Mama Aida said, passing Mary Jo. "Somebody has a decision to make."

Yes, she did. About a lot of things. Today though, she would focus on helping a family in need and not worry about something as silly as romance. She'd had it once and could very well live without it now.

"Good morning, Bill," Mama Aida said, climbing onto the seat. "It's a beautiful day for a house building."

"That it is." Bill smiled at Mary Jo. "Stash that basket in the back and we will be on our way."

"Here, Mary Jo, you should sit in the middle because I have the baby."

Mary Jo didn't know what having the baby had to do with where she sat but rather than have her mother-in-law cause an argument, Mary Jo did as instructed. Every bump in the road caused some part of Mary Jo to come into contact with a part of Bill. The constant contact kept her emotions fluttering and her mind clouded. She couldn't say for sure, but she would bet her best Sunday dress that was part of Mama Aida's plan all along. There wasn't a lot of room in the truck cabin with three people.

They rolled onto the Simpson property and parked next to several other trucks. Bags of concrete rested against a tree. "We're going to build a solid foundation for this house."

"Most folks around here like a crawl space," Mary Jo said. "They store potatoes under there."

"And get termites and dry rot." Bill slid from the truck. "It's only an option, Mary Jo. I'm not here to make them do anything. I'm here to give them better options."

She slid out his side. "I understand that, but you shouldn't—"

"Force my opinions on anyone. I know." He slammed the truck door then left her standing there while he marched to the waiting men.

Mary Jo made a beeline for Dean. "You shouldn't be telling people that you proposed. I haven't given you an answer."

"Good morning." He kissed her cheek. "I have no doubt you'll make the right decision."

"It may not be the one you prefer." She whirled and stormed over to the women, doing her best not to wince when she stepped on a rock. For a moment, she rethought her refusal of Bill's gift of shoes, but stubbornness welled and won the battle.

The women fussing around the quilt rack turned as if one body and smiled.

Mama Aida laid Rose on a blanket in the grass. "We've just been discussing your proposal."

"Mama Aida! You know I've not said anything." She glanced from one face to the next. "I'm sure everyone in the hollow will know within seconds of my making a decision." Which, if she got any more pressure, would be a resounding no. She sat in the chair closest to Rose and threaded a needle.

Mary Jo listened with half an ear as the other women gossiped about the community. It wasn't until she heard Daisy's name that she perked up. "What about Daisy?"

"Why, her and her new husband are returning to Pilgrim Hollow. At least, that's what her mama said. I reckon the girl will want her baby back." Widow Larson, the community's oldest resident at the age of ninety-one, nodded. "But, that's what good people do, and that Daisy Mason is not good people."

"We shouldn't speak ill of others," Mary Jo murmured, out of habit from being a teacher. No, she just *thought* ill of others. She sighed and prayed again for the ability to forgive the young woman who took from her and left a baby in exchange.

She smiled down at the cooing Rose. After caring for the baby for several weeks, it would be incredibly difficult to give her back. But, a mother who abandoned her child, then got married, was still preferable in the eyes of a court than a woman unmarried. Mary Jo stared to where Bill stood on a ladder.

Mama Aida was right. Bill would make a wonderful husband. So would Dean. One had proposed, one hadn't. One would stay in Pilgrim's Hollow, one would leave. Decisions of the heart were never easy.

Aaron Simpson had opted for the crawl space. Bill smiled as he hammered in a nail; the man thought a concrete floor on the smokehouse might be a good idea. But some people thought he had strange ideas.

"I don't understand her hesitation." Dean stood below the ladder, speaking with one of the other men, a deacon at the church if Bill wasn't mistaken. "Why wouldn't she give me an answer right away? Especially now that she has an infant to care for."

An answer? He had to be speaking of Mary Jo. Instead of striking another nail, Bill poised his hand as if to pound but listened instead.

"I've a mission in life," Dean said. "I've a house, a church, and I'm respected in the community. Any woman would be lucky to be my wife."

The man had proposed to Mary Jo? Bill's foot slipped on the rung; he grappled for a hold and dropped the hammer. It missed Dean's head by inches. "Sorry." His grip slipped and he bounced down the ladder like an automobile on a road full of ruts. He lay on the ground, unable to breathe for several seconds and stared into the men's faces. "I'm...fine."

"Get the doctor." Dean placed a hand on Bill's chest to prevent him from rising to a sitting position. "Don't move. You could be more hurt than you realize." He prayed for Bill to have a quick recovery with no lasting damage.

Bill started to speak then his world grew dark. When he awoke, he was not in his bed. His head pounded. Moving just his eyes, he noticed white walls. A porcelain doll atop the bureau was a dead giveaway he wasn't home.

"Don't move." Mary Jo stepped into his sight. "You have a concussion and two fractured ribs. The men brought you to my house."

The thought he was lying in her bed almost made him stop breathing again. "Water." He cleared his throat. "I could manage sitting if you help me."

She grabbed a pillow from the foot of the bed and helped him sit, so she could prop it behind him. "Let me get you something to drink. Are you hungry?"

He gripped her hand as she started to leave. "How long have I been here?"

"You fell yesterday." She flashed a grin. "Not long at all. You had us worried, Bill Wright."

Rose cried from another room as Mary Jo bustled out. It pained Bill to take a deep breath, but he wouldn't be a burden on the Stevens women. Especially Mary Jo. If the perpetual crease between her eyes was any indication, she had enough to worry about.

"Here you go. A nice hot cup of coffee and some chicken soup Mama Aida made." Mary Jo pulled up a small table. "I'll feed you." She dipped the spoon into the soup then lifted it toward his mouth.

He put his hand around her wrist. "I can feed myself, thank you."

She scrunched her nose and sat back. "Do you need an aspirin?"

"Don't waste your medicines on me. I know how expensive they are."

She smiled. "The doctor left them for you. I'm sure he'll add them to your bill."

"No doubt." He ate a few spoonfuls of the delicious soup. "My compliments to the cook, but I'm ready to lie down again."

She rushed to move the small table. "Do you want me to leave the extra pillow?"

"Please. It helps to sit at an angle." He closed his eyes and listened for her to leave. No padding of bare feet. Was she going to sit and watch him sleep? He'd never be able to if that were the case. He groaned.

"You're in pain. Let me run for the doctor."

"No." He opened his eyes. "I can't rest with you watching me."

"Why not?" She frowned. "The doctor said you had to be watched."

"Not every second!"

"Don't shout. You'll make your head ache."

"It already aches."

She sighed and tucked the sheet more firmly around him, which brought her face wondrously close to his. Before he could change her mind or she could pull back, he kissed her. "Think about that next time a man proposes." He closed his eyes and turned his head.

"Oh." This time she stomped out, leaving him to fall asleep with the feel of her lips lingering on his. When he woke again, dusk had darkened the room.

Mary Jo sat slumped in a chair, asleep.

Using care, Bill sat up, holding his left arm tight against his side, and swung his legs over the side of the bed. He bit back a groan as he stood.

Mary Jo immediately shot to her feet. "Where do you think you're going?"

"Japan."

"What?" Her eyes narrowed.

"The outhouse, Mary Jo."

"Not by yourself."

He stepped past her. "That is not something you can help me with."

"I can go and make sure you don't fall. I'll wait outside, of course."

He cut her a sideways glance. "Do you really think you'd be much help if I did fall?"

"Stop being so hard-headed, Bill Wright, and take help when it's offered."

He stopped moving and faced her. Laughter bubbled up and out, causing him to clutch his side harder. "Are you hearing yourself? You're one to talk about accepting help."

She put her hands on her hips. "Help and charity are two completely different things."

"No, they're not." He headed again for the back door.

She followed. "Yes, they are."

"How?"

Her mouth opened and closed. "Well. . .I. . .uh. . .never mind, they just are."

"Hmm-hmm." He stepped outside and shuffled to the new building on the property. "Stop, Mary Jo. Not one step closer." He opened the door to the outhouse, did his business, and exited to see her sitting on the bottom step to the porch.

The moon came through the branches of a cedar tree and cast silver highlights on her head. Her chin rested in the palm of her hand. One leg was bent to support the arm connected to her hand. The other foot drew circles in the dirt. Bill wished for a camera to capture the moment. He'd call it *Beauty Waits*.

What would she do if he kissed her again? The first time he'd managed to catch her by surprise. He wasn't sure he could again. He grinned.

"What's so funny?" She stood and came toward him.

"Private thoughts." With his right hand, he caressed her cheek. "You really are a beautiful woman, Mary Jo. Inside and out."

Rose cried from inside the house.

Mary Jo whirled around and raced away from him.

Chapter 6

Two days after his accident, Bill told Mary Jo she was smothering him, and he left. "I have work to do," he said. She pounded the bread dough on the counter. "Don't we all?" What really made Mary Jo upset was not his leaving, but the fact he hadn't tried to kiss her again. That one simple kiss had made her more confused than ever in regard to Dean's marriage proposal.

Why had Bill taken such liberty? He'd be leaving soon. By winter, most likely. Where would that leave her?

"I'll finish up. Go on, or you'll be late for school. It rained, so take my shoes. No sense showing up to work with mud on your feet." Mama Aida placed Rose in her carrying basket. "She's going to be too big for this soon. We'll need a proper crib. I reckon it's time for her to start staying home with me."

"Are you sure?" Mary Jo dusted off her hands.

Mama Aida nodded. "I've gotten attached to the sweet little thing. She's good company."

"Thank you." Mary Jo planted a quick kiss on her cheek, grabbed her school bag and the shoes, and then dashed outside. She hated to get the shoes muddy, but she hated what might be in the mud more. She squeezed her feet into the shoes and headed to the school. The moment she stepped into the road, the mud squelched halfway up the shoes. Mama Aida would never lend them to her again.

She stepped to the side of the road as a vehicle stopped beside her. "Good morning, Bill. How's the ribs?"

"Smok'n." He grinned. "They're fine. Would you like a ride? Those too-small shoes have to be torture."

She opened the door and climbed in. "What is your obsession with whether or not I have shoes?"

"I'm here to—"

"Help. I know." She set her bag in her lap. "I do appreciate the ride. It looks like rain again."

The truck strained to get down the road. "I think I should have walked," Bill said. The truck's back rear tire slid into the ditch. The truck listed sideways. Bill pressed the gas.

The tires spun, flinging mud. Mary Jo peered out the window as the clouds released their burden. "Do you have an umbrella?"

"No. There is a blanket behind the seat, but I think you should wait out the rain."

She cast him a horrified look. "I'm the teacher. I can't *not* show up to school."

"How do you anticipate getting there?" He pointed out the window. "You'll be soaked in a minute."

She reached for the door. "I have a responsibility."

"Fine. I'll go with you."

"Not necessary." She turned and bent over the seat to retrieve the wool blanket. "Perfect." Doing her best to appear as confident as she pretended to be, she clutched her bag, threw the blanket over her head, and slid out into the rain and down the ditch on her backside.

Bill came scrambling after her. "Are you all right? I tried to tell you to come out my side, but you seem to have an aversion to spending any amount of time with me. *Ahh!*" His feet slipped, landing him on his back beside her.

Mary Jo's eyes widened then laughter bubbled out of her. She lay there in the downpour, covered in mud, her school lessons being ruined, and laughed at the ridiculousness of their situation. Within seconds, Bill laughed with her.

He slipped and slid, finally getting to his feet and held out a hand to help her. "Don't need this anymore." He tossed the sodden blanket toward the truck.

Mary Jo grasped his hand. "I need to get word to the school that I'm going to be late."

"Why don't you head home? I'll leave a note with Dean before coming back here with help to get my truck out." With his forefinger, he brushed wet hair from her cheek. His gaze settled on her lips. "Mary Jo Stevens, I'm going to—"

"Hey!"

She turned to see Dean, wearing a sensible bright-yellow raincoat and galoshes, standing at the edge of the road. "Did you have an accident? Is everyone all right?" He held up an umbrella. "I came to walk you to school, Mary Jo."

"Raincheck," she whispered in an uncharacteristically flirty gesture. Using small bushes to grab hold of, she dragged herself out of the ditch.

"You're a sight." Dean unfolded the umbrella.

"Not much use for that now."

"I meant to be here earlier, but someone needed prayer."

She blinked away the water on her lashes. "That's what makes you a good pastor. Nothing comes between you and a parishioner."

"You make that sound like a bad thing."

"Not at all." She tossed Bill a wave. "Dean, please let my students know I'll be late. The umbrella will be very useful once I'm cleaned up. Thank you." Trying not to let the pained look on Dean's face stop her, she turned toward home.

"Wait." He put a restraining hand on her arm. "Was Bill going to kiss you? Because from up here, it looked like he was going to kiss you."

She glanced at his hand. "Just brushing mud from my face. I'll return the umbrella to you later."

"Mama Aida invited me for supper. I'll see you then." Shoulders slumped, he trudged in the opposite direction.

Over her shoulder, Mary Jo watched him go. She had to tell him she couldn't marry him. She'd do her best to let him down gently, but if another man's kisses could affect her the way Bill's did, then she wasn't yet ready to settle down. She glanced to where Bill stood, next to his truck, kicking mud off his shoes by use of the tires. If Bill were to propose, she might rethink those words.

The Arkansas clay was like glue. It didn't help that Bill's good mood disappeared the moment he caught sight of Dean looking like the rubber duck of good will. He had half a mind to give his regrets on passing on supper with the Stevens women and staying home to sulk. But, home-cooked meals were a rarity, and he'd be a fool to pass up time spent with Mary Jo.

After his tumble into the ditch, his ribs reminded him they weren't fully healed. He grabbed the muddy blanket from the ground, held it over his head in a futile attempt to prevent being more soaked than he was, and sloshed, sucked, trodded his way to find someone to pull his truck out of the mud.

As he approached the small cluster of buildings that made up the town of Pilgrim's Hollow, he encountered Dean, the last man Bill wanted to see at that moment. Realistic or not, Bill felt in competition with the man for Mary Jo's affections. Which was ridiculous when he thought about it. Who would want a man who didn't stay in one place when they could have someone who served God?

Bill did his best to serve God. Attended church, said his prayers, read his Bible, did the job entrusted to him as if doing it for the Lord. . .but there was something even more when a man's job was preaching the Good News, wasn't there? His father would tell him it wasn't the job that made a man but what was in a man's heart.

"I found someone to pull your truck out of the mud." Dean waved a man forward. "Larry, here, has a hitch."

"Thank you." The pastor's smile looked forced, but here he was, helping Bill. He had to have seen him almost kiss Mary Jo, and yet he went looking for someone to help.

"Not a problem. I've got to go wait at the school for arriving students." He turned and hurried away.

By the time the supper hour rolled around, Bill was exhausted from a day spent digging out his truck. The rain had stopped. Nature's colors were bright and clean, the air fresh. The bright spot in the day was that he was having supper with Mary Jo. He stopped at the side of the road and picked a fistful of wildflowers.

When he approached the Stevens' front porch, it was apparent Dean was also invited to supper and had the same idea about flowers. The two men stood and stared at each other then, as one, they climbed the stairs.

"You want to knock?" Bill asked.

"You go ahead."

Bill knocked and stepped back so the other man could enter first.

Mary Jo answered the door. Her eyes widened. She sighed and muttered, "Mama Aida." She shook her head. "You two come on in. I have no idea what game my mother-in-law is playing, but we've a good roast on. Might as well not waste it. Thank you both for the flowers." She took them and put them into one group.

This was not going to be the night Bill had looked forward to. But he'd have to be a gentleman and make the best of things.

"There they are. The men vying for Mary Jo." Mama Aida stood in the doorway to the kitchen. The blue frilly apron she wore made her look ten years younger. "Sit. We're ready to put the food on the table."

Bill glanced at Dean, who shrugged, then led the way to the dining room. The large wooden table looked ready for Thanksgiving. Mama Aida had apparently used their finest dishes. What was she up to?

He stood behind his seat, as Dean did behind his, and waited for the women to sit. Once they did, Bill sat and spread his napkin in his lap. He filled his plate with food from the dishes being passed, waiting to hear the reason he and Dean had been invited. Mama Aida chatted on like a magpie as they ate, keeping him in suspense.

From the high spots of color on Mary Jo's cheeks, emotions ran high. She looked close to exploding.

When she'd finished, Mama Aida stood. "Why don't you three young people go sit on the porch a while. I'll clean up this mess." When no one moved, she shooed her hands. "Go."

Mary Jo sighed and stood. "We might as well. She'll stand there until we do." She tossed her napkin on the table and marched to the front porch. She sat on the swing, barely big enough for two.

Bill, out the door first, joined her there and flashed Dean a grin as he took one of the rockers. "This is cozy." He set the swing in motion with a push of his shoe's toe.

"Did Mary Jo tell you that I proposed?" Dean glared.

"I heard that around town. I also heard she hasn't answered."

Mary Jo sucked air sharply through her nose.

Dean narrowed his eyes. "If I weren't a man of God, and if this wasn't the twentieth century—"

"You'd what?" Mary Jo leaped to her feet and planted her fists on her hips. "Challenge Bill to a duel over me? The two of you are more ridiculous than Mama Aida. Strutting around like roosters, as if I'm the last hen left in this hollow. I'll not have it. Go home." She stormed into the house and slammed the door.

"That didn't go well." Bill stood.

"What are you hoping to prove?" Dean faced him. "I believe things were settled between me and Mary Jo until you arrived and caused confusion in her heart. What will she do when you leave?"

"You'll be here to pick up the pieces." Bill clapped him on the shoulder and strolled away, whistling. As soon as he was out of earshot of the house, he stopped and leaned against a tree. He could act as if he didn't have a care in the world, but the longer he stayed in Pilgrim's Hollow, the more he had second thoughts about leaving.

He glanced back to where the house shone under the moonlight. If he stayed, how could he support Mary Jo without a job? If he left. . .how would his heart survive?

Chapter 7

Why are you in such a hurry to marry me off?" Mary Jo glanced over Rose's head at Mama Aida, who sat in the other rocking chair.

"You're still young. Your life shouldn't be spent taking care of me." She stared over the lawn.

"I think I'll be the best judge of how I spend my life."

"It worked out well for you when you gave away your shoes." She flicked a look at Mary Jo's bare feet. "It'll be summertime, school will be out, and the road hot. I reckon you'd best work on building up those callouses."

"It was the right thing to do." Mary Jo rested her cheek on the baby's head.

"Stop lying to yourself. You acted impulsively, got gypped, and you've been struggling with forgiving that girl ever since. Especially when she run off and left that baby."

Mama Aida was right. Even after several months, it was a daily struggle for Mary Jo to forgive Daisy. "You may be right on that account, but it still doesn't give you the right to feel as if you need to find me a husband."

"You have two fine men vying for your attention. Pick one." She pushed to her feet and stomped into the house. If Mary Jo didn't know better, she'd think Mama Aida was pressing the issue that she had shoes and her daughter-in-law didn't.

When Rose's eyes began to close, Mary Jo carried her inside and laid her on a pallet in the corner. Maybe not the best cradle, but the basket was no longer a viable option. "I'm headed to the mercantile," she told Mama Aida as she headed out the door.

The rising temperature warmed her back, promising summer was on its way. Next week was the last week of school, and the children had been practicing poem recitations and math equations for a program put on for their parents.

Mary Jo slid her hand into the pocket of her dress and felt the coins jingling inside. It should be enough for a pair of shoes. She'd set aside a few cents a week for this purpose, and excitement bubbled inside her.

"Good morning, Mr. Wilson." She headed straight for the counter. "I'd like to buy a pair of shoes."

"Good morning, Mary Jo. We've some women's oxfords over here. I'm sure there's a pair to fit you." He led the way to a shoe rack. "It's all over town how you turned down a pair Mr. Wright repaired for you. One of the students said he's going to get them all shoes. Is that right?"

"That's what he said." It had been over a month and still no shoes, but the students hadn't given up hope.

"He's a good man."

"Yes, he is." Mary Jo picked up a pair of shoes and slid her feet into them. Perfect fit. "I'll take these."

"Good, sensible shoes."

"Yep, that's me. Sensible Mary Jo." She paid for her purchase.

"I also heard that tonight's class is to teach the women new recipes. My Betty said she plans on bringing whatever she makes to the school program. A fresh batch anyway." He grinned.

"With the Depression going on, Bill said he has ways of making desserts that don't require as much sugar. Imagine that." Mr. Wright shook his head.

"So, the community has accepted him?"

"For the most part. How can they not? When he isn't teaching, he's helping repair a pump, a barn, you name it, and I think Bill knows how to do it. He's a well-rounded man."

"Good and well-rounded." Mary Jo smiled and left the mercantile. Her toes, used to the freedom of going barefoot, protested at first, but by the time she'd walked a ways, the shoes started to loosen a little.

"Mary Jo, wait up." Dean jogged to her side. "Do you have a minute to come by the church? I'd like to make sure I understand where you want everything for next Friday night's performance."

"Sure." Glad to see he didn't seem grieved after last night's supper fiasco, she gladly went along with him.

"New shoes?"

She grinned. "Bought them myself."

"You are a very proud woman, Mary Jo Stevens." He opened the church door and let her go in first.

Bill knelt behind the podium, hammering nails into a two-foot-high, makeshift stage. With nails in his mouth, he couldn't speak, but gave Mary Jo a nod.

"I can still use the podium for Sunday services then move it onto the stage afterward. Where do you want it placed?"

"Stage left, please." She stepped onto the stage and stared over the empty pews. The parents would easily have a clear view of their student. "This is wonderful. It's a shame to build it and tear it down."

"Who said anything about taking it down?" Dean waved his arm. "I'll put a baptism over there and the choir can stand there."

"That's wonderful. Nothing wasted."

"It was Bill's idea." Dean shrugged. "He knows what he's doing." He took Mary Jo by the arm and pulled her to the side. "I think I may know where your heart lies, but my proposal still stands. I'm here if you want me. I won't put any pressure on you."

She tilted her head and stared into his blue eyes. "Thank you." Stress fell off her shoulders. She couldn't say for sure her heart belonged to Bill, or that she didn't care enough for Dean to marry him, but she knew with all certainty that she didn't know what she wanted.

Bill had noticed Mary Jo's shoes the instant she stepped into the church earlier. Now, she stood next to him and patiently waited while he got ready to address the women.

"First, we wash our hands." He smiled over the crowd. As word spread, more and more women made the trek into town to attend his classes. "Once we've done that, we bake. The first cake I'd like to show you is a chocolate cake. With supplies being as scarce as they are during this time, you can use coffee and vinegar to enhance the chocolate cake. Mrs. Stevens, if you will."

As she measured the ingredients, he continued with his demonstration. "This recipe takes no butter, milk, or eggs. Instead, we'll use water, oil, and a mix of baking soda and vinegar as a rising agent. This is a thick, heavy, decadent cake."

The women leaned forward eagerly. No one took notes. Bill knew from experience they would commit the recipe to memory just by watching.

"While the chocolate cake bakes, how about a double-tiered vanilla? Again, no milk or eggs, but it's worth saving your sugar rations for." By the time the night drew to a close, a chocolate cake and a vanilla cake stood on the sideboard of the church's fellowship hall. "I have pamphlets here with these recipes and many more. Please take one. Even if you can't read, they also contain pictures to guide you."

"You have been a blessing to this community, Mr. Wright." Mrs. Wilson, the general store owner's wife stood before him. "So many times the frugality of these lean years keeps us from enjoying treats. These recipes will allow us to enjoy them again."

Other women murmured their approval and everyone took a pamphlet. Bill smiled, pleased with his progress in Pilgrim's Hollow. He turned his attention to where Mary Jo stacked the dishes they'd used into a box. Bill was almost finished with what he had come to the hollow to do. Soon, he had an all-too-quickly-approaching decision to make, and his smile faded.

"That went very well." Mary Jo handed him the box of dirty dishes. "You should be quite pleased with yourself."

"I am."

"Then why the long face? These women can't wait to try out the recipes."

"My time here is drawing to a close."

Her eyes searched his face. "Then stay."

"I want to." He cupped her face. "My job is important. Look how we've improved the lifestyle of these people."

"How you've improved it." She stepped back.

"Without you these people would never have given me the time of day, Mary Jo. You've been an invaluable assistant."

"One of many, I presume." She headed for the door.

"What does that mean?" He hurried to catch up with her.

"Surely you have someone helping you every place you go."

"It's usually an older woman, such as a mayor's wife or the preacher's wife." He kept a tight grip on the box of dishes to keep from touching her again.

"It seems I was a pleasant diversion from the norm."

Why did she seem so angry with him? "Have I offended you in some way?"

She stopped next to his truck. "Not at all." She opened the door and climbed in before he set the box in the back.

They drove to her house in silence. When he stopped to let her out, she reached for the door handle. "When do you leave?" she asked softly.

"That depends on my boss. I send him weekly reports."

She nodded and pushed the door open. She rushed inside her house.

Bill removed the box of dishes from the truck bed and set them on the porch. Backing up, he scanned the windows, waiting for her light to come on. When it did, she stood at the window, her form highlighted. With one hand on the curtains, she stared down at him.

He gazed up at her for several seconds before shoving his hands in his pockets and shuffling back to his truck. If she asked him to stay, he would, and figure out the rest. What would she say if he were to tell her of his feelings for her? She was much more than an assistant. She was his other half.

He drove to his small house and lit the gas lamp. He didn't mind so much not having electricity. The lamp was more than sufficient for the tiny, one-room building. He dug a sheet of paper and a pencil from his briefcase and sat down at the table.

As he wrote his weekly report, Mary Jo's face swam before him, making it hard to concentrate. He set down his pencil and stared at the words he'd written. There had to be a way to prolong Bill's stay. Was there another way he could serve Pilgrim's Hollow, other than as a demonstration agent?

Right now he had a steady paycheck in a time when few had such a luxury. If he were to set up some type of business, he would have to rely on the poor members of the community for his livelihood, and if God led him to marry, his family's welfare as well.

"God, what do I do?" He folded his arms on the table and lowered his head. He was a smart man. He did his best to follow God's will. There had to be a way to follow God's leading and have what his heart desired as well.

Chapter 8

Y ou are the sweetest thing." Mary Jo blew a raspberry on Rose's stomach. The baby grinned, revealing toothless gums, and waved her fists in the air. "To think I was upset at getting you. Silly me." The baby had turned out to be a great blessing. Not just to Mary Jo, but to Mama Aida too. Lifting Rose to her shoulders, Mary Jo turned.

Mama Aida, a stricken look on her face, stood in the doorway. "We have company."

"Oh? Who?" Why would company affect Mama Aida so negatively?

She turned toward the front room, leaving Mary Jo to follow. "Well, then. Let's go see who it is." Mary Jo patted Rose on the back and followed Mama Aida.

Ice water filled her veins at the sight of Daisy, her hair cut in a modern bob, face made up, sitting on the sofa. A smile curved her ruby lips as Mary Jo entered the room. "There she is." She held out her hands for the baby.

Mary Jo drew back. "Not so fast."

Daisy's eyes narrowed. "You can't keep me from my baby. My husband is waiting in the car. We're headed to St. Louis."

"She's right, Mary Jo. You have to give Rose to her."

Tears filled Mary Jo's eyes, blurring the face of the young woman in front of her. "All right. I'll fetch her things." She handed Rose to Daisy, who held her at arm's length.

Rose immediately began to wail. The sound ripped at Mary Jo's heart as she quickly placed the baby's few items of clothing into a small box. Wiping her eyes on the sleeve of her dress, she hefted the box, squared her shoulders, and went back to face Daisy. "It isn't much," she said, setting the box on the sofa, "but it's enough. Do you have my shoes and dress?"

Daisy frowned at the still screaming Rose. "No, and I'm right sorry about that. I left the shoes in Little Rock. They got scuffed up pretty bad. The dress got stained when I spilled coffee." Her gaze flicked to Rose's feet. "It's a good thing

170

you have another pair, isn't it?"

"Quite." Mary Jo took a deep breath. *Forgive*, the Bible says. *Seventy times seven.*

"Well." Daisy awkwardly held Rose against her chest. "I'd best—" A horn honked outside. "That would be Davey. Thank you for your help." She propped the box on one hip, Rose on the other, and raced out the front door.

Mary Jo's legs refused to hold her. She collapsed onto the nearest chair and covered her face with her hands. When would life stop throwing unexpected blessings her way and then, once she saw the blessing for what it was, rip them from her?

"I'll, uh, be in my room." Mama Aida sniffed and shuffled away.

It would probably be best if they grieved together, but Mary Jo didn't have the strength to follow her mother-in-law and give out comfort she didn't have to give. She glanced toward the open front door. A lone, tiny sock lay white against the wood floor, starting her tears anew.

No. She would not do this. She had students to fill the empty hole in her heart. Preparing lessons will help her over the tough days ahead. With purpose, she marched out the door, closing it behind her, and headed for the schoolhouse.

The dark recesses of the building kept the warm spring day at bay and suited Mary Jo's dark mood. Without opening the windows, choosing to light a lantern instead, she sat at her desk and gazed over the empty chairs. Five days until the end-of-the-year performance. How would she fill her days during the summer?

Her students would be home, Bill would have moved on. . .only she and Dean would be left, and he had his flock to shepherd. She sighed and reached for the stack of math problems to grade. The numbers blurred.

Not able to concentrate, she sat back. Perhaps she could write a book. She'd thought of it on more than one occasion. Or she could submit her ideas for a series of elementary-age Sunday school lessons. Yes, she could keep herself occupied.

A shadow filled the open door of the schoolhouse. After a pause of several seconds, Bill rushed down the aisle between the desks and knelt in front of Mary Jo, taking her hands in his. "I just heard about Rose. Are you all right?"

His question and the sympathy on his face started her tears again. She shook her head as the tears fell.

"Sweetheart." Bill sat against the wall and drew her into his arms. His hand made soothing circles on her back. "I'm here. I'm here for as long as you want me."

They sat there until Mary Jo cried herself dry. It wasn't until then that she realized how improper it would look should someone come in. She whispered a thank you and got to her feet.

"I had no idea I'd grow to care so much for that little one." She fumbled on her desk for a tissue.

"Use mine." Bill handed her a clean handkerchief. "Can I buy you a milkshake?"

She blew her nose then tilted her head to the side. "That sounds like a celebration rather than a mourning."

One corner of his mouth curved. "Just something sweet to make you feel better."

"Then I accept." She started to hand him back the handkerchief then decided to wash it first and stuck it in her pocket. She turned down the lantern and followed Bill outside.

After the dim inside, the bright afternoon sun blinded her. She stopped on the steps and blinked, waiting for her eyes to adjust.

Next to her, Bill kicked at a small rock in front of him, clearly deep in thought about something. Then, as if remembering she was there, he turned and grinned. "Ready?" He crooked his arm toward her.

"Very." Forcing her sadness aside for the time being, she placed her arm in his and did her best to focus on the beautiful day and the promise of a special treat.

Mary Jo's forlorn expression and body language, as Bill watched her sitting behind her desk in the school, had him postponing the news he had to share. He was still praying for something to change, anyway. A door to close or another to open, so as to make his future more clear.

He held the drugstore door open. It wasn't until Mary Jo stiffened that he realized this was where Daisy had worked. A place the girl had gone almost every day, including today. Mary Jo turned to leave so fast that her face buried in his chest.

He planted his hands on her shoulders. "I'm sorry. Let's go to the diner." He steered her outside.

"I know I'm being ridiculous," she said as they walked across the street. "But the sight of her holding Rose earlier almost started me crying again. I know Rose is her child, but the pain will take a while to fade."

"No apology necessary. I understand completely." He grinned down at her. "I'll buy you dinner and a milkshake."

"Which I will gladly accept." Her returning smile had his heart skipping.

A girl around the age of sixteen led them to a booth and handed them each a tattered menu. "I'll be back for your order."

"I know what I want," Bill said. "Mary Jo?"

"Yes. Cheeseburger, fries, and a strawberry shake."

"I'll have the same." Bill handed the girl the menus then reached across the table and took Mary Jo's hand. "Tell me what I can do for you."

"I'm not one of those you came to help, but thank you." She pulled her hand free.

"You're a part of this community. Same as anyone." She was also the most stubborn woman he'd ever met. A trait both exasperating and endearing.

"No, there's nothing you can do." She glanced at the window, where Daisy, a young man in a suit, and a crying Rose rushed by.

"You'll marry and have children of your own someday."

She shot him a sharp glance. "How can you be so sure? I'm a widow, remember? God didn't bless me with children in my first marriage. Besides, maybe I don't want to get married again."

"Do you?" He held his breath waiting for her answer.

She exhaled, long and slow. "I think I do. I've been so very lonely." Her eyes widened. "I'm so sorry. You shouldn't have to hear of such nonsense. What does a woman like me really have to complain about?"

"Do you mean a caring, compassionate woman, with a heart as big as these mountains? What does she have to complain about?" He straightened as the waitress set baskets lined with wax paper in front of them. Nestled in each basket was a mound of french fries and a cheeseburger so wide it would be tough getting it to fit in his mouth. "You're a woman who gave away her only pair of shoes to a student who deceived her. You took in the care of that very same student's infant, only to have said student return to claim her child. Only a saint would not complain and, as wonderful as you are, you are not a saint." He winked and shook salt over his fries.

She laughed. "What do you mean I'm not a saint? You just listed some rather admirable qualities."

"You, Mrs. Stevens, are too stubborn to be a saint." He held out his hand. "Let's pray." He prayed for a blessing over the food and that God would still Mary Jo's heart and make His way known to her. "Amen."

"You really are a good man." She popped a french fry into her mouth.

"With God's help, I strive to be."

"In your line of work, you must see atrocities and down-trodden people. How do you keep going?" She glanced at the sparsely populated diner. "Especially during a depression like this? Most of the people in this community can't afford sugar, yet you're teaching them dessert recipes. They make soap, doing their best to make it last, and you teach them cleanliness. You've come across adversity, disbelief, and dislike, yet your smile never fades and you trudge forward. How?"

"It's the love of my job and my fellow man. I truly believe what I'm doing is worth the hardships."

"Don't you want to settle in once place and work for yourself?"

He studied the pretty face in front of him. She didn't seem to be striving to be contradictory. The look in her eyes said her questions were genuine. "Yes. The older I get, the more I believe it may be time to settle down. I'm working on it, actually."

Her cheeks darkened, and she ducked her head. "That's good."

He cleared his throat, wanting to steer the conversation into smoother water. He didn't have definite answers yet. "Are you and the students ready for the program Friday night?"

"Definitely." Her face lit up. "The students have worked so hard, and they're so excited. Coming back to Pilgrim's Hollow was the best thing I ever did." She chuckled. "Mama Aida was fit to be tied when I told her we were returning to where I grew up. But, in the end, she had nothing for her to stay behind for. I think she likes it here."

"That's another admirable quality you have. Not many young women would live with their mother-in-law after the death of their husband. Especially when the mother-in-law seems determined to marry you off."

"I am sorry about that disastrous supper." She groaned.

"There's nothing to apologize for." He smiled and dug into his hamburger.

When they'd finished eating and forcing milkshakes into already full bellies, they strolled slowly toward her house as the sun began to set over the mountain. He stopped her at the bottom of the stairs. "I think we were interrupted the morning of the rainstorm."

"Oh?" She peered up at him.

"I was going to kiss you again." He cupped her face.

"Oh." Her breath, smelling faintly of strawberries, caressed his face.

"Since no one appears to be around. . ." He lowered his head, closed his eyes, and placed a lingering kiss on her lips that removed all thought of leaving, staying, or his future. All there was remained in the moment.

Chapter 9

Mary Jo beamed at her students who stood on the stage. Their dress rehearsal had gone without a hitch. Some had memorized their presentation, others glanced at notes. It was going to be splendid.

She clapped and stood from her seat in the front row. "Bravo, everyone."

"I second that." Bill struggled to carry boxes into the church.

Mary Jo hurried to take the smaller one off the top. "I hope you didn't watch the entire thing. You won't enjoy it tonight."

"No, I caught the hymn singing. Like a choir of angels." He flashed a grin to the students. "I am fulfilling my promise, although you no longer need shoes. Line up, boys and girls. Everyone gets a new pair of shoes for tonight."

Mary Jo peered into the box. Brown shoes in all sizes. "How did you manage this?"

"I wrote a letter to my church." His smile never faded as he handed out shoes for the students to try on. "They always provide in abundance when someone is in need."

"Their families won't let them accept charity," she told him softly.

"It isn't charity." His eyes twinkled. "I paid every single student a penny for helping me clean the church. They'll purchase the shoes with that penny. Penny jar is on top of the organ."

She glanced over. So it was. One by one, the students, shiny new shoes on their feet, proudly put their penny into the jar, while filling the sanctuary with the music of joy. "You truly thought of everything." Bill had come so far in understanding the people of Pilgrim's Hollow.

After paying for their shoes, the students removed them, tied the laces together, slung the shoes around their necks and thundered out the door, shouting, "See you later, Mrs. Stevens."

The week had started with heartbreak. Now, her heart overflowed with the blessings that still surrounded her. She'd miss Rose every day of her life, but life went on, and there were others who needed her. She rubbed her hands together and faced Bill. "Is that last pair mine?"

"They were meant to be." He laughed and handed them to her. "For the next time you need to give away your shoes."

She laughed with him. "Thank you."

A heavy silence filled the church as they stared at each other. Last night's kiss lingered between them. Mary Jo wanted to ask Bill about his plans for the future, whether she could get him to stay, but fear filled her heart.

"Good afternoon." Dean entered, a wavering smile on his face. "A herd of happy children just ran past me into the sanctuary. You're a good man, Bill." He thrust out his hand.

Bill gave a wry smile. "That jar of pennies is a donation for the church. I'll see you tonight, Mary Jo. Send word if there is anything I can help you with."

"I will, thank you." She turned to Dean when Bill left, set back by the hard glint in his eyes. "Is something wrong?"

"Was he going to kiss you in the house of God?" Dean's face reddened.

"Of course not. He'd handed out shoes and made twenty cents for the church." Oh. She dug in her purse for a penny. Not finding one, she dropped in a nickel. "Twenty-five cents."

He crossed his arms. "You've made your decision regarding my proposal, I gather."

"I suppose I have." She blinked back tears. "I know there can be nothing between Bill and me since he'll be leaving soon, but knowing that I can care for another man shows I'm not the wife you need."

"I'm willing to wait until your heart sorts itself out."

She tilted her head. "It won't. I'm so sorry, Dean."

He gave a curt nod. "God will send me a wife if that is His will. I need to be patient." He hung his head then squared his shoulders. "Let's get ready for the program."

When they'd finished readying the church, Mary Jo hurried home to change into her best dress.

Mama Aida, wearing her fanciest hat, met her at the door. "I've made you a sandwich and laid out your clothes. You'd best hurry. It wouldn't do for you to be late."

"I'll eat on the way." She dressed quickly, ran a brush through her hair, then twisted her hair into a bun and raced to grab her sandwich from the table. "I'm ready." She bolted out the door, taking bites of ham and cheese between slices of bread.

"Why are you so late?" Mama Aida hurried to catch up.

"It took longer for Dean and me to fold the pamphlets." It had taken longer for sure, but the awkwardness between them hadn't helped.

Thirty minutes later, Mary Jo stood in front of a church fuller than it had ever been on a Sunday morning and smiled at the sea of proud faces. "I know I arrived as teacher only a few months ago, but the students have learned and worked so hard that I know your hearts will swell. Without further ado, I present the students of Pilgrim Hollow school." With a wave of her arm, Mary Jo stepped aside and let the children take over.

When the last hymn was sung, the church exploded with applause and whoops. There was no other place Mary Jo preferred to be at that moment. Happiness overflowed from a heart wounded for too long. So great was the emotion, her legs threatened to buckle.

She continued clapping as she realized she'd not only *not* forgiven Daisy, but she hadn't forgiven her husband for dying. For five years, she'd carried bitterness in her heart. Through the noise around her, she forgave them and let the tears stream down her cheeks. Tomorrow. . .she might have to dig up the strength to forgive again, but she could. . .with God's help.

Bill couldn't take his eyes off Mary Jo. Her face was radiant, even with the tears. His heart lurched.

He'd received a letter that morning from his boss, requesting a meeting. Usually that meant reassignment. How could he leave? How could he stay?

She turned her head and beamed his way. He returned her grin even though his heart was shattering.

"Bill?" Mr. Wilson tapped him on the shoulder. "Daisy Mason is outside and wants to talk to you."

"Me?" What did the vixen want now? He pushed through the throng of parents fighting their way toward the stage and practically stumbled outside.

Daisy stood next to a battered Ford truck. At her feet was a box. In her arms sniffled Rose. "I ain't cut out to be a mama." She thrust the baby at him. "I know Mrs. Stevens is busy with the program and all. Will you give her the baby?"

"Her name is Rose." Bill took the baby and glared over her head.

"I wrote a letter and had it notarized, giving Mrs. Stevens the right to raise my baby. She can make it more official if she wants." Daisy tossed a look over her shoulder. "My husband said the. . .*Rose* cries too much." She lowered her voice. "I think he might hurt her if I keep her. Tell Mrs. Stevens I'm sorry." She scrambled into the truck and gravel flew as they roared away.

Bill held Rose above his head and peered into her tiny face. Her cries had stopped, but tears still glistened on her soft cheeks. "This is the second time you've been left with me. Do you think God is trying to tell me something?" He grinned and tucked her close to his chest with one arm and scooped up the box with the other. "We're going to make a woman very happy."

He entered the church and found a place in the back, around from the throng. Parents gathered their children and headed next door to the fellowship hall for cookies and punch. Bill couldn't erase the grin on his face when Mary Jo turned and her eyes widened.

She moved slowly toward him, her gaze not leaving the gurgling baby, who reached for her the moment she caught sight of who was coming. "Oh, Rose." Mary Jo hugged the baby close. "How?"

"Daisy couldn't do it, so she said for you to have her."

"This has been the most perfect night in more months than I can count." She kissed the top of the baby's head. "Let's go see Mama Aida." She tossed Bill a smile then motioned her head for him to come with her.

Mama Aida shrieked when she saw Rose and came running. "Oh, my." She covered the baby's face with kisses. "My grandbaby is back."

Mary Jo laughed. "I guess you can call her that now." She explained what Bill had told her then gripped his hand and squeezed.

He kept a firm hold even when she tried to pull away. He needed to tell her he had to leave in the morning, but how could he erase the happiness from her face? Perhaps he thought too highly of himself and she wouldn't care as much as he thought for him to be gone.

"Aren't you happy, Bill?" Mary Jo gripped his arms and stared into his eyes. "Rose is back."

"I'm thrilled. You'll be a good mother."

She paled. "You're leaving, aren't you?"

"I have to." His heart sank. "Let's not talk about it tonight. This is a night of celebration."

She licked her lips and caressed his cheek. "I will miss you." Then, she turned and left, her shoulders slumping a bit. One of the children ran up to her, wrapped their arms around her waist, and returned some of the glow to Mary Jo's face.

Bill did his best to imprint her face on his heart and in his mind. If God chose to bring him back this way someday, she'd most likely be married to Dean. For a while, Bill had entertained the idea of asking Mary Jo to travel with him. That wasn't possible now. The road was no place for a baby.

He continued to watch as her students pulled her further away from him. Once she disappeared among the many bodies, he shoved his hands into his pockets and left. Before heading to his place, he propped an envelope against her front door. He wrote of his feelings, how much he wanted to stay but couldn't, and how he wished her all the best in the future.

Swiping the back of his hand roughly across his eyes, he shuffled away.

Mary Jo had looked for Bill as people left the church. Not finding him, she realized it best that he wasn't there to say goodbye. She didn't think she could bear it. She walked home with Mama Aida, listening to her mother-in-law's happy chatter about Rose's return and how much she had always wanted to be a grandmother. She smiled and laughed, trying to ignore the dull pain in her heart.

Bill had a job. A job that took him places. He couldn't be tied down by a hillbilly schoolteacher who barely had the money for a pair of shoes when she needed them.

Spotting a white rectangle at the door, she quickened her pace. Scrawled across the front was her name. She tucked the letter into her pocket and opened the front door to allow Mama Aida to carry in Rose. Mary Jo set the box containing the baby's clothes and diapers in her room and sat on the edge of the bed to read the letter.

> *Dear Mary Jo,*
> *I tried to find a way to stay. I'm still trying in fact, but my boss has summoned me. Leaving isn't easy, I want you to understand that. I hope, no, I pray, God will return me to Pilgrim's Hollow, but if He doesn't. . .then, please don't wait for me.*
>
> *Am I being presumptuous? Perhaps we're nothing more than friends, but the tenderness of your lips against mine gives me hope that you maybe feel a little more than friendship for me.*
>
> *I lied a few sentences up where I asked you not to wait for me. Do wait. Give me a month. If you don't hear from me within that time, then marry Dean.*
>
> *My Love,*
> *Bill*

Mary Jo choked back a sob. Silly fool of a man. She couldn't marry Dean. Her heart belonged to Bill. She'd wait for him. For as long as it took.

Chapter 10

S ummer came with its heat and humidity, and still no word from Bill. Mary Jo sat on the porch, rocking a sleeping Rose, and wondered why she'd been so foolish as to wait for him. She shrugged. It wasn't like she could marry anyone else. Dean had transferred his attentions to the pharmacist, and Mary Jo was happy for him.

School began tomorrow, lessons were prepared, and the tiny town of Pilgrim's Hollow had grown by three families, with the opening of a new wood mill. Mary Jo might be lonely, but she was content.

She pushed the rocker into motion with her bare toes and smiled. Now that she had shoes, she found going barefoot during the day was cooler and more comfortable. Her pride had been a silly thing.

Dean's sermon at church that morning had been about pride and how it could be man's downfall. He spoke of how pride often led to a person not forgiving someone. Mary Jo could see how that could be. While it was no longer as big of a struggle for her to forgive her husband for dying or Daisy for the things she'd done, that ugly monster still visited on occasion.

"I'm headed to town." Mama Aida, still dressed in her Sunday clothes, rushed down the steps.

"You've sure found excuses to go to town a lot lately." Mary Jo grinned. Mama Aida had been making eyes at the new pharmacist's father. "Enjoy yourself."

"Oh, hush." Mama Aida grinned and set off down the road.

Once she was gone, Mary Jo pulled the well-read letter from Bill out of her pocket. She read the words again then opened her hand and let the wind carry the letter, and his words, away. Tears pricked her eyes. Refusing to shed another tear over him, she blinked them away.

Rose's body grew heavy in Mary Jo's arms. She stood and moved to place the child in the newly built crib before going to the kitchen to check on the Sunday roast. A meal she'd be eating alone, it seemed. She closed the oven door and turned.

A shadow stepped into the doorway.

She screamed.

"It's me." Bill limped into the light. A fresh scar ran from his hairline to just above his eye.

She stared. "What happened?" She stepped forward and brushed his bangs away from his face.

"May I sit?" He motioned to the kitchen table.

"Of course. I'll make coffee." Her hands trembled as she measured the grounds. She gripped the countertop. Was it possible he hadn't been able to contact her? He was here now. That was the most important thing. She made the coffee, letting silence fall between them. When their mugs were full, she sat across from him at the table and slid his drink to him.

"I left here at the request of my employer. My intentions were to finish out the spring lineup of jobs and resign. On the way to Little Rock, I hit a slick spot in the road and crashed into a tree." He wrapped his hands around his mug. "I don't know how long I lay there in the rain before someone found me, but I've spent the summer in a coma. The doctor said my first word when I woke was your name."

Her throat clogged. "I thought you had filled me with false hope." She reached across the table and placed her hand on his. "I'm so sorry."

"I love you, Mary Jo. I have no idea what the future holds for me. . .for us. . .but I'd like you to marry me anyway." He gave her a crooked smile. "I'd get down on one knee, but I doubt I'd be able to get back up."

She darted around the table and wrapped her arms around his neck. "I don't care what the future holds. We've a home as long as I'm a teacher. With your skills, I have no doubt you'll find work." She kissed him. "Oh, yes, Bill, I'll marry you."

Bill stood in front of the small brick building, sporting a hand-painted For Sale sign. Could he? He pushed open the door and was greeted by the smell of ink and paper.

"Mr. Wright." The owner of the Pilgrim's Hollow *Gazette* held out his hand. "I'm not a bit surprised to see you here. You'd be perfect for the job."

Bill laughed. "I haven't said I'll buy it yet." Him own a newspaper? "How many subscribers do you have?"

"Not many. Maybe fifty, but more people are coming all the time. A young man like you could change the name of the paper and deliver in neighboring towns and hollows." He shook his head. "I'm too old, and the missus wants to move to Kansas where our daughter is."

"I should probably discuss this with my fiancée, but. . .yes, I'll buy it." He needed a job to support his new family. This sounded perfect.

After heading to the bank and signing the papers, he strolled past the school. Recess was in session, and the love of his life stood on the steps. Her face lit up at the sight of him, and she met him halfway.

"This is a lovely surprise."

He stepped close, not touching her because of the watching students, and lowered his head. "Ready for Saturday?"

"More than ready. What's that?" She reached for the folder in his hand.

"I've got a job. Well, actually, I, uh, bought the *Gazette*. Do you mind?"

She caressed his cheek. "You'll be perfect. I've got to go, but I'll see you for supper, right?"

"You can help me come up with a new name and plan." He tapped her nose and left as she called the students inside.

He couldn't remember a time he'd been happier. God had spared his life from a horrible accident, he was marrying the best woman on the planet, and he now had a way to support her. The overflow of blessings humbled him.

He marched up the steps to the church and made his way to the altar. Staring at the simple wooden cross hanging behind the podium, he gave thanks and asked for a blessing on his upcoming marriage. He turned to see Dean waiting.

"Welcome back, Bill." Dean held out his hand. "You look a little worse for wear, though."

"But, I'm still breathing." He returned the pastor's handshake. "Thank you for agreeing to perform the ceremony this weekend. No hard feelings?"

"Not at all. All either of us wanted is for that beautiful woman to be happy. I believe you are quite capable of undertaking that job." He smiled. "Besides, I've found someone whom I believe may actually care for me more than as a friend."

"See you Saturday." Bill clapped him on the shoulder and strode from the church. After a stop at the mercantile to purchase a pad of paper and two pencils, he headed for the lake to jot down his ideas for the new paper.

He wanted to not only list the breaking news, but weddings, births, deaths, and accomplishments of the community. He wanted this to be the people's paper.

As it came close to time for school to dismiss, Bill hurried to Mary Jo's house to speak to Mama Aida. He wanted to make sure things were ready for his wedding surprise.

"Of course, they're ready," she said when asked. "All they needed were a bit of polishing." She handed him a pair of white shoes. "You sure have a strange way of being romantic."

Finally, the day of her wedding arrived. Mary Jo felt as if Frank would approve of Bill, not as a replacement, but as someone to take over where Frank couldn't.

Times were too harsh for a new wedding gown, but Mary Jo had been able to alter her gown to appear as new. A lace collar, a sheer overlay over the sateen skirt, it barely resembled the dress she'd worn seven years ago.

Mama Aida hovered in the doorway, tears shimmering in her eyes. "Don't you forget your old mother-in-law, now that you have a new husband."

"Oh, Mama Aida. You're my mother, the mother of my heart. How could I ever forget you? Besides, you'll still be living with us, silly goose." Bill hadn't thought for a second not to say yes when Mary Jo had asked.

Mama Aida's gaze traveled from the hat and veil on Mary Jo's head to her feet. "You look very pretty." She sniffed.

"Thank you. Are you ready?" She'd chosen Mama Aida to give her away.

The pharmacist's father, Mama Aida's beau, pulled up in his coupe. "Don't the two of you look lovely?"

"Thank you for the ride, Mr. Rhodes." Mary Jo slid into the backseat, leaving the front for Mama Aida.

"Wouldn't dare let you walk to your wedding."

Ten minutes later, Mary Jo stood outside the church's double doors and waited for the wedding march to sound. She clutched a bouquet of wildflowers in her hands. "What's taking so long?"

Mama Aida peeked through the doors. "Bill isn't there. Neither is the pastor."

Ice water trickled through Mary Jo's veins. "What if Bill is having second thoughts?"

"Don't be ridiculous. He'd be a fool not to marry you. Oh, there they are. See? I told you not to be silly. Hold my hand."

"I'll drop my flowers. Just walk beside me."

"I'm nervous."

Mary Jo laughed. "I'm the one getting married."

"It'll seem strange having a man in the house again."

The music started. "Thank you, Mama." Mary Jo planted a kiss on her cheek.

"You're welcome. . .daughter. Now, let's get you married." Mama Aida thrust the doors open.

Mary Jo laughed and hurried after her. Slightly out of breath, she stopped and faced Bill, who held something behind his back. "Hello," she whispered.

"Hello." He glanced at her feet. "Barefoot?"

"I couldn't think of marrying you any other way." She smiled.

"Not even with slightly used white ones?" He held out a pair of open-toed shoes. "I promise to never let you be shoeless again."

"You silly man." Tears trickled down her cheeks. "Would you be my prince and slide them on my feet?" She sat on the front pew as laughter filled the church.

Bill knelt beside her, wincing slightly, and put the shoes on her feet. Then, using the pew to help him stand, held out a hand to her. "Let's get hitched."

She laughed. "Yes, let's." Still holding hands, they faced a smiling Dean.

The pastor gave them a nod, and then began, "Dearly beloved. . ."

Cynthia Hickey grew up in a family of storytellers and moved around the country a lot as an army brat. Her desire is to write about real, but flawed characters in a wholesome way that her seven children and five grandchildren can all be proud of. She and her husband live in Arizona where Cynthia is a full-time writer.

Between the Moments

by Maureen Lang

Chapter 1

Kansas
1879

Mary Elliot hurriedly tugged at the stiff laces of her shoes, having waited to put them back on until the last possible moment before disembarking. Shoes were certainly not the only thing she must get used to wearing, but they were among the most uncomfortable. Particularly these! Fashion might require two-inch heels, or so she had been told, but they were silly for traipsing the world.

Gripping the single bag she'd traveled with across Africa, across the ocean, across half of America, she stepped onto the train platform. Mary had learned weeks ago when the ship landed in New York that the sky here was as blue as the sky over Cape Colony, the clouds still white or gray depending on their mood, the ground still brown or green or dried to muted shades. If she closed her eyes, when she opened them again she might imagine herself still at the African mission.

But that was silly too, to entertain dreams as childish as they were hopeless. She'd been forced to choose family over duty. A duty few people on the board of the London Missionary Society felt she needed to fulfill, reminding her it was her parents' mission to work with the Khoikhoi tribe, not hers. Nonetheless she'd refused to leave her parents' mission post for nearly a year after both had succumbed to fevers. But when the LMS finally sent replacement missionaries, Mary had been ordered "home" to family.

If the missionary society had known this last leg of her long journey was as far as it had proven to be, that Topeka was days and not hours from Chicago, they likely would not have approved of her chaperone letting her finish alone. But Mary had convinced them it would be easy to travel this relatively short distance by herself considering how far she'd already traveled. Grandfather Moorely was expecting her—although not a soul among the thinning crowd seemed to match her imagined picture of him. Certainly no older gentleman, with underlying kindheartedness or otherwise, appeared to be looking for her.

Eventually her gaze was drawn to a group lingering at the farthest edge of the platform. Though they were dressed like other Americans, they were clearly African.

Perhaps they might know of him or could direct her to his home.

"*Halau!*" She added a wide smile, the universal welcome. Then she asked, in the language shared by so many in the southernmost regions of Africa, if they knew of the Moorely residence.

Six sets of eyes turned to her filled with equal measures of curiosity and wariness but not a trace of understanding.

"You'll get further in English around here," said a voice from somewhere behind them.

Mary tilted her head in the direction everyone had turned, to a man seated comfortably on a bench. He wasn't African, though from under his tipped hat Mary glimpsed black hair long enough to touch the top of his denim collar. Looking up at her, however, were the bluest eyes she'd ever seen. He was sitting against the station's office, his long legs spread out while he whittled a small piece of wood held steady against the cut of his knife.

"Oh, yes, of course," Mary said, silently chiding herself for wanting to believe even for that brief moment she was back in Africa among the people she'd grown up with. "I'm looking for my grandfather, J. W. Moorely. He must have been detained, so I'd like to find my way to his home if someone can direct me?"

"You shore not from 'Merica," said one of the children closest to her. "I ain't never heard anybody talk like you done before—or now."

"I suppose my English sounds more British than American," admitted Mary.

"Afraid we're new to Topeka too, ma'am," said one of the women. "We're waiting for a guide ourselves." She was old enough to be Mary's mother, and by the twinkle in her eye Mary guessed she was at ease filling the maternal role no matter who seemed in need of one.

"Would you mind terribly if I wait with you? Perhaps your guide will know my grandfather."

"I know him," came that same voice from the bench. He hadn't bothered to stand when he'd spoken either now or earlier, signaling he was less than a gentleman. So despite his pronouncement, his youth and handsomeness, she decided immediately she was safer with the Africans. She said nothing to encourage him.

He stood at last, and he was as tall as she'd guessed from those long legs that had been sprawled in front of him. He tucked his knife into a beaded pouch that hung at his waist—a beautiful holder, a kind Mary had never seen before. But he covered it with his jacket before she was finished admiring it. Then he handed his carving to the boy who'd spoken a moment ago. The man had shaped the wood into a horse, and the boy's eyes widened at the unexpected but welcome gift. After running his thumbs over the flowing mane, he held it up for the woman at his side to see.

Mary let her gaze return to the blue eyes of the man now approaching, wondering if she'd been too hasty to judge him less than a gentleman. He wore a brimmed hat, not the pith helmet or safari hat worn by her father and other missionaries, but this kind would certainly keep the sun off his head and neck as well. He shoved it back now, better to see her no doubt, but left it on his head as further evidence he wasn't quite the gentleman most Western societies expected a man of his age to be.

"Moorely's on the outskirts of town," the man said, his gaze now leaving her face to take in her form and linger on the hem of her dress, as if looking specifically for her footwear. She glanced down too, holding aside her hem, and to her mortification saw she'd missed loops on both of her shoes, giving her laces a decidedly untidy look. She stiffened, unsure if he was still within the boundaries of politeness because he continued to stare at her. "Pretty long walk for somebody who doesn't like shoes. Dusty too."

Pulling her bag into a grip with both hands, she lifted her chin. "I'm accustomed to walking and don't mind dust. I'll thank you to point me in the right direction."

He eyed her a moment longer, as if deciding whether or not to speak. "I can take you."

An instant refusal was on the tip of her tongue. He was, after all, a stranger to her and not altogether. . .mannerly. Yet there was something in his eyes that intrigued her, that hint of kindness behind a veneer of devil-may-care self-protectiveness. She could hardly look away, even as she told herself she must follow the many rules of etiquette the ladies of the mission society had drummed into her whenever Mummy and Daddy suffered their overseeing visits. Mary had always complied, being a fast learner, if only to keep them from insisting Daddy send her to a *proper* school instead of letting her stay with her parents in the various villages they called home.

Besides, he'd made a gift of that horse to a child, and that said more of him than his other shortcomings.

"That would be very kind of you," she said at last.

He took her elbow, starting to lead her away, but the boy who'd been the recipient of the carved horse called after them.

"Sir!"

The man beside her turned, and so did she. "Thanks for the horse!"

He grinned, tipping his hat more formally than he had toward Mary just a moment ago. But the boy spoke again before either of them had taken another step.

"Ma'am," he sang out again, "what's that language you used? Ya know, when you first come up on us?"

She turned fully to the boy then, bending to meet him eye-to-eye. He was a handsome youth, large eyes, perfectly smooth bronze skin, his hair shorn close to the head. "The language of the Khoikhoi, from Africa. That's where I'm from."

"*You're* from Africa?" It was the older woman now, not the boy at all.

Mary stood tall again, nodding. "I was born there."

Now the maternal eyes that had been so friendly earlier narrowed with suspicion. "We from there too, only when they come for our forefathers they used chains."

"Yes," Mary said sadly. "It's still a blight, selling people from tribe to tribe. My parents and I did all we could to fight such a horrific trade."

Now the woman's brows rose, and a hint of affability reentered her dark eyes. "It's over at last, leastwise here. Thank the Lord for that."

Mary nodded, extending her hand. "My name is Mary Elliot," she said. "If you're staying in Topeka for any length of time, perhaps we'll meet again. I do hope so."

The woman stared down at Mary's extended hand so long Mary feared she'd made a mistake in initiating a greeting she'd enjoyed with all of the visitors to her parents' home. At last she took Mary's hand, shaking it firmly.

"I's Cisley and this here's my boy, Kitch." She introduced the others then, and Mary vowed to remember them all, just as she always did when meeting new people. "Topeka's our new home, so we'll be here if you will. Not so sure your kind can mix with us, though."

Mary laughed. "I suppose I know nothing of how things are run here, but I very much hope we'll see each other again. Soon."

Mary was vaguely aware that the man beside her, the very one she'd decided to trust enough to transport her safely to her grandfather, had not participated in the introductions. Yet if they were new to town, he could hardly know them either. Had he something against these newcomers? Or did he simply think an introduction a waste of time, if he had no intention of seeing any of them again? She meant to find out before stepping another foot alongside of him.

"And you are. . . ?" she asked, so everyone could hear his response.

"Eddie," he said, low, then added more loudly, "Tucker."

He didn't offer his hand, not even to Mary, but at least he'd offered another scant tip of his hat. Then he turned to her. "I've got to pick up the mail; it's why I met the train. After that we'd best be going. Looks like rain might move in."

He was likely right about the change in the weather, and in a moment he excused himself for the window at the station, where a line had dwindled away. She saw him receive a package while she waited with the others, chatting. She learned Cisley and her family had come from Missouri after hearing Kansas would welcome "their kind"—former slaves, freed less than half a dozen years ago. Mary marveled at Cisley's courage, who admitted she didn't know what kind of life they would face. Who did? Certainly not Mary.

Mr. Tucker approached again, the packet under his arm, and Mary waved goodbye.

"Finding them again won't be hard," Mr. Tucker said as he directed Mary to a wagon beyond the station house. "They might not have too much trouble getting work if they stay in the city, but if they do live here, it'll be in the same spot as all the others. Might as well be a reservation for all they know."

"A. . .reservation?"

Mr. Tucker nodded, his lips tight. "Where they shove people away they don't trust."

"How awful."

He might have answered, but after helping her up to the seat in his wagon, Mary heard a voice calling her name.

"Mary! Mary Elliot!"

An older man, older than her yet surely not old enough to be her grandfather, hurried along the road leading to the station, not looking her way. His call was like a summons announcing his search before he'd even reached his destination.

"I'm Mary Elliot," she called.

The bustling man didn't hear her, just kept running. Mr. Tucker issued a shrill whistle then shouted, "She's right here."

The man turned abruptly, looking relieved as he redirected his path to hurry to their side. Mr. Tucker didn't wait for the man. He went around the wagon and hopped up behind the reins.

"Miss Mary Elliot?" he asked, belatedly taking off his hat as he looked up at her from beside the wagon.

"Yes, that's me," she said.

"I'm Alwin, your grandfather's man. He's—he's in the carriage, but we were stopped by an upturned honey wagon just down the road. We waited and waited for it to be cleared away, but they're still working on the mess."

"Oh my," Mary said, imagining upturned vats creating a sweet, sticky mess. "I hope all that honey doesn't bring every bee—and bear?—to town."

She saw Mr. Tucker and Alwin exchange a glance and guessed she'd somehow misspoken. Although there were no bears in Africa, she was certain her mother once told her about such creatures here and how they liked to eat honey.

"The mess might attract pests," said Mr. Tucker, "like rats and even those bees you're worried about. But it's not the kind of honey you seem to be thinking of. This kind of honey's only good for fertilizer. Manure."

Even as he explained, a faintly unpleasant scent reached Mary's nose, indicating Alwin must have braved the accident to reach her.

"If you don't want your guest traipsing through the muck," Mr. Tucker continued, his tone as bored as if explaining the obvious to an errant child, "then go on back to Moorely and let him know I've taken her back. We'll leave from this end of town and circle around to Moorely land."

Alwin's brows lifted with relief but only for a moment. In the next instant he looked curious then concerned then outright disapproving, all directed at the face of Mr. Tucker.

Mr. Tucker shook the reins, urging the horse forward.

"I'm afraid Mr. Moorely wouldn't agree to that!" Alwin cried out, but his protests were left in their wake.

Eddie would have chuckled at the look on Alwin's face as he directed his horse away, but he decided that might appear more rude than necessary. It didn't matter that the town would never trust him with one of their innocents—and Mary Elliot was clearly that. She'd find out sooner or later not to spend time with him, but at the moment he decided that discovery should come later.

Mary Elliot, however, was looking back at Alwin. To her credit, her face held more curiosity than alarm. "Was there a reason beyond my lack of a proper chaperone that he thought I ought not allow you to take me to my new home?"

"Yep." He decided to leave it at that but expected it wouldn't take long for her to press him.

"Something I should know about? Worry about, perhaps?"

"I suppose you could worry what people will think, but I'll get you there safe and sound. Nehemiah—that's my horse—and this buckboard are trustworthy. So am I."

"But others don't think so? At least," she added, after a glance to Nehemiah then back to him, "so far as you go?"

He shrugged.

"I see," she said.

He wondered what conclusions she'd drawn. She didn't look worried, which pleased him, probably more than he should let it. He might not mind shoving a finger in the eye of Topeka's polite society now and then, as he was doing right now, but that didn't mean he could spend more than five minutes with any girl in town. Especially a Moorely granddaughter.

"Listen," he said after a moment, "if you plan to cavort with the Exodusters you'd better not care what others think. But you should care, if you want to please that grandfather of yours."

"Exodusters?"

Once again he was pleased, since she'd followed the conversation in the direction he preferred. Away from Moorely. "You know, after the Exodus."

"Oh, I assumed that much. But who are they? And why are they called Exodusters?"

"Those Africans come from slave states along the Mississippi—well, what used to be slave states. It's like an Exodus from there to Kansas because they can own land here. Not that there's much good land left," he added, then even lower, "after all the parcels the government already handed out."

"You don't approve?"

He supposed he ought to clarify just what he didn't approve of, especially since she'd gone so far as to call herself an African. It was a bit soon after meeting her to be so honest, but since he heartily doubted he'd get to spend much time with her anyway, it probably didn't matter what he said. "It's the government I don't approve of, if you want to know the truth. They took hold of the land even though it shouldn't really be owned at all."

"But. . .surely there are benefits to owning land? To plant crops and let the land sustain them?"

He shrugged. "The land offers plenty on its own without scraping into it with a plow, demanding the same ground produce so much year after year."

She smiled, but it wasn't what he would call receptive. She appeared almost. . . sad. "I've never met anyone who disapproved of farming."

He thumped the reins and Nehemiah picked up the pace. "I guess I better not disapprove too much," he admitted, "since I am one. Or my family is. Farmers, that is."

Her brows came together and her mouth set, creating a small dimple to one side. He nearly couldn't tear his eyes away, he was so captivated. "How can you disapprove, then?"

"I go along with it because that's what they do. But I don't have to like it, do I?"

"No, I suppose not. But what would you rather do?"

"Hunt. Fish. Raise horses maybe. My Apache father taught me how to train horses, and even though I've only trained a few for my mother, that's what I enjoy more than farming." Then he glanced down toward her feet, which she'd braced against the buckboard. "You can take your shoes off if you want. It's nearly a half-hour ride."

She pulled back her feet, and for the barest moment he thought she might take him up on the offer. But she only tucked them out of sight.

"If worse came to worst," he continued, "I'd get a job in town. But my brother needs my help, and so I'm a farmer."

"Even though you hardly like it."

"I'm getting used to it."

She laughed, and that dimple deepened. "How is it you're only now getting used to something you were surely born to do, having a farming family?"

"I wasn't always with them."

"Oh?"

Once again, the thought crossed his mind that he was talking too much, at least about himself. He wasn't used to that. Everybody in town already knew his history. Which probably meant he ought to tell her his version of it before somebody else did—including that grandfather of hers.

"I spent seven years away from my family," he said slowly. "Learning another way of life. One that lived off the land but never took it for granted or called it mine. It's a gift to all of us, from the Creator."

"I'm in accord with that," she said, raising a hand to sweep in the fields appearing now that they were outside of town. "This is certainly a gift from our Creator. But did you live elsewhere? School perhaps? I'm the daughter of missionaries, and sending children off to school is common practice."

He shook his head. "I lived with the Apache. Grew up with them." Preferred them. . . but saying that aloud really would be going too far, so he squashed the words even if he couldn't entirely squash the sentiment. In these last six years since his return, he was glad to be reunited with his mother. His brother was another matter altogether.

"Who are the Apache?" she asked.

He grinned at her lack of education, at least the kind that mattered around here. "Whatever school they sent you to never let you read any of those silly dime novels, did they? I guess you don't know this grandfather of yours, either, but didn't he ever write to you, share with you what it's like around here?"

"But I didn't go away to school. I lived with my parents the entire time."

"So didn't they tell you about America? Weren't they from around here?"

"My mother was born here in Topeka," she said. "My father in England. London, actually. They were missionaries with the London Mission Society. Mother did talk of Topeka fondly, and of her mother and sister, but both died some years ago. Her father, my grandfather, apparently didn't approve of her going off to Africa."

"What happened to her? Why aren't you with your parents now?"

"They died a little over a year ago. Yellow. . .yellow fever." She'd paused when her voice started to wobble, so he said nothing. He knew what it was like to lose a parent; he'd lost two fathers and may as well have lost one mother, even though the woman who gave birth to him was still alive—something he thanked God for, even as he silently asked her forgiveness for hurting her feelings just about every day.

Mary sighed as if to regain her composure, which didn't entirely work because there was still the trace of a frown on her forehead. "I tried taking up their work at the Rehoboth Mission, but the LMS—that's the London Missionary Society—decided it wasn't my place to do so. They said I was too young and hadn't gone through proper schooling and training. What? said I to them. My entire life was perfect training, but they refused to let me stay on. I went to my father's family in London, but my London grandfather insisted I come here, at least long enough to make a proper choice between the two branches of family."

"Fair enough, I suppose," he said. He didn't know the first thing about London or anywhere outside of what used to be Indian Territory, but he imagined she'd probably end up choosing London. It seemed far enough away to imagine more justice there.

He looked at the rolling landscape around them, reminded that this country was still beautiful, even with its flaws. The land offered so many shades of green he couldn't describe them all, along with tans and golds and yellows against the widest sky the eye could see. Straight up it was clear blue, a sharp contrast to the front lines of white clouds being chased by dark gray ones moving in from the west. It all reminded him of no less than God Himself. No wonder so many Apache had given their lives to hold on to it.

"Mr. Tucker," she said, her voice softer than it had been so far, "is it because you lived with the Apache that Alwin didn't want you to take me to my grandfather's?"

He eyed her. "You're pretty quick. That's it exactly. What made you guess?"

"Observing tribal loyalties, I suppose," she said. "Back home—that is, in Africa—there are frequent fights between tribes. People have such a hard time trusting those who aren't one of their own. I suppose it's the same everywhere."

He felt a grin growing on his face, despite his wish not to be too friendly. Eddie had no friends. There wasn't an iota of doubt that her grandfather wouldn't let him anywhere near her.

For the first time since he'd been plucked from the reservation and returned to his mother, Eddie found himself wishing he could fit back in to a place that would have been his had he never been abducted. At least enough to be accepted as Mary Elliot's friend.

Chapter 2

The home belonging to Mary's grandfather was just as she'd expected it to be. Her mother had drawn a picture of it for her, the brick facade, the wide porch with white columns in the center and corners, gardens on each side. She'd even provided a floor plan that included all eighteen rooms, as if she'd been etching the memory for herself. Because of that, Mary already knew her mother's bedroom was next to the one that once belonged to her mother's younger sister, the aunt Mary had never known.

It was a far larger home than the one belonging to her grandparents in London. The small size of that house had been Mary's first guess as to why they'd so easily advised her to go. Her father's parents had always been kind, but they were mostly strangers—busy strangers, with her grandfather a vicar and her grandmother's days filled with charity work. On those rare occasions when she had visited England with her parents, Mary sensed the three of them were in the way. That still proved the case when Mary had arrived alone. She'd briefly hoped her London grandparents would find a place for her, a niche to fill, a job for her to do. Perhaps if she'd stayed long enough they would have, eventually.

"You don't have much baggage for a visitor to this house," said Mr. Tucker as he jumped to the ground. He came around to assist her.

"Have you delivered other guests here, then?"

"Not a single one. But I've seen a guest or two leave the station with Alwin. Let's just say he often had to bring a carriage for the guests and a separate wagon—or two—for the baggage and servants they brought in tow."

She took another look at the tall house, wondering if any such visitors were inside even now.

"I'd probably best get you to the door before either the rain or your grandfather catches up," said Mr. Tucker as he reached for her.

She let him swing her down to the ground, smiling as she felt feather light in his strong arms. When he let his hands linger at her waist after she was safely settled, she hadn't the faintest intention to protest. Or move away. Instead, she looked up at him, once again marveling at the blue of his eyes. Her own were plain brown, just like those of both her parents. It was easy to look at his eyes, especially seeing a hint he might be as interested in gazing at her face as she was in gazing at his.

"I should thank you properly for the ride," she said, and her voice was softer than she'd meant, but her throat was suddenly dry and her heart sped so unexpectedly she couldn't speak any differently. "Perhaps you might come to dinner? It's bold of me to offer an invitation to a home that isn't really my own, but it does seem the least I can do."

His smile automatically broadened her own, but then he frowned and her rushing heart nearly stopped with disappointment. "Do you—not want to?"

"Oh, it's not that," he said, with such assurance she immediately believed him. Then a sound from afar caught his attention, and Mary looked to see a carriage coming up the long lane at a much faster pace than the one Mr. Tucker had used bringing her here. Mr. Tucker cocked his head toward it. "It's that."

John William Moorely—J.W. as many in town knew him—might be well over sixty, but he was as agile as someone twenty years younger. He was out of that carriage before it was entirely stilled from its rapid approach.

"Young man," he called, rounding Eddie's rig to stand before them, "you have something to learn about manners if you think you can get away with carrying off my granddaughter like that. Get off my property."

Beside him, Mary gasped. "He didn't—"

J.W. Moorely cast a quick, cold glance Mary Elliot's way. Eddie had half a mind to step in between before the look reached her. That wasn't the way a grandfather should greet a granddaughter he'd never met.

"I'll see to you in a moment," Mr. Moorely said, and even if Eddie had somehow been able to block the icy stare he wouldn't have been able to soften the unmistakable stoniness in the tone before it reached Mary's ears. "Good day, Mr. Tucker."

Eddie hesitated. Heaven knew he'd been rude to the likes of Mr. Moorely before. Going against the older man's wishes wouldn't bother Eddie in the least. But there was Mary to think of now, and if it took crushing his impulse to repay bearish behavior in kind, he would do it. He wouldn't have her receiving a backlash once he inevitably went on his way.

"I'll go, Mr. Moorely," he said evenly, removing his hat for good measure, "and I apologize if I stepped out of line. But we were already leaving the station when Alwin beckoned us, and it seemed just as easy for me to bring Miss Elliot home since it's on my way. I didn't know how long your rig would be stuck. She'd likely have gone along with your man if we knew you could end her journey as fast as this."

Then he replaced his hat and jumped back up to his wagon, resisting the urge to look back at Mary.

It was a good thing he wasn't counting on that dinner invitation.

Mary watched Eddie Tucker's departure as long as she dared, entirely ignoring the stare she felt aimed at her from her grandfather. Perhaps she was afraid to look at him, but she was also sure she would have watched Mr. Tucker as long as he was within sight.

"Come inside the house," her grandfather said then led the way without another word as if he hadn't a doubt she would obey.

The door opened before her grandfather had reached the porch's top step. Evidently the home wasn't empty after all. Mary had little more than a glimpse of a young maid who stepped into the shadows as Grandfather led Mary through a wide, polished foyer and into a sunlit parlor.

"I expect you'll want some refreshment and then to rest," said Grandfather Moorely. He went to a side table and poured a drink from a crystal decanter, but rather than offering one to her he downed the amber liquid then set aside the empty glass before facing her again with a frown.

Myriad thoughts assailed her. Her mother had once told Mary that if she ever met her American grandfather, the first thing Mary must know was that his heart might seem hard, but he did have one. To find it she must convince him she would not be bullied. Her mother said her father respected only one kind of person, and that was someone who wasn't afraid to speak in his presence—as formidable as he was. That was the very word she'd used, *formidable*, and Mary had to admit it fit.

"Grandfather," she said slowly, deciding her mother had only let her down once in her life and that was by dying. Mary ought to believe the rest and follow her advice. "I feel the need to speak on Mr. Tucker's behalf. He was polite and kind, and I believe you were rude to him."

The utter shock on her grandfather's face made her wonder if her mother's advice had been wrong, after all. Perhaps he used to welcome a display of backbone, but he may have changed during the many years since her mother had lived under this roof. Or perhaps he only welcomed such a thing in a man. Some men were like that, or so Mary's father used to say.

"Mary." He stated the name all by itself, rather flatly and without emotion, apparently neither as an opening salvo nor the first gentle wave of conversation. He was silent so long she wondered if he meant to speak to her at all. He even turned away, pouring and consuming another amber drink from the crystal glass nearby.

Finally he faced her again, this time staring at her so intently it only reinforced her original opinion, which had begun to ebb during his silence. She thought he'd been unsure of himself, unsure what to say, how to respond, but from the hardness on his face she wondered if he'd been tamping down a foul temper instead. So she said nothing.

"Mary." This time the single word was a bit softer, much to her relief. "I will overlook your behavior today because you are new to town, new even to this country, as I'm reminded by the British clip to your tongue. I see you've taken more after your father than my daughter." One brow now dipped as he continued looking at her. "Though you look more like my younger daughter, Sarah." He cleared his throat, looking away briefly. "Being new, there are many things you'll need to learn. Evidently the first thing is to stay away from that man. He's not to be trusted, neither civically nor personally."

"Civically? What do you mean?"

"He spent seven years living with Apache savages, and from all accounts he was returned to his very own mother against his will. Everybody knows he holds no gratitude to the army or to the American government for rescuing him. He's anything but a patriot, and likely no gentleman, either. No proper young lady should be seen with him. But," he went on a little louder even though Mary opened her mouth to speak, "what's done is done. You didn't know any better, but now you do. I've taken the initiative to invite my nearest neighbors to dine tonight, and they have a daughter about your age. Between Mrs. Babineau and her Lauralie, you'll learn soon enough how to get along here in America."

Mary wasn't sure how long her spine had been so stiff that it rendered needless the whalebone in her corset, but that rigidity spread to her shoulders as well. She ought to count, to breathe, to calm herself the way she'd been taught since the youngest age, but she immediately dismissed all caution.

"*Grandfather* Moorely," she began, holding steady his widening gaze, "or should I call you *Mr.* Moorely? You speak of Mr. Tucker as being less than a gentleman, yet here you stand before me drinking what I can only assume are spirits! A gentleman does not drink in front of a lady, particularly one who has just completed a journey of several thousand miles. I've traveled across the tip of southern Africa then up the ocean, from one side of Britain to the other, then back across the ocean to this continent, and finally over half of this immense country. For the last part of that journey, at least from Chicago to Topeka, I was entirely alone. Did you think to ask why the chaperone of the London Missionary Society provided isn't with me? Did you think for a moment to say, 'Welcome to your new home, my dear, *dear* granddaughter, how good it is to finally meet my only surviving relative'? Instead you've done nothing but berate my behavior and claim how ignorant I am and that you will address my supposed deficiencies this very day, without even a hint of that repast you alluded to. So you'll forgive this further display of my no doubt many flaws as I go to my room—I assume you've put me in the one that once belonged to my mother—where I will take a nap. If you do not wish me gone, I would ask that a plate of food and drink be sent to me upstairs. And do not bother to show me the way. In spite of what you think, my mother provided sufficient education for me, even about this house, beginning with a floor plan indicating which room was hers."

Then, with the hope that she exhibited more confidence than she felt, Mary swept toward the hall. If only her shoelaces had been properly tied, she might have made a regal escape. Instead, she heard only the faintest flapping of the sturdy shoe ties before stomping on one and falling straight to her knees. Why, oh why, must one wear shoes anyway?

"Took you long enough."

Eddie said nothing to his older brother, just jumped from the rig and went around to loosen Nehemiah's harness. He hated all these trappings on a horse but had to admit they were needed whenever he used the wagon. Before picking up the mail from the train, he'd gone to the livery for feed, the smith for a repaired wheel, and the mercantile for a bolt of material Mama had been waiting for.

"Glad you missed me," said Eddie.

"I didn't," Sherman said, "but the weeds did. I left half a field of beans for you to tend, so you better get to it."

Weeds again. Sherman couldn't look at a planted crop and tolerate a single one. To Eddie's way of thinking, it was the ground's way of reminding them it would grow what it wanted.

Together, silently, they unloaded the goods Eddie had brought back, but when all that was left was the fabric, Sherman fairly shoved Eddie aside as they both reached for it. "I'll bring that in. Those weeds are waitin' for you."

Eddie said nothing. He didn't like taming the ground the way his brother did, but working outside was far better than sitting inside or working in the barn, especially if Sherman was under the same roof.

Chapter 3

Mary would have struggled to her feet, tugging ignominiously at her skirts, but in one quick instant she was on her feet again, pulled up and into her grandfather's arms. He hugged her, but only for a moment, before putting her at arm's length, a look of unexpected concern wrinkling his brows.

"Are you all right? Did you hurt yourself?"

She'd had the wind—and the pride—knocked right out of her, but she regained her breath enough to offer a little laugh. "It's obviously true a haughty spirit goeth before a fall. My apologies, Grandfather. I shouldn't have spoken to you that way. I'm not really so awful, I promise you. I'm actually quite nice. I suppose I am just tired, although Mother always said rudeness has no excuse."

He patted her shoulders, as if suddenly aware he was touching her, then removed his hands altogether. "I'm the one who ought to apologize. You were right, each and every word. So, tell me now, your mother really provided you with a house plan?"

Mary nodded. "Right down to the cellar. Evidently she used to hide there when—"

"...she was expected to practice piano," they finished in unison.

He now tucked her arm in the crook of his, leading her from the parlor. "Let's start over, all right? Pretend the last half hour didn't happen?"

She nodded, even if some small part of her didn't want to forget all of it— at least meeting Eddie Tucker. That was something she must work out, though, if Grandfather Moorely insisted she not see him again. Goodness, she needed friends if she was to be happy in America, and she ought to be able to choose whom she spent time with, oughtn't she?

Mary led the way upstairs and directly to the room that would indeed be hers. On their way, they passed another door, one that had belonged to Sarah.

"Mother said she missed her sister Sarah nearly every day of her life," Mary said softly.

"She's not the only one," Grandfather said quietly, and Mary believed him. She had lost her mother, but he had lost his one remaining daughter. A realization that, if it had come earlier, might have helped contain her outburst.

"Do I really look like Sarah?" she asked gently.

He eyed her again then nodded. "You do indeed. I'm surprised your mother never told you."

"She always said Sarah was the beauty of the family. Perhaps she was trying to limit my pride, which as you've seen is healthy enough without more fuel."

For the first time since her arrival, Grandfather Moorely smiled. It reached all the way to his light brown eyes.

"Now go and take your nap," he suggested, "and I'll make sure a sandwich is sent up, and coffee—or, I suppose, being half English, you'd prefer tea?"

She smiled. "Yes, actually, with milk. And a sandwich sounds lovely."

He patted one of her shoulders again. "You'll have all you want. And don't worry about that dinner I mentioned. I'll cancel—no, postpone—it. I'll send word they should come tomorrow or the day after. Let you get settled in first. How does that sound? You'll like the Babineaus."

"That sounds lovely too. Thank you, Grandfather." Then she stood on tiptoe and kissed his cheek before going inside the room that had once belonged to her mother.

Eddie picked up the bowl of carrots just as his brother's fingers grazed the edge. Glazed carrots, just the way he liked them, and he knew his mother had made them for him. Sherman preferred plainer food, like potatoes or beans. So Eddie piled the carrots high on his plate, and only then did he pass the considerably lighter bowl on to his brother.

"Did you hear me, Eddie?" his mother was saying. "That material you picked up today should be plenty for me to fashion new suits for both of you. I'll want to take your sizes tonight, so I can get started right away. That dance is only two weeks off, so I'll need to make fast work of it."

"What dance?" Eddie wasn't really interested since he had no intention of going, even knowing his mother expected him to attend. He needed to know which barn, which church, or which public hall to avoid on the night this dance was scheduled.

"The harvest moon dance," she said, "over in Mr. Moorely's back barn. It's the one dance all of Topeka is invited to."

"You know he won't go," said Sherman.

Eddie didn't deny it. Not only did he not want to go, he doubted Mr. Moorely wanted him there, despite the invitation supposedly being for the entire town.

"I was hoping you'd escort me this year, dear. Sherman will be taking Polly."

Eddie winked at his mother, knowing she was far more likely to let him do as he pleased if he cajoled her. "I'm sure you can get Mr. Halford to take you, Mother. And you'd have a better time too. I can't dance."

"Not the way we dance, anyway," mumbled Sherman.

"I'll see Mr. Halford there, of course," came the reply, a touch more firmly than Eddie liked to hear coming from his mother. Her tone might have been sharpened with irritation by Sherman's comment, that allusion to his penchant for native dance, but there was something else in his mother's tone. Determination. "If the only way I can get you to go is with me on your elbow, so be it."

"I don't see why you want him to go," Sherman said, his mouth nearly stuffed full of fried chicken. "Can't be much fun for him."

Eddie wished he could believe his brother spoke out of compassion, but knew better. Rather than acknowledge the obvious, he decided to pretend some measure of sympathy had gone with the remark. "He's right, Mother. They aren't any fun at all."

"I'm lucky Polly speaks to me, with him for a brother," said Sherman, clarifying his sentiments along the vein Eddie expected.

"This is exactly why you need to attend this particular dance, Eddie," she went on. "This year a contingent of army officers and their men will attend. I thought. . .that is, I hoped, if you're there and prove to everyone you don't hold anything against their work, it might go a long way."

Eddie stopped chewing, despite his prior enjoyment of the carrots. When his mother looked at him, she stopped speaking altogether. Surely she wasn't thinking of the same soldier he was, because if he was expected she probably would have been afraid to let Eddie anywhere near him.

"What do you think has changed, Mother? Have they stopped holding honorable people on reservations? Have they stopped crushing their way of life? Stopped killing them? When that happens, I'll tolerate their company. Better yet, I'll learn to dance your way. Maybe."

Then he stood, letting the chair behind him scrape the floor and nearly topple over before Eddie stomped from the kitchen. He'd spend tonight on the prairie—worship there, sleep there. Forget, if he could, all of the injustices of this world.

Chapter 4

Mary took a deep breath, deciding the air here was different from home, after all. The breeze wasn't nearly as inviting as that carrying the mimosa along so many African riverbanks. The grass was different too, and so was the wildlife. So far, she'd spotted nothing larger than a gopher.

She'd awakened far earlier than anyone else in the household, despite the fatigue she'd felt the day before. Going to bed before the sun had even set had no doubt been to blame for her early-morning stir. So she'd quietly dressed, stopped in the kitchen for a glass of milk and hunk of bread before slipping out the back door. She hadn't bothered to take along her shoes, knowing they would only get discarded along the way.

The ground itself was soft and verdant, at least closest to her grandfather's home. It was rife with clover that was so comfortable to her bare feet that she wondered if it grew naturally or if her grandfather had planted it intentionally. Either way, each step was cool and velvety, like the finest English carpet.

There was a river in the distance and a thick band of trees growing tall alongside. She would go there and splash her toes in for refreshment.

It was farther than she'd expected, so she broke into a trot. It reminded her of all the footraces she'd laughed over with friends she'd left behind, although she conceded her long skirts and petticoat would have hindered any runner, even without the corset she'd set aside today.

The river was in the exact direction she wanted to go. East. She wondered how far east were the so-called Exodusters. She supposed she could ask her grandfather for the use of a cart or horse, but if she could make it on foot she'd have far more freedom to come and go as she pleased.

As she neared the river, the ground offered different growth, small shrubs and discarded pine needles. Closer still to the water, the ground was loamy, nearly like a sponge that invited her to hop. If only she'd had such a place near the huts and cottages she'd lived in when she was younger, she'd never have come home!

Jumping over a fallen log, she saw it too late—a snake, colored with circular markings. Surely it was as startled as she when she landed right on top of it. In that very instant she felt the sharp prick of a bite. She cried out, more from fright than pain, then looked again at the reptile that slithered away more quickly than she would have guessed such a creature could move.

Finding a rock to sit upon, she examined her injured ankle, seeing twin puncture wounds. A wave of dizziness nearly overwhelmed her. Colorful snakes. . . Father always said to avoid them. It was God's way of painting a warning on which ones to avoid.

Her light-headedness nearly made her faint. Was it the poison, already coursing through her veins? Was she to die here and now, alone in this wild country? No one would find her here, at least not very soon, and she was unsure she could make it all the way back to Grandfather's even along the softest pathway.

"You all right?"

Mary wasn't sure where the voice came from, only that the wooded banks seemed to echo the question as if it had come from an angel. Perhaps it was her guardian angel, here to comfort her, save her, or fetch her to heaven. Oh, what foolishness now. Surely the poison had reached her brain, addling her mind.

But then a very real shadow stepped into her line of vision—a familiar shadow belonging to the man she'd found herself thinking of so often since her arrival yesterday. Eddie Tucker looked down at her, a rifle slung along his back. He was clad in buckskin and the softest leather shoes she'd ever seen.

"Oh, Eddie!" Never mind that she addressed him by his first name, she was too glad to see him, knowing she wouldn't die alone. Who would care about propriety at such a time? "I—I was bitten by a snake! A colorful one, so surely it was poisonous. I'm afraid!"

Even as Eddie bent before her to inspect the bite on her ankle, he was already frowning. "I saw the whole thing." He cocked his head upward. "I was up in that tree, waiting for a deer. It was a red milk snake, Mary."

She was so dizzy she fought again the feeling she might faint. "So I'm. . .going to die?"

He looked at her, grinning. "We're all gonna die someday. But if you die from the bite of a red milk, you'll be the first."

"My father always said God added color to snakes to warn us away."

He nodded. "For a red milk, it's likely to protect them, not us."

"Then are you saying I won't—?"

He was already nodding. "Red on yellow kills a fellow. Red on black, venom lack. In fact, I hope you didn't scare the thing away. It kills rodents I'd rather not have getting into my cache."

Then he scooped her up into his arms and sloshed through the shallow river. Mary found herself still befuddled, although she was suddenly less certain of the cause. Snake bite, or the fact that Eddie Tucker was carrying her away?

Eddie might have marveled at his own behavior, if he allowed himself to think about it long enough as he made his way through the thicket. He didn't hesitate to take her to the one place he invited no one—not that he knew many people well enough to shun. But he hadn't even taken his mother here, to show her where he spent so many nights away from home.

Far up the bank, still under the shade of hundreds of pines and oaks and maples, he found the plot of ground that was as close to his own as Eddie dared call anything. He pushed open the door, a door he'd made himself with sticks and sapling trunks, secured with tree roots and long, sturdy plant shoots. Then he placed Mary carefully on the pile of deer skins and blankets that served as his bed. It was cool, dry, and comfortable, but even as he was sure of that he looked around at the roughness of the place. He'd built many shelters over the years, depending on the season, and this design was his own, and one of his favorites. Sturdy sapling walls, fir branch roof. Unlike similar wickiups or the teepees he built for colder weather, this kind of shelter didn't allow an indoor fire. But the air was inviting under the treetops, and he had plenty of blankets to chase away any trembling Mary might suffer.

He put the softest blanket over her then left without a word, going to the cellar he'd dug out some time ago. Only a knowing eye would see the outline of the top hatch, with grass covering it in the summer and fall, leaves or snow in winter and early spring. He'd carved stairs out of the earth itself, stabilized them with more timber, but used the cavern mostly as he'd found it: a dry underground cave perfect for storing whatever he liked.

He grabbed a small clay pot of honey then returned to Mary.

"Does it still hurt?" he asked, kneeling beside her at the foot of his make-shift bed.

"A bit," she said. "Not so much as when I thought I was soon to be at death's door."

"Hold still a minute," he said, opening the jar and pouring some of the honey into his palm. Then, gently, he rubbed it into her ankle, well covering the wound and surrounding area.

"What's that you're doing?"

She'd asked curiously, neither with suspicion nor alarm.

"Applying honey." He didn't dare look at her face. At first the idea of applying the natural curative seemed nothing more than what anyone would do. Polite, if not expected from a concerned neighbor. But now, coming to his senses, he realized he was nearly massaging the ankle of a beautiful young woman. What a fuss would be made if anyone were to come upon them. He'd probably be arrested, and she whisked away before she'd be labeled an outcast like him. His throat tightened, but he managed to keep his fingers steady until he reached for the sheepskin towel he used after swimming. Then he rubbed his hands clean and looked at her at last.

To his surprise—or relief, he wasn't sure which—she was looking around the dimly lit hut without a trace of distaste. He hadn't expected someone dressed so finely to think of this as anything more than a hovel, even if it was. But her eyes were wide and curious, her brows lifted as if impressed by the tiny sparkles of light filtering through the branches suspended up above.

"What is this place?"

"I use it when I go hunting and fishing," Eddie explained.

"Did you build it?"

He nodded.

"Is this the kind of shelter you lived in when you were with the Apache?"

He settled himself more comfortably on the hard ground across from her, cross legged. "My family preferred teepees—long poles tipped together at the top. It makes a sort of upside down cone, with the poles covered with deerskin." He looked around, trying to see it for the first time.

"Where I come from, huts are round. And taller. Though they are made of the same sort of branches, and rather than fir trees they're covered with reed mats." She grinned. "I've spent many happy days in huts like this. With friends. Good friends."

She held his gaze and his heart tripped, despite warnings erupting like kernels of corn popping out of flames. Anything, even friendship, between them, was impossible. So he diverted his gaze, turning away altogether to replace the lid on the small clay pot of honey.

"Why didn't you build the other kind of shelter, then? A teepee, did you call it?"

Without thinking, without considering all he was revealing, he answered. "This kind doesn't draw as much attention."

"Unwanted attention, you mean," she said, and he nodded. Then she added,

"Perhaps America and Africa aren't so very different, after all. There are all kinds of wars in Africa, natives against settlers, natives against natives, settlers against settlers. I suppose it happens everywhere man goes."

He caught her gaze and held it again, his pleasure soaring. No one—no white person, at least—had ever looked at him with the kind of understanding she seemed to be offering. No sooner had that thought taken shape than images of her grandfather returned, cooling Eddie's increasing warmth. He ought to make sure she left quickly, even if he couldn't very well see her all the way home—or at least not so her grandfather would spot him.

"How is your ankle?" he asked. His voice felt tight, awkward, and he wondered if it sounded that way to her ears. "Do you think you can walk?"

She grinned. "Now that I'm calmer, I can admit it doesn't hurt. I was a bit of a ninny, wasn't I?"

"No," he said gently, and the word wasn't more than a whisper. "I'd expect nothing else from someone who believed they'd been bitten by something deadly."

"But I should have known," she said. "I must remember that rhyme."

He nodded slowly. "Yes, it comes in handy." He really was a dolt but couldn't think of a single intelligent thing to say. Never before had he missed the kind of education enjoyed by most young men his age. He'd been able to read before the Apache took him, but in the half-dozen years since his return he hadn't spent much time reacquainting himself with the books on his mother's shelf. Well, only with the Bible and that was because he hadn't realized how much he'd missed it.

Eddie stood, holding out a hand to pull her up. Once accepted, he was reluctant to let her go, but after leading her to his door, he did.

"I can take you to your grandfather's clover field," he said. "But I don't think he'd like to see me on the house grounds."

She put a hand to his forearm, a look of distress crossing her lovely face. "I apologize for how he treated you yesterday. It was horrid, and I told him so."

His brows shot up. "You did?"

"I certainly did."

He cocked his head. "I bet it didn't change anything. Look, Mary, I can see you're sweet. But you know we can't be friends, right?"

"I know no such thing. Unless you do not want to be my friend?"

His first impulse was to gawk and question her sanity. Who wouldn't want to be friends—or more—with her? Instead, he looked away, nearly drowning in an unexpected wave of shyness. He'd never felt such a thing before. There were some advantages to being an outcast; it had made him bold not to care what others thought. But now...

"All I know," he said, still not brave enough to look her in the eye, "is that it's for your own good if you steer clear of me."

"Because you would rather live with the Apache?"

He'd been leading her away but now stopped to face her. "Is that what your grandfather told you?"

"He said you were brought back against your will."

Eddie ran a hand through his hair, the thick dark strands that had been similar enough to the rest of the Apache that he hadn't immediately been spotted as a captive when the tribe he'd lived with was gathered up and sent to the reservation. How could he explain something he was still trying to figure out? He remembered those months after he'd first been taken, having been snatched from the field he'd been working in with Sherman, pulling weeds even then, how he'd pined for his parents, and for his brother. Yes, pined for the brother who had been taken too but had managed to get away. Without Eddie. Without coming back for him. The pain of that memory still sliced Eddie's gut.

And then, as the months went on and he'd become part of a new family, one who loved him, taught him how to live, he'd grown to love them. Loved the mother who had cherished all the children in their village but had never had her own, until Eddie. Respected and honored the father who taught him the Apache way of life, the man who on his deathbed had charged Eddie with the care of his wife, Eddie's Apache mother. None of that meant Eddie had ever stopped loving his first family, even after years had gone by and he'd almost forgotten them. Memories of when he was little almost seemed to belong to someone else as he still struggled to connect the boy he once was to the man he was now.

"It's not easy to explain," he said finally. "I liked the way the Apache taught me to live. They were good to me. My Apache father died, and I miss him more than I miss the man who was my real father, a man I barely remember. I still miss my mother. But I know I was born into my family here, so I guess I shouldn't be doubting God."

"You do believe in God, then?"

He snorted. "I've always believed in God. In fact, my Apache mother is more a Christian than half the people right here in Topeka. She never read a word of the Bible, but she was already worshipping the Creator when I was taken in by her. When I used to talk about the Bible, she thought it all made so much sense she adopted Jesus right along with me. I was only seven, but she thought God brought me to her to teach her about Him."

"Is this woman, your Apache mother, still on the reservation?"

He nodded.

"My grandfather believes you're not to be trusted—civically, as if you don't trust the authorities that brought you back. How do you want to live, Eddie? Where do you want to live?"

It wasn't a long or complicated question, yet no one had ever asked him such a thing before. Not even the mother who had given birth to him.

"I live in between the two ways of life. I can see benefits to both. But that means keeping to myself, because people still remember the fight over this land." If he was to be honest, he had to add, "I haven't minded until the last couple of days. Now. . .I guess I wouldn't mind fitting in a little better, if it meant we could be friends."

Her smile was so wide, so genuine it spread easily to her eyes.

"So let's see what we can do about that, shall we?" she asked. "Starting by having you take me all the way home?"

Chapter 5

Mary had no idea of the time, except that it was likely still well before lunch. Grandfather had told her when he'd come back with the tea the day before that he expected his neighbors the following afternoon. She was fairly certain she would have plenty of time to change her clothes and greet them properly.

If she'd had anything to say about how to spend the afternoon, she'd have invited Eddie. As they neared her new home, it was all she could do not to insist he stay.

However, as they rounded the gardens to enter through the front door, she was met with the sight of two carriages and half a dozen men on horseback. Men of all ages, some young, some older, some white, others African. Alwin was behind the reins of the Moorely carriage, and he was the first to spot her.

"There she is!" came his call, followed by several others, including confused questions, "Is that her?" and "What's she doing with him?"

Mary spotted her grandfather, who was mounted on one of the taller horses. Rather than dismounting, he directed his horse in her direction until he was standing before them both, the original stern visage back in place on his handsome face.

"Where have you been, Mary?"

"I went for a walk," she said. "To the river."

Grandfather's eyes narrowed as his gaze went from Mary to Eddie than back to Mary. "That's quite a distance. Why didn't you tell anyone where you were going?"

"I suppose it didn't occur to me," she said. "I've never had my whereabouts checked before."

"And you, Mr. Tucker?" Grandfather asked, his tone laced with steel. "How is that I find you once again in the company of my granddaughter?"

"I was hunting along the river and wanted to make sure she was returned safely."

Grandfather started to speak again but Mary took a step closer to his mount. "I was bitten by a snake, Grandfather, and Mr. Tucker helped me."

Now Grandfather's brows went from two straight slashes to gather in concern.

"What kind of snake?"

Eddie answered for her. "A red milk, sir."

"Go inside, Mary," Grandfather said. "See Mrs. Warren, the housekeeper." Then he turned his back on both of them, calling for the others to dismiss.

Mary looked at Eddie, who offered an almost imperceptible shake of his head. Without a word, she understood his intention. He wanted her to say nothing more, so she did not, hoping her parting smile communicated something else to him too. She knew where to find him now.

She had barely made it up to the porch before Grandfather had dismounted and followed her. But instead of a maid opening the front door, another woman stood there—an older, strikingly attractive one, alongside a girl who was every bit as plain as the other one was pretty.

"I'm Mrs. Babineau," said the older woman. She wore a deep burgundy gown, gathered tight along the bodice and pleated at the waist to be gathered for a bustle at the back. An open skirt revealed a lighter shade of burgundy to contrast the silk of the overskirt. "And this is my daughter, Lauralie."

Mary's gaze went from one to the other. Where Mrs. Babineau was dressed to attract the eye, her daughter was the opposite. She wore a simple dark brown skirt and pleated white shirtwaist. Her hair was braided, twisted tightly together atop her head.

"Our nearest neighbors," said Grandfather as he approached Mary from behind.

"Oh, I do hope I haven't miscalculated the time?" Mary said. "Grandfather said you were coming for lunch, but honestly I thought it far too early for that."

"Yes, we are here a little earlier than we expected," said Mrs. Babineau with a half-smile directed at Mary's grandfather. "But J.W. sent out an alarm when the maid reported you missing this morning."

"Yes, well, that was an overreaction on my part," said Grandfather, putting a hand on Mary's back. "Go on, then, have Mrs. Warren look at that wound."

"Wound!" Mrs. Babineau put out a hand, as if to take Mary by the arm. "What's happened?"

"Snake bite," Grandfather said, "but nothing to worry about if the thing was identified properly."

Mary was about to claim she had little doubt of anything Eddie said but thought better of questioning her grandfather, at least in front of his guests.

An hour later, bathed and dressed in one of the gowns her mother handed down— fatally out of fashion but comfortable nonetheless—Mary rejoined her grandfather and the Babineaus at an outdoor dining table that overlooked the clover field and trees in the distance. Mary couldn't help but smile, knowing the vantage would forever bring Eddie to mind.

"I'm so glad you've come to stay with your grandfather, Mary," said Lauralie, though she spoke so softly it was almost difficult to hear her, and she didn't allow her gaze to meet Mary's.

"Yes," Mrs. Babineau added cheerfully, "your arrival is perfectly timed for the harvest dance. It'll be a wonderful time to introduce you to the town. Isn't that right, J.W.?"

He nodded. "We're hosting out-of-town guests, as usual. This year we'll have several officers from the army. They're arriving on Friday."

Despite the modesty of every African home in which she'd lived, Mary's parents had often hosted visitors. Other missionaries, sponsors, LMS staff and overseers. Never, however, military. But it didn't worry her. She'd helped her parents be gracious hosts even to the strictest LMS sponsor. Surely military men were much the same in their disciplined behavior.

By the end of the afternoon, Mary had high hopes of becoming good friends with Lauralie Babineau. They'd made arrangements to go into town the next afternoon, with Mrs. Babineau as chaperone.

Mary had also learned Mr. Babineau had passed on some years ago, leaving Mrs. Babineau a widow. That was rather a relief, since Mary spotted Mrs. Babineau's gaze lingering on Grandfather in a way that appeared far more than simply neighborly.

Eddie welcomed the endless expanse of the clear afternoon's blue sky. As he headed back to the woods, he couldn't help remembering how easy it was to welcome Mary into the forest he usually shared with no one.

Sudden awareness of the smile on his face conjured the same warning Eddie had already failed to heed. The truth was he could caution himself every hour until a half-dozen moons came and went, but he knew his heart wouldn't listen. It was already too late, even if he was bound for disappointment.

Besides, he had another matter to dwell on. Army soldiers would arrive any day now. Vance Saxton might be among them. Saxton was only one of many soldiers posted at a camp outside the reservation, their job to "guard" the entire population. Only Saxton made frequent tours inside the camp, not to note needed improvements, not to help them learn to farm the land that likely wouldn't produce much anyway—Eddie had a far better idea of how bad the land was on that reservation now that he knew what good land could produce—or check on water supplies, schools, or any other detail that might have improved life on the reservation. Saxton came, instead, to count heads, to report missing Indians, interrogate those left behind.

Eddie had grown to hate the man, because he'd seen suffering but did not care. It had been Eddie's own fault, though, that Saxton noticed him. For months Eddie had blended in with his people. His skin never tanned exactly the way young warriors' skin did; his hair was neither black enough nor perfectly straight enough to entirely blend, but both skin and hair were close enough to escape a second glance.

It was Eddie's budding hatred that had given away the one feature he could not hide: he'd leveled a burning stare at Saxton. That was when Saxton had noticed Eddie's blue eyes.

Saxton had taken him the moment he'd spotted that gaze, pulling him forcefully away from the mother clinging to him. Saxton had spoken words Eddie no longer understood, but he had understood the actions.

Saxton himself had escorted Eddie to the camp where other soldiers lived. He'd been fed, given clothes he didn't like, shoes that hurt his feet. But that was as far as any kindness went, if he could have called it that. Two moons passed before Eddie received much attention, two months where the only people he knew, his family, were so close and yet he'd been allowed no contact with them. He'd tried going back but was put in a locked room, one with only a single window too high to see through, a place that might have made him cry if he'd been any younger. His Apache father would have been proud of him, but Eddie was glad he had not lived to see the treatment of his people.

Then, one morning just as the sun was rising, Eddie was put on a horse with Saxton, and along with a half dozen other men they left the camp and headed east. He'd delivered Eddie to his first family. His first father was dead, his brother a stranger who seemed to resent him, and his mother the only one who tearfully, happily, received him. She'd been grateful to the man Eddie hated.

Army soldiers had been through Topeka other times through the years, and always Eddie looked for the one.

Maybe this time.

Chapter 6

T
he carriage ride into town the following afternoon was laced with laughter, initiated more often by Lauralie than anyone else. Mary observed that while Lauralie was quiet when in the presence of men even as old as Grandfather, it was quite the opposite when she was in the company of only her mother and Mary.

They visited several shops, although Mary did not purchase a single item. Mrs. Babineau, however, bought herself a new hat, a new parasol for Lauralie, and new gloves for all three of them. Mary protested, but Mrs. Babineau heard none of it.

While Mrs. Babineau made arrangements for the parcels to be delivered, Mary and Lauralie wandered outside the hat and glove shop. It was a lovely cool autumn day, and the town bustled with activity. Mary eagerly scanned the crowds, knowing all were strangers yet hoping to spot a familiar face, one in particular, but also the African faces she'd met at the train station the other day.

"Do you know anything of the Exodusters, Lauralie?" Mary asked.

"Oh, goodness, yes. Everyone in Kansas does. We're the state who stood for freedom, you know, even before the war. There was an awful fight between those who wanted to join one side or the other. And Mama supports the KFRA."

"The KFRA? What is it?"

"Kansas Freedman's Relief Association. An organization to help the Exodusters settle in."

"Surely everyone supports such a goal?"

Lauralie's frown engulfed her narrow face as thoroughly as her smiles did. "It's amazing, isn't it, how different people of considerable faith and intelligence can come to vastly different opinions? I'm afraid not everyone thinks Mama is using her funds wisely to support the KFRA."

Mary scanned the busy street again. "Do you suppose we might go by the east side, then? I've heard that's where many of the Exodusters live."

"We can ask Mama."

"I met a lovely woman at the train station, and I'd like to see how she's getting on."

Mrs. Babineau agreed without hesitation to visit the east end of town, even if the Babineau stable hand driving the carriage did raise a hesitant brow. But he didn't protest, so before long they arrived at an end of town that seemed much farther away than only minutes from the better neighborhood in which they'd shopped.

The Exodusters lived just north of the river, near a conglomeration of railroad yards. There were makeshift buildings, one of which was likely a hospital based on the sign, alongside what looked like a warehouse and commissary. All of that stood in the shadow of another tall building, where most of the people were gathered just outside the front.

"I know it seems rough here," Mrs. Babineau said, "but it's actually improved from what it was when so many new arrivals all came at once earlier this year, most without much to their name. That tall building is the Barracks, where at least everyone has a dry roof, a bunk bed and cook stove. The KFRA is trying to match people to jobs and offer education, and of course see to everyone's health."

"Sounds precisely like something my parents would have been involved in," Mary said, feeling the sting of a tear which she promptly ignored. Grief stirred over their loss, but she wanted no pity. "Is there some way I might be of help? Perhaps in a school? Is there such a thing, for the children, I mean?"

"We'd love to start a kindergarten, of course," Mrs. Babineau said, "but so far we have education only for the older folks, those in need of jobs. As for your helping..."

"I'm stronger than I appear," Mary assured her quickly, "and I do have training. I've worked with my parents for years."

"Oh, it's not your qualifications," Mrs. Babineau said. Then, rather than looking at Mary, she exchanged a glance with Lauralie, who looked as though she was trying not to frown.

"What is it? Why shouldn't I help?"

"It's your grandfather," said Lauralie, when her mother's lips looked tightly shut. "Oh, Mama, don't you think she'll figure it out, now that she's living with Mr. Moorely?"

"Then it's for her to discover, not for us to gossip about. Especially since it concerns J.W., who is my dearest friend."

Now Lauralie winked at Mary, all trace of any frown gone. "Do you know what 'dearest friend' really means? Sweetheart!"

"Lauralie!"

But Mrs. Babineau was smiling now too, at least with her eyes.

"Mary," said Mrs. Babineau, "your grandfather has been a widower for several years now, and I've been a widow even longer. We've been neighbors since I first came to Topeka and friends from that day. Your grandmother was perhaps my dearest friend. I suppose it's not surprising that J.W. and I still enjoy one another's company. Perhaps you should know that he's asked me to marry him."

Mary smiled. "That's delightful!"

"But Mama said no," Lauralie told her. Now her mother took Lauralie's hand and held it, as if with it she could control her daughter's mouth.

"I didn't say no," Mrs. Babineau admitted. "I said not yet."

Mary didn't want to suggest that two people of somewhat advanced age hardly had time to dally, yet her surprise likely spoke such words for her. Mrs. Babineau leaned across the carriage to pat one of Mary's hands.

"I'll be perfectly frank, my dear. I do love your grandfather, except for one thing. He is rigid. Change is especially difficult for him. I admit it's not easy for me, either, especially as I age. To J.W. an unprecedented number of newcomers is too much, too quickly. He seems to be coming around, because I've asked him to invite the Exodusters to the harvest dance, and he has. But I'm afraid until he shows me he can adjust to another change—surely one of the biggest since his wife died—I'm hesitant to say yes."

"I've brought change," Mary said. "And he invited—" She cut herself off. Her father's parents had said Grandfather Moorely's letter encouraged her to come. Yet she hadn't actually read that letter, so perhaps he'd merely invited her as his duty. There was, after all, little true evidence he'd welcomed her arrival. Her eyes widened as realization crystallized. "Oh, goodness. He did not want me to come, did he?"

Mrs. Babineau now squeezed Mary's hand, and her gaze softened with sympathy, proving it was true. "You're *exactly* what he needs, though. For his sake, and for mine too. You can do what I can't, living under his roof. I'm afraid you'll be the one to draw the rough sketch, so to speak, of how he'll handle change. I'm sorry if he's crusty in the process."

"May I add something?" Lauralie said then went on without waiting for an answer. "Just remember, Mary, God brought you here. Maybe it's to prove your grandfather isn't already in the first stages of rigor mortis."

Then Lauralie giggled, even as her mother looked horrified but a moment later grinned along too.

As the afternoon went on, even the realization that she would be a test of her grandfather's ability to change didn't dim Mary's enjoyment. She saw Cisley and Kitch, and Patty who was Cisley's cousin. She was about Mary's age and size, excited about going to a fine Topeka home the next day to see about a job.

Mary took another look at Patty and worried the poor condition of her shoes and clothing might reveal just how desperately this girl needed a job. Would someone be less apt to hire her because of that? Pay her less than a fair wage? And so just after Mrs. Babineau hinted they needed to leave, Mary slipped out of her boots and shawl and handed them over, refusing to be dissuaded even under the surprised gazes of Mrs. Babineau and Lauralie.

Eddie urged Nehemiah along after leaving the butcher shop where he'd sold his meat. He wasn't especially eager to return home except for one thing: the Moorely place was on Eddie's way, and spotting a glimpse of Mary was likely all he could hope for from now on.

Once outside of town, he noticed a carriage on the road up ahead. It was open, with three bonneted heads barely visible above the back of the polished barouche. They traveled at a leisurely pace, so he was soon close enough to recognize the carriage belonging to the neighbor between his mother's farm and the Moorelys'. His heart picked up a beat as he identified one of the three occupants as none other than the young woman on his mind.

Eddie nearly obeyed his first instinct, to urge on Nehemiah to catch up. But the usual caution held him back, though it was harder than ever to heed. He wanted to see her; what's more, he had some confidence she'd be happy to see him too. But he'd already been turned away by J.W. Moorely, and every ear in town had heard long ago that J.W. was sweet on Mrs. Babineau. Although neither she nor her daughter treated him with the icy regard many others adopted, he reminded himself he'd never given them cause. Lauralie had never cast her eye his way, and neither had his gone to her.

Still, he was willing to risk finding out just how many hurdles he would have to cross if his interest in Mary refused to be ignored. Knowing where the Babineaus stood was probably something he should find out, given the closeness of his two neighbors.

"Good afternoon!" he called, wondering how the Babineaus would react to his friendly greeting—something he'd never done before, not just to them but to anyone in town.

As he directed Nehemiah alongside the carriage, all three sets of eyes—four, after he counted the driver—shifted to him with initial interest. Out of the corner of Eddie's own eye he saw the driver's frown first. Not unexpected. He looked next at Lauralie, whose rejection could easily be added to many others, but she only smiled. Mrs. Babineaus' rejection mattered more as far as potential access to Mary was concerned, but he wasn't rebuffed there, either. The gaze Eddie saved to look at last, and longest, was Mary's. He was suddenly too caught in her smile for anyone else's surprised reaction to matter.

"Mrs. Babineau," he tipped his hat her way, "I hope we don't need a more formal introduction, though I believe you're acquainted with my mother."

That was partly why he'd been so bold just now; Mrs. Babineau was one of the few women in town who hadn't cooled their friendship with his mother over the years.

"Good afternoon, Edward," she said, and somehow even though she'd never addressed him in all the years he'd been back, he wasn't surprised that she spoke so formally. That mattered less than the warmth behind it.

Eddie greeted Lauralie next but let his gaze return quickly to Mary. "I'm glad I ran into you. How is your ankle?"

She smiled. "Entirely recovered."

"But not exactly shielded from danger, since you gave your shoes away," said Lauralie. She spoke with a mix of surprise and maybe, though he wasn't sure, admiration too.

"Barefooted again, Miss Elliot?"

"It's the most natural way to walk," she said.

"Except around snakes," he countered.

"Or in the city, or in bad weather," added Mrs. Babineau. "I offered to buy her a new pair, but she said she had another and reminded me we're expected to dinner soon."

"All of which is true," Mary said, still looking at him. "I hope I didn't frighten away your colorful rodent-catcher?"

"I spotted him this morning. All seems well, though I did see him looking both ways as he slithered along."

She laughed. "Then perhaps we both learned something."

He knew he couldn't linger, even though he searched his brain for another topic to continue the visit. But there was no reason he could admit to, except dawdling, and so he pulled on Nehemiah's reins to let them pass. "Good afternoon, then."

Just as they were almost ahead, Mary turned back and called to him. "Oh, Mr. Tucker! I hope to see you at the harvest dance!"

He didn't dare nod or even wave—or admit there was suddenly nothing on earth that could keep him from that dance now.

Chapter 7

Nearly an entire week had passed since Mary's arrival, and although she was getting acquainted with her grandfather he was still more aloof than companionable. She hoped by not demanding his time he would become better accustomed to her presence.

So she went on frequent outings, spending several afternoons with Lauralie. But as much as she enjoyed her new friend's company, Mary could not deny her favorite outings came in the morning, when she crossed the clover field and ventured into the woods.

She had no idea how often Eddie visited his little hut. That first day when she'd gone there, the shelter had appeared entirely the same as when he'd first brought her there. The second day she wondered if she imagined it looked different but convinced herself the blanket he had draped on her after the snake bite hadn't been folded when they'd left. And so the next day she'd planned ahead, writing a note telling him she would be out walking on most mornings and hoped to pay him a neighborly visit.

Two days of rain had followed, making her own pining heart difficult to ignore. What good was it to know how to find Eddie Tucker if she couldn't go to him?

Today, however, surely he would be there if only a couple things were true: that he had seen her note, and he wanted to welcome her.

The ground wasn't quite dry under the shade of the trees, but the air was cool and clean. Mary knew better than to hop over logs, particularly near the river, and so this time she watched where she stepped. As she approached the too-quiet shelter, she prepared herself for another day of disappointment. Perhaps she ought not encourage these feelings growing inside of her. Especially since her grandfather would likely lock her in her room if he knew she was being so bold in seeking Eddie's company.

As she'd done on previous occasions, Mary stood outside the hut and called his name. Only the same silence returned to her. Gently, she pushed opened the door. If her note was still on the blankets, she would know he had not yet seen it. As disappointing as that might be, it was her only hope for an explanation of his continued absence. If he had seen the note and was staying away, surely that was worse?

She could smell the sweet pine roof, feel the warmth of the dry enclosure away from the breeze. Instantly her gaze went to the bed, and her heart sunk. Her note was gone, but he was not here.

She ought to leave, never come back. And yet something else caught her eye. A pair of shoes sat at the end of the blankets, made of some kind of brushed leather, beaded with half circle designs at the toes. Though they were cut high like boots, surely they were too small for Eddie. She stared at them, her heart pounding, an urge to try them on nearly consuming her. Never before had she actually wanted to wear shoes, but these looked as if they would not only protect her but would neither pinch nor stay wet very long, nor trip her with long laces, nor let her slip on wet ground or pavement. They fairly begged for her touch, the hide having been worked until smooth and supple.

She had been staring so intently she didn't hear the sound until it was right behind her, the soft footfall on the leaf-covered ground just outside the door.

"I see you found my gift for you."

She turned, her heart leaping anew. There was no question to what Eddie referred. "They're. . .for me?"

"Try them on," he invited. "I made them from your footprint near the river, but it would have been easier if I'd had your actual. . ."

His voice faded, as if he wondered whether it was proper or not to refer to her limbs. Perhaps she should blush, but she was too pleased. Instead, she scampered to the blankets and sat, taking up the moccasins with a sigh of pure pleasure. They were just as soft as they looked.

"Imagine my dismay that shoes are handy in this climate. I never worried about where I walked when I lived with my parents. But these! These are meant to be worn, and enjoyed."

She slipped them on, holding her skirts out of the way so she could admire the footwear without thought to propriety. Eddie watched, looking pleased by her happiness.

She hopped up, testing the fit by closing the few steps between them. "Thank you, Eddie!" Then she did what came naturally, what she would have done had anyone else given her a gift not only useful and beautiful but made of his own hands and with his own time. She threw her arms around his neck and kissed his cheek.

Then she realized how close he was. How bold she'd been. Still, she didn't pull away, especially when his arms went around her waist, completing the embrace. She leaned back only far enough to look at his face, silently telling herself she should mind her manners, remember her grandfather's warnings, remember. . .but nothing would make her break away from him, not so long as he seemed content to hold her close.

He too seemed to realize the hug was anything but casual. Though he had smiled while watching her enjoy his gift, he now looked at her intently, searching her face as if for a sign. To pull away? To continue? Surely he would see nothing but welcome.

When his mouth came down on hers Mary leaned ever closer, relishing the contact. His lips were cool, welcoming, as eager as her own. She'd never in her life been held this way, kissed this way. Yet it felt so natural, so real, so right. She didn't want it to end but knew it must—even as his lips left hers and she sighed with a sense of delight more deeply felt than ever before.

"I—hadn't meant—" he whispered, "that is, I didn't plan to do that."

"No? Because it felt so right to me, as if it was planned from the day we met."

He shook his head, backing away a full step but leaving his hands on her hips. "I may not have planned this moment from the day we met, but I did think of such a thing often enough since then."

She grinned. "As have I."

But no sooner had she said as much than he was already frowning, an expression she knew herself to be absolutely incapable of at the moment.

"It may not matter what we think," he said slowly. "This town, your grandfather in particular, probably has plans for you that definitely don't include me."

Even if she'd tried, she could not match either his serious tone or his frown. "My grandfather is my grandfather," she admitted, "but he's still somewhat of a stranger to me. Why must I do as he says and not follow my own wishes?"

"Because. . .because he's family."

She nodded and tightened her grip around his neck. "Kiss me again, Eddie. I don't want to think about anyone but you right now."

And so he did.

Eddie dragged himself from Mary's embrace, not knowing which he feared more: letting her go, or being incapable of letting her go. Ever. He knew this was impossible. Somehow he must convince her of that, and convince himself as well.

He gently tugged her arms from his neck.

"Mary, there is nothing I'd rather do that spend every free moment with you—"

"Very well, then! I'd like that too. I'm not a typical mild Mary," she said with a laugh that was as mesmerizing as her kiss had been. "If I thought we might be doing something outside God's approval, that would be another matter entirely. But why would God object to our caring for one another?"

He moved outside their embrace, taking two steps back—as far away as the narrow shelter allowed. She obviously didn't see the extent of the problem, so he pointed to the shoes he'd made for her. "You can't even wear those if you want the town to accept you. I made them for your morning walks, out here where no one will see them. Doesn't that tell you something? I already care for you, Mary. Enough to want to spare you from the kind of treatment I get."

Her smile barely dimmed, even as she put a hand on his shoulder. "I admit I don't understand the attitudes of the people here. But I don't think the Babineaus would treat me any differently."

"They will if your grandfather says anything about it."

She was smiling broadly again, and it was all he could do not to be caught up in her optimism. "Then we'll have to change his mind, won't we?"

Eddie made his way back to his own home after seeing Mary to hers. He'd walked her all the way to the door, but the house appeared vacant except for the maid who greeted her. So he'd left without the confrontation with her grandfather that he'd tried preparing himself for ever since they'd left his forest shelter.

He wasn't sure if he felt like celebrating or wringing his hands. He was already half in love with her, the other half held back by a fraying rope made solely of his caution—for her sake, not for his. Even as he'd made those shoes, he knew the risk he was taking by presenting them to her. The risk she would take if she wore them. He'd meant to make her promise not to wear them except in the forest.

At his house, Eddie opened the door that led directly into the kitchen. There was plenty to do in the field today, but he'd left his water pouch inside and wouldn't get to work without out it.

"There you are!"

The angry tone startled Eddie, not having seen his brother since the day before and nothing, at least as far as Eddie knew, had transpired to renew harsh feelings.

"I thought you were in town selling wheat today?" Eddie asked Sherman. A moment later his mother entered the kitchen too, a look of concern on her face.

"I finished as soon as I could," Sherman said, stopping only a few feet from Eddie. He poked his finger into Eddie's chest. "Listen, you better stay away from that Moorely girl. The whole town is talking about you, and that's the last thing I need. Polly's family doesn't need a reminder that you're my brother."

Eddie held Sherman's stare, despite his racing heart. No one knew he'd seen Mary this morning; no one knew he'd made shoes for her. Surely no one had seen her in them—yet! "I don't know what you're talking about."

Sherman opened his mouth as if all too eager to repeat what he'd heard, but their mother took a step between them. "He says there's gossip in town that you were with her earlier this week when Mr. Moorely was looking for her."

Eddie wanted to be relieved, but wasn't. There was only worse to come if he saw her again. "I can't help what others say." He looked past his mother to level a stare at Sherman. "I guess you're hoping somebody would just come along to steal me away again."

"Of course he isn't!" Mother said, although Sherman remained mute. His mother pulled on Eddie's arm to turn him to her, to focus on her and not his brother. "Tell me about this girl."

Eddie wished he could tell his mother all of it, how he hoped—against his better judgment—for a future with a woman who might just be able to ignore the sympathy he couldn't deny holding for the Apaches he'd lived with for so long. Tell her he believed Mary was bold enough, strong enough, not to care if the entire town shunned her right along with him. But it was just that which kept him from telling his mother everything.

"I met her at the train station and again when she was out walking in the woods where I hunt. She was bitten by a red milk, and I calmed her down when she thought it was poisonous. I saw her home. I didn't know Moorely had rounded up his work hands to start a search for her."

He'd recounted their history with such a facts-only tone that even Sherman appeared mollified. Eddie wasn't about to admit any more than what he'd shared; it was the truth, just not the whole of it.

"It sounds as if she's been friendly," Mother said, with so much hope in her tone it rekindled Sherman's wrath.

"That's why he needs to stay away from her! The whole town is talking about how old man Moorely was fit to be tied and kicked him off his land."

Eddie said nothing, even when Sherman stepped closer again.

"You need to be invisible, little brother. For my sake and for Ma's."

Then he strode from the house, letting the door slam behind him.

Eddie's mother frowned after Sherman, but when she turned to Eddie a smile overtook her face.

"Do you think she'd come for dinner?"

The invitation astounded him, and he might have laughed if only to imagine Sherman's reaction. Instead, he slowly nodded.

Chapter 8

Mary didn't take off her moccasins for the remainder of the morning. She marveled at their comfort, at the way her feet felt both protected and strangely free. She admired the neat, even stitching, the creative placement of the colorful beadwork, the inviting touch of the folds that reached her mid-calf. Only when hearing the rumble of multiple horses outside did she consider taking them off, knowing her grandfather might not approve. She went to a parlor window and looked outside. Grandfather had brought company: at least a dozen men, all on horseback, all in dark blue army uniforms.

She hurried upstairs, as much to avoid reaction to Eddie's gift as to delay an inevitable meeting with so many visitors. Surely her grandfather would think her in the way of such a large contingent of male guests.

Mary's retreat lasted until an hour before dinnertime. Grandfather himself came to her door, letting her know she was to dress for guests and he would return to escort her down.

Which he did, precisely one hour later.

"Our guests will be here for the next few days," Grandfather said, holding out his arm. "Army folk who pass through every now and then. I have business with them, but some have been good friends to this town. Saved a few of us old-timers from Indian attacks a while back. One even did a favor for the family of that young man you seem bent on showing up with. Yes, Martha told me that Eddie Tucker sought you out on your way home from town the other day. You oughta know that young man's mother is grateful to at least one of our guests here tonight. He's a captain now, the one who brought Tucker back to civilization. Even if he doesn't seem grateful for that, at least his mother is."

It was on the tip of Mary's tongue to say then she was grateful to this captain as well, lest she might never have met Eddie. But instead she merely descended the steps at Grandfather's side, her toes pinched into old shoes making her wish she'd dared to wear the ones Eddie had made for her.

Rumbling male voices and laughter greeted Mary before they reached the threshold. She was glad to see Lauralie and her mother there, and fewer men than she'd seen arrive earlier. Only four soldiers were present, each of them some kind of officer if she could guess by the decorative trim on their uniforms. The rest of the men must have been relegated to eat elsewhere.

Mary intended to go to Lauralie's side, who stood behind her mother while she spoke to a beribboned older officer. But Grandfather loudly cleared his throat as he took Mary's elbow, effectively silencing the room.

"Gentlemen, I'd like to present my granddaughter, Miss Mary Elliot."

Mary nodded briefly, acknowledging the greetings, and would have moved on if one man in particular hadn't stepped forward. Grandfather seemed to welcome his attention, patting the man's shoulder.

"Mary, this is the officer I mentioned just now. Captain Vance Saxton."

"Captain," she said, curtseying politely. He was as tall as her grandfather, at least a dozen years older than Mary, judging by emerging lines feathering his eyes and deepening creases around his chin. Yet he had a youthful, vibrant air about him. He bowed, adding a wink to his grin.

"Your grandfather's description of a pretty young thing pales to your beauty, miss," he said smoothly.

She wished she didn't feel the warmth of a blush creeping upward but had never conquered control of such things. "You're very kind, Captain."

"The captain is on his way back to Arizona Territory. I thought you might compare descriptions of Africa to the places he's seen, Mary. Yes, I know there aren't any giraffes or elephants here, but there might be some similarities elsewhere. Both places are untamed, uncivilized for the most part. Isn't that right, Vance?"

He smiled again at Mary. "Certainly I can't speak for Africa, but the Arizona Territory is as vast a place as anyone can imagine. I admire you, miss, for your travels at such an age, and I'm interested in hearing about where you used to live."

The small, homesick part of Mary longed to talk about Africa, about its people and rivers and plains, the snow-capped mountains in the distance, scorching sun, cool winds. And even though it had been more than a year since the deaths of her parents, one after the other from fevers, she could barely think of her fondest memories without the piercing pain of loss.

Still, she had learned well from her father not to give in to whatever feelings threatened her, and so she bit her trembling lip, took in a fortifying breath to forestall sudden tears, and looked from the captain to her grandfather. "My mother and I used to write to you, Grandfather, all about the places we lived. Mother sent pictures she'd drawn, as I recall. I've been meaning to ask if you still have such sketches? I'm sure they could reveal Africa far better than my words. Perhaps Captain Saxton might enjoy them."

It was true she had been wanting to ask her grandfather such a question, fearing his resentment of Mary's father, of where they lived, of their very mission, might have inspired him to get rid of such letters and pictures. To her surprise, the gaze that met hers seemed every bit as sad as her own.

"Yes, I'd forgotten. I do have them, Mary. We might look at them together soon." She nodded. "I would like that."

Mary was unable to spend much of the evening with either Lauralie or her mother, since each of them seemed to be there for the sole purpose of conversing with men who evidently had too few opportunities for the polite company of women. Eventually, Mary relaxed and enjoyed herself, though one stubborn thought emerged. Her grandfather seemed to be making sure she was at Captain Saxton's side. With Grandfather at the head of the table, the captain to the right, she to the left, Grandfather kept the conversation among the three of them, as if the rest of the table were another party altogether.

Captain Saxton was pleasant enough, and he certainly seemed to admire her grandfather. Mary found herself wishing she could thank him for bringing back Eddie but knew that would surely risk Grandfather's temper. Still, she couldn't help imagining how much more she would have enjoyed the evening if Eddie, and not the captain, sat opposite her.

Eddie winced when one of his mother's needles pricked his skin.

"This would be much easier if you stood still," she said.

At least she was almost finished with this new suit. She was adjusting the length of the sleeves and pant legs, the final touch. She'd asked him to bring out the long mirror from her room, and under the bright light of a trio of oil lamps he could see how he looked.

The reflection clashed with how he imagined himself. He looked like someone else.

Eddie's eyes widened. He looked like his first father. Eddie barely remembered him but had seen the framed photograph often enough, with a five-year-old Sherman standing stiffly beside their father, Eddie himself a two-year-old perched on his mother's lap. Somehow, he both welcomed and opposed the realization.

His mind went to his Apache mother Onawa, as it always did when he felt her memory slipping further away. He'd never abandoned his dreams of somehow joining that world with this one, that mother with this mother.

As he stared at himself he vowed not even his growing love for Mary would stop him from achieving such a dream. Somehow.

"I'll ask Mary to dinner for tomorrow night," he said softly.

Then he sent up a prayer for God to help make it possible.

Chapter 9

Mary slipped on her moccasins and tiptoed down the stairs, through the kitchen, and out the back door. It was the closest exit to the clover field, the most direct path to her destination. The sun hinted its arrival at the eastern horizon, offering enough light to see the outline of the forest in the distance.

"Good morning!"

The deep voice called from the back porch, the very spot Mary liked to have breakfast because it afforded her favorite view. But today it wasn't empty. Captain Saxton was just rising from one of the chairs, evidently having been enjoying the view himself.

Mary tightened the sweater she'd grabbed on her way out of her bedroom, not stopping, merely calling over her shoulder, "It's my favorite time of day, Captain. A time to thank God for His many blessings while outside enjoying them. Good day!"

Then she hastened her step, sailing without effort over the dew-dropped clover, thanks to the moccasins making easy her way.

Eddie stood outside his wickiup. He hadn't bothered bringing his hunting rifle today, knowing it would have been nothing more than a prop to fool Sherman into thinking he was off hunting. No sense pretending, at least here at home.

He returned to the log he'd dragged from its usual spot farther upriver, knowing Mary was more apt to cross here. He traversed the water again, making sure the furrow he'd dug on each end held the log securely in place. He didn't want a dunk in the river to cut short his time with Mary.

After climbing up the opposite bank, the horizon came back into view. His heart leapt at the sight, having nothing to do with exertion. There she was, as graceful as a young deer, her hair flowing freely behind her as she danced closer with each step. Rather than waiting, he bounded forward, meeting her just outside the edge of the forest.

It was as natural as breathing to take her into his arms, to greet her with a kiss. Not only were they alone, she wasn't too shy to return the embrace, the kiss, with the same sort of expectation, as if it was like breathing to her too. It was all Eddie could do to pull away, reminding himself seclusion in her company might be a dangerous thing. Not only could he not trust himself, he was beginning to think he probably shouldn't trust her, either. One of them had to keep their wits.

"My grandfather has visitors," she said.

While at the same time he asked, "Would you come to my home for dinner tonight?"

"Oh!" she laughed. "Dinner, did you say? With your family?"

He nodded. "Yes. I'll call for you at six if you can."

"Of course! I'd like nothing better."

"And these visitors. . .you won't be expected to stay because of that?"

"Perhaps, but I'd much rather dine with you. All of the guests are soldiers, and I'm quite out of place with them."

Something tightened around Eddie's heart, a coldness he wouldn't have thought possible while standing so close to Mary. "Soldiers?"

"Yes, on their way back to Arizona. Grandfather says they've been here before, that one of them brought you to your mother."

A bolt of lightning struck at Eddie's heart, but it was so hardened it deflected any pain and left behind yet another layer of hatred.

"I didn't know they would be staying with your grandfather." He thought speaking would deflect the rawness inside of him, hide it, but she was looking at him as if she saw everything.

"You knew they were coming?"

He nodded. Surely she saw what spread from his heart to his brain, all the way out to the tips of his fingers. She shifted away, far enough to place a hand on each of his arms and look at him with concern, as if he'd suddenly come down with an illness.

"Who are these soldiers, Eddie? Why don't you want them here?"

"Oh, I want them here. Especially Saxton."

"But I thought. . .that is, I'm sure my grandfather is right to believe your mother is grateful to him. But you aren't?"

It was all he could do not to spew out the truth, knowing the man he hated was so close. But how could such hatred not frighten Mary, or at least repel her? He'd had years of hiding his pain of the town's rejection and mistrust. He could hide this too.

He breathed in deeply, taking one of her hands and leading her along. He knew he couldn't take her to the wickiup, not even with this new turn of emotion blinding him to all else, but they could sit on the riverbank.

"I can accept it was for the best that I was brought back, for my mother's sake. I was born into my family, and that was God's doing, not mine, not the army's, not the Apaches'. So I'm here." He was able to muster a smile through the hate still swirling through him, the first sign of hope he really could master all of his feelings, no matter how powerful. "Since you arrived, I've never been more glad to be here."

She raised a hand to lightly stroke the side of his cheek, and he nearly shivered. He wanted to kiss her again, to forget such serious talk, but knew he couldn't.

"I don't hate Saxton for bringing me back," he told her. "I hate him because of the way he treated the Indians on the reservation. Like they should be grateful for having been conquered. Like prisoners. Like. . .like people who don't matter."

"But Eddie," she whispered, leaning closer, letting her head rest on his shoulder, "I see something so personal in your eyes, something more than injustice."

He pulled away far enough to look at her. How had she known? Could she read his soul? "It's true. I hate him for the way he took me from my Apache mother, without time for goodbye before throwing me into a prison for weeks, when I could have stayed with her until they found my family here. The last time I saw my Apache mother she was crying. It was like being stolen all over again."

Her gaze held his, as if she was inviting some of his painful memories from his heart to hers so they could share the burden. "I'm sorry," she said at last, but then her brows slowly lifted as if struck with a dose of something good, something hopeful. "God must have loved your Apache mother very much, though."

He grimaced. "That's a strange way to show it."

But Mary was already shaking away his mild objection. "He brought you to her. Didn't you tell me she adopted Jesus right along with you? Is God's love ever more apparent?"

Slowly, he smiled along with her, the hate, anger, resentment, and bitterness receding again, stuffed back where he'd learned to store them all these years. This was the first time, though, he hadn't wrestled so hard to overcome them.

"Come in here, Mary," said Grandfather from one of the few doorways she never graced, the one to his office. It was at the back of the house, unavoidable from the path she'd used to reach the stairway used by servants.

Grandfather closed the door behind them, and instead of taking a seat behind the massive desk claiming most of the room, he stood in front of it. He motioned to a chair nearby, which was dark leather and deeply padded, but Mary was too stiff to appreciate its comfort.

"I see you've found new footwear."

Immediately she tucked her feet under the chair, letting the hem of her skirt hide them.

"I do not understand you, girl," he said. "You hide those shoes as if you know it's wrong to wear them."

"No, sir! Forgive me, but I hid them fearing your anger, not because it's wrong."

He paced once then twice along the length of the room before speaking again. "Vance told me he saw you leave this morning. Further, he saw with his spyglass that you met that young man on the other side of the field."

"Spyglass is certainly the correct term," she murmured.

"I've been remiss by not hiring a chaperone for you," he said firmly, ignoring her words.

Her gaze darted to his. "I've never had need of one!"

"And you wouldn't now, if you heeded half of what I tell you. Or if you were married."

She'd been about to protest, but those last few words stopped her. Sudden hope flared, since she was already wishing for that too. "I have no wish to hurry things, Grandfather, but if an engagement will help, that might be acceptable."

He was shaking his head as if he knew something she did not. "If you think for a moment I'd entertain the thought of you marrying that renegade, you had better think again. Now, Captain Saxton is someone more in line with my hopes. He's been married but widowed, and proven to be a good husband, a good father. Has a little girl waiting for him in Arizona, and you could be a fine influence."

The idea of marrying anyone other than Eddie, especially someone Eddie had just described to her as cold-hearted, horrified her. She gaped at her grandfather for a long moment unable to speak. Upon seeing his gravity, her hands began to tremble.

Slowly, she rose. "Grandfather," she tested her ability to speak then swallowed, taking in a fortifying breath before beginning again. Grandfather was so much taller she decided to take a step away, to put the chair between them. "I know you did not want me to come here, but I refuse to believe you would marry me off at the first opportunity. I have no intention—none whatsoever—to entertain the idea of marrying Captain Saxton. In fact, if you continue to refuse me the freedom to see Eddie, I shall return to Africa. I'm sure the LMS will appreciate my continued interest in taking up where my parents left off."

Then, though she heard him speak, object, demand her return, she ran from the room without looking back.

Chapter 10

The following evening, Mary crept down the back stairs, avoiding the one that creaked. She mostly hoped to escape the notice of her grandfather, but even Mrs. Warren couldn't be trusted not to summon him immediately. Mary would leave through the kitchen and circle around to the front porch to wait for Eddie.

With each step, myriad pleas filled her mind. Prayers and defense, guilt and assurance. Did honoring father and mother include a grandparent who couldn't possibly know what was best for her? *Please, God, soften Grandfather's heart! Or change mine—and Eddie's...*

Even as such words took shape, she knew her heart would never be so transformed as to accept the plan her grandfather had in mind. Marry a man who was not only a stranger to her but one whose true nature was in question?

Her silent pleas halted abruptly as she came to the corner of the garden at the side of the porch. She was too late! Eddie was already there, and although a maid may have opened the door, Grandfather stood with one palm on the frame and the other on the door itself, as if prepared to slam it shut.

"Grandfather!"

Her call stopped him as his gaze passed over Eddie's shoulder to meet hers. She hurried up the steps, holding out a hand. "Please don't send Eddie away. He came to take me to his mother's house, to dine with them."

"I think I've made my wishes clear," Grandfather said, shifting one hand to the doorknob as if still prepared to close Eddie out.

"I believe we both made our wishes clear," she said.

"As long as you live under my roof, you'll do as I say."

Mary opened her mouth, but Eddie stepped into her line of vision. "It's all right, Mary. He may be wrong—this whole town may be wrong—but I know it's probably best for you if you don't come."

"But, Eddie! How can it be right to bend to what others think? Especially if they're as wrong as you and I both know?"

Eddie crossed the porch to close the distance between them, taking the hand she reached out to him. "Do you want me to carry you away with your grandfather's anger chasing us?" He shook his head. "I want you and your grandfather to know I want only the best for you. I may be that best—I hope I am—but riding away with me right now isn't right."

Mary wanted to argue, to pull Eddie to her side and have them both jump into his wagon and ride off. Let Grandfather stew alone in the cloud of anger he'd created! Yet she knew such a cloud wouldn't be left behind at all, that Eddie was right. Why, though, must she be the one to give in?

As if he'd read her thought, Eddie leaned closer and whispered, "Patience is worth a try, at least for a start."

Then he let go of her hand and returned alone to his wagon.

Mary watched him go, her moccasin-clad feet fairly itching to follow him.

"What did he say to you just now?" demanded Grandfather.

She wanted to say it was none of his business; she wanted to let out the anger inside; she wanted to strike him with words that would hurt because that was how she felt. But she held her tongue.

"Did he tell you to go off to those woods? To meet him? Because if he did, I'll see you chaperoned every minute of the day if need be."

Mary sucked in a puff of air but realized what Eddie had just done. Poured hot coals—of kindness—upon this man who was so clearly wrong.

"He said we ought to be patient with you, Grandfather, which is far more generous than I find myself wanting to act. Now if you'll excuse me, I do plan to eat dinner, but I'll take it in my room so you may have your guests to yourself."

Eddie urged Nehemiah along, nearly in awe of his own unexpected behavior. He'd arrived early to the Moorely place, fully expecting resistance from J.W. Eddie hadn't known how to handle conflict over Mary, but did know when he was around her it was easier to cling to the kind of honor both of his mothers had tried instilling in him.

He wanted to believe if God could change Eddie's intention just now, to whisk Mary away despite J.W.'s protests, He could change J.W. too.

But even with that comfort, another truth wagged venom at him, one Eddie feared his wish to impress Mary might not be enough to extinguish. Saxton was there, in that very house.

Somehow it was easier to believe God could soften Eddie's attitude toward J.W. than remove his ill will toward Saxton. It would take a miracle to keep Eddie from confronting the man, especially with the upcoming dance providing the perfect opportunity.

Chapter 11

"You're welcome to come along, because one way or the other, I'm going."

Mary lifted one expectant brow as she waited for Lauralie's answer. Since yesterday, Lauralie had been installed in Sarah's bedroom as Mary's "companion," displacing one of the officers who had previously occupied the room.

Both Mary and Lauralie knew she'd been assigned as guard, shadow, and snitch, but Grandfather's fatal mistake had been in thinking Lauralie's loyalty to him or even to her mother was greater than to Mary. Or, more aptly, to young love.

"Oh, I'm going," Lauralie assured her but was still frowning. "Only if your grandfather spots us walking through the clover he'll know I'm not doing the job he brought me here to do. He might replace me, and then where will you be?"

Mary shrugged. "At the very least, it will take time to replace you. Shall we go, then?"

Mary didn't bother using either the back stairway or the rear door. Instead, they walked boldly out the front—though once they left Mary conceded it hadn't been such a bold act, after all. The entire house seemed empty; even the servants were busily out of sight with preparations for the upcoming harvest dance.

Meeting Eddie with Lauralie in tow wasn't ideal, but since it was the only way to do so, it was the best choice. She hoped Eddie would agree.

As they approached the wood, Mary spotted Eddie just swinging down from a tree limb—perhaps the very perch he'd used when he'd first spotted her not so very long ago. She marveled that they hadn't known each other far longer. With Eddie almost constantly in her thoughts, it was as if she'd known him forever.

His smile engulfed them both. "I'm surprised your grandfather installed such a friendly guard."

Both Mary and Lauralie laughed at how quickly he'd assessed the situation. Then Mary stepped closer, slipping her hand into Eddie's as they walked farther into the shadows of the trees.

"I'm not at all convinced my grandfather will have a change of heart by tomorrow's dance. How do we know he won't turn you away?"

"I don't see how he could," said Lauralie, even though Mary had clearly directed the question to Eddie. But Mary looked at her eagerly, welcoming her words. "Remember, my mother made sure the harvest dance is open to everyone in town. Rich neighbors and poor, farmers and farmhands, even the Exodusters."

"Then certainly that means you too, Eddie!"

He shook his head. "But I'm the one most interested in spending time alone with you."

"True," she said slowly. A thought was just beginning to form, one she perhaps should mull before sharing but didn't. "I told my grandfather the other day that if I wasn't allowed to choose whom I spend time with, I would return to Africa and take up my parents' work—"

"What!"

She looked between them in surprise, both having uttered the same reaction. "I suppose I wasn't entirely rational at the moment, because I truly do not want to leave." She cast a grin Eddie's way but knew Lauralie was becoming the kind of friend she wanted for life. "The fact is, I do want to follow the example my parents set for me, and independence would allow me the same freedom my mother assumed when she left this very same home. But I needn't go all the way to Africa to do the work God designed me for. If I could be useful, I could be independent here, a missionary without leaving America. Missionary to the Exodusters, for example, or even to one of the reservations you described, Eddie."

Eddie rubbed the back of his neck, his brows furrowed. "It's one way to leave your grandfather's nest, I suppose. He would have nothing to say about your choices then."

"Precisely!"

"But how would you live?" Lauralie asked. "I mean, who would support you if not your grandfather? It's one thing to want to help the Exodusters, or the Indians, but I must say finding someone to take care of your needs would be difficult. The Exodusters, at least the new arrivals, aren't in a position to take care of you along with their own needs. I'm not sure it's any different on a reservation."

"It isn't," Eddie said.

"And anyway," Lauralie went on, "I thought you were going to marry—"

She stopped herself suddenly, as if she'd been too forward on Mary's behalf. But what else could she assume, given the need for her current role as chaperone?

Mary supposed she ought to look embarrassed, as if she'd discussed her hopes with Lauralie and would soon be expecting Eddie to propose. But she hadn't a trace of dismay; instead, she looked at Eddie with an unabashed smile. To her delight, he smiled in return.

Eddie probably shouldn't be smiling like the lovesick calf he was. No matter how patiently he forced himself to jump the hurdles set up between him and Mary, there was no guarantee her grandfather would ever change. Or the town. The thought of Mary being shunned right alongside of him was intolerable.

So he let his smile fade, reality, as always, bringing caution.

He put a thumb to Mary's chin, not caring if such a display of affection embarrassed Lauralie. "I'll be at the dance tomorrow night, doing my best to fit in." Even as the words left his mouth, he knew that was a promise he would struggle to fulfill, with Saxton there. "But I can't change how people think of me. Your grandfather doesn't want you under my shadow. He doesn't know it, but I agree with him there. I don't want that either."

She put her hands over his. "Then we'll have to draw you out of those shadows, won't we?"

Chapter 12

The evening air was cool, necessitating shawls for both Mary and Lauralie as they made their way over the clover and to the Moorely back barn. It was in the opposite direction of the wooded area serving as Mary's meeting place with Eddie, and the field was already filling up with carriages, buckboards, wagons, horses, and mules. Mrs. Babineau had arrived earlier that afternoon, helping the girls to get ready.

Mary looked down at the gown she wore, loaned with some insistence by Lauralie's mother. Mrs. Babineau had ordered the dress made for Lauralie last year, but Lauralie refused to wear it, citing the midnight blue satin overskirt and shimmery bodice was something her mother, not Lauralie, would wear.

She had also been provided a new pair of shoes, delivered to her room with a crisp note from her grandfather that simply stated, "Wear these tonight." Deciding it was better to appease such an inconsequential demand, she complied. But now as she walked the clover to the barn she couldn't help wishing she could have worn her moccasins.

The barn was a tall structure void of any stalls or other impeding walls but for various beams holding up its considerable roof. Soon, she was told, the entire facility would be converted to house a new venture Grandfather was working out with the army. Stalls were to be added for horses, she thought, though she couldn't be sure since Grandfather hadn't discussed it with her.

There were more people gathered than Mary had expected, even for a town as large as Topeka. Many were already dancing to the cheerful tunes of musicians stationed on a loft, out of the way but where their music could rain down and fill the barn from end to end. They were in the midst of a fife and drum polka, rousing the dancers below.

After circling the room, Mary had not spotted Eddie. She might have kept moving, except two figures stepped in her path. One was Captain Saxton who requested a dance, while the other soldier asked Lauralie.

Mary stiffened but knew she could not refuse even if she admitted she'd never excelled in the woefully few dance lessons she'd had. Worse, though the polka ended, a violin took up the gentler notes of a waltz. The kind of dance she had envisioned sharing only with Eddie.

Eddie's pulse throbbed through his veins, pounded at his temples. He'd just endured a pair of battles to get here, one to quell his own dark eagerness to confront Saxton and the other with his brother. Fighting with Sherman had been the last thing he needed, the reason they were late, but something Polly had said made the explosion unavoidable—even if it had ended with the first sign of hope that his brother didn't really hate him, after all.

The clashes would be worth it to dance with Mary, especially in plain sight of the entire town. The vision had been enough to demand he surrender to God the residue of anger between him and his brother.

But there she was—in the arms of the man he'd just begged God's help to cool his hatred of.

"Eddie."

He heard his mother's gentle voice, a sharp contrast to the renewed storm inside. Her tone was nothing more than a reminder of what she'd said earlier, the statement Polly overheard, the one that started the argument with Sherman. *"Remember my gratitude to the man,"* she'd said.

Gratitude!

Jealousy filled him along with old hatred, muddled with his resistance to his mother's wishes. He knew only one thing: to conquer this feeling, he knew he couldn't share the same roof with Saxton.

Mary caught sight of Eddie, and she was at once struck by two things: how handsome he looked in the dark suit and how intensely he stared at the man currently guiding her in the waltz. She wanted to fly to Eddie's side but knew to do so would only give fuel to her grandfather's ire. Surely he was watching her behavior tonight, even if he did seem happy to be dancing with Mrs. Babineau at the moment.

"Your grandfather will have a hard time accepting that you care for that young man," said Captain Saxton.

She looked up at him in surprise. He must have seen her spot Eddie, but to speak of something clearly not his business was unexpected.

"J.W. isn't unreasonable," he went on. "He wants what's best for you."

She looked at him, suddenly suspicious of his motives. Was he about to suggest himself as a better choice?

"Yes, he assured me of that," she said. "But I believe I know myself better than he does. After all, until recently he didn't know me at all."

"Still, he's a man of experience, wisdom. He loved both of his daughters, and now you're what remains of both. The daughter of one, the image of the other."

"I hardly think that gives him the right—"

Though Captain Saxton was smiling, he shook his head. "I would like to make a suggestion, if you'll grant me a moment. I, too, have some experience you might benefit from."

Surely he *was* about to petition for her hand! She started to pull away, but his grip grew more firm.

"I married a young woman my family didn't approve of. Your grandfather might not have approved, either, if he knew who I'd married. But I regret not one single moment, even if I might have handled it better than I did."

Mary let her hand remain in his, waiting for him to continue.

"The only antidote to prejudice, the only way to bridge differences, is with love. I assure you, your grandfather does love you. But I'm not sure he believes that feeling is returned. Is there a way you can follow your own wishes but at the same time find a way to convince your grandfather he might have a place in your heart too?"

She stared, perplexed but soon convicted. Had she shown her grandfather even a hint of a granddaughter's love since her arrival? All she'd done was avoid him or stand up to him, even defy him!

Mary eyed Captain Saxton curiously as the dance came to an end. How could this man be the same one who had treated Eddie so harshly?

Eddie paced the clover, a good distance from the barn. The only reason he'd come was to dance with Mary—not to watch her look up into the face of his one enemy with such a rapt look in her eyes.

He should go. Between the unexpected realization he'd discovered about his brother and the image of Mary apparently enjoying Saxton's company, all he wanted was to find his forest shelter and spend the night alone.

Chapter 13

T here you are!"

Mary turned expectantly to Lauralie's voice. Eddie had disappeared again, and both had been searching for him. Surely she'd found him!

But Lauralie was alone.

"I spoke to Polly, Sherman's bride-to-be. They rode here together, and she said Eddie and Sherman had an awful fight on the way. Evidently they often argue, but he might not be in the mood for a party where he thinks he isn't wanted."

Mary's spirit could not be any heavier. How was he to gain acceptance if he never joined in such parties? If Captain Saxton was right, and she suspected he was, then the love must start somewhere. Loving thy neighbor was one of the first rules she'd learned, and if his neighbors hadn't offered any, it was left to Eddie, and even to her, to do so even if they believed others undeserving.

"Will you keep looking for him with me?"

Lauralie squeezed Mary's hand. "You know I will."

Eddie kicked at a stick lying innocuously on the ground. Why hadn't he left when he'd meant to? As much as he wanted to be with Mary, his anger at Saxton had rendered Eddie weak rather than strong. His jealousy was groundless, he knew that, but Eddie was still disgusted with himself. Without Mary there, would he have gone up to the man and landed a blow Saxton wouldn't see coming?

Indecision drove him from the barn and kept him away. Revenge wasn't his; it said so in the Bible. But Eddie's fists fairly itched to get at the man who had provided one of Eddie's worst memories.

Lurking in the shadows, he kept his gaze on the barn door. He must either go inside and act the man he knew Mary expected him to be, or leave. He doubted he could stay without confirming to his neighbors he really did hate the army who had "rescued" him. That he really was savage.

Eddie remained, still torn between wanting to please Mary and wanting to satisfy his own version of justice, until a figure emerged who was the cause of his turmoil. Vance Saxton.

Instantly, Eddie's pulse quickened. He would wait until the man was outside the spill of light and then face him. How satisfying it would be to pummel the man. . . .

Eddie waited quietly, knowing if Saxton wandered in the wrong direction Eddie might lose the opportunity. But if Saxton walked this way. . .

The man sauntered closer. He wasn't even looking ahead; he was looking up at the sky, as if the stars held more interest than the party. The opportunity couldn't be simpler!

Eddie sprang from the shadows, but even in the darkness he knew Saxton recognized him. To his credit, he appeared entirely calm before Eddie's stark hatred.

"I think I owe you this." Then his fist connected to Saxton's jaw with a satisfying thwack.

Saxton stumbled back but did not fall. Eddie waited, both fists up, ready to continue the attack. Saxton straightened, but rather than raise a return fist, Saxton charged Eddie, pushing him backward until the side of the barn stopped them. The move was so unexpected, and the older man so surprisingly strong, that Eddie was left immobile for a split second before using the solid wall to push himself off, ready to hit the man again.

"Stop!"

Eddie barely heard the call, refused to accept it was Mary even though part of him shrank at the sound. Saxton dropped his hold on Eddie's shoulders, freeing him, though Saxton did not raise his fists to meet Eddie, but rather his palms. That, combined with the shadows of three faces in particular, stopped Eddie cold. First Mary. Then his mother, and finally Sherman.

Sherman, who had called Eddie a savage even as recently as on their way to this dance. To which Eddie had reminded him he was the same kind of savage Sherman would've become if he hadn't run away all those years ago. The look on Sherman's face had said more than words, though the words did follow. Yes, he'd run, Sherman admitted. Run like a coward, one word that had never occurred to Eddie. All these years, he'd thought his brother simply hadn't cared. But the truth was he'd never been angry with Eddie. All these years he'd been angry with himself for not suffering what Eddie had, for leaving him behind. For feeling like a coward.

It was time Eddie proved he wasn't a savage, that if he'd learned anything from his Apache family he'd learned honor and respect. Eddie needed to prove that to Sherman, his mother, and most of all to Mary.

Perhaps Saxton was the first to see the change in Eddie, that the anger had drained away. Was it that which made Saxton present a hand rather than a fist? Eddie stared at the invitation, uncertain the offer of a handshake was sincere—or that he wanted to accept.

"Maybe you did owe me that punch," Saxton said. "You're probably not the only one."

Eddie had taken too long to accept the hand, and so Saxton let it fall back to his side. He turned to Eddie's mother then, briefly bowing his head. "Mrs. Tucker, it's nice to see you again. If you don't already know, your son has reason to remember me harshly. That's partly why I made sure to come back. To apologize."

"Apologize, Captain?" asked Eddie's mother. "For bringing Eddie back to me?"

Saxton shook his head. "No, ma'am. For the way I did it." He turned now to face Eddie again. "I was fresh off a battleground back then, son. Saw a number of friends killed. I was ready to lay blame on anybody who ever killed a soldier, and that included Indians. But I was only seeing one side, until someone took the time to set me straight."

Eddie wondered who that could have been, remembering how zealous Saxton had been while guarding the Apache reservation. Whoever it was, the impact must have been great, if Saxton's words were to be believed.

But Eddie wouldn't ask; he wasn't certain how to feel about this sudden turn of events. All these years he'd dreamed of revenge upon an unrepentant soldier who'd torn Eddie from his Apache mother's arms. The Saxton in front of him wasn't the Saxton Eddie remembered.

"There's a party going on in there," Saxton said, as if they were all friends and had only briefly forgotten the reason they were together. He held out his hand once more in Eddie's direction. "And if I were you, I'd show J.W. Moorely you know how to dance with that granddaughter of his."

The words helped Eddie let go of his hesitation. It was as if the man knew his best reason for coming to this party, and even approved.

Eddie shook the man's hand.

Chapter 14

"E ddie," Mary whispered as she returned to the harvest dance on his arm, "you have a lot to tell me."

"Yes," he agreed, "but you'll have to suffer my clumsy dancing if you want to hear about it."

She laughed, letting him sweep her into his arms for a waltz as she confessed she'd had only rudimentary dancing lessons herself.

"It's been a busy evening," Eddie said, "and I can tell you all about it, but I'll start by saying I'm having a hard time believing half of it—or understanding any of it."

"Lauralie told me you and Sherman had some kind of argument."

"That was the first surprise. I learned something about my brother I never suspected. He isn't angry with me for not wanting to come home all those years ago. He's angry with himself!"

"For treating you badly since you've returned?"

Eddie shook his head. "When I was taken all those years ago, the two of us had been far from the house, clearing weeds from a crop. Sherman was chased too but managed to get away. I saw him run off, and I thought he'd come back for me. I guess he did go for help, but it was too late. He's been blaming himself all these years." He frowned. "I thought he was worried about sharing the farm with somebody who hadn't helped build it up to what it is today."

"Do you suppose you'll get along better now?"

Eddie shrugged. "Old habits are hard to break, but maybe."

Mary's gaze roamed the room before resting on her grandfather. He was talking to Captain Saxton. "And. . .Captain Saxton? What of your feelings about him?"

She saw his gaze wander in the same direction. "I'm not sure what to make of that. Maybe once the surprise wears off I'll hate him again, but right now I don't think it's possible."

Mary leaned close enough to whisper softly, "Maybe God's taken that hatred right out of your heart."

He eyed her with such approving scrutiny her heart twirled in tune with the dance. "You might be right about that."

In Eddie's best dreams of the evening, he'd danced every dance with Mary.

But that didn't come true, even if the night had brought something unexpectedly welcome. How astounding that Saxton's simple words so thoroughly deflated Eddie's hope for vengeance. Mary was surely right about divine intervention, but this could be proven only with time.

His dream of dancing solely with Mary was interrupted without contention. She danced with her grandfather—who was in surprisingly high spirits considering Eddie's attention to Mary—then Sherman and another soldier Eddie didn't know, while Eddie danced with his mother, then Mrs. Babineau, Lauralie, and even Polly. Not even Mary's second dance with Saxton could rekindle Eddie's initial anger.

He and Mary mixed easily with the Exodusters who had come—not many, not nearly all who lived in town—and he marveled at her ease in mingling between one group and another. She was already making plans to help with a school for children, just as soon as it could be arranged.

When the music dwindled and the food and drinks had been consumed, Eddie knew he would have to say good night. The beginning of the evening was nearly forgotten. Eddie wasn't sure he would be allowed to call on Mary, but he had a sliver of hope that hadn't existed before tonight.

No sooner had he reached the house at her side than her grandfather invited them to join him inside, as if he'd been waiting for an opportunity. To make sure Eddie went quickly on his way?

Neither his level tone nor his impassive face hinted at what he wanted to talk about, but Eddie feared the evening might end as unpleasantly as it had begun when he saw Saxton lurking in the shadows of the parlor where J.W. headed.

"Eddie, Captain Saxton would like to speak to you."

Eddie exchanged glances with Mary, who looked more curious than wary.

"I have news of the woman who raised you with the Apaches," said Saxton.

Eddie's gaze flew to Saxton.

"She's well," Saxton said quickly, as if guessing what conclusions could be drawn. "I told her I hoped to see you, and she wanted you to know she is happy and looks forward to hearing about you."

"Happy? On a reservation."

Saxton had the grace to look uncomfortable. "She says her faith has taught her to be content in all things. You ought to know she comes to my home often, to help me care for my daughter. Her mother, my wife, was Cocheta. Do you recall Cocheta?"

Eddie could scarcely believe the words. Of course he recalled the young woman his mother had cared for. Cocheta's father had been killed in battle; her mother died of the fever that swept through their village. She was several years older than Eddie and had been like a sister to him.

"You—were married to. . . ?"

Saxton nodded, and the news struck Eddie anew. If Cocheta was Saxton's wife, it meant she had died.

As if reading Eddie's grief, Saxton said quietly, "In childbirth. But our daughter is a gift I treasure beyond anything."

Eddie felt Mary's hand return to his arm, and automatically he placed his own hand over hers, needing her comfort.

"I told Mary earlier that love is the answer to hatred, and I thought you deserved to know who was able to change me from the brute I was when you knew me to. . . well, I can only say I am not perfect, but I am a better man than I was. I take special comfort from the apostle Paul, who once persecuted God's elect until he was changed into one of God's most ardent followers."

The words slowly took meaning as J.W. neared him. Mary was still at his side, but his gaze was fixed on Eddie. "I only found out tonight about these details, and I must say the entire evening has given me plenty to think about. But tonight you showed interest in our town, our society, for the first time. If you hope to see my granddaughter again, I expect this won't be the last time you try getting along with this town."

Then J.W. turned to Mary. "You said to me not so long ago that you'd rather go back to Africa than do what I say." His tone had deepened somewhat, but there was still a sparkle in his eye. "You are your mother's daughter, and I don't doubt you meant such a threat. If the only way I can keep you here is to allow this young fellow in your life, so be it. I've heard he's good with horses, and I'd like to find out how good. If he's willing, he can prove his talent by helping me invest in my new venture: breeding and selling the finest horses in the state."

Mary dropped her hand from Eddie's arm and pitched herself into her grandfather's embrace, who patted her back and cleared his throat as if unaccustomed to her affection.

"Thank you, Grandfather!"

"Now, now, I didn't say he's good enough for you, but I won't fight your choices." Then he extricated himself from Mary's embrace to eye Eddie narrowly again. "My horses will include sales to the army. Think you can work with me on that?"

Eddie spared a quick glance Saxton's way before answering. "Yes, sir. I look forward to the opportunity." As Mary slipped her hand in his again, Eddie added, "I have only the best intentions for your granddaughter, sir."

"Just don't take her to Africa."

Epilogue

ddie stroked the top of his wife's hand. *His wife.* He could hardly believe she was his, even though there hadn't been a single doubt in his mind that was exactly what he wanted from the moment he saw her getting off that train with her badly laced shoes.

He did not take Mary to Africa, though he was at her side as she worked with the Africans in Topeka. But he did take her for a visit to Arizona to see his Apache mother, Onawa. She was as happy to see him as he was to see her, but knew the moment he witnessed her with Saxton's daughter that she would not leave her, even for a place in his home in Topeka.

Now Eddie worked with J.W. Moorely, a match he once imagined impossible. But he'd learned Mary's grandfather wasn't as hard-hearted as Eddie once believed, especially after marrying Mrs. Babineau. He liked to think J.W. trusted him now, certainly with his horses, but even with his granddaughter's happiness.

He drew Mary close to his side. "You know I loved you from the moment you got off that train, don't you?"

He'd told her so many times before and waited expectantly for her to add the rest. "Yes," she said with a contented smile, "and every moment in between."

Maureen Lang writes stories inspired by a love of history and romance. An avid reader herself, she's figured out a way to write the stories she feels like reading. Maureen's inspirationals have earned various writing distinctions including the Inspirational Reader's Choice Contest, a HOLT Medallion, and the Selah Award, as well as being a finalist for the Rita, Christy, and Carol Awards. In addition to investigating various eras in history (such as Victorian England, First World War, and America's Gilded Age), Maureen loves taking research trips to get a feel for the settings of her novels. She lives in the Chicago area with her family and has been blessed to be the primary caregiver to her adult disabled son.

Promise Me Sunday

by Cathy Liggett

For the LORD *seeth not as man seeth; for man looketh*
on the outward appearance, but the LORD *looketh on the heart.*
1 SAMUEL 16:7

To thine own self be true.
WILLIAM SHAKESPEARE

Chapter 1

S tanding with a wooden mallet dangling from her hand, idly waiting her turn, Adeline McClain didn't have to guess that she hadn't been first choice for a sixth player for the game of croquet her cousin Shannon had organized.

While her highbrow cousin thought Adeline lacked social graces, Adeline thought Shannon fell short in the way of tact—at least where Adeline was concerned. Shannon hadn't hesitated to bluntly tell Adeline how her good friend Mary Elizabeth had suddenly taken to bed with the onset of an awful headache and was sorry to have to cancel. Who else but Adeline could Shannon turn to last minute to complete the afternoon gathering of three young ladies and three young men?

Adeline remembered a time about a year ago when she'd first arrived at her uncle William and aunt Martha's well-to-do household how Shannon's insensitivity and borderline rudeness used to rankle her. But as if she were waving away a pesky fly, she shooed the thought from her mind. Like Mama used to say, a tiger can't change its stripes, so why dwell on something that wasn't likely to change?

"We need to get to the Cape again before summer ends."

"Don't forget, we have an open invite from the Stanford family."

"When can you go?"

"When can't I go?"

Tidbits of conversations floated her way as the other players stood scattered around the lawn, taking their turns, the young women clad classily in their long colorful skirts and the young men in their day coats.

She was rarely included in their conversations as they laughed and talked among themselves. But that was all right. On such a beautiful day, she was simply happy to be outside where there was plenty around her to delight in. Watching the leaves rustle on the trees. Gazing at the clouds gliding by. Not to mention listening to a bevy of birds twittering all kinds of pleasantries to one another from the branches of a shade tree that graced the expansive lawn.

Luckily for her feathered friends, the July eastern seaboard sun was far more forgiving than any middle-of-the-summer days she remembered growing up in Arkansas. Back home during this sweltering time of the year, the birds might not have had the energy for so much chattering. The creeks would be all dried up by now and the grass would be wilting and turning brown. Yet here in the north, the tips of the soft, well-tended grass sparkled fittingly like tiny diamonds, laid out all around her uncle and aunt's prominent homestead. Or rather, what was better known as the Dougherty estate.

No, it wasn't anything like home here. Not at all like the open land and the enchanting woods where she used to roam. Places where she could enjoy so many of God's critters and pretty creations every season of the year. But just as the squirrel scampering up to its nest in the tree, she'd made a home in her new surroundings with her Bostonian relatives the best way she knew how. Finding comfort and peace wherever she could, which sometimes wasn't that easy but—

Something flitted across her line of vision, making her blink.

What was that?

Oh, there it was again, dancing a path past her.

Curious as always, she raised her hand over her eyes, looking all around. But left or right, up or down, she couldn't see a thing. She was just about to give up her search when suddenly she felt something. A tiny something. And there it was on the back of her hand which held her resting mallet.

A butterfly! Black with iridescent blue hindwings, it was quite a beauty. So delicate and perfect, just like ones she used to draw in her sketchbook. A sketchbook of sorts anyway, something her mama had made for her using wrapping paper from the dry goods store. It had been a treasured birthday gift two years earlier, along with a small tray of watercolors her mama had saved up for.

Oh, Mama! The memory made her heart flutter like the winged creature itself, bringing on a mixture of sadness and happiness all at once. How she missed the home and the days she used to share with her! How she missed her mama most of all!

It was times like these that always had her wondering about sketching again. If she did, would it bring any kind of comfort? Or would it only make her heart long even more for what she used to have?

"Adeline!"

Her head jolted upward as Shannon's voice shot across the lawn. The butterfly flickered at her jerky movement, spread its wings, and was immediately gone. Along with the special moment the two of them had shared.

"Addled Adeline. That's what I should call you. It's your turn. You're holding up the game. Can you please pay attention?"

"I—there was fluttering, and—" She started to explain, but the five pairs of eyes staring blankly at her seemed to insist that she needn't bother. Actually, that wasn't totally true. Only four sets of eyes were on her. Everett Brighton's were not. She would have instantly noticed if Everett was looking her way. His eyes were hard to miss, because they were a color that always reminded her of the same striking bright hue of a blue jay's crest. She only knew that because she'd seen plenty of blue jays in her life. She'd seen Everett plenty of times as well.

As the heir to the Brighton's ever-expanding market and restaurant, his name was at the top of all of Shannon's invitation lists. And not just Shannon's, but Aunt Martha's and Uncle William's too. The entire Dougherty clan had it in their heads that Shannon would surely become Mrs. Everett Brighton one day. Coming from two well-heeled families, Everett and Shannon would undoubtedly be a perfect match when the time came.

Adeline could see why her cousin would want to be paired up with Everett. Mostly because out of all of Shannon's friends, he was the one who usually had a kind smile for Adeline. At the very moment, however, his eyes were downcast, hidden from her view. He seemed to be examining the mallet in his hand intensely, as if seeing it for the very first time. Was he embarrassed for her? Irritated? Or plain bored?

"Sorry, y'all," Adeline blurted quickly.

Then with a movement as brisk as her apology, she stepped forward, sidled up to her green ball, pulled back her mallet, and swung hard. Unfortunately, a little too hard and with too little aim. Her renegade ball bolted like a streak of lightning with a path just as unpredictable, bumping and jumping over the lawn not anywhere close to its intended wicket.

Instead, the ball seemed to have a mind of its own. She watched as it cruised its way over the grass, appearing to be on a determined course, headed straight toward—oh, no, Shannon's red ball!

Closing her eyes, she made a wish the ball might change its way, only for the fact she wasn't in the mood to encounter her cousin's wrath. But before she could finish her wish, she heard the clash, loud and clear. Opening her eyes, she spotted her green ball at rest and her cousin's ball, shot off to the right. A long way off to the right.

With that, all eyes were on her once again. This time, even Everett's. And most particularly Shannon's. Her glare shone as brightly as the afternoon sun, but not nearly so kindly.

"Adeline!" Her cousin shouted across the lawn again. "How could you? That was my ball!"

Obviously, it hadn't exactly been her intention to send Shannon's ball flying off course. But since it had happened that way, she couldn't say that she was sorry either. It was only a silly game, after all. Yet Shannon was taking the matter much to heart.

Throughout the entire game, Shannon had been so involved visiting with her friends, she hadn't come anywhere near Adeline. Now she threw her mallet to the ground and pounded a path toward Adeline, closing the distance.

Even with her huffy walk, Adeline couldn't believe how Shannon's skirt swayed daintily around her. Her nails looked freshly and evenly filed as she aimed a pointed finger in Adeline's face.

"Just because we're on opposing teams, you didn't have to go out of your way to hit my ball, Adeline."

"I wasn't trying to hit your ball. Really. I wasn't."

"Oh, like that's the truth. You came after my ball because I called you Addled Adeline. How childish can you be?"

Adeline wasn't at all surprised that Shannon had shifted the tables, making her out to be the one to blame. She'd done the very same thing to her plenty of times before.

"It *is* the truth, Shannon. But let me ask you this," she said boldly, not caring any longer about the consequences, "isn't that how you so kindly explained the rules to me? Aren't we allowed to go after the opposition's balls in our path?"

"She's right, Shannon. Those are the rules. That's part of the game." Everett's voice came out of nowhere but seemed to be everywhere, silencing everything else around them and tempering Shannon's ire.

Adeline couldn't have been more thankful that he was standing up for her, even when he was on Shannon's team. And even when her own teammates hadn't said a thing to back her.

At first Shannon appeared shocked that Everett had spoken up on Adeline's behalf, giving Adeline one of her most evil looks. But just as quickly, she turned and spoke to him with a voice as sweet as a sparrow's song.

"Of course, Everett. You are so right." She let out a long sigh then fanned her face with her hand. "Oh, I don't know what came over me. It must be all this heat. Why don't we take a break and get something icy cold to drink? It's so hot, especially in these long skirts and long sleeves. Although,"—she turned to Adeline—"some of us might not need a cold drink at all. You're probably not quite as warm as the rest of us in this simple frock of yours."

With a look of disdain, Shannon reached out and lifted a corner of one of Adeline's favorite dresses. It may have been simple, indeed, in comparison with the other girls' croquet wear, but the pale, yellow dress with a white bodice was special to her. Her mama had sewn it for her just a few months before she'd taken ill.

"Oh, my word, Adeline." Shannon looked down at the ground and Adeline flushed, knowing exactly what her cousin was seeing. "Are you truly barefoot again?" Shannon gasped. "Poor Mother and Father. Don't they have enough to deal with, taking you in the way they did? I certainly hope they don't get wind of more barefoot antics. Dearie me!" She raised her hands and turned to her friends. "Well, it just proves what they say, doesn't it? 'You can take the girl out of the South, but you surely can't take the South out of the girl.'" She shrugged and waved a hand toward the patio. "Come on, it's time for some lemonade, friends. Or should I say, 'Come on, y'all?'" She mimicked Adeline, causing a few snickers to erupt from the group.

Before heading for the terrace, Shannon took one last look at Adeline and shook her head as if she felt extremely sorry for her. But Adeline knew that just wasn't true. Not one bit. Shannon had never been sympathetic at all. Not at the loss of Adeline's mama and her own aunt. Not at Adeline's plight to make a space for herself in a new and quite different kind of place.

Instead, Adeline could see the slightest hint of a devious smile on Shannon's lips. And the merest glint of pleasure in her eyes. All signs of how very glad Shannon was to have something else to report to her parents. Something more to ensure Adeline looked like a hapless, hopeless backwoods orphan girl in her aunt and uncle's eyes. Rather than them seeing who she was—a girl trying not to lose the very person she was raised to be.

Chapter 2

W ell, if other Northern girls are anything like you, Shannon, then I'm surely glad I'm not from anywhere near this neck of the woods. You might think I'm some back-country hick, but I'm proud of where I come from."

Everett stood back, watching and listening, partially amused but also somewhat concerned, as Adeline paced back and forth in her bare feet across the brick walkway of the Dougherty's stately garden. It had taken him less than a minute of observing the pretty, unpretentious girl to realize she was airing her mind, spewing out all the things she could've said to her cousin.

But hadn't.

Instead, after Shannon made her derogatory comment about Southern girls in front of the group, Adeline had been the bigger person and bit her tongue. Not that she cowered by any means. Or at least not that he had seen. No, she held her head high. Even when the others laughed and then laid down their mallets and walked arm-in-arm up to the terrace, leaving her behind. As if she wasn't worth giving another thought to.

He, however, had been noticing lately that thoughts of Adeline wouldn't leave his mind so easily. Glancing over his shoulder as he trailed behind the others, he watched how she quietly gathered up her shoes from under a nearby shrub. Then, without putting them on—perhaps her small way of getting back at Shannon—she'd followed her own path, as she always seemed to do, marching off toward the garden.

Totally intrigued, he couldn't help himself. Falling back from the group, he stealthily headed in Adeline's direction. There, in the middle of every kind of flower and scent, she appeared perfectly at home to voice everything on her mind.

"And let me tell you another thing, Cousin," she continued, this time even more animated, shaking a warning finger in the air like a pastor in a pulpit. "You sure don't want to be in the habit of judgin' others like you do. No, you don't."

Her finger stopped wagging long enough for her head to shake back and forth. "Maybe you don't know it, or maybe you weren't raised to be God-fearing like me, but our heavenly Father sure doesn't take too kindly to us judgin' each other. Not when we're all His children and equal in His eyes—whether you think so or not."

Her intense lashing out at Shannon in one breath, and then in the next, her good-hearted gesture of turning the other cheek and trying to bring Shannon's lost soul into the fold, made him smile. And chuckle.

At the sound, Adeline turned around and looked at him. Mouth agape, obviously shocked by his presence, her face grew more flushed by the second. A perfect match for the cluster of pink rosebushes bursting with blooms nearby.

He could feel his ears heat as well, the observer caught by the observee. "I, uh—" He cleared his throat. "I hope I'm not interrupting anything." He flashed what he knew from prior encounters with the opposite sex to be his most captivating smile.

"Why, no. You're not interrupting anything, because I'm quite finished now." She'd gathered her wits quickly then smoothed her dress, folding her hands primly over her skirt. "I do believe I've run out of things to say."

"You're sure? Because I don't mind waiting if there's more you want to vocalize." He grinned again. A very big grin.

Why on earth was he working so hard to charm her? It wasn't exactly like he was hurting for attention from females these days.

This girl, however, with her natural beauty and down-to-earth ways made him curious. More curious, he realized, than he'd ever been about a female before now. That's why he'd followed her to the garden. His intention wasn't to rescue her. Far from it. From what he had seen, she could manage on her own. He just wanted to learn more about the girl who seemed to have a love and flair for living that the rest of them, even given all their wealth, didn't possess.

"In fact. . ." He paused, growing more contrite. "I feel as if I owe you an apology."

"Whatever for?" She looked honestly puzzled.

"When I sided with you on the croquet field, Shannon grew even testier with you than she had been. I do believe she had a problem with me agreeing with you."

"Ah, yes. No doubt about that." She nodded her pretty head vigorously. "But don't you worry. I won't hold it against you." The eyes he knew to be blue-green twinkled at him. "I can't rightly imagine Shannon will either. I don't suppose you'll be left off any of her invitation lists because of it."

"You think not?" He furrowed his brows with mock concern.

She caught on to his act and smiled. "I'm sure not. But I've got to tell you—" Her tone went from jesting to instantly sincere. "I do appreciate you being the voice of reason out there today. It was mighty kind of you, Everett."

She suddenly looked self-conscious as she tucked a stray strand of golden hair behind her ear. Because she was thanking him? Or because it was the first time she'd ever addressed him by name? He pretended not to notice her discomfit.

"You're quite welcome, Adeline. Or should I call you Bruiser? You're quite a ruffian with a croquet mallet in your hand."

Her eyes glistened even more. When her unbridled laughter erupted, he felt like he'd won a prize. "I think ya better not. Please don't, in fact. You'll only get me into more trouble all over again."

With that, she sat down on the wrought iron bench at the edge of the walkway, appearing to relax in his company. He was certainly glad about that and happy that he'd made the decision to follow her.

Although when he thought about it, there really hadn't been much of a decision to make. Had there?

If she didn't sit down, Adeline thought she might just plain keel over. Her legs were as shaky as anything. She'd seen Everett Brighton plenty of times and in plenty of situations, but never like this. Never so close and never just the two of them. Alone.

Instead of joining the others, he had followed her to the garden. But why? And now he was brushing off some leaves and dust from the other end of the bench, acting as if he wasn't about to make an exit from her flowery haven any time soon.

"Mind if I join you?" he inquired politely. Though by clearing off the section of bench, hadn't he already made up his mind what he intended to do?

"Of course not," she said as easily as she could manage. Just being so close to him had her insides swirling madly like a whirling tornado whipping across the prairies.

"Are you sure you don't want any of Shannon's lemonade?" she asked, thinking the offer might dissuade him from staying too long. Not that she exactly wanted him to leave. Why, he was the handsomest of all the young men who came visiting at the Dougherty house. It wasn't just the pleasing contrast between his nearly black hair and his clear blue eyes either, both shining, one like night and one like day. It was the kindness in his eyes and the humor in his words that could draw a girl in.

Which all should've made her relax, but being around him made her nervous for other reasons too. She didn't even want to think what Shannon would have to say if she discovered them there together. He was, after all, Shannon's future. Her love to be.

"I can get plenty of lemonade at the restaurant, and I do. I'm fine." He settled back deeper into the bench.

Right away the seat she always lingered and lounged on felt as if it had decreased in size significantly, just like her intake of breath.

"Pretty place." He glanced around. "I don't think I've ever noticed it before."

"I think I'm the only one who comes here. Well, me and Mr. Henry, who takes care of the grounds and garden. He's very nice and teaches me about the plants and all he does to take care of them."

"So, you come here often then?"

"I sure do. I find it peaceful. Like a little piece of home for me." She sighed, gazing straight ahead at the plants. Anywhere except at him.

"Does Arkansas have a lot of flowers?"

His question shouldn't have taken her so much by surprise. Of course, he'd have knowledge of her circumstances and where she came from. How wouldn't he have heard? But that he cared to remember, that was something unexpected. She couldn't help but look his way.

"Why, no. Not so much like this. Mr. Henry laid out this garden," she explained. "He told me all about why he put roses here and zinnias there and where the lupine grows best. Whereas, back home I was surrounded mostly by wildflowers, shooting up in all kinds of places. I used to love to take walks in the woods and fields to see them all."

"And just by chance were some of those walks in your bare feet?"

She steadied her eyes on his to see if he was mocking her or truly simply asking her. When there wasn't a speck of judgment in his eyes, she nodded eagerly. "Definitely. A lot of them."

"How did your mother feel about that?" This time his forehead creased, but with true concern, causing her to laugh.

"Oh, if only you knew my mama. If you did, you'd know nothing tickled her more," she said, remembering those special times with her mother. "Sometimes Mama would take off her shoes and join me."

"You must miss her," he said, warmly. Sincerely. Causing the lump of emotion that she'd grown so accustomed to, to rise in the back of her throat.

"I truly do. I can't even tell you how much." Her voice quivered. "Some days when I'm longing most for her, I sneak down into the kitchen to visit Miss Clara. I know I'm not supposed to. I'm not supposed to mingle with the help or to cook. But being with Miss Clara as she goes about her work is a great comfort to me, just like this garden is. It's what I remember. What I used to do with Mama. Cook. Bake. Enjoy the outdoors."

"Hmm." He shook his head, seeming lost for words for a moment. "It sounds like you've had to make a lot of adjustments."

"A few. Yes." She fiddled with her hands in her lap. "But I don't want you to think I'm not grateful. When Mama passed, it was very kind of her brother and his wife to take me in the way they did. They sure didn't have to. They've been so generous and have bought me so much too. So many dresses and—"

"Let me guess. . ." He made a show of ducking his head to peek at her bare feet and the pointed shoes lying close by. "Shoes?" He glanced back up at her, his eyes glimmering.

"Oh, yes. And shoes." She smiled, appreciating his attempt to lighten their talk. "So many I've never stopped to count them all. Although I sure don't know why I need so many. I've gone most of my life with one pair. Or one pair at a time anyway."

"Well, I don't have a sister, only a brother. But I guess most women like a variety of shoes. I hear Clancy Baker does a great business selling them."

"I'm sure you've heard right. What I've learned over the past year is that every social event seems to require a different pair of shoes." She grimaced. "But honestly? My skin just doesn't feel right in a lot of them."

"Or your feet either?" His lips twitched.

"Are you making fun of me?"

He broke into a full-fledged smile. "Now would I do that?"

She shrugged. "I don't rightly know," she answered. However, deep inside, she knew he was very much teasing. Good-naturedly. Even from this short conversation, she was quickly getting used to his sense of humor. And enjoying all the smiles he could so easily draw out of her with just a few words. It made her feel like she wanted to confide in him even more.

With the onslaught of that startling realization, she abruptly changed the subject. "But I've been doing all the talking, and you all the listening. How about you? Do you have a special place you like to go to relax?"

"Not currently." He frowned. "But while you were talking, it reminded me of something I used to do. Before I got overly busy with work and social obligations."

"You mean as a young boy?"

He nodded, his face lighting up as he recalled the distant memory. "Yes. I'd say from the time I was around seven years old until I was about twelve. There was a tree at the edge of our property. The perfect climbing tree. Whenever I wanted to be alone—get away from my nanny or my brother—or just things, I'd climb as high up in that tree as I could. I'd sit in the branches for hours where no one could find me."

"It's good to have a place like that, don't you think? Just with you and God and nature?"

He nodded again. "Here's to special places." He reached out and plucked a rose from the nearest bush. "And also to special people."

For a moment, a very surprised moment, she thought surely he was going to hand the flower to her. But before she could find out, a voice suddenly snapped like the crack of a whip across the quiet space.

"Everett! What are you doing? Have you lost your way?" Shannon stood there, hands flying to her hips. Although to Adeline's way of thinking, the confused expression on her cousin's face asked an entirely different question. Had Everett lost his senses? Being there with *her* the way he was? When he had a better option? As in Shannon?

"Not at all. I wanted to—"

Adeline wasn't sure what Everett was about to say. Before he could utter another word, and perhaps get her in deeper with Shannon, she interrupted with an explanation. A false one, God forgive her!

"He brought my shoes to me." She bent over, picked up the heeled pair, and held them in the air for Shannon to see. "From the lawn. I'd forgotten them."

"Well, of course you did," Shannon said snidely. Then dropping her arms to her side, she changed her tone, sounding sweet as Miss Clara's peach pie. "Everett, you are so very thoughtful. Now you must come so I can reward you for your troubles. I have a tall glass of iced lemonade, waiting just for you."

"Yes, you need to go get cooled off." Adeline glanced at Everett, hoping to urge him along with her eyes. "Thank you again for fetching my shoes. It was mighty kind of you. Why, I'm slipping them on this very minute."

She bent over, taking her time putting on her shoes, hoping he would take her hint. She held her breath and finally let it out when she felt him get up from the bench and follow Shannon from the garden.

Once she had her shoes on, she walked over to the stone wall that ran all around the garden. Peering over it, she watched as the two of them sauntered over the lawns to the terrace.

267

If appearances told all, Adeline had to admit, Shannon and Everett did look like a match. Like the roses and baby's breath that Mr. Henry planted alongside each other, one complemented the other. They looked like a pair who belonged together.

Chapter 3

Everett, your shenanigans have put your father and me in a most embarrassing situation. And there you are, leafing through today's mail, acting as if you don't even care what others have to say."

His mother had caught him off guard, verbally attacking him the minute he walked through the front door. Tossing the mail back onto the entryway table, he sighed. Not exactly what he wanted to come home to after a long day of work.

"Mother, you have me wondering if Mr. Alexander Graham Bell has done us a disservice after all. Ever since that telephone was put into our house, you've become more interested in what our neighbors have to say."

He made a show of shaking his head in a disappointed way, hoping his blunt remark would put an end to his mother's nagging. Put the focus on her bad habits instead of what she considered to be his. Mostly so he could enjoy the rest of his evening in peace.

However, his comment only served to fuel her irritation with him even more.

"That is not so, Everett," she said, eyes wide at his audacity. "I will have you know, I did not hear about your rendezvous in the garden with Shannon Dougherty's cousin by way of a telephone call. It was from Martha Dougherty herself—from her very lips—when I saw her at women's club this morning."

Rendezvous? He had to smile at that. Such a surprising and shocking twist on what had merely been an innocent meeting and conversation. Although. . .it did leave something to the imagination, didn't it? Now that his mother mentioned it, a rendezvous with Adeline McClain did sound like an interesting suggestion.

"It was hardly a rendezvous," he objected. "I was curious, and wandered off briefly. I'd never been in the Dougherty's garden."

"Exactly. Or ours either for that matter." His mother's eyes narrowed at him the same way they always did when she caught him up to something. "So, I rather think it was Shannon's cousin and not the floral fragrances that drew you there. Which hurt Shannon's feelings immensely and left Mrs. Dougherty very much displeased."

"And you in a dither." He grimaced apologetically, attempting to help his cause.

It must have worked. His mother's tone softened some. "Everett, you know very well that it has always been thought you and Shannon are a perfect match. We think very highly of the Dougherty family and feel the two of you would do quite well together."

"Yes, well. . ." He shrugged, keeping his reply intentionally vague. He wasn't about to get involved in that conversation right now. Walking away, he scuffled toward the parlor, partly because he was tired and wanted to sit down. But mostly to escape the same talk about him and Shannon that he'd been hearing since he was a teen.

Settling into a chair, he loosened his tie, hoping his mother's little talk was over. But he feared it wasn't when she followed behind, sitting down in the chair across from him.

She was a kind woman, his mother was, and very well-meaning. But so rigid when it came to the expectations of their social rank. It seemed to him she lived in constant fear of falling out of the good graces of other people—even those she didn't know. Eyeing her worried face, a tinge of sadness crossed over him as much for his mother as for himself. She'd never be the joyful, carefree mother like the "mama" Adeline described to him in the garden.

Or would she?

"You know, Mother, I've been thinking. . ." He sat up from his slouching position, making the effort to lean forward. "What would you say about the two of us—you and me—taking a walk sometime?" he ventured. "Perhaps through the grove of trees that run at the edge of our estate? Or we could stroll through the public gardens if that suits you better." He paused and frowned. "I don't think we've spent time like that before. Or at least not since I was a young boy. Wouldn't that be nice? Even a rowboat ride on the pond near—"

"Really, Everett? You're talking about a walk at a time like this?" Her expression was a mixture of hurt and frustration. "You're avoiding everything I've been speaking of. Please listen to me, will you?"

So much for trying to initiate a warm, fuzzy time together. He let out another weary sigh. "Actually, Mother, I've heard what you're saying plenty of times."

"I don't believe you have, Son. Or at least you're not behaving as if you have. So, I shall repeat myself." She inhaled as if trying to tame her temper then exhaled a deep breath before continuing. "Your father and I—we have expectations."

Ah, there was that word again. The one he'd been hearing for years.

"We'd hoped we could pin those expectations on your older brother, but of course, you know all the problems with Garrett. His carousing. His drinking. He's been a total embarrassment, not to mention an extreme disappointment. You're our only hope, Everett." Her eyes pleaded. "All of our faith is in you. You're the one who will be taking over our business."

Funny, how that had always been said, yet no one had ever asked his thoughts on the matter.

"We count on you to uphold our family's good name."

"And haven't I been doing that, Mother?" He could feel his temper flicker as his voice rose. "Haven't I been handling my responsibilities at the restaurant? Overseeing the staff, making sure things are running smoothly?"

"Yes, and all we're asking is that you don't do anything foolish to hamper that. Especially nothing to rouse anger from the Doughertys. You know William Dougherty has powerful friends in powerful places."

It wasn't in him to bring added worry or stress to his mother. He knew enough of that trickled down onto her from his father, and she got socked with it plenty of times from his brother. As a result, he'd always been the "good" son.

As much as he wanted to argue that because of that fact she should trust his judgment—which included having the right to choose which girl he spoke to and when—he let the issue go. His mother apparently wasn't open to any kind of understanding at this moment, and after a day hard at work, he wasn't in the mood to protest. Instead he conceded. At least outwardly.

"Of course, Mother," he said tersely. "I'll try not to disappoint you." And then a thought suddenly hit him. Something to placate her, and please him as well.

"I'll tell you what. Instead of sending over our delivery boy to the Doughertys with items they ordered for Shannon's birthday gala, I'll take them myself tomorrow. Pop my head in and say hello."

There was no denying the glint of joy that instantly sprang to his mother's eyes. "That's an excellent idea, Everett." She clapped her hands. "A great excuse for you to drop by and visit with Shannon for a bit."

He nodded agreeably, but felt slightly guilty as he did. Shannon wasn't the person he hoped to visit at all.

"You're telling me your aunt and uncle had words with you about going barefoot and not behaving like a proper lady of the house?" Miss Clara's hands stilled over the bowl of dough she was stirring and stared at Adeline, her eyes as round as the morning's sun.

"I know. It's silly, isn't it?" Adeline leaned over the kitchen's sizeable butcher block table and plucked a strawberry from the bowl there. "Why is it so wrong for me to enjoy warm, lush grass under my feet? It was only a game of croquet." She shrugged, recalling how sternly they had reprimanded her. "They just don't understand."

"And I don't either, missy."

"Beg pardon? I thought you said ya'll had been barefooting before and liked it very much."

Adeline gave an incredulous look to the woman who reminded her so much of her mama. Though a different race and different color, so often Miss Clara felt like the closest thing she had to real kin. Her shoulders were ample and welcoming, a soft place to lean into in troubled times as Adeline had experienced in months past. Her dark eyes were always warm and affectionate, even with no words spoken. But now Cook's shoulders lifted and squared noticeably. Her gaze narrowed, sharpened. "I mean that I don't understand you." She frowned.

Adeline pulled her head back. "Excuse me?" she repeated.

"I appreciate you are your own person, Miss Adeline. I really do. And I would miss your visits very much if you stopped dropping by the kitchen. You fill a very special place in my heart. But, honey," she said softly, "I'm afraid you're going to get yourself into deeper trouble with your aunt and uncle if you don't try to conform at least a little more. Starting with being here in the kitchen with me. It's not the place you should be." She glanced around and quieted her voice even more. "Associatin' with the help is another thing ladies of your stature aren't supposed to do neither. And you well know it."

"Oh, well, about that. . ." Adeline waved a hand and stood up straight, unable to keep a self-satisfied smile from spreading across her face. "I outsmarted them."

Miss Clara quirked a curious brow. "Oh, you did now, did you? You outwitted your very well-educated uncle and your sophisticated aunt?"

"Absolutely. I mentioned that if they wanted me to act like a lady of the house, I needed more practice. I asked if they wouldn't mind my starting with the kitchen, being more in charge. I said I could check in on you and the staff, making sure you do your jobs correctly."

At that, Miss Clara's other brow raised and her chest puffed in indignation. "And just what would you know about that? About running *my* kitchen?"

"Just everything that you want to teach me," Adeline answered quickly with a demure grin.

Miss Clara laughed wholeheartedly. "Oh, Adeline. I'm going to miss you when you're gone."

"Where am I going?"

"Why, someday you'll run off and get married. Have a home of your own."

"Married? I'm not thinking that'll be happening any time soon." Especially when the young men who came around would barely talk to her. Well, all except for—Everett. Unbelievably, her cheeks began to tingle just at the thought of him. Hastily, she worked to shift her mind. "How are things going with Olivia's wedding plans? Did ya'll finish her dress yet?"

Miss Clara's eyes immediately lit up at the question. Adeline knew how excited she was about her daughter's upcoming wedding and how thrilled she was with Olivia's husband-to-be. "Oh, I have to admit I go home all tired from working here, but then you wouldn't believe it, missy. As soon as I pick up that wedding dress and start to stitch, why, a whole new energy seeps into my tired bones. Hours later, I have to force myself to stop so I can get some sleep."

"I bet it's a beauty. I hope I get to see it finished," Adeline replied. Yet, even as she said the words, a hollow feeling settled over every part of her. With no mama, no papa, when and if the day ever really did come for her to marry, who would be there for her? To help her plan the special day? To stitch a dress for her? To give her away?

As she watched Miss Clara go about her business, she tried to shake the onslaught of sad thoughts streaming through her head, breaking her heart. She was glad when a rustling at the back door distracted her.

"I'll see who it is," she offered.

Several steps later, as she stood at the back entry, she couldn't have been more surprised by what she saw. There was Everett with boxes stacked up to his chin, trying to knock on the door with his elbow.

Seeing how he was struggling with the load in his arms, she hurriedly opened the door. As she did, she felt an embarrassed sort of warmth rising inside her. How thankful she was that he couldn't read minds! If he could, he'd know how much she'd been thinking about him the past couple of days since his visit to the garden.

Of course, one conversation didn't mean a thing, she knew. It only meant she was silly for thinking about him so much, going over their conversations again and again in her head. But she hadn't been able to stop herself. She also hadn't been able to forget how being so close to him right at first had her heart beating as crazily as a flag flapping wildly in high winds. It had taken a while, a little time, and his deep-blue eyes looking so kindly into hers, for her to relax some.

Although right at the very moment, seeing him again, her heartbeat overreacted once more, picking up its pace, getting completely off rhythm.

"Special delivery," he greeted her with a grin.

Oh, seeing him was special indeed. She tried to concentrate on the load in his arms and not how that smile of his made her feel. "An especially heavy delivery, from the looks of it," she said. "Want to set the boxes over there?" She pointed to the butcher block.

As he made his way to the center of the room, she followed alongside him wishing she could be of help.

"Is all of this for Shannon's party?" she asked as he hoisted the boxes onto the table.

Preparations for Shannon's birthday gala had been taking place all around the house lately. Shannon and Aunt Martha had been especially busy, making endless trips to various shops and boutiques for weeks, trying to find the perfect gown for Shannon's event.

"I'm assuming it's the soda water and other drinks for the party," Miss Clara chimed in. "Right, Mr. Brighton?"

"That's exactly what it is." Everett brushed some dust from his pants legs. "How are you doing?" he asked Miss Clara.

"Busy as always," she answered. "But I'm doing well. Thank you for asking."

"You're most welcome. I'm glad to hear it." He nodded politely before turning back to Adeline. "I thought I'd bring the boxes by myself. Although now I'm thinking I may have to give Jonathan Simpson a raise. . ."

Adeline noticed Miss Clara give her what seemed to be a conspiratorial wink behind Everett's back but wasn't quite sure why. She also wasn't sure who Everett was referring to. "Jonathan Simpson?" She looked at him, puzzled.

"He's our usual delivery person," he explained. "I didn't realize how heavy those crates can be. I'm probably not paying him enough to manhandle those things."

"Is he out sick today? Your deliveryman?"

"No. I just. . .I thought I'd stop by."

"Oh." If he was dropping in, she assumed he was doing so to see Shannon. As her aunt and uncle had explained in their talk with her, in terms they thought she might understand, Shannon was their "show" pony. And Adeline? Well, she was the kind of pony who ran wild.

Obviously, Adeline preferred to think of herself as a carefree, free-spirited creature rather than a wild one. "Wild" left a bad taste in one's mouth—even her own. But apparently that's how her aunt and uncle saw her. They also told her that she, too, could be a "show" pony one day if only she would follow in her cousin's footsteps.

There was no telling them that God made all kinds of ponies, with different personalities and reasons for being on His earth. And that maybe He didn't want her to be a show pony after all. She could tell they certainly didn't want to hear any of that from her.

"I can go get Shannon for you," she told Everett. "I think she's in the front parlor. I believe I heard her playing piano earlier."

"No." He laid a hand on her arm to stop her. "Actually, I—well, I remembered what you said about liking the kitchen and that you come here as often as you can, so I . . ." He paused and looked around as if not sure he should go on.

Was he meaning he was there to see her? Not Shannon? Could that be?

Confused and feeling awkward, she tried to quickly think of something to make them both feel more at ease. "Miss Clara baked some mighty delicious gingersnaps this morning. Would you like to try one or two?"

Before she could cross the kitchen and reach into the jar of cookies, the kitchen door squeaked open. There stood Shannon with Aunt Martha right behind her.

"There you are!" Shannon's eyes lit on Everett as she and her skirts waltzed into the room.

"We noticed your carriage from the parlor window and kept waiting for you to knock on the front door," Aunt Martha remarked.

"I had parcels to bring in," Everett explained. "The back door seemed most logical."

"Of course. For the gala." Aunt Martha nodded.

"It's so nice of you to deliver them personally." Shannon tilted her head, giving Everett an adoring look. Yet he appeared more irritated than pleased by her doting. To Adeline, his entire demeanor seemed to change.

"Yes, well—busy day at the restaurant, so I need to get going." He gave a polite nod to each of them and started to go.

"You can't stay a bit longer?" Shannon asked sweetly.

"Shannon just learned a new song on the piano. It's quite a difficult piece too," Aunt Martha added. "One I'm sure you'd like to hear."

"Sounds wonderful," Everett said, but Adeline knew he didn't mean it. She could tell by the flatness in his voice. "But I need to get back."

"Of course, Everett." Shannon sighed wistfully. "You're an important man, and I understand completely."

"You are coming to Shannon's party, aren't you?" Aunt Martha inquired, though her voice sounded slightly demanding.

"The party?" He gave a sideways glance at Adeline. "Sure. Wouldn't miss it."

"That's good, because I'm expecting you to be my first dance of the evening," Shannon announced instead of asked, truly her mother's daughter.

To which Everett grimaced. "I'm not much of a dancer." He shook his head. "Now, the O'Malley boys, they're the ones you want to ask. They're far better than I am."

Aunt Martha acted as if she hadn't heard him. "Yes," she said, "we're expecting Shannon's first dance to be with you. And many more after that, Everett. It's going to be a wonderful evening. For both of you."

"Yes, well. . ." Everett's jaw clenched. In Adeline's estimation, he suddenly didn't look all that happy that he'd made the delivery himself. "I need to get back to work," he repeated.

"Tell your parents we said hello." Aunt Martha got in the last word, because Everett didn't say a thing. His only reply was a half-hearted wave goodbye which he delivered over his shoulder.

Chapter 4

The gala in Shannon's honor had been going on for the past half hour, yet Adeline still stood gazing in wonderment at everything around her. She knew Mr. Henry and the other groundskeepers had been working for days to prepare for the event, but she never imagined their labors would produce such a breathtaking sight.

It didn't even matter that only the slightest sliver of a crescent moon graced the summer skies. The Dougherty's lawn and brick patio were perfectly lit up, glimmering romantically with lanterns of all sizes and shapes placed everywhere. Men and women in finer clothing than she'd ever seen before waltzed on the painted black-and-white checkered dance floor topping the lawn. Other couples strolled arm-in-arm through the floral-trimmed trellis up to the patio where the crystal and sterling silverware that adorned the tables sparkled like jewels in the glow of shimmering candlelight. Inside the circle of candles, assorted roses from the Dougherty's garden poured from slender vases, at least two feet tall, creating lavish centerpieces.

Shannon may not have been a princess in the truest sense of the word, but she was Bostonian royalty in a way, and every detail of her party supported that fact. For at least the third time, Adeline sighed appreciatively at the beautiful surroundings.

"You look very nice tonight, Adeline." Her aunt was suddenly at her side, jarring her thoughts. "I think that dress suits you well."

"Why thank you," she replied, smiling inwardly. Why wouldn't her aunt think the dress suited her? She'd been the one to select it, hadn't she? "You look beautiful, Aunt Martha, and elegant," she said truthfully, admiring her aunt's exquisite lace gown and perfectly coiffed hair. "But then you always do."

Her aunt peered down the bridge of her nose and smiled. "Yes, well. . .you must be so uncomfortable among us since you haven't been bred for such things, Adeline," she said, tucking one of Adeline's stray hairs behind her ear. "Poor girl."

Her aunt's harsh words caught her so off guard she wobbled uneasily in her tight, heeled shoes. Which led her to remembering how many times her aunt had also warned her not to be going barefoot at the party—as if she'd even consider doing so at such a highfalutin event. She started to protest her aunt's comment, to tell her what she thought true good breeding consisted of, but then recalled her mother's advice. "If you can't say something nice," her mama would always say, "don't say anything at all." And she couldn't think of something nice, so. . .

Obviously, her aunt wasn't aware of her niece's discomfort. She let out a wistful sigh. "Ah, lovely, isn't it?"

Of course, that was one thing Adeline could agree with her about. "Yes. It's all beautiful. The lights. The roses. The trellis."

Her aunt chuckled beside her. "Yes, that's all pretty too. But I was speaking of Shannon and Everett."

She nodded to the pair on the dance floor where Shannon was giving Everett her usual adoring gaze and standing oh-so-close to him. At least in Adeline's opinion she was far too close.

"Perfect, aren't they?" Her aunt practically swooned.

It wasn't like she hadn't noticed the two of them together. Who could ignore them? They were an extremely attractive couple, easily drawing attention. But she'd tried to keep her mind and eyes elsewhere—like on Mr. Henry's handiwork—because of the feeling stirring up inside of her. A feeling she wasn't accustomed to. Plain old jealousy.

"I think I'll get a cup of punch." Her mouth suddenly felt dry.

"Be careful not to spill it on your dress," her aunt warned. "And remember how we taught you to walk in your shoes? One foot in front of the other. No teetering, or our guests may suspect you've been drinking something more than punch."

Again, her mother's words rang out in her mind. Keeping mum, with barely a nod in reply, Adeline turned, making her way to the table laden with drinks and appetizers at the edge of the dance floor. As she did, she noticed a bespectacled man about her own age who was off to the side, looking just as uncomfortable in his fancy attire as she was suddenly feeling. She almost made a path toward him to invite him to dance, but then immediately thought better of it. It wouldn't be proper, would it, in this environment? A girl asking a boy? And this evening was about all things proper, wasn't it?

Picking up a delicate crystal cup, she had to smile musing about how shocked her aunt would be if she made such a forward invitation. She was just about to dip the ladle into the fruity punch when a male voice—*his* voice—came over her shoulder, shaking her from her thoughts. Shaking her, period.

"Here. Allow me."

Everett's hand brushed against hers stirring a warmth within her as she let him remove the ladle from her grasp. "You look much too pretty to be lifting even a finger." He winked at her.

"Why, Mr. Brighton." She caught her breath. "You do say the kindest things."

He eyed her quizzically. "I thought we were on a first-name basis."

She smiled. "I was simply trying to be as formal as the occasion."

"Then, Miss McClain. . ." He took the crystal cup that hadn't yet touched her lips and set it back on the table. "May I formally ask you to share a dance with me?"

She'd been watching him song after song, wondering what it would be like to share a dance with him. But not imagining she ever would. Yet here he was asking her, and in the most flattering way.

He bowed deeply, one hand at his waistline, the other sweeping outward in a grand gesture. Then he stood up straight, offering his arm to her.

She hoped in the dim lights that he couldn't see the way the warm flushes she was experiencing were surely reddening her face. "I've got to warn you, I'm not much of a fancy dancer," she admitted. "But I promise to try not to step on your toes. Not too much anyway."

"It's okay." He smiled. "It's my job to lead you."

"Oh?" She put a hand on her hip.

He laughed. "Is that a problem? Me leading?"

"Well. . ." She hesitated, biting back a smile. "It's not like I'm some farm animal that needs a nose ring and leading around, you know."

"Trust me. I know." He grinned, holding up his right hand. "I promise to only lead on the dance floor."

She'd been teasing him all along. After all, when she looked up into his kind eyes, she knew she would let him lead her just about anywhere.

"Okay, then," she conceded. "I'd like that very much, thank you." She held out her hand, but then just as quickly withdrew it. All kidding aside, she was suddenly feeling timid. "Oh, Everett. I don't rightly know about this."

"About dancing? Or—your cousin?"

He did know her well, didn't he?

She leaned her head toward the opposite side of the dance floor where Shannon was standing with a group of her friends.

Everett's lips tightened. "Well, you shouldn't be concerned. I danced the first

279

dance with Shannon as I was asked to. And a few after that," he pointed out. "I've lived up to my promise. Now you need to live up to yours."

"My promise?" She frowned.

"Yes. Your promise to try not to step on my feet. And I mean to hold you to that." His eyes met hers as he offered her the crook of his arm once more.

This time she took it and let him lead her onto the checkered squares. The clarinet quintet had sounded wonderful while she was standing on the outskirts of the dance floor. But now, with Everett's hand on her waist, hers on his broad shoulder, and their free hands joined together as one, the music sounded more glorious than she could've ever imagined. Like she was floating in a dream. One she didn't ever want to wake up from. . .

"So far, you've been keeping your promise," he whispered in her ear, his breath feeling temptingly warm.

"Maybe because you're a good lead. On the dance floor," she added, and noticed his smile. How she enjoyed making him smile that way. "This is so different for me," she admitted, looking up into his eyes.

"How so?" His head tilted to one side.

"I'm more familiar with square dancing than waltzing."

"Hmm. I don't think square dancing would work too well at this event."

She laughed. "I believe you're right. It's more suitable for a barn-raising party. My parents held one once," she shared. "When I was ten."

"Well, I'm sure you were a cute square dancer then, just like you're a pretty waltz partner now." His gaze intensified. "You have the kind of beauty that fits in anywhere you are."

His eyes seemed to skim her hair, her face, her eyes. All the while, his hand growing tighter around hers, his arm pulling her closer to him.

The feel of his touch, the very nearness of him, stole her breath for a moment. She wobbled in her heeled shoes and he caught her, his hand deftly glued to her waist, fitting there so perfectly. Righting her. Leaving her trembling from the top of her swept-up hair to the glittering shoes covering her toes.

She looked up into his eyes, realizing she'd never had someone touch her, notice her, look at her that way before. She staggered again, and his reaction was more of the same. He pulled her even closer.

"Oh, Everett. . ." she whispered.

"Yes?" He gazed down at her.

"I think. . ." She shifted her eyes to her feet. "I think something is wrong with my shoe."

Though he hated to admit it, it was probably a good thing Adeline's shoe was causing her problems. Otherwise, given one more minute, he may have done something improper and impulsive when she looked up at him. Like kiss her sweet-looking lips. That's how good she felt in his arms.

"What do you say we head over there?" He nodded to the closest place for her to limp to, a wooden bench perched under a tree at the edge of the lawn. There, they could sit and face the garden she was so fond of, out of the way of the other dancers and out of sight as well. Not giving anyone a reason to be talking about them.

"That would be fine." Adeline nodded.

Waltzing her to the side of the crowded dance floor, he discreetly slipped her off, onto the lawn, hoping no one would be the wiser. With his arm securely locked around her waist, he could feel her lean into him as he helped her hobble toward their destination.

Once seated, she sighed. "I'm not sure I even want to look. These were new shoes Aunt Martha just bought for me. She's going to be terribly upset."

"It's not like you tried to damage them," he countered, though he knew what Adeline was saying was true. Her aunt wasn't the most understanding person. "Maybe it's not too bad. Here, let me have a look." He started to slip off the bench and kneel at her feet. Something he wouldn't typically do for just any girl.

"Don't be silly, Everett." She caught his arm, pulling him back onto the bench. Then she reached down, slipping off both heels.

"This wouldn't be your excuse to get out of these contraptions, would it?" he teased. "Although I wouldn't blame you," he said, studying the pointy shoes in her hands. "How do you wear those things?"

"It's the ribbon." She held up the shoe in question. "It's broken. A huge part of it is totally gone."

"A ribbon isn't such a big deal, is it?"

"It is when it's decorated with jewels." Adeline groaned. "Aunt Martha isn't going to be happy about this."

"But I'm sure your feet have to feel much better." He tried to cajole her back into her former good mood.

"Oh, they do." She sighed. "For sure, they do." She held up her feet, wiggling her toes. "Though I have to tell you, even with my feet in pain, I really enjoyed our dance, Everett. Have you always been a good dancer?"

He laughed at her naiveté. "See, that's where you're wrong. I'm just an okay dancer. I pretended to be better than I am to lure you to the dance floor."

"I sure hope that—"

He had seen that expression on her face before. The worried one. The concerned one. He put a finger up to her lips to stop her from saying more.

"Don't even say your cousin's name, Addy."

The lips beneath his touch began to spread into a smile. Relieved, he pulled his hand away.

"Mama used to call me Addy," she told him.

"It's a natural fit for you, I think."

At the mention of her mother, he almost shared that she had inspired him to ask his mother about taking a walk sometime. But then, remembering the outcome of that conversation, he decided not to bring it up. It wasn't something he really wanted to think about right now anyway. Besides, he'd rather talk about Adeline. Listen to her stories.

"So, fill me in about the barn-raising dance," he said. "Just in case I ever get invited to one, I'd like to know what I'm in for. How to act. Dress." He teased her and felt pleased when she laughed.

"I sincerely doubt that's an invite you'll ever receive. Not in the world you live in."

"Well, just on the off chance." He smiled. "Besides, I'd really like to know." Which was true. Lately he found he enjoyed learning everything he could about her.

"Okay, then, I'll tell you." She sat up straighter and turned toward him. "Compared to this event. . .well, it's just different. To start with, it's held inside a barn. A new barn that smells unbelievably good, or at least good to me. Like fresh hay and brand-new wood. So right off, it's not as fancy as this party here. There's music. But mostly fiddles instead of violins and a cello and a clarinet and all. And people don't go buying a bunch of new dresses and pants for just one night. They put on their Sunday best instead. And there's lots of food. But it's food everyone brings a little of so there's a lot for everyone. If that makes sense."

"It does." He nodded. "And you said you were ten. So that means children come with their parents?"

"They sure can," she said.

"Sounds like it really stuck out in your mind."

"Oh, yes. It's one of my favorite memories. It's the last time I saw my mama and daddy looking so happy. The next week, my daddy left early one morning to go hunting and—well, Mama and I never saw him again." Her lips trembled slightly, but she pursed them together tightly as if forcing herself not to shed a tear.

"I'm so sorry, Addy." He placed a hand over hers. "I shouldn't have pushed you to talk about it."

"No, don't be sorry." She gave him a forgiving look. "You didn't know. Besides, I like talking about home and thinking about it. That night was so special for me. A great memory. Unforgettable. I got to dance with my daddy." Her voice broke. "He put my feet up on his boots and clomped around. I thought I was the luckiest girl in the world. Mama and Daddy were so happy. Gazing into each other's eyes, dancing like the night would never end. It was magical and—"

Before she could finish her thought, Everett felt a hand clamp down on his shoulder. Startled, he jumped in his seat.

"Everett!" his mother whispered loudly. "What do you think you're doing with this—this—" She didn't finish her sentence, but she didn't need to. The implication was clear to him, and apparently to Adeline too. He felt her stiffen beside him.

"I don't know where your mind is taking you, Mother, but it's nowhere good." He placed a strong hand over hers and removed it from his shoulder. "I'm merely helping a young *lady*," he emphasized the word, "in distress just as any proper gentleman would do."

"Helping? Do you think anything about this situation is helping anything?" his mother nearly screeched.

"As I was about to tell you, Miss Adeline's shoe came apart, and she was stumbling on the dance floor. She needed to sit down."

Just as he was explaining himself, he heard Adeline explaining herself. To her aunt. Who had apparently snuck up around the other side of the tree with Shannon in tow.

"I'm only barefoot because I had a problem with my shoes, Aunt Martha."

"Oh, it's more than an issue with your shoes, young lady," her aunt fumed. "What are you trying to do, dragging—luring—Everett all the way over here?"

His head turned at that. Seeing the hurt look on Adeline's face, he couldn't hold back any longer. "Now that's quite enough," he growled. "Adeline didn't drag me. She didn't have to," he said curtly. "Not at all. Her shoe merely—"

"Watch your tone, Everett!" his mother scolded. "You need to apologize right this instant for speaking to our hostess that way."

Standing up, he jabbed a finger into the night air. "I will apologize for my tone. But that's all. Nothing else, you hear? You women are completely overreacting."

"Is that so, Everett?" His mother eyed him warily.

"Yes, Mother. It is."

But even as he said the words, and as he watched Mrs. Dougherty send Adeline retreating from the party at her command, he knew he had spoken falsely. What his mother and Mrs. Dougherty suspected might be going on between him and Adeline was true. At least on his part. It was very true.

Chapter 5

Adeline walked up the long, shadowed hallway to her uncle's study. Assuming she was going to have to answer to her aunt and uncle this morning, she had barely slept all night. The humiliation of being sent away from Shannon's party had kept her on the brink of tears in the darkness.

When she wasn't dwelling on the unfairness of that situation, her mind turned a switch, and thoughts of Everett seeped in. Recalling his kindness and protectiveness. His eyes smiling into hers as they floated across the dance floor. The feel of his arm around her waist. All of which had a calming effect on her. But only a temporary one. Just when she'd feel her body relax, her aunt's cruel words would ring out in her head, starting the emotional cycle all over again.

And now here she was, standing in front of her uncle's door, thinking—hoping—her encounter with her aunt and uncle wouldn't be as dreadful as the scene she'd been conjuring up during the pitch-black hours of night.

I didn't do anything wrong, after all. Maybe I've been overthinking this. Maybe Aunt Martha only wants to apologize.

Sucking in a deep breath, she raised a hand to knock on the door. Then stopped. Hearing strained voices coming from the other side, she placed her ear against the cool, dark wood, trying to listen.

Then wished she hadn't.

"I can't take much more of her, William." Her aunt's high-pitched voice rang clear. "She's such an embarrassment. I've tried to make her one of us. But she refuses to change."

Instantly Adeline's mouth went dry, her shoulders slumping at the weight of the words.

"Martha, please. I can't change the circumstances. My sister is dead. She's my niece. What can I do?" her uncle pleaded. "Besides, it's only been a few months. Can't you please give things more of a chance?"

"A few months?" Her aunt's sardonic laugh floated through the door. "Where have you been, husband? She's lived with us for a year. Not that you would notice. You're absorbed in your work while I deal with this problem daily."

"Daily? Are you sure you're not exaggerating, Martha?"

Her aunt didn't answer the question. "And if you'd open your eyes," she replied instead, "you'd see what it's doing to your daughter."

"Shannon?" She could hear her uncle's chair scoot on the wooden floor. "What does she have to do with Adeline going barefoot?"

Adeline was just as puzzled as her uncle sounded.

"Your niece is trying to steal Everett Brighton from your daughter, William. Not that you would notice—or even care."

Steal Everett? That wasn't true. Was it?

"Oh, so now you're saying I don't care about our daughter?" Her uncle's voice rose in indignation.

"Well, if you did," her aunt retorted, "you'd send your niece from this house."

"To live where, Martha? Where would that place be?"

A heavy, despondent feeling settled over Adeline. Things were far worse between her and her aunt than she imagined. She knew they didn't exactly see eye to eye, but she'd never realized how much the woman truly loathed her.

"Your niece isn't even respectful enough to show up on time for our talk with her."

"It's only a minute past nine, Martha." Her uncle's reply sounded unusually gruff.

If Adeline hadn't wanted to confront her aunt and uncle before, she really and truly didn't want to now. But there wasn't any way out of it. At least nothing she could immediately think of. Trembling from her head to her toes, she swallowed back tears and knocked on the door.

"Come in," her uncle said.

Everything looked as she expected when she opened the door. Her aunt stood in front of her uncle's desk with her hands on her hips, her expression tight with displeasure. Her uncle sat back in his chair behind the large mahogany desk, his head lowered as he peered over his spectacles, his eyes reminding her of her mother's. Although not as kind, given the circumstances, and now seeming to be drooping with weariness. "Please have a seat, Adeline." He pointed to the pair of chairs in front of his desk.

She took a seat as directed, choosing the one farthest from her aunt and closest to the door.

Even though the morning sun poured in glorious rays through the windows of the room, the air was uncomfortably chilly to her, causing her arms and fingers to feel deathly cold. Her initial inclination was to sit on her hands to warm them, but she caught herself, realizing that may not be perceived as very ladylike.

"Obviously, you know why you're here," her uncle started.

"I'm here because of Mama."

At the mention of his sister, her uncle gave her a benevolent look. "No, I meant why you're here in my study this morning, Adeline."

"Oh, yes. That." She nodded gravely. "But this time was different, Uncle William. I was having a difficult time with my shoe. The ribbon holding together my shoe broke when I was dancing with—" She glanced up at her aunt whose expression showed no mercy, nothing but disapproval. "When I was dancing," she repeated, ending the sentence there, deciding it better not to mention Everett's name.

"But as your aunt has pointed out to me, and to you more than once, there are certain things you're expected to do while in our keep. Yet it's plainly disrespectful that you continue on in the way you have after you've been given so much and—"

"Uncle William. Aunt Martha," she interrupted. "I'm not meaning to be disrespectful. I'm truly not. Why, I appreciate everything ya'll have done for me. It's just I think God makes us all different ways, and He makes us care about different things and—"

This time her uncle interrupted her. "And as His commandment states, He expects you to honor those who are acting as your caretakers."

"Well, of course," she stammered. "I just meant—"

"Adeline." Her uncle's stern, raised voice quieted hers. He sat forward in his chair while she cowered slightly in hers. "No doubt you're your mother's daughter. It wasn't easy on my family all those years ago when she left this life. When she ran off to marry that roughrider person from Arkansas whom she met on the outskirts of town."

My father, rough? That wasn't so at all. He was gentle and loving and. . .

"So many years went by and we hardly ever saw her. Or you. And yet, when she grew ill, and reached out to me about you, I was happy to oblige." He leveled his eyes on her. "What I'm saying is. . .Adeline, if your mother truly didn't think this—this comfortable way of life—was good for you, why else would she have contacted me? She must have had regrets about the life she'd led. She must have realized that our way of life is better. And now I'm trying to follow your mother's wishes. Your aunt is too. We expect you to do the same. No more of your antics, do you hear?"

Her heart felt broken in two, tormented, wanting to say so much. Her uncle may have thought he knew his sister. But nothing he said was true. Her mother loved her father more than anything in the world, more than all the fancy dresses or jewelry or homes that money could buy. The only reason she wanted her brother to take Adeline in wasn't so she could be molded and changed. It was because her mama wanted to protect her and didn't have anywhere else to turn.

But if she argued the fact, it would only cause more turmoil, wouldn't it? Not knowing what to do, she nodded. "Yes, Uncle," she said even though she didn't agree. "Yes, I do hear. I apologize to you. And I apologize to you too, Aunt Martha."

She looked up at her aunt, trying to be respectful. Trying to forget all she heard behind the closed door. Hoping to ease the tension between them once and for all.

But her aunt glared at her with outright contempt, her eyes dark with hatred. And in that moment, Adeline knew the truth. The woman didn't like her. More than that, she never would.

Even if Adeline did everything right according to her aunt, she still wouldn't want Adeline there. If she was a social princess, her aunt would be afraid of Adeline stealing Shannon's limelight. If she was what she was—herself, and not so socially inclined—there was reason to cite her for that too.

Especially since, even without trying to, she'd drawn some friendly attention from someone special. From Everett, the handsome, successful Brighton son. The sole heir to the Brighton fortune. The man whom her aunt had chosen for Shannon, and for Shannon alone.

The restaurant had been busy for lunch, but there hadn't been much of an early dinner crowd. Even so, Everett was glad when he could finally turn off the lights and lock the back door behind him.

The summer's dusky light and a slight breeze greeted him, which would make the walk home a pleasure after being cooped up all day. If only he felt like going there. All day long, he'd found his thoughts straying to Adeline, hoping all had gone well with her aunt and uncle. The evening before, he'd tried his best to get Martha Dougherty to hear him out. Though she'd listened politely, her closed expression conveyed that his words on Adeline's behalf had fallen on deaf ears.

Of course, it wasn't just the shoe event that had Adeline on his mind. It was more than that. The way she'd felt in his arms while they were dancing. The way she'd smiled at him so sincerely, making him feel like he was the best thing that had happened to her in a long while.

It would be a little out of the way, but he could walk by the Doughertys' instead of heading home. See if Adeline might be sitting out in the garden. . .or strolling the grounds.

The thought of seeing her immediately renewed his energy, lightening his steps. Until he heard someone call his name. He stopped in his tracks.

"Everett."

There it was again. It was her voice, wasn't it? Which he couldn't believe, since he was just thinking of her.

Glancing around, he looked for clues as to where she might be.

"Adeline?" he called out.

Still he saw no signs of her, until a few broken-down delivery crates tumbled from the top of several waste cans and Adeline stepped out from behind the mountain of trash.

The instant surge of joy he'd felt hearing her near retreated quickly at the sight of her. Red, puffy eyes looked up at him. The peaceful expression she always wore had been replaced by a sad, forlorn look. He'd never seen her so despondent.

"Addy." He grabbed her elbow. "Are you okay? What's going on?"

"I hope you don't mind me waiting here," she quickly apologized.

Mind? Was she crazy?

"I don't know where else to turn, Everett."

No matter what was upsetting her, he was glad she'd turned to him for help. He nodded to the back door. "Let's go inside where you can sit down." His hand slid down to meet hers.

"No." She took her hand away. "I don't want to get you into trouble."

"Everyone's gone for the day. It'll be fine. But you're not, apparently. So, let's go in."

Once again, he took her by the arm, and after unlocking the door, ushered her inside. The last rays of the day's sunlight streamed in the windows as he sat her down at one of the tables.

"Can I get you something to eat? Drink?" he offered.

She shook her head.

"How about a new set of eyes? Yours look awful." He took a handkerchief from his pocket and offered it to her.

At least she grinned slightly at that as she took the handkerchief from his hand.

But just as quickly as her smile had surfaced, it faded. She dabbed the cloth at the corner of her eye, stopping a tear from trickling down her cheek.

"She hates me, Everett."

"She?"

"Aunt Martha. I had to meet with her and Uncle William this morning."

"I was wondering how that went. I feel badly I wasn't there for you, Addy. After you were banished from the party last night, I tried to explain about your broken ribbon to your aunt again. I take it that didn't help?"

"Uncle William said they're giving me another chance. To become respectable."

His ire rose instantly. "You? You're not respectable? I've never heard a disrespectful word come out of your mouth." A flash of her in the garden shot across his mind. Even then she'd held her tongue, not talking back to Shannon during the croquet game. And the night before, she hadn't protested or raised her voice to her aunt. Not once. Even though he had.

"It doesn't matter. What matters is, when she looked at me—when Aunt Martha looked at me today—I knew what I hadn't known before."

He raised his brows, questioning.

"No matter what I do, Everett, she's never going to be all right with me living in their house." She shook her head and a tear escaped. "If I follow all her fancy social rules, or if I don't, it doesn't matter. One way or another I'm trouble to her. Either I'm an embarrassment to her because I'm not acting just right and fitting in, or I'm a threat because I'm getting attention from someone in Shannon's circle."

He knew instantly that she was speaking of him. He probably should've known better than to put her in that position. But he hadn't been able to help himself.

"Addy, it's just a rough patch you're going through. It'll get better. I promise." At least that's what he'd told himself. Given time, if their feelings continued to deepen for one another, wouldn't things simply work out?

"I can't make Aunt Martha happy, Everett." She shook her pretty head again. "But more importantly, I feel sure that she's not the one I'm supposed to make happy. God is. And He made me a certain way because that's the way He wanted me to be. I don't know if I can change or if it's even right to try."

"You shouldn't have to change, Addy." You're perfect, he wanted to say.

"That's what I'm thinking. So, I came to you because I need a job, Everett. And you're the only person I know well enough to ask."

"A *job*?" That was the last thing he thought she'd be asking him for.

She nodded. "Something in the back of the restaurant. Washing dishes or cleaning. Whatever it is, I don't even care. Just so I won't be seen by any of my aunt and uncle's acquaintances. I need it badly, Everett."

"But, Addy, I don't see how that will help your situation."

"It's the only thing that can, Everett." She looked him squarely in the eye. "I need to earn enough money to get back to the place where I can be accepted as I am. I need to go back home. To Arkansas. That's where I need to be."

Chapter 6

Two weeks after he had given Adeline a job, Everett found himself doing exactly what he'd done other mornings before. Looking up from his book-keeping tablet, he watched her mop the restaurant floor as if it was the most interesting thing he'd seen since the first time he'd viewed a sky full of stars through a telescope.

How a woman could look so lovely toiling away, he didn't know. But she did. Golden strands of hair, escaping the kerchief around her head, curled prettily around her face. And her movements were as fluid and graceful as a dancer's as she swayed with the mop, making sweet humming sounds as she did.

It was a sight he never tired of, and how he found her several mornings of the week. He'd never come to work at the crack of dawn when Charlotte had been doing the cleaning for him. But on Adeline's work days—which were every other day—he bounded out of bed. He didn't want to miss seeing her before she finished her chores and was gone.

This time she caught him eyeing her. "Am I doing something wrong?" she asked.

"No. Not at all."

In fact, she couldn't have done the massive amount of cleaning any better. Still, it hadn't been an easy decision to make when he had given her the job. It had left him with a mix of feelings. He'd been happy to see her eyes light up when he handed over the key to the restaurant, telling her she could take over Charlotte's place for a while. The timing had been right, since Charlotte had hastily left for New York to take care of an ailing parent.

On the other hand, the thought that he was giving her the opportunity to leave Boston—and him—once she saved up enough money, left a strange emptiness inside him. As one who was used to a privileged life, having everything he wanted or needed, it wasn't a feeling he was used to. Or comfortable with.

"Am I humming again?" she asked him.

"You always hum when you work," he pointed out.

She was so opposite any young girl in his social circle who would've been humiliated to do a cleaning job, let alone hum while doing it. She'd also sweetly said she'd pray for Charlotte and her family's well-being, which had touched him too.

"I guess I probably do, and didn't realize it." She stopped, crossing her hands over the top of the mop handle. "Is it bothering you? You're trying to do your ledgers, aren't you?"

"It's fine. I can do two things at once. Add and subtract and listen to you hum."

"That's three things." She grinned.

"Oh, you're right. Maybe I'm not so good at this math stuff after all." He laughed. Something he seemed to do a lot of around her. "What were you humming by the way?" he asked curiously. "It's pretty."

"Oh, a hymn called 'All the Way My Savior Leads Me.'" She paused to wipe her brow. "If it's bothering you, I promise I'll stop."

"I don't think you can stop." The girl was naturally and usually happy. It was sort of contagious in a way.

She chuckled as she wrung out the mop. "You know, I'm not so sure I can either. Guess humming while doing chores just kind of comes natural to me."

His thoughts exactly. "I don't remember hearing that hymn in church."

"Oh, it's one my mama taught me."

Of course, he wasn't all that interested in the hymn. He was just trying to keep the conversation going long enough to figure out how he could ask to see more of her. Outside of the restaurant.

Adeline had been vague in telling him how she'd been getting out of the house early in the morning to come clean the restaurant without anyone knowing. She'd mentioned that since she had been given access to the kitchen, most of the family thought that's where she was keeping herself. And as for Miss Clara, she assumed Adeline was spending her early morning hours in the garden. She'd also mentioned that no one seemed to mind or care much about where she was anyway. He wondered if that was the case on Sundays too? Their day off.

"Have you been to the public gardens?" he asked, knowing how much she loved flowers. Maybe the gardens were a way to entice her?

Suspending her mopping, she gave him a puzzled look, and no wonder. Going from hymns to gardens was only making sense in his mind, not hers.

"Only once since I've lived here."

"Would you like to go sometime?" Unbelievably he found himself a little nervous asking. Something else he wasn't accustomed to.

"With you?"

He looked around. "I don't see anyone else asking. Yes. You and me."

"Well. . ."

He swallowed hard as she paused. She sure wasn't making this easy for him, was she?

"Sure," she drawled slowly, much to his relief. "But I don't know. . .how would that work exactly?"

Yes, how would that work?

"Maybe we could go on Sunday after church. Unless you think the Doughertys will have plans."

"No, I can go after church." She didn't hesitate. "How about I walk to the gardens and meet you there?"

"It's fairly far, and we'll be doing a lot of walking once we get there." He scratched the back of his head. "I think I should pick you up."

She nearly gasped.

"Not at the house," he added quickly. "At the corner of Lane Street? That's only a few blocks from the Doughertys'. At say, one o'clock?"

"That sounds perfect, Everett." Her eyes shone. "Thank you for asking."

He nodded. "Thank you for saying yes."

It was barely a few minutes after he settled back into his work, and Adeline into hers, that he heard her humming again. Another tune he didn't recognize. But it sounded less serious than the hymn. More up-tempo and upbeat. Maybe that was just a coincidence. Or maybe it meant she really was thankful he asked and was looking forward to their outing just as much as he was.

Oh, no! Is that one of Shannon's friends?

Adeline's heart quickened as she glimpsed a girl she thought she recognized standing on the sidewalk across from Lane Street.

She couldn't have been happier earlier in the week when Everett had invited her for a walk in the public gardens. She enjoyed his company very much and was finding herself missing him on her days off. Even in the wee hours of the morning just having him sitting at a table silently going over his ledger or inventories, his presence felt comfortable and natural to her. But standing on the corner of Lane, waiting for him to pick her up in his buggy, she couldn't quell the anxious feeling mounting every minute, through every part of her.

She'd never been one to use a parasol much. She'd always found them a bit silly and enjoyed the sunshine far too much to bother with shielding her face. Yet now each time a person even close to her and Shannon's age passed on the street, she was afraid that it might be someone who would recognize her and go mentioning it to her cousin. Angling the parasol to hide her face, she'd turn the other way, pretending to look at something in the opposite direction. Or like now, she swung completely around from the street, acting as if something behind her had caught her attention.

It was silly, she knew, to be so on edge given the fact that she'd be heading back to Arkansas, leaving as soon as she had enough money saved up. But she couldn't help herself. She'd been experiencing bouts of anxiety like she never had before. Even feeling like someone was following her some mornings as she made her way to the restaurant.

She hadn't mentioned her unease to Everett, mostly because she had no proof. And, of course, more than anything, she hoped she was wrong. The last thing she wanted to do was to get into another squabble with her aunt and uncle at this point. Or to get Everett into any kind of trouble. It would be far better to make a quiet exit when she left for Arkansas. For everyone. Especially for him.

"Adeline?"

She spun around. Looking up at Everett's boldly handsome face, an easy smile playing at the corners of his mouth, her apprehension instantly melted away.

"I'm so glad you're here," she said, thinking he was much like the dashing knight coming to save the princess in one of the stories her mama had shared with her.

As she closed her parasol and put her foot on the step of the buggy, he reached out and took her free hand. Once she was settled in next to him, she noticed how smooth and clean-shaven his cheeks were, and the fresh scent of soap drifting from him. It was the same way he'd looked and the same pleasant scent that had delighted her when they were dancing weeks before, causing her to smile to herself. It was nice that he'd gone to the extra trouble for their daytime excursion. Because, of course, she had as well. She'd taken great care with her appearance for this special outing, even adding extra pins in her hair so it wouldn't go drooping so quickly. Which, so kindly of him, he readily noticed.

"Your hair." He glanced at her in the coziness of the closed carriage, his eyes taking her in. "You've done something different with it. It looks pretty."

She started to tell him about the added pins she'd put in, so it wouldn't come undone so easily, but then decided no man wanted to hear that kind of information.

"Thank you," she said instead.

"You're welcome." He smiled then turned to the horses and lifted the reins. "So, tell me, how was your morning? Beautiful weather we're having, don't you think?"

With that, as the horses fell into a comfortable cadence, they did as well. Laughing and talking, even riding along quietly at times, they easily found a perfect rhythm with each other.

It wasn't until they reached Arlington Street that Adeline noticed her nervousness resurfacing again.

On her first visit to the gardens, she'd been impressed by the stately statue of George Washington that hailed visitors at the entrance off Arlington. It was a grand sight, and she enjoyed learning about its sculptor. But now she only saw the monument as a problem. The area around it attracted too many people. Women, men, families, couples, all milling around the statue, admiring the flowers close by, or resting on nearby benches. Increasing the chances of seeing someone they knew.

Stiffening in her seat, she glanced at Everett and was about to express her concerns. But she didn't have to.

"Don't worry," he spoke up, reassuring her. "We're going to a quieter section of the gardens. It'll be fine. You'll see."

Then he placed his hand over hers, saying even more than his words ever could have. At his touch, she instantly felt a caring warmness, a feeling like she'd just come home.

She only wished he never had to move his hand from hers.

Chapter 7

Adeline glanced over at Everett, walking beside her through Boston's public gardens for the third Sunday in three weeks, and sighed with contentment. She had always liked Sundays. Growing up, she knew the Sabbath as a day of rest and peace and enjoying God's blessings. After church service, she and her parents would sometimes picnic with another family or explore the outdoors on their own before settling in to make an early dinner. And when her daddy passed, her mama held on to those traditions, making sure the two of them did much the same.

Even their farm animals seemed to know Sunday was God's day. She couldn't remember a Sunday when a mare had to push a foal into the world or when her daddy had to go scouting for food. Not that that couldn't happen, she knew. But in those ways and in so many others, their family had been blessed for sure.

And now, God was doing it again. After a year of feeling somewhat lost, especially on Sundays, since her relatives rarely went to church or even made a point of sharing the day together, He'd brought Everett into her life. A very special someone, to enjoy every passing moment of a Sunday afternoon, just as she had when her mama and daddy were alive.

How good of Him! How good!

Overwhelming gratitude gushed through her, bringing a surge of tears to her eyes. "Thank You, Lord!" she whispered, glancing up to the heavens. "Thank You!"

"Did you say something?" Everett looked her way.

"Oh, I—I was just saying thank you." She swiped at her eyes.

"Don't mention it," he said blithely. Then stopped and scratched his head. "Wait. Thanks for what?"

She laughed. "I wasn't saying thank you to you. Although I really do appreciate you bringing me here. Mostly I was thanking God for bringing me here. And for bringing you into my life," she said boldly, not holding back. She couldn't help herself. Her feelings for him over the course of the weeks had become too strong.

He didn't seem the least bit rankled by her admission. In fact, his eyes lit up as he spoke. "I wouldn't have it any other way, Addy." He squeezed her hand. When he seemed to realize what he was doing, he let go.

"So. . ." He cleared his throat. "You talk to God that much, huh?" He eyed her quizzically.

"Don't you?" she asked.

"Not quite." He gave a slight chuckle. "I think we were brought up to see God in a whole different way. I see him as a rule maker. A judge. A stern commander. You see Him as—well, I'm not sure. How do you see Him?"

"As my Father," she shared honestly. "Someone I can talk to anytime, anywhere, because I know He loves me. But I agree, God has rules, just like my daddy did."

"But—" He plucked a leafy twig from a tree bowing over their path. "From what you've mentioned to me about your dad, we see our fathers differently too. My father rules with an iron fist. He has expectations that must be met. And there's always major disappointment if I don't meet those expectations and follow everything just the way he wants it. To the letter."

"That must be hard on you and your brother," she sympathized. "Maybe my daddy was easier on me because I was an only child and his little girl."

"Oh, no. It's because my father doesn't forgive easily—sometimes not at all. He gave up on my brother Garrett a long time ago." He looked away as he spoke, seeming uncomfortable, causing her to wonder if he'd shared this with anyone before.

"Does that mean you never see your brother?"

"I see him once in a great while," he said, tearing one leaf after another off the shoot. "Garrett still stays at the house when he wants to. My parents won't abandon him completely. But my father refuses to communicate with him. That only makes Garrett behave even worse. In my opinion."

"Hmm." She didn't have any experience with those sorts of family dynamics. "Well, I guess no one is perfect. It's not like I didn't disappointment my daddy sometimes too. But even when I did, I knew he still loved me."

"And that's the difference." Everett tossed aside the nearly leafless twig. "That's not something I know about my father."

His mood seemed to dip like the sun, which had ducked behind a cloud. Lips tight, his features drew into a pained expression. No doubt, she'd touched on a topic that he felt very deeply about.

"God never stops loving you, Everett. Not any of us." She offered what she knew best.

"Well, if that's the case, I'd like to see Him the way you do, Addy."

"It isn't like you can't." She smiled at his candor. "You just have to—I don't know—" She raised her hands in the air, looking for the right words. "Pray and change your thinking some."

"Pray and change my thinking, huh?" He shook his head as if that was too much to think about.

"You could try. I mean, if you wanted to."

She made up her mind she wasn't going to press him. Sometimes pushing someone just made them back away. But as they walked on, the sun peeked out again from behind a cloud and suddenly his mood seemed to lighten again along with it.

"I'm taking your advice, Addy," he said.

"I'm glad I could help," she said, thinking that perhaps he meant he was going to go home and pray later. Or maybe even ask her more about how she prayed. But instead, he sauntered over to the nearest tree.

Putting out a hand to steady himself against the trunk, to her utter surprise, he did what she least expected. He lifted his feet one at a time, taking off his shoes and socks.

"Everett, what are you doing?"

Adeline looked at him as if he was stark raving mad, which, given her predilection for going shoeless, was rather ironic and humorous.

"What does it look like?" He held out his hands and nodded down at his bare feet. "You said going barefoot brought you closer to God. I decided to give it a try."

"Well, I didn't exactly mean it was my bare feet that did it," she stammered, looking perplexed.

"Ahh. . ." He scrunched his toes in the sun-warmed grass. "You're right. This feels good. Like a piece of heaven." He glanced down at her shoes. "What are you waiting for? Aren't you going to join me?"

"I don't know. . ." She looked all around them, searching for anyone who might be passing by, he imagined.

"So now I'm the improper cad and you're the proper lady?"

"Why, no, it's just that—" She stuttered again indecisively.

"It feels really, really good. You know it does." He tried to tempt her. "Here, let me help you take those off." He stepped closer.

"There is no need." Her voice flared just the slightest. Her hands flew up, resisting. "I can manage on my own."

"As always, I have no doubt about that. But, please, allow me to help." He knelt in front of her. "Come on, Addy. Just place your foot here." He patted his thigh.

She wasn't so easily persuaded, but then finally raised her skirt slightly, placing her shoed foot on his thigh. For all his supposed gallantry, he had an extremely difficult time untying the laces.

"What on earth?" he groused, his fingers fumbling, seeming to botch up things even more. "Could they make these designs any more difficult to deal with?"

"They're women's shoes, Everett." She giggled at his ineptness. "They're not meant to be practical."

"You're loving every moment of my bumbling, aren't you?"

"I am." She laughed some more. "But also enjoying your gentlemanly ways."

"Aha! Finally!" He removed her first shoe and placed it on the ground.

"Second foot." He patted his thigh again and was slightly quicker at untying the laces this go around.

"There. You are now a free woman." He stood up and faced her. "Feels great, doesn't it?"

"Oh, so good!" she agreed, arms out, spinning around.

"I rather feel like I'm ten again," he admitted.

"Me too," she chirped.

"What do you say? Race you to those trees?" He pointed to a line of beech trees to the south of them.

"What?"

She looked confused, but he leaned into a runner's stance anyway, not giving her time to decline. "One. Two—"

"Three!" she shouted, bolting ahead of him.

He was laughing so hard at how she'd duped him, that he didn't move at first. Then seeing how she most likely was going to beat him, he took off running, sprinting as fast as he could.

By the time he caught up to her they were only a few feet from their goal. He slowed down versus passing her up and declared the race a tie.

"I almost beat you," she rasped gleefully, bending over to catch her breath.

"Almost is not quite enough. Besides, I *almost* let you beat me."

"You did, huh?" She put her hands to her hips.

"Definitely."

She looked so pretty standing there, her face flushed, her eyes wide with merriment, her hair disheveled in the most becoming way that he needed to distract himself. Quickly. Picking up a small fallen branch from a nearby tree, he swung it in the air like a baseball bat.

"Have you gotten to see the Beaneaters play?" she asked as she leaned up against the largest beech, shading herself, her arms behind her back.

"You know about the Beaneaters?"

She never ceased to surprise him.

"Well, of course I do. I'd like to see a game of theirs, but never have."

"I used to want to be one of them."

"A baseball player?"

He nodded.

"Were you good at it?"

He shrugged. "Some people thought I was. But it didn't matter. My father wouldn't go for it."

"I can't imagine him not letting you give it a try." She sighed. "Seems to me you'd be good at anything you put your mind to. You're smart, and knowing you like I do, I'm sure anyone would want you on their team."

It wasn't just her compliments that made him want her. Although he certainly didn't mind hearing what she had to say about him. But the way she was gazing at him—with such a sweet sincerity shining in those blue-green eyes of hers—it was like nothing he'd ever seen before. The grand slam right to his heart.

"What's past is past," he said, tossing the stick aside. Seeing her standing there, he couldn't have cared less about his long-ago dream. He was only concerned about the here and now. And her, of course.

Taking a step closer, all he knew was that he wanted to kiss her. But then suddenly, unbelievably, he caught a glimpse of something out of the corner of his eye.

Turning his head, it wasn't a something but a couple of someones. An acquaintance, Thomas Wilberforce, and a young woman, strolling around the bend of the concrete walkway off to the right of them.

"Quick! We need to get out of sight." He grabbed Adeline by the arm and pulled her to the rear of the trees, knowing she couldn't afford to be seen by anyone they knew.

Leaning her against the smooth bark, he hovered over her, sure they wouldn't be sighted. But not so sure he could contain himself as the scent of her hair and her very closeness tempted him.

"Is it safe?" she whispered, looking up at him.

"I don't know," he answered, his mind only on her. "Is it?"

He didn't wait for her answer. He couldn't resist her any longer. Reaching for her hand, he drew her into his embrace and did what he'd been wanting to do for a long time.

He kissed her.

Chapter 8

Adeline had snuck out of the house the day before to meet Everett for their Sunday outing. Now in the still of night, she was sneaking out again. Not to see him—but because of him.

Trying not to awaken her relatives in the upstairs bedrooms, she clutched a stuffed burlap sack to her side and crept down the steps as quietly as she could. All the while, she prayed none of them would creak and betray her.

Her prayer answered, she descended the last step then tiptoed across the house's entry, through the dining room. Then froze when the white-paneled door leading into the kitchen squeaked.

Heart pounding, she looked over her shoulder, glancing up the long staircase, listening for any commotion. When all seemed to be silent, she crossed into the kitchen, easing the door to a close behind her. Lightly padding across the kitchen floor, she stood at the back door and drew in a deep breath.

Should she, or shouldn't she?

As much as she didn't want to, she had to, didn't she?

Gently undoing the lock, she clutched the door handle and opened the door slowly. Lightly stepping over the threshold, she turned and with two hands brought the door to a silent close behind her.

The air was beginning to get cooler at night. Such a welcome relief from the heat that had engulfed her while creeping around the house. Slipping along the side of the house, she headed for the sidewalk. Only to stop abruptly in panic.

Hair stood up on the back of her neck. Her heart quickened in her chest. Was she being watched? It certainly felt like she was. Daring to look back at the house, she scanned the yard. . .the windows, but couldn't see anyone. Not a thing.

Letting out her pent-up breath, she started off again down the sidewalk, toward her destination.

It was probably quite natural to feel like she was being spied on. After all, she wasn't used to sneaking around the way she was. But she hadn't come up with a better idea.

Knowing she'd be leaving Boston, weeks ago she'd sorted through her closet and all the fancy things she'd been given. She certainly couldn't take much with her and surely wouldn't be needing such fine things back home, especially such frilly shoes. She'd remembered Miss Clara saying that Adeline and her daughter were two of kind, wearing the same size, so she packed up her shoes to give to Olivia.

But how to get them to Miss Clara and Olivia wasn't so easy to figure out. There was no way she could give the shoes to Miss Clara at the house. If the cook was caught with them, or if one of the staff found out and snitched, that would cause trouble for them both. Hugging the sack of shoes to her side, Adeline was doing the only thing she knew to do. Making a trip to Miss Clara's residence in the dark.

She just hadn't counted on making the journey this soon.

But then—

Everett. . .

He had kissed her. And his kiss had changed everything.

She reached up to her lips, touching them, still remembering their Sunday afternoon together. Unable to forget the sweetness of his kiss. The gentle urgency of his lips intensified every feeling she had for him. And when he broke away from her and gazed into her eyes, telling her how special she was to him, she'd been speechless. Unable to say a thing. She'd been amazed that he felt the same way she did.

Yet the two of them—they were as wrong for each other as they were right. Their backgrounds too different. His parents far too put off by her. As much as it hurt and broke her heart, things would never work between them. How he could even imagine they would, made no sense whatsoever.

She wasn't about to be the ruin of him, hurt his reputation or his relationship with his family. She'd been planning to leave anyway. And had enough money saved up. May as well be sooner than later.

But as determined and set as her mind was, her heart faltered. She could barely stand only seeing him every other day of the week. How on earth was she going to manage not seeing him at all?

She had to leave. For his sake, she had to go.

And for my sake?

Abruptly, she stopped on the sidewalk, frozen with indecision. Everything inside her ached, feeling so torn. What if she never cared for anyone the way she did for Everett—not ever again?

Turning, she glimpsed at what was behind her then turned again, peering into the darkness that laid ahead. And in that moment, right or wrong, she knew what she had to do.

One by one, step by step, she headed back to where she'd come from. Because for her sake...she needed one more week, one more perfect Sunday in the park with Everett.

Then she would let go and do what she'd planned to do all along. She would get on a train and leave. Tearing herself and her heart away from the only man she'd ever loved.

It wasn't the way Everett had imagined starting his Tuesday morning. Not with his long-time cashier and hostess staring into the empty cash register drawer, looking just as flummoxed as he felt.

"I promise you, Mr. Brighton, I didn't do it," she said. "I didn't take the money."

"I believe you, Evelyn," he said, because he sincerely did. "You've worked for my parents for years, and—"

"I don't steal or lie or cheat." She interrupted him. "It's not in my nature. Never has been, never will be."

"I know." He patted the older woman on the shoulder. "It's all right."

He could see she was getting flustered, her cheeks and neck turning bright crimson. He certainly didn't want her blood pressure shooting sky high, causing him to have to make a mad dash with her to the nearest clinic. He didn't need that kind of fiasco along with the present trouble this morning.

"Don't worry." He tried to soothe her. "I'm probably overlooking something I did yesterday."

Though he couldn't imagine what that would be.

Walking to the center of the restaurant, he rubbed his forehead, trying to remember if he'd done anything differently the night before at closing time. But, no. He'd checked the kitchen for any fire hazards as he always did, making sure everything was turned off. Scooted in some chairs. Righted the menus. Turned off the lights. And locked the door behind him.

When he opened this morning, true, it did feel like something was missing. But it always felt like that on days that Adeline didn't work.

Yet, obviously, today was even worse. He was not only missing Adeline, but also all the money in the cash register. Money that had been there the evening before. Money that he was planning on depositing today.

But, again, it made no sense. How?

Glancing all around the restaurant, nothing looked out of place. Or damaged. Not one broken window. Or mangled lock. Or busted door. It was so mind-boggling, he was lost in thought when he felt a hand touch his shoulder.

"Everett?"

He turned to see Shannon Dougherty staring at him.

"Are you all right?" she asked, her eyes wide with concern.

"Me?" He shrugged. "I'm fine."

"You are?" Her brows lifted in surprise. "Well, if I were you, I'd certainly be upset. Evelyn told me all about the missing money. Such a shock!"

"She told you?" Did he hear that right?

"Don't be mad at her. I sort of guessed, actually." She gave him an apologetic look. "Open cash register. Upset cashier. I assumed something bad had happened."

He glanced over at Evelyn, hoping she wasn't telling any of the other customers. Luckily it was early, and there were only a few. As far as he could see, it appeared his cashier had pulled herself together now. Looking prim and proper, back to business as usual, her face had calmed to a light pink.

As he knew from past experiences, Shannon did have a way of weaseling information out of people. He needed to caution himself as well.

"I haven't seen you here for a while." He changed the subject. "And so early today too. You're having breakfast instead of lunch for a change?"

"Yes." She beamed. "I woke up famished and thinking of you."

"Of me?"

"And the restaurant too." She batted her lashes. "Though I must admit, I think of you often, Everett."

Would she ever let up? He pretended not to hear her flirty comment. "There's a seat over by the window." He pointed as far away from him as he could. "Lots of sunshine there for you to enjoy," he added as graciously as he could.

She smiled broadly. "Always so sweet and thoughtful, aren't you? Thank you, Everett." She started to head toward the table then stopped. "Funny thing is, I don't see any broken windows. How did your thief get in? Through the back door? Was that busted in?"

"No, nothing broken into," he said, then was instantly sorry he'd shared any information with her. No one needed to know his business, especially her.

"Interesting." She tapped a finger to her cheek. "It's as if someone had a key to get in." She brightened. "There's the answer to your mysterious robber. Who has a key besides you?"

It wasn't as if the same thought hadn't crossed his mind. But he'd pushed it away. Adeline was the only other person with a key. But that didn't make sense. It wasn't believable. She'd never do something like that. It had to be someone else.

"Did you go out anywhere last night? Maybe dropped your key someplace?"

Shannon shot off more questions.

Discreetly as he could, he felt for his key in his pocket. It was there and had been in the same place this morning when he left for work as it always was. On top of his chest of drawers.

"No, I was home last night."

"So was I. Unlike Adeline." She shook her hat-topped head. "I can't imagine where that girl went. I heard something and saw her sneaking out of the house late. Though I didn't tell Mother and Father." She sighed. "Why should they have to know? She's already such a handful for them."

Adeline? Sneaking out?

That news hit him hard. It was all he could do not to react in front of Shannon, to let his jaw drop open in disbelief.

Was Adeline so serious about leaving town that she'd creep around in the middle of the night and steal from him?

No, it couldn't be. It couldn't. He wouldn't believe it.

"I need to run to the bank. Excuse me." He nodded curtly. "Enjoy your breakfast, Shannon."

"I certainly will." She flashed her usual effusive smile his way.

He rarely was in the mood for one of Shannon's faux smiles, the ones that looked like she practiced in a mirror. But this morning he really wasn't up to one, his mind trying to sort through the events of the morning—and now the possibly disturbing news about Adeline.

Things got even worse when he turned to walk back to the front of the restaurant. There was his father. Approaching the cash register.

"Father!" he called out. "What brings you in so early this morning?"

"I need to borrow change for the deli." His father waved. "I'll get to the bank later and get you repaid."

It wasn't an unusual request. They often exchanged money and change back and forth, lessening their trips to the bank. But today was an altogether different matter.

Evelyn put a hand to her mouth and stepped back from the cash register, not saying a thing as his father made his way around the counter and opened the drawer. Everett stood watching the scene unfolding before him, feeling paralyzed and unable to stop it.

His father's eyes might as well have been question marks as he looked down at the empty drawer then up at Everett. "Where's all the money?"

For a moment, he thought about lying to his father. Making something up. But his mind was in such a state of confusion, nothing was coming to him.

"Everett. I asked you a question. And I expect an answer," his father's stern voice commanded.

"I, uh, I don't know."

"What do you mean you don't know?"

Everett shrugged. "I found it empty this morning. I'm trying to figure things out."

"Did you call the police?"

"And tell them what?" He held up his hands. "Nothing's been broken into or damaged."

His father's eyes quickly scanned the restaurant then came back to him. Everett dreaded what he knew his father would say next.

"You said you hired a new cleaning person. That's the only other person with the key, correct?"

Everett hesitated. Then nodded glumly. "I suppose."

"You suppose?"

"Well, I'm wondering if perhaps Charlotte had an extra key made and somehow someone found it somewhere." He grasped for an explanation. For anything but the facts in front of him.

"Someone spotted a key and knew it would unlock our restaurant?" His father shook his head. "Who has the other key, Everett. Why won't you say?"

Adeline.

Her name was engraved on his heart. Always on his mind these days.

Addy.

He enjoyed calling her that nickname and watching her smile.

But no way did he want her name to come out now. To cross his lips.

He stared at his father. "I'll take care of it, Father."

"Everett, I'm going to ask you one more time, and I want the truth." His father fumed, leveling his eyes on him. "Whom are you protecting? Tell me. Now."

Chapter 9

Adeline had been enjoying her morning in the garden, sketching the last of the season's roses while trying not to think about Everett too much on her day off, when she was wanted in her uncle's study.

With every step back to the house, she sifted through reasons why she might have been asked to see her uncle this time of day. It wasn't due to any barefoot drama, that was for sure, and she hadn't been caught doing anything else wrong. She couldn't imagine why she'd been summoned.

By the time she walked down the hallway to his study, she'd half-convinced herself she was being called in for a pat on the back. That notion quickly flew the coop, however, when one foot into his office, her musings were replaced by shock.

Not only was her uncle, aunt, and Shannon gathered there, but Everett and his parents too. Their faces were all so glum, her heart sank. Her fear mounted. And her sketchpad nearly fell from her grasp.

Everyone was silent, even Everett. Her only greeting came in the form of a few terse words from her uncle.

"Adeline." He nodded. "Take a seat."

"I'd rather stand, sir, if that's okay with ya'll," she said. She'd sat in those chairs of her uncle's before and knew very well how small they made her feel.

Casting a sideways glance at Everett, she tried to get a read from him, some sort of insight. But he didn't even look like the Everett she knew. His face was pale and drawn, his eyes dim. Instead of his usual reassuring smile, he eyed her warily, then stared at the floor in front of him.

His noticeable indifference felt like a physical blow, making it difficult for her to keep standing. It was everything she could do not to fall into one of her uncle's chairs after all.

What on earth is going on?

Her alarm quickly turned to panic.

"Is anyone hurt? Is everything all right?" she asked.

"Everyone is fine," Uncle William answered.

"That's good to hear." She gave a sigh of relief.

"But every*thing*," he emphasized, "is not."

She raised a brow.

"We know about your job at the restaurant," her aunt blurted out from across the room. "You've been seen going there in the morning. Everett confirmed that it's true."

This is what the gathering was all about? Evidently, she hadn't been imagining her feelings that someone was following her. This was all her fault. In hindsight, she should've told Everett. Or at least forewarned him. No wonder he seemed so put out and would barely look her way. And no wonder that her aunt was the first one to speak up. Contrary to what Adeline believed, taking a cleaning job was an embarrassment to the family, especially to her aunt. A disgrace to the Dougherty name.

But it wasn't her aunt that she cared about so much. It was Everett. She hated the thought of getting him into any kind of trouble on her behalf.

"I begged Everett for the job," she spoke up. "I thought by working I could get on my own somehow. You know, not have to bother ya'll so much. Maybe even repay you for your kindness someday," she added, deliberately leaving out the part about her plans to move back to Arkansas.

The entire time she tried to explain herself, her uncle looked the other way, totally avoiding eye contact with her. But now that she'd finished, he turned his head and she was stunned to see what she'd never seen in his expression before. Total and utter disgust.

"But embarrassing your aunt with a job like that wasn't enough for you, was it?" He practically spat the words at her, his cheeks redder than she'd ever seen them. "You couldn't stop at that, could you, Adeline? You had the gall to steal money from the cash register too."

"I—what?" she stammered, his accusation completely blindsiding her. "Whatever do you mean?"

She looked at her uncle with imploring eyes, begging for the benefit of an explanation. He clearly wasn't about to give her one, shifting in his chair, dodging her gaze.

Continuing to feel helpless, she glanced around the room at one person at a time, seeking clarification from someone. But the atmosphere had grown even chillier. There wasn't so much as a kind or warm response from anyone. Her aunt stood firmly, arms crossed over her chest, practically snarling at her. Mr. Brighton was taciturn, his jaw clenched in silence. Mrs. Brighton's lips curled upward as if she had a bad taste in her mouth. Understandable, since she'd expected Shannon to be the target of her son's affection, not a nobody from out West. Shannon, as always, had a glint in her eye, very much enjoying the uncomfortable encounter.

And Everett. For the slightest moment, he raised his head to look at her, and she wanted to break down and cry. So many times, he'd regarded her with pleasure in his eyes. With appreciation and warmth. Friendship. And yes, even hints of so much more than that. . .with love. But never had she seen him scrutinize her the way he was now. Casting questioning glances her way, so much doubt dimming his eyes.

"I didn't steal anything. I wouldn't." She looked at Everett, suddenly not caring about anyone else except him. Everett had to know that of her. To know the truth.

Still he said nothing. Only her aunt spoke up again. "Of course, you would say that. But you're not as clever as you think. Shannon saw you sneaking out of the house last night. You can't deny that, Adeline."

Shannon had seen her? Is that who had been following her all along?

"But, I was only going—" She stalled, trying to think of a way to tell her story without getting Everett or Miss Clara involved in her problem. But nothing would come to her quickly, which no doubt left her looking guiltier than ever.

"The facts are the facts, young woman," Mr. Brighton interjected, his hands clenching into fists at his sides, leaving her understanding why Everett was intimidated by him. "Nothing was damaged during the robbery at the restaurant last night. No windows broken. No doors busted in. You're the only other person who has the key." Mr. Brighton narrowed his contempt-filled gaze at her. "And you were seen going out last night. You're not even denying that. If you didn't steal the money, then are you saying Everett took it? He's the only other person with a key."

"I'm saying nothing like that at all, sir." She shook her head vigorously. "I'm mighty sure he didn't take it."

Mr. Brighton shrugged a shoulder. "A few months ago, I would've said the same thing. Lately, however, I've been starting to doubt my son's judgment. I'm not so sure he's the right person to take over the business." He spoke of Everett as if he wasn't even there. "The decisions he's been making have not fared too well."

She knew very well what Mr. Brighton was referring to—the decisions Everett had made regarding her. Meeting her in the garden. Helping her at the gala. Giving her a job. It seemed most all his troubles began and ended with her. And now, because of her as well, his father may even strip away the family business from him?

"Matthew, please, enough of that subject," Mrs. Brighton insisted. "This isn't the time or the place."

"I'm not saying anything that isn't true," Mr. Brighton replied huffily, scowling at his wife before turning back to Adeline. "If you pay back the money, we've agreed not to press charges. I don't wish to sling our good name or the Doughertys' through the mud over this."

Staring at Everett and his parents, hugging the sketchpad to her heart, she couldn't believe her ears. Nor believe the situation she was in, or be sure what to do about it.

All she knew was, that for a time, Everett had chosen her over his parents' protests with his attentions and his kindness. With his trust. His sweet kiss. Yet, in the end, that hadn't worked out so well—not for either of them. To the point where weeks ago, she'd felt like she had to leave Boston. And to the point where now his father was ready to take his livelihood and future away from him.

There was no way she could—or should have to—admit to something she didn't do. But maybe if she offered to pay back the money, it would keep Everett from any future issues with his family. If she knew anything, she knew family was important. She'd give the world to have her mama and daddy back again. Besides, she'd planned on leaving anyway. But Everett? He was here to stay.

And the truth of the matter was, all the evidence did point to her. Even she couldn't imagine how the money had been taken or who could've stolen it.

"I—I'll pay the money back," she said at last. Her heart ached as she said the words. She didn't want Everett to think badly of her, but she also couldn't stand feeling badly for him.

"I knew it." Her aunt's head shot up. "I knew you stole the money. You are one embarrassment after the other. That's what you are." She glared.

Adeline bit her trembling lip, trying to hold back tears, trying not to rebut the accusation again even though she wanted to. "I'll get the money from my room now."

"And the key," Mr. Brighton said.

"Yes. And the key." She nodded, not even bothering to so much as glance at Everett as she left the study.

Climbing the stairs to her room, she realized she had no idea how much money was kept in the cash register. The only thing she could do would be to put aside enough for a train ticket and return nearly all the rest of her earnings. That wouldn't leave much to live on once she got back to Arkansas, but none of that seemed to matter in this moment. None of it as painful as knowing that there'd be no more walks or talks or hours spent with Everett. No more of anything with him at all.

By the time Adeline made her way back downstairs with her envelope of money, Mr. and Mrs. Brighton had already left in their carriage, and her aunt and her uncle were nowhere to be seen. She assumed Uncle William was still in his study working and Aunt Martha in her room nursing a migraine, which was her typical response after most confrontations regardless if she had a headache or not.

Only Shannon remained in the entryway with Everett, rubbing his shoulder, consoling him with news of something to "take his mind off things"—another party scheduled for that coming weekend.

He heard her footsteps before jabbering Shannon did, glaring up at her as she descended the stairs. His contemptuous stare was like a dagger to her heart, causing her feet to falter. Almost falling, she grabbed the bannister, holding on to it tightly the rest of the way down.

Without taking his scornful eyes off her, he spoke to Shannon.

"Shannon, would you mind giving us a moment alone?"

Her cousin didn't look pleased at the request, but she nodded at Everett anyway. "I'll stop by the restaurant tomorrow and give you the details of the party, Everett," she said before departing the room.

As soon as Shannon was out of hearing distance, Adeline started to say how sorry she was. But after being silent throughout the earlier encounter, Everett let out everything that had been on his mind.

"I don't know how you could do this me, Adeline. To us." He shook his head. "You said you believed God has rules for us to follow. But all of this has me wondering if you're just a barefoot, free-spirited girl who doesn't think the rules apply to her."

"That's not who I am at all, Everett, You know that, don't you?"

"All I know is that my parents have questioned my decisions to be around you all along. And now I'm questioning myself too." His jaw clenched as he paused. "Honestly, Adeline, I don't know what I believe anymore."

She couldn't hold back her tears any longer. As they flowed down her cheeks, she started to explain everything to him. But the look of disdain on his face said he wouldn't believe her anyway. In the end, it didn't matter. The two of them weren't meant to be together. Not in this world—his world. Still, she hated for them to part this way.

Placing the envelope into his hand, she took one last look in his eyes. "I only hope someday you'll believe me," she said, because it really was the most she could wish for. She would never see him again; she'd never know if her wish came true.

Chapter 10

I t was barely four a.m., the morning sky still dark outside her bedroom window, as Adeline stood staring at the two plump bags sitting by the side of her made bed. After the confrontation the evening before, she'd been up all night, never changing into a nightgown, feeling it best to be packed and out the door early before Miss Clara arrived for work.

She had no clue about a train schedule, when one might be heading to Arkansas. But it didn't matter. The time had come. She'd rather sit for a day or more in the train station, if she had to, than be in her relatives' house any longer.

Yet. . .there was still one last thing she needed to do before leaving.

Taking her sketchpad from her travel bag, she opened it and placed it on the bed in the glow of the lantern on her bedside table. Kneeling on the floor, she bent over the pad with pen in hand, trying to find the words to say goodbye to the people who had felt most like family to her. First there was a thank-you note to Mr. Henry. And then, of course, Miss Clara.

Dear Miss Clara,

Before I head back to Arkansas, I want to thank you from the bottom of my heart for being the closest thing to kin and home that I had here in Boston. You've been a mighty big comfort to me at a time when I really needed much comforting and kindness. Though I've only known you for a year, I feel like you've always been a part of my life. You can be sure I will carry your memory with me for a long, long time. Because of that, I need you of all people to know I didn't take the money. I only paid it back because I didn't want Everett to get in more trouble. I was out that night, that part was true. I was headed to your house to bring this bag of shoes to you, thinking I was heading back to Arkansas real soon. But then on the way there, I changed my mind. I wanted to stay in Boston a bit longer. But I guess I'm leaving now anyway.

Please give the bag of shoes to your daughter. If anyone questions you about

them, this note will be proof that I wanted Olivia to have the shoes and that you
did nothing wrong. Since the shoes were gifts to me, I feel I can do with them
as I wish. Maybe a pair will even work with the pretty wedding dress you've
been stitching. Fancy shoes or not, I know being your girl, she will be a beautiful
bride, inside and out.

Happy wedding to ya'll, and thank you again for everything.

All my love,
Adeline

Of course, Mr. Henry and Miss Clara weren't the only ones she'd miss. There was also—Everett. How she'd miss him most of all! How she wanted to tell him everything in her heart. But she couldn't. She shouldn't.

Resolutely she tore Miss Clara's letter from the pad, not expecting to see the sketch of the pink rose underneath. How ironic that she'd been sketching a rose symbolizing the first day she and Everett had met on the same day they'd parted ways.

Once again, she wondered if she should have argued more the night before when they all stood staring at her so accusingly. Maybe she should have fought for herself. But to what end? It wasn't as if Everett's parents or her relatives had taken much of a liking to her. That's why she'd been planning to leave anyway. Everything in Everett's life would be better without her in it. But, oh, how she would miss him!

Picking up the pen once more, she added a postscript to Miss Clara's letter.

P.S. Inside the bag of shoes, you'll find a sketch of a rose.
If you get the chance someday, please deliver it to
Everett and tell him

She paused, not sure what to say. Tell him thank you for the way he made her feel so loved? For the way he'd made her heart dance? For the way he listened to her, made her laugh, filled her and her days?

Even though all those things were true, she couldn't say them now. Not after what had happened. She closed her eyes and tried to think. Finally, she jotted down the last few words:

thank you for his kindness toward me.

With that, she tore the picture of the rose from the sketchpad then placed it and the letter inside the sack of shoes.

For the second time that week, she tiptoed down the staircase as quietly as she could, carrying the bag of shoes in one hand and a carpet bag filled with the same items she'd brought to Massachusetts the year before in the other.

After depositing the sack of shoes in the kitchen, she let herself out the back door, her heart pounding. This time, she realized she wasn't worried that she'd get caught. She was more fearful that she wouldn't and sad that no one would care to come looking for her.

As much as she needed to go for her sake as well as Everett's, as much as she'd talked about returning to the place she'd always called home, it wouldn't be the same as it had been. Not only difficult because she'd be completely on her own, but also because she'd be leaving a part of her heart behind. With Everett.

Immediately, tears pricked her eyes at the thought of him. That seemed to be happening a lot in the last ten hours. So much sadness pouring out of her. She knew he'd captured her heart in a way no one had ever done before, but she hadn't realized how empty her being—her entire world—would feel without him.

But her mama had raised her to be strong, to try to be a David when there was a Goliath of problems confronting her. She had to trust God would help her and her heart find a way. Find a home again.

Stopping to place her note to Mr. Henry in the birdfeeder in the garden, she then started down the driveway, her steps feeling just as leaden as her heart. But she tried to be positive. She'd have to be if she hoped to get through all that loomed ahead of her. God was already providing a good morning to be walking to the train station. No rain. No people on the streets. Just her. And her alone.

Chapter 11

The pounding on the restaurant door early in the morning took Everett by surprise, causing the screwdriver in his hand to slip from the head of the screw. He didn't know why it had taken him so long to finally fix the loose hooks where Adeline had hung the mop and broom. But with the confrontation the night before still fresh on his mind, and so many conflicting thoughts of her still twisting his emotions, somehow it seemed like the thing to do.

"We're closed," he yelled grumpily toward the front door. "Come back at nine."

Still the pounding continued, harder than before. He shook his head in disbelief. Why today? He was in no mood for aggravation of any kind.

"I said we're closed!" His ire spiked.

Another heavy fist sounded in reply. Testing his patience even more.

"For the love of. . ." he grumbled, tossing the screwdriver aside.

Stomping to the door, he flung it open with all his might.

"Are you deaf or some—" He barely got the words out when he recognized the woman standing there.

"Miss Clara?"

"Mr. Brighton, sir." The cook nodded her hello.

"I'm sorry for yelling. I thought—"

"I'd say all our nerves are on edge today." She waved away his apology. "I'm sorry too. Sorry to bother you. But do you have a minute? I've got a lot to say."

"About?" He stared at her, more confused than ever.

She sifted in her pocket and brought out a piece of paper. "Adeline wanted you to have this. It's something special she drew."

Taking the sheet, he stared at the sketch of a delicate pink rose. The significance wasn't lost on him. Right away he knew it was a rendering of the rose he'd almost given her the first day he'd approached her in the garden. Simple yet beautiful, that's the way Adeline had drawn it. That's the way he'd seen her too. Or at least at one time he'd thought of her that way. Now it seemed she'd been more conniving than he'd ever imagined. Or was she? His mind began its debate all over again.

"You came all this way to deliver this?"

"No." The older woman shook her head. "But the rest I've come to say is a bit difficult and may take a while."

"So, you'd like to come in?"

"I would, Mr. Brighton, thank you."

Admittedly, he was curious about what she could have to say. Closing the door and locking it behind her, he ushered her over to a table. "Can I get you anything? Fresh coffee?"

"No, thank you," she said formally. "I'll just say what I have to and then leave you to decide what you wish to do. There's not much time." Crossing her hands on the tabletop, chin up, she looked at him as if she meant business.

"All right." He nodded, figuring her comment about time meant she needed to get back to her job. "Tell me what you came to say."

"It wasn't Adeline who took the money, sir."

He'd been prepared to hear Miss Clara out, but the abruptness and absurdity of her initial words startled him. "You don't say?" he replied a bit sarcastically.

"She left a note for me this morning, telling me she was leaving for the train station. She said she didn't steal the money."

She'd left? His heart lurched. It was probably better this way, he knew. What else was there left for them to say to each other? But still. . .

He closed his eyes, rubbing his hand over his forehead. When he opened them again, Miss Clara was staring at him. "Look, Miss Clara, I know how fond you were of Adeline and how close the two of you were. I was extremely fond of her as well. At one point in time anyway. But it seems she played tricks on both of us. You have to see that."

He'd expected to see a pained expression on the cook's face, but instead a slight smile twitched at her lips.

"I figured that's how you'd be seeing things, Mr. Brighton. I can't say as I blame you. But Adeline was only out that night because she'd planned to deliver a sack of shoes to my daughter then changed her mind. The truth is, your brother and Shannon took the money, sir."

He flung back in his chair, hating that he was having to defend his lame brother over a girl he'd been so attracted to. "Miss Clara, don't you see? That makes no sense. For one, why would Garrett and Shannon take the money? It's not as if they need it. And two, how would they get the key? Plus, last night Adeline didn't say anything of the kind."

"That's because she didn't know it was them who took it."

He blinked at the woman, frustrated. "Because they didn't; she did. Last evening in her uncle's study, Adeline admitted that she'd taken—" He stopped midsentence, the scene from the prior night flashing through his mind. No, she never had admitted taking the money, had she? She'd only said she'd pay it back. Her eyes hadn't looked sorrowful because of something she'd done wrong. She was sorry for him. She'd implicated herself to help him. He'd misinterpreted everything.

"Oh, I can't believe this. . ." He groaned as a sick feeling flooded his limbs. "I've made a terrible mistake. Haven't I?"

Miss Clara nodded solemnly. "You refused to believe her even when she was telling the truth."

"But I still don't understand, Miss Clara. How does it all make sense?"

"Well. . ." Miss Clara's hands came uncrossed as she used them to explain. "Mr. Henry came to me first thing this morning. About the same time that I found Adeline's note and the bag of shoes in the kitchen, he found a thank-you note for him that Adeline had left in the garden." She took a breath then continued. "He asked me what was going on, and I told him about everyone being there the night before. And what all that happened—at least as much as I could tell from Adeline's note. Right away, he put the pieces together."

"What pieces?" So far, he hadn't heard anything of significance.

"Mr. Henry said he'd been at McQuire's Pub Monday night, and your brother was there too."

Garrett at a pub? Not surprising. "That's not hard to believe."

"But your brother wasn't the only one there." She leaned forward to deliver the rest of the story. "Shannon was at the pub also. Evidently, she'd been waiting outside for your brother. When Mr. Henry left McQuire's, he saw the two of them out there talking. He overheard them mentioning a key of some kind, but he had no clue what that was all about. Not until this morning when he put two and two together."

Garrett and Shannon? "They plotted the robbery together?"

"Definitely," Miss Clara replied. "Shannon masterminded the whole thing to make look it like Adeline took the money from the cash register because Shannon wants you for herself. And it sounds like your brother wanted to use your misjudgment where Adeline was concerned to look better in your father's eyes."

If it was true, it wouldn't surprise him. His brother would do anything to make him look bad, and Adeline had the same kind of relationship with Shannon. No love lost there either.

Yet in his mind, it wasn't as neat and tidy as that. There was still a loose end.

"The thing is, Miss Clara, Garrett doesn't have a key to the market or the restaurant. Only my father and I do—and Adeline did too, of course."

"True." She nodded. "But evidently your brother knows where you keep your key. He slipped in late and took it from your room. Then put it back before you ever knew it was gone."

There it was. The key mystery solved. Of course, his brother would also know what a heavy sleeper Everett was and how easy that would be to do. Over the years he'd slept through any number of things that had roused the rest of the household.

"And you know Shannon would do anything to make Adeline look bad in your eyes," Miss Clara added. "Less competition that way."

He stared at Adeline's picture of the rose again, recalling the day he'd given it to her. Well, almost given it to her. It had felt like a special moment between the two of them. Adeline looking at him like he was a hero of sorts, about to hand her the world in the form of a simple flower. But out of nowhere, Shannon appeared. Like a wedge, she'd come between the two of them then too, hadn't she?

"Just so you know, Mr. Brighton." Miss Clara leaned in. "Mr. Henry and I have already spoken to Adeline's uncle about this."

His eyes widened at that bit of news. "You have? That's brave of you."

"We had to. Adeline is special to both of us. We'd risk losing our jobs for her any day."

"And Mr. Dougherty. . .what did he have to say?"

"He didn't believe us at first, of course. He asked us to step out, and he called Shannon in. Oh, that girl. *Mmm-mmm-mmm.*" Miss Clara paused, shaking her head in disbelief. "She has such a twisted way of looking at things. Very few values. I personally think it has a lot to do with her mother. That woman can be so—"

"Miss Clara." Everett twirled his finger in the air, trying to bring her back to the facts. "Mr. Dougherty's reaction?"

"How else could he react? Shannon went into his study thinking she was so clever that she came up with the idea to get Adeline on your bad side, that she told her father all about it. He couldn't believe it. He was appalled."

"He stood up for Adeline?"

"And for what was right."

Thank You, God! He found himself offering up his gratitude. "I suppose doing what's right runs on that side of the family. So that means he went to get Adeline from the station? Are they back home yet, I hope? I need to see her."

"Actually. . ." Miss Clara's warm eyes settled on him. "He just sent me here to ask if you'd be so kind as to go. After all his grousing with her, he thought you might have a better chance of bringing her back. If it helps her to know, Shannon and her mother are packing now. They'll be in the Hamptons for the next month until things simmer down. Mr. Dougherty is also on his way over to speak to your parents."

It was all resting on him?

Adeline's future and his own?

"I don't know if she can ever forgive me." Doubt tugged at him.

"Well, there's only one way to find out now, isn't there?"

"You're right." Jumping up from the table, he stuffed the sketch of the rose into his pocket for good luck then tossed Miss Clara the key.

"Would you mind putting a note on the door, saying we're closed today? Then sticking around to let my help know what's going on? I hope I'll be back with Adeline in an hour, but if it takes all day, I plan to keep trying."

A broad smile crossed her lips. "I'm happy to help, Mr. Brighton. Now go." She shooed him. "Go get your Adeline."

Bolting out of the restaurant, that was his plan. He only hoped Adeline was still in Boston. And if so, he hoped he could find the right words to make her stay.

Chapter 12

The railroad station had been nearly empty when Adeline first got there in the dark of the morning. Even though it would be hours before her assigned train came clacking up the tracks, she purchased her ticket and sat down to wait.

As the hours slipped by and the dawn of a new day lightened the skies, other travelers scurried around her. Normally she would have found pleasure in the waiting, happily whiling away the time, eyeing individuals in the crowd, curious about their life stories and making up tales about them on her own.

But not this morning. Not when her heart felt too troubled and broken. Right now, she couldn't think about anyone else but herself—and Everett.

Was he feeling the least little bit the same way? Was he missing her at all, or was it just another day to him?

Not only that, she couldn't stop wondering and worrying about him and his parents. Were things between them back to normal again? Like they used to be before she came into their lives?

She sighed, hoping the money she'd given him would help mend the rift between him and his parents. At least that would make it all worth it to her. It hadn't been easy. Every time she thought about how they thought the worst of her, she felt sick. Yet given the situation, it had seemed like the right thing to do. And the right thing. . .no, it usually wasn't the easiest, she learned.

Just like her leaving the way she was. It wasn't simple at all. Not only was she hurting from the loss of Everett in her life, but now she barely had any money left after paying for her ticket. When she'd first started planning to go back to Arkansas, she hoped to have more money saved up. Funds to live on once she got back home.

No, that's not true.

What she'd really been hoping, in the deepest parts of her heart, was that she'd never have to leave Everett. Wishing that somehow, some way, they'd be together, because she'd fallen so completely in love with him.

Letting go of another long sigh, she glanced at the clock. And instantly stiffened. Throughout the morning, the hour hand had moved with agonizing slowness, but now there were only minutes left before her departure time, causing her heart to race. In less than a quarter of an hour, she'd be boarding the train and heading west to whatever life awaited her there.

It took all the strength and willpower she had left inside her to force herself out of her seat. As she stood, her legs felt weak from sitting, heavy with dread. Picking up her bag of belongings, she hugged it to her side as she nervously inched her way across the platform, joining the group of travelers waiting there.

Most of the others had eager smiles on their faces, watching the approaching train come up the tracks. But she was feeling anxious in a whole different way. Instead of eyeing the train, she gazed up at the sky.

Oh, dear Father God, please be there for me, will ya? Just like You always have. Please be there to guide me, to keep me safe, to take my life in whatever direction that You—

"Ad-dy! Addy!"

She started. Had she really heard her name?

Glancing around at the people surrounding her, she saw that no one seemed to be paying her any mind. She must have been imagining things.

"Adeline!" The shout came again.

Yes, coming from down the way. Someone was absolutely calling her name.

Standing on tiptoes, she tried to see over the heads of the men next to her. And there he was. There was Everett, running up the platform, his shirt half untucked, his tie flapping loose, looking more disheveled than she'd ever seen him. And more handsome than ever too.

Cradling her bag in her arms, she started to burrow her way through the group of businessmen next to her. At the same time, Everett was trying to make his way in. Until finally, they were standing as close as could be, facing one another.

"Everett? What are you doing here?" What a gift it was to see him one last time! She thought she'd never have the chance to lay eyes on him ever again.

"Adeline, look at me." He reached out, grasping one of her hands in his own. "You can't go."

"But I—I have to." She choked on the words. Was he saying she couldn't leave because she was in more trouble? Or because he still cared? She was so confused.

"I can't let you go." He threaded his fingers through her own, linking their hands together.

"Everett, the train leaves in less than ten minutes." She nodded toward the locomotive inching its way up the track. "It's the best thing for both of us. Just let me go."

"I don't care when it leaves. You can't be on it."

Without warning, he tightened his clasp on her hand, drawing her from the throng of passengers. Deepening his hold on her as if she could disappear at any moment, he led her to the side of the station away from the crowd. Then reaching for her bag, he dropped it to the ground, and this time took both of her hands into his.

"We need to talk, Addy," he said with an intensity she'd never heard from him before.

"I can't imagine what else there is to say," she replied honestly. "I already spoke the truth. It wasn't me, Everett. I didn't take the money."

"I know that now." A look of remorse instantly shadowed his face. "It was Shannon and Garrett. The two of them, working against us."

"Our own kin?" She gaped at him, not wanting to believe it was true. "But why? How?"

"I'll explain it to you later, I promise. But right now, I don't care about that." A new light shone in his eyes. "I only care about you. And me. And, Addy. . .I'm sorry for ever doubting you." He gazed at her intensely, his eyes searching hers. "Can you—will you—forgive me? Please?"

Once again, like the night before, it tugged on her heart to see him so distressed. "Everett." She squeezed his hands. "It's not your fault. I should've never begged you for a job and all. I put you in a bad position."

"That's not true. You put me right where I wanted to be. With you. And that's where I hope to be, Addy. Now and for all our days." He dipped his head. "Say you'll forgive me." His voice deepened with earnest. "Say you'll stay with me."

She looked in his pleading eyes. Those blue, blue eyes. Oh, how she loved him! Her mama and daddy would have loved him too, wouldn't they?

The instant they came to mind, she remembered what the two of them would say when they had a spat or lost their tempers. "It takes a strong person to say they're sorry," her daddy would always go first. "And just as strong of a person to forgive," her mama would chirp back. Then they'd kiss and make up.

But it wasn't only their example that had her in the forgiving mood. It was easy to forgive Everett because she loved him so.

Looking at their hands that were still joined together, she said, "I'll forgive you if you forgive me for causing so much trouble."

A broad smile broke out on his lips. His features relaxing, instantly relieved. "You're trouble all right," he teased. "But I can handle it. I love you, Addy."

Her heart overflowed, hearing those words come from his lips. She let him pull her close, into his warm embrace and a kiss she didn't—couldn't—resist. Pressing his lips to hers, he caressed her mouth as much as kissed it. So tender and sweet and loving in ways she'd never felt before.

But although she wanted to love him for always, to be held in his embrace for all time, none of it changed anything. The reality was the two of them were far too different. A relationship between them would never survive. There were too many outside forces pitted against them.

"Oh, Everett!" she whispered. Pulling away from him, she could feel the emotion welling up inside her, her eyes glistening with tears. "I love you too. But I can't—" She paused, working to muster up her resolve. "Even though I didn't steal anything, I can't go back. Nothing else has changed. I still don't fit in your world."

"I just told you I love you, Addy. With all my heart." He held out his hands to her again, appearing crestfallen. "You said you loved me too. That's all that matters."

"Is it? I'm just not sure. The world I came from isn't like yours." She shook her head. "I don't think we're supposed to be judging each other or trying to impress the next person by what we wear and who we're seen with and such. I feel like we were all made for something more, the kind of stuff that's inside of us. That's what counts to me."

"But don't you see, Adeline? From all that's happened over the past few days, that very thing has been proven."

"Maybe to you, but to all the others—your parents and my relatives—I don't think they see it the same way."

"Trust me. They do. Your uncle knows the truth and is sorry. My parents are asking for your forgiveness too. Even Mother caught me on my way here, insisting that I run after 'the love of my life.'"

"Your mother? She said that?"

"Absolutely. My parents hope you'll stay because they can't deny how much I care about you. And now they know they can trust my judgment."

"I don't know. . . I'm not sure what to do."

"I think it's clear."

"What do you mean?"

"You and me. I'm the clear choice for you, my love." Pulling her close again, he leaned in. "Addy, I promise you I will do everything in my power to grow our business, so we can head west and build a home there."

Looking up into his eyes, she chuckled. "You don't need to go promising me all that, Everett. I just need the promise of your love."

"I'm happy to say it again." He kissed her hand. "I love you, Adeline."

"And. . ." She paused.

"And what?"

"I need you to promise me one more thing."

He straightened, taking her seriously. "I can do that."

"Can you please promise me more Sunday afternoons?" she asked. If they had those moments together, they could get through anything, she was sure of it. "Just like the ones we've had?"

Her request brought an added glint to his eyes. "You mean strolling through the public gardens?"

"Uh, huh."

"Arm in arm. Or holding hands?"

"Of course." She shivered just thinking about it, so happy to be planning a future by his side.

"And in our bare feet?" His eyes twinkled even more.

She laughed. "Why, Everett Brighton, you know me mighty well, don't you?"

"And I love every part of you."

He leaned over to kiss her again, his ardent lips sealing the promise of his love on Sundays—and every other day of the week. . .every week of the year. . .for many years to come.

Cathy Liggett is an award-winning author who enjoys writing sweet romances and women's fiction. She and her husband live in southwest Ohio and spend most of their free time walking and spoiling their boxer mix, Chaz. They are always happiest when their greatest blessings—their two grown children and most delightful son-in-law—are home for a stay.

Lady's Slipper

by Kelly Long

Chapter 1

S hoes? Whatcha think we need shoes for, boy?" The old mountain man spit a line of chew off the porch and into the summer grass.

Jacob Reynold ran a hand over his eyes. His vision optimized in time to see the bearded gentleman stick out a hideously toenailed bare foot.

"Lookee here. I got some of the best feet around, and I ain't never owned a pair of shoes." He wiggled his toes for emphasis, and Jacob tried not to mind the yellow calluses on the sole of the protruding foot.

"I understand. No shoes. But sometimes, shoes can be of help in the cold—for children and women, of course."

The man laughed, displaying toothless gums and a wide tongue. "Women? Ha! Now I see whatcha really after!"

"No. . . . I'm here to distribute shoes. Look, I'm supposed to meet Miss Fern Summerson who has offered to be my guide up the mountain."

The old man thumped back in his willow bent rocker, silent for a moment. But soon he leaned forward and beckoned Jacob closer with a conspiratorial whisper. "Son, you best take my advice and hightail it outta here. Fern Summerson lives atop this mountain and knows every inch of it—that's true. But Summerson Mountain here is named for her daddy, and his daddy, and his daddy before that. And the whole bunch of 'em Summerson men would sooner spit in your eye than say hello—and they've got quick tempers too."

"Yes," Jacob nodded, unimpressed. "The mission board was careful to tell me all that you've said and much more. But God called me to deliver shoes to the people of Summerson Mountain, and deliver them I shall. . .with His help, of course."

"Humph!" The old man shook his head. "Suit yourself then. But I can tell ya, you're headed for a mess of trouble."

Fern Summerson ran barefoot and fleet down the mountain trail. She was already more than half an hour late, but her little brother had insisted she help him catch fire salamanders by the well wall and she'd somehow lost track of time. Now the words from the mission board's brief letter played out behind her hazel eyes.

"Missionary from Williamsport to arrive on Summerson Mountain the tenth of June. Please aid as guide in distributing goods to those in need."

Fern could imagine what an arduous trip the missionary, Mrs. Deborah Cummings, had to take—part mountain roads and part open boat travel on the moody Susquehanna River. It would most likely be overwhelming for a woman who also brought heavy goods to give to the people of the remote Allegheny Mountains, the foothills of Appalachia.

Fern caught her breath when she reached the mountain's general store and smoothed her light-green slip of a dress. At nineteen, she was an accomplished seamstress, having learned to make her own clothes at her grandma's knee. And today she wanted to make a good impression on the missionary lady whom she corresponded with on a regular basis.

She ran up the sagging white steps of the mountain store, barely glancing at the stranger with a loaded pack mule who stood outside talking to Jeb Richards.

"Here now, Miss Fern!" Jeb called to her, and she sighed to herself, but turned to hear what the old man had to say.

"Jeb, I'm rather in a hurry—"

"To meet the missionary, right?"

Fern let go of the screen door. "Oh, did I miss her all together? I thought—"

"Her. . .is right here." Jeb grinned, pointing a gnarled finger.

Fern looked to where the tall stranger was taking off his hat. "Miss Summerson, I'm Jacob Reynolds, from the missionary board down Williamsport way."

Fern frowned in confusion. "But you're a—man." The word sounded thin and hardly adequate to describe the handsome russet-haired missionary who stood straight and tall before her.

"Uh. . .yes. Yes I am, Miss—"

"Please, call me Fern. Everyone does. But where is my pen-friend, Deborah Cummings? We were to meet for the first time in person."

"Mrs. Cummings took ill at the last moment."

"Oh," Fern exclaimed. "I hope she's not bad off. She's very special to me."

"I don't think you have cause to worry, Miss Sum—er Fern. A head cold only, I believe."

"I see," Fern murmured then smiled. "All right. Well, as promised, I will be your guide on the mountain and help in any way I can." *Even though my father may have something to say to that when he finds out you're a man. But my sister. . .she'll be over the moon. . . .*

Jacob was surprised at Fern Summerson's cultured voice; she spoke English with a beautiful tone and none of the distinctive dialect Mr. Barefoot had favored. And there was a kindness about her face, an empathy that seemed to reach out and encompass those she looked upon. He felt it more than any pointed glance from some fashionably dressed lady passing on the street—Fern Summerson seemed to be able to see clean through to a man's heart. *And I am losing my mind—it must be the heat. I'm here to deliver shoes. Period.*

Jacob watched her bid farewell to the old man on the porch and then dart up the mountain path that seemed faint in the dappled sunlight. He clung to his hired mule's bridle and tried to get the beast moving in one direction. But Clog seemed to have other plans, which in no way included bearing his burden with placidity. The mule pulled against him, and Jacob narrowly avoided a kick to his shins.

Jacob almost laughed out loud. A week ago, he was sitting in a stuffy office writing support letters for local mission families, and today he was in the wilds of Pennsylvania. The latter was by far the more pleasant of the two places, despite the mule's disposition.

"Are you making it all right?" Fern's voice called back to him from above. He gave Clog an unrelenting pull that finally seemed to orient the mule.

"Yep!" Jacob called. "What's our first stop?"

"Only a bit further. The Mortons live up above here."

Jacob caught up with her in time to hear the whoops and calls of several boys. "Whoo-ee, Ma! The missionary's come! Whoop! The missionary's come!"

Jacob smiled at the enthusiasm of the boys. It boded a good start to his work on Summerson Mountain.

Fern was pleased that the Morton family was the first they came to—the boys were always grateful for anything that might come in a pack or barrel, and this time they had a flesh-and-blood minister to bring them aid. She slanted a glance at Jacob through the light fringe of her bangs and found his smile to be infectious as he worked at the pack straps.

In Fern's experience, missionaries of the day usually brought Christian reading materials or good-wearing secondhand clothes or small toys for the children, like doll babies, pocket knives, and yo-yos. But it was the inevitable treats, chocolate bars and candies, that so endeared the missionary to the children of the backwoods.

"Can I help you with the packs?" Fern asked, coming to pet the muzzle of the mule.

Jacob gave her a fast smile, and she was struck by the emerald depths of his eyes. But then she shook herself mentally and came around the mule to help lift down a heavy cloth sack.

"My," she commented, almost as excited as the boys jumping around. "You've brought a lot if the weight of the bag is any indication."

"Yes, ma'am."

He lifted the flap of the material and put one hand inside to rummage mysteriously while the young boys waited with bated breath. Fern watched the smile on Jacob's face grow as he pulled out a solid-looking, dark-brown pair of. . .

Chapter 2

S hoes!" Jacob said triumphantly, but then he noticed the smiles slipping away from the eager faces.

What's going on? These are great shoes! A shoemaker who was going out of business in Philadelphia had donated a lot of sturdy styles and sizes. Why did everyone look dejected?

Jacob sought Fern's gaze for a clue to the seemingly odd behavior, and she stepped a bit closer. He caught the fresh scent of mint from the top of her hair and forgot about the shoe he held momentarily—but then she stretched on tiptoe and whispered to him.

"Perhaps if you'd start with a toy or some candy? They so look forward to the rare treat."

Jacob blinked. "I don't have any of those things. I brought good, sensible shoes."

"Shoes? He brought us shoes, Ma! What'll we do with dumb ol' shoes?" One of the young Morton boys looked like he was about to cry at the prospect of shoes until his mother grabbed him by the ear.

"Foolish child! Hush! Now we be grateful for what the Good Lord gives us, and that's final. Round up yer sisters and let's see what fits yu'uns here. Sorry, Preacher. We'll take the shoes and be glad for 'em."

But Jacob felt a funny foreboding in his belly that the Mortons' reaction was going to be universal. It was confirmed when the honey-haired Fern bit her bottom lip as she looked down at the pile of shoes.

"All right! All right. . .it appears that I've forgotten a sack." Jacob smiled at the family. "Miss—ah—Fern, if you'll hold on to Clog, I'll hike back down to the general store where I've left some of my gear. I'll be back shortly."

He headed back to the trail before Fern could comment and hastened the relatively short distance back to the general store. The old man with the bare feet was still sitting on the porch and Jacob sighed inwardly, knowing he wouldn't be able to pass the fellow without receiving a comment or two.

"Ha! Ye're back already! Whatcha do with Fern—scared her off, didn't ya?"

"No, I, uh, simply realized I needed a few things from the store that I'd forgotten." Jacob caught the latch on the screen door with gratitude, but the old man's voice echoed inside.

"Ha, boy! Ya didn't bring nuthin' but shoes, right? Shoot—the young'uns ain't gonna take hearty to that!"

Mr. Clarey, the storekeeper, hollered outside in a booming voice. "Jeb! You hush up now and let the boy alone! He ain't supposed to know everything about everything! Now, come on in, Mr. Reynolds—what can I do for you?"

Jacob eyed the big storekeeper with relief. "I need to look at your toys and some candy."

Mr. Clarey smiled. "Ah, you need a little sweetness to make your shoes more palatable?"

"Something like that." Jacob smiled. He liked the first impression he'd had of Mr. Clarey when the storekeeper had readily offered to give him some space for the rest of the shoes.

"Well, I can tell you I don't get much stock in for toys—times are tough."

"Do you have anything?" Jacob asked trying to keep the note of desperation out of his voice.

"Well. . . .I got some fancy marbles in last week. They're not made of clay but of imported glass. Wanna take a look?"

"Yes!" Jacob didn't try to contain his enthusiasm as he followed the storekeeper behind the counter.

The marbles were beautiful, cleanly round, with a wonderful swirl of color captured inside each one.

"Yep, they're right nice. But maybe a bit too costly for a missionary."

"How much?" Jacob asked, still studying the small glass balls.

"Oh, say two dollars for a hundred of 'em. I got leather pouches to put 'em in too."

Jacob nodded. "Deal. What else do you have?"

"Well, I got wooden tinker sets in the back that I lay out for Christmas. And lemme see. . .I got a bunch o' little things like bird calls—'course the kids are right good at calling on their own. I got airplanes, wooden horses, baby dolls, and all kinds of suckers and hard candy—"

"Mr. Clarey," Jacob interrupted with a look of apology. "Could you pack up a sack with say, fifty dollars' worth of toys and candy in it? And maybe a few treats for the mothers? I'll add in a few dollars if you could do it right away. Fern—uh Miss

Summerson—is waiting for me up ahead."

The storekeeper appeared taken aback and leaned over to mutter in Jacob's ear. "Son, ya don't have to spend a good summer's salary—I'd be glad to donate some of the marbles."

Jacob smiled. "You're a kind man, sir. But my earthly mother was able to endow me with plenty, and my heavenly Father enjoys an abundant expenditure now and then—especially if it'll aid in my preaching and visiting."

Mr. Clarey slapped the counter. "All righty then. I'll have your order comin' right up!"

Fern accepted Mrs. Morton's offer of rose tea and secured the mule to the front porch hitching post. Then she entered the small cabin and sat down at the rough-hewn table. Her stomach grumbled as she'd had little for breakfast after serving the others at home. But Susan Morton served freshly baked bread with the tea, and Fern delighted in the blueberry preserves and freshly churned butter that came as accompaniment. The Morton children gathered round too, and Fern loved the homey sound of silence as everyone chewed with enthusiasm.

"It's so nice here," Fern commented with a smile.

"Why ain't it nice at yer house, Miss Fern?" Billie, the oldest boy, spoke clearly, and Fern saw his mother give him a quelling glance.

"That ain't none of yer business, Son."

Fern's smile grew. "Oh please, Susan, let me answer—it's all right. You see, Billie, since my mother died, my father has been a bit—well, angry at God."

Billie snorted. "I think your pa's plain mean, and I—"

"Billie!" his mother hollered. "That's enough."

Fern answered softly. "My father is—well—he can be mean and gruff, but I hope that a tender heart still lingers beneath his demeanor, Billie."

She would have continued had not the tall missionary appeared in Sue Morton's doorway with a bulky and tantalizing-looking sack in his arms.

Jacob felt a little like it was Christmas instead of high summer. He enjoyed the expressions of expectation that turned his way. He was especially pleased to see Fern Summerson's gentle look of delight, and he couldn't help smiling at her. But then, the younger children drew around him with wide eyes, and he moved to the table.

"Thank you, Morton family—Mrs. Morton—and uh—Fern for reminding me that everyone deserves some cheer and fun—along with the occasional new shoe.

And now"—he reached into the sack and rattled around—"I have something beautiful for you." He pulled out two small leather drawstring pouches and put the sack on the wood floor.

He opened one of the pouches and poured ten glass marbles into his hand. Even in the filtered light from the cabin's two windows, the glass shone clear, and the yellow, red, and blue iridescent streaks seemed to glow with all of the enticement of a lit flame.

"Woohee," Billie exclaimed softly. "What are they?"

"Marbles," Jacob said just as softly. "But they're also a way to remember that you can invite God to live in your heart and that when He comes, He brings marvelous color into your soul and world."

"That's a beautiful thought." Fern spoke with tenderness in her voice, and before he knew what he was doing, he'd taken one of the marbles and slipped it between her slender fingers.

"To remember," he said gruffly. Fern closed her fingers around the glass and smiled up at him.

"Thank you," she said. "Children, what do you say to Mr. Reynolds?"

There was a chorus of gratitude as Jacob handed out a few pouches and admonished them all to share. Then he pulled a prettily flowered apron from the pouch and handed it a bit awkwardly to Mrs. Morton. "Mothers need to remember the beauty of God in their hearts as much as children."

Mrs. Morton moved around the table and reached to give him a big hug then she tenderly stroked the beautiful cloth and nodded with tears in her eyes. "I'll remember, Preacher."

Chapter 3

Fern let her fingers trail gently over the leaves of mountain laurel that lined the path as they climbed deeper into the secrets of the mountain. She'd slipped the marble in her dress pocket and was glad of its slight weight. She glanced over her shoulder now and then to make sure that the missionary was keeping up with his mule. She didn't talk much, because she was caught up with thoughts about what had happened in the Mortons' cabin. She'd never seen a man preach the Gospel with such beautiful simplicity, and she felt a growing interest in Jacob Reynolds.

"Poison ivy."

Fern startled from her reverie and looked back. Jacob indicated a vine with a nod of his chin. "I'm allergic to it," he explained.

"Oh, I'm sorry. We'll have to be careful. It doesn't bother me."

"It's an acquired allergy," he said. "You have to get it to get it."

They both laughed together and Fern felt a yearning in her heart to experience such companionship—even for a few moments. At home, no matter how much she tried, there was always discord with her sister, Daisy, and the negative attitude of her father. It was only with her little brother, Seth, that she found life's joy. Yet, here was this stranger, a man of God, softly treading into her heart. She drew a deep breath and told herself she was being foolish—Jacob Reynolds would be gone in less than two weeks, and she'd probably never see him again.

"Where to next?" Jacob asked cheerfully.

She looked back at him, and he saw the hesitation on her face.

"What is it?"

"Well." She spoke in soft tones. "I had thought we might not stop, actually."

"Is there some reason? I don't mind ministering to anybody as we go."

She smiled at him. "Of course, but the Kelley cabin is sometimes difficult."

He nodded. "Please let me try—or maybe I mean, let God try with me."

"Yes, you're right."

She turned and took a faint path off to the left. Jacob followed eagerly. Then he began to notice that the woods grew darker and more overgrown by subtle degrees. Something in his spirit urged him to pray, but he wasn't sure why.

Fern stopped in front of him as if to listen. He heard the faint sounds of some stringed instrument. For a brief moment, he was reminded of an orchestral violin in the mournful harmony of the distant notes.

He watched as Fern seemed satisfied with the music and continued on the path once more. Jacob moved to follow, but Clog had other ideas and fought him with every step.

They finally came to a clearing where a sagging and desolate cabin held sway. The music stopped abruptly as they walked toward the place, and Jacob had the curious sensation that they were being watched from all sides.

A woman with an ill-fitting housedress and unkempt hair slipped out onto the porch. "You know better, Fern Summerson, than to bring anybody 'round here."

"It's all right, Lucy. Jacob is a visiting missionary."

Jacob heard the kind patience in Fern's voice and kept silent as the woman on the porch seemed to debate some choice within herself. But before she spoke, an eerie wailing filled the air and then the music started again.

"John is playing very well," Fern praised.

"The Lord knows he can't do much else," the woman said. Jacob stepped forward.

"John is your son?" He asked the question and was startled when the woman began to sob. The sound rose as did the weeping noise of the strings. Jacob stared down at Fern in confusion.

"Lucy doesn't believe John is. . .normal," she whispered.

Jacob nodded. He didn't truly understand, but he did recognize that something was very wrong with the situation.

Lucy stopped her mournful cry and locked eyes with Jacob. "Preacher man, you tell me why God give me a curse in place of a whole child?"

"I—I don't. . ." Jacob faltered, but only for a moment. "You're wrong, Lucy Kelley!" He called the words out with growing conviction. "Your—John has a gift. His playing of music conveys great strength of emotion!"

"You ain't seen him!" Lucy yelled back. She turned and ran into the cabin.

"What is wrong here?" Jacob asked Fern when he noticed her young jaw set as though against tears.

Fern shook her head. "It's an old story. Many people here believe that if a person looks or acts differently, they are cursed in some way. Lucy blames God, as you can tell."

"And—John?"

He watched her eyes stray to the trees beyond the cabin. "Come," she said finally. "I will introduce you."

Fern was conscious of the tension in her body, wondering how Jacob would react to John. *But after the beautiful analogy he gave with the marbles, all should be well.*

She led him to a tall tree at the back of the cabin and stopped to call up into the thickly leafed limbs. "John? It's Fern. Could you come down and meet the missionary?"

"He ain't never seen the likes of me, I bet." John's voice was soft, even melodic, and Fern nodded, glancing at Jacob.

"All of us are created to be unique, John," Jacob called. "The Master's hand crafts each of us, and we breathe the breath of life. That makes us brothers in Christ. I would surely find this journey unmet without having touched hands with a brother."

There was a dense rustling in the tree, and John dropped from the limbs to the ground. He rose to his feet slowly and Fern smiled. "Hello, John." She looked straight into his single blue eye and paid no attention to the distorted face that resembled something from a child's darkest nightmare.

She knew 'twas something wary and almost feral in John—he'd been scorned so much. But Jacob held out a strong hand and took John by the shoulder in warm greeting and praise.

"John, your music rivals what I've heard played in symphonies back in the city. It is beautiful and alive, even in its pain."

Fern waited, her breath held, to hear John's response.

"I fiddle some."

Fern almost laughed in relief. John had spoken three words that acknowledged something other than his appearance. Jacob Reynolds had a way of talking to a man's soul.

Jacob walked through the woods and back to the cabin with John and Fern. It seemed important that he speak to both Lucy and her son and explain that John was no cursed thing, despite his appearance. He knew that the relationship between mother and son needed repair somehow. Dear Lord, Jacob cried out in his spirit. *Please help this family. . .this need is so great, so much more than shoes. . .to change a mother's heart and mind. Oh Lord, be glorified in this situation.*

They entered the cabin; it was dark and dreary. Lucy stood at the sole window with her back turned. Jacob glanced at John and saw the boy hang his head in his mother's presence. Jacob drew a deep breath and spoke with authority. "Lucy Kelley, you have a son, a beautiful son. His face may be crooked, but his soul is straight. His music speaks to that and is a gift from God."

Lucy turned, and Jacob watched Fern hold out a placating hand, but the older woman cried out shrilly. "God don't give me no gifts! Only—him!" She pointed to John. "His daddy done run out on me when he saw him." She shuddered. "And you come in here like some high and mighty—"

"Stop!" Jacob commanded, and Lucy's shoulders sagged. "You're a selfish woman and an unkind mother. I will encourage John to build his own cabin—far from yours. Perhaps one day God will heal your heart and your mind. The boy is no curse."

"Please, Lucy," Fern soothed. "Listen to Jacob."

But Lucy turned her back on them and stood silent in stubborn resolution.

"Is there a church or meeting place on the mountain here?" Jacob asked. Fern heard his attempt to change the air about them after the visit to the Kelley cabin. "I thought maybe I might preach a bit even though my main job is to bring shoes—and sweets—to the folks on Summerson Mountain."

"At the top of the mountain, on my father's land, there's a small white church where we gather. Most of the older men take it in turns to lead the service, and there's usually a good amount of people who come."

"I must confess," he said, sounding rueful, "that I've heard a fair amount of gossip about your father. I'm speaking in apology. I never judge a man, and I try to understand his heart." He laughed. "I sound like a pious fool, but it's true, nonetheless."

"No," she returned in sober tones. "I think it's wonderful that you try and see a man's heart. My father seems to have lost his when my mother died."

"I'm sorry."

"She was a believer, so I know she's in heaven, but my father seems to find no consolation in that."

"Sometimes grief takes a while for a man to work out."

She nodded, and they hiked on in companionable silence for a while. Then Fern stopped and pointed. "There's a natural spring over here, if you'd like some fresh water."

"That would be wonderful."

She nodded and led the way to the rocks.

Jacob led Clod to the little stream of water that ran from the spring in the rocks. Someone had left a tin cup there, obviously for all to drink. Jacob handed Fern the cup and looked at the ground while she drank. He didn't want to appear as though he were watching her, though he longed to do so. He was surprised at his interest in the girl but decided it had something to do with the way she blended in and was part of the beautiful mountain itself.

"Would you like a drink?" She held out the cup and he took it eagerly, thirsty from their travels so far.

He bent to where the water ran, sparkling and crisp, and felt the immediate refreshing coolness through his fingers on the cup. Then he drank deeply and filled the cup twice more. He smiled at her when he put the cup back. "As the Lord is Living Water, this sweet liquid is but a mere taste of heaven."

He felt her curious look and shrugged awkwardly. "What is it?"

"You," she returned. "You seem to have a way of making everyday things part of God. It is a gift, I think."

He looked down at her honey-colored hair and its clean part and thanked her with sincerity. "You have a gift too, Fern Summerson."

"Now what would that be?"

He stretched out an arm to encompass the vastness of green and light surrounding them. "God gives you all of this, every day, and I think your spirit too is much like its beauty."

He saw her blush and wondered if he'd spoken out of turn. But then she lifted her gaze to his and nodded. "I am blessed to live here. What is it like in the city?"

"Ah, it's a far cry from this place. The city is incredibly dirty—there's dust from the railroad, the coal that's transported, and the stirring up from the automobiles and horses that travel through the streets."

"And yet you live there?"

"Yes, I do. The missionary board has its headquarters there, and it's where God has called me—at least for now." He gestured with his arm once more. "But this— this is truly a respite."

"I'm glad." She smiled. "But now, we should head on. There's rather a feisty clan of folks who live along the next ridge."

"Feisty?" he inquired with a lopsided grin.

"Well, they're the Bodleys. Their cousins, the other Bodleys, live farther on. And the bunch of them become rather worked up now and then and become—um—feisty."

"I see," Jacob said, not really seeing at all. But he decided that an adventure lay ahead.

Fern bit her lip and hoped that the wild Bodleys would be on their best behavior. She was sadly disappointed. No sooner had she and Jacob walked into the clearing that marked their property when the sound of a gunshot rang out with startling force. Fern turned in time to see the missionary duck and his hat go flying off into the weeds.

"Oh my," she muttered.

"Yes," Jacob said grimly. "Oh my."

She watched him straighten to his full height and stalk ahead of her into the clearing. "Jacob, please, I wouldn't—"

"Come out, ye brood of vipers, and repent!" Jacob called the words out and even Fern recognized the boldness of the challenge. Clearly, he had dealt with tough men before.

Fern clutched Clod's reins and waited to see what would happen next. She knew if she jumped into the fray it would only weaken Jacob's reputation as a preacher, so she waited.

Jacob stood with his hands on his lean hips and straightened his strong back, clearly presenting a ready and fearless target.

Fern saw Bud Bodley, the eldest of the clan, come out onto the porch, laughing in a hoarse breath. "Ah now, preacher, we just meant a little fun—even the Lord Hisself drank wine and busted the rabble out of the temple courts."

"So you know enough of the Bible to be dangerous," Jacob called. Bud laughed again.

"Let's make a deal, preacher boy. You say I'm dangerous with the Good Book, but how dangerous are you with a gun? Let's say if you can shoot three tin cans offa that stump over yonder, I'll let ya come in and say your piece."

"And if I don't succeed?"

Bud coughed. "Then let's say, I'll be aimin' a little lower than yer hat next time."

Fern's fingers tightened on the reins as Jacob approached the lean-to porch. Bud's sons had come out of the house and stood alert and ready with their rifles. Somehow the mood had switched from rough teasing to dead seriousness, and Fern was terrified that she might actually see Jacob get shot.

Chapter 4

Jacob had been a scrawny kid growing up and had no father figure to teach him how to deal with bullies. So he'd learned the hard way, in back alleys, getting pummeled and even knifed once. All of this ran through his mind as he accepted the revolver one of the younger men handed him. Jacob checked if it was loaded, tested its weight and grip in his hand, and walked out to where one of the boys had set up three cans with peach labels on a thick stump.

Jacob extended his arm and took a slow breath. Then he shouted, "If I wait upon the Lord. . ." He fired and one can flew clean off the stump. He called out again, "I shall find new strength. . ." He fired again and a second can gave a disconsolate ping as it hit the ground.

"Wait a minute, here," Bud Bodley said, coming down off the porch. The old man drew abreast of Jacob and looked up at him. "So you can shoot, and I ken admire that. But, preacher boy, can ya do it blindfolded?"

"Let's find out, shall we?" Jacob bent so Bud could tie a turkey-red handkerchief around his head then straightened and fired. "Praise God!" Jacob said loudly as he pulled off the blindfold and saw the empty stump. He calmly handed the handkerchief back to the man beside him.

"Hoowee, boy. Ya didn't tell me you was some fancy shooter! That ain't playin' fair!"

"Neither is blindfolding a man. Now, Mister Bodley, it will be my distinct pleasure to come into your home and say my piece."

Fern had to resist the strong urge she felt to embrace Jacob after the shooting, but she smiled up at him and was glad to lead Clod forward to the sagging hitching post.

"Fern—how's yer daddy doin'?" Bud asked cheerfully. Fern wanted to roll her eyes at the change in his attitude. The man was as quicksilver as a serpent, and she was always on her guard around him though she didn't truly fear him—except for those moments outside with Jacob.

"My father is about the same," Fern answered politely. Then she nodded a greeting to Mrs. Bodley, a sallow-faced and sulky woman. *But I guess I would be sulky too if I had married Bud.*

Mrs. Bodley put a basket of nuts on the table in a careless fashion then went to a rocker in the corner and began to rock in sullen silence. Bud and his sons scrambled to grab the nuts and carelessly dropped the shells on the dirt floor as they ate them.

Fern took in the air of despair that clung to the house and wished there was something she might do to help relieve the sense of hopelessness that called scorning a visiting pastor a fun pastime.

But here again, Jacob seemed up for the challenge. He waited patiently until, by his very silence, the men stopped eating.

"If you all are through and would come back outside, I've brought a few things along that might be of use to you," he finally said. "You too, ma'am." He indicated Mrs. Bodley, who rose with apparent mistrust but came forth just the same.

They all ambled out onto the porch, and Fern hurried to help Jacob unstrap one of the packs on Clod's back. It appeared that there might be just shoes for the Bodleys' dirty bare feet, but then Fern saw something in Jacob's face soften. His emerald eyes gleamed as he reached into a different sack. He brought out a handful of pink netting wrapped around hard candies. The whole Bodley clan surged forward and waited while Jacob passed round the candy. Then he pulled forth a single red sucker of a tiny horse and handed it to Mrs. Bodley.

Fern was amazed to see a tear trickle down the hard woman's face. She knew then that what suffering had done to Mrs. Bodley might be undone by simple acts of kindness.

"Now," Jacob said with a smile when silence reigned because everyone was enjoying their candy. "Mr. Bodley, if you'd do me the pleasure of sitting on the porch step, I have one more gift from the Lord."

Bud Bodley hunkered down on the step, sucking his candy while Jacob reached into the sack on the ground and pulled out a black pair of steel-toed boots. Fern watched in wonder as Jacob knelt in front of the man who so shortly before had threatened him. But Jacob's big hands were gentle as he eased one of the old man's dirty feet into the loosely laced boot. Then Jacob rested his hands on his thighs and looked up at Bud.

"Here now," the old man grunted. "Steel-toed boots. Why, I haven't owned a pair of boots since I wuz a youngster. Pa would drink up all the money he made." Bud paused abruptly as if he'd revealed too much then cleared his throat. "You keep 'em, Preacher. They're too fine fer the likes of me."

Jacob shook his head. "No. The Lord taught with grace. And people need grace the most when they deserve it the least. So, the boots are yours, Mr. Bodley. Come, I'll put the other one on for you."

Fern swallowed back tears of joy when Bud took Jacob's hand to help him to his feet. Then the old man stood straight and tried a few awkward steps. He smiled at Jacob, a mostly toothless grin. "They're fine—just fine."

"Ya look good, Pa," one of the boys on the porch ventured.

Fern watched Jacob lift his head to look at the boy. "You will look good too. I've got these boots in a range of sizes, and I'll fit you all out."

There was a round of cheering, and Fern wondered who this missionary was to have such wisdom in dealing with those who were hard or brokenhearted.

When they finally left the Bodleys', the gloaming was setting in and lightning bugs began their flickering waltz over the bushes along the path. Jacob realized then how tired he was after such a long, and at times, difficult, day.

He glanced ahead to where Fern was moving in spritely steps before him and Clod and had to smile. He had been conscious of her throughout the day, and he wondered at the warmth he felt for a girl he had only met this morning.

"I feel like I've known you a very long time, Jacob Reynolds." Fern turned to face him.

Jacob almost tripped over his own feet at Fern's clear admission. Any female he'd encountered at home would never have made such a plain statement—they would have been coy or flirtatious. But here was Fern, silhouetted by the beauty of the coming night, speaking sweetly and with innocence in her hazel eyes. Truth deserves truth, he thought, then looked at her with sober acknowledgment. "I feel the same way, Fern Summerson."

She smiled, her small teeth pearly white in the increasing dusk. "Thank you," she said simply.

He nodded, longing for some way to respond, but she spoke instead. "I know you must be tired. I made arrangements for you to stay with Grandma Birdy this first night. It's not far ahead, and she is a delight."

"Grandma—Birdy?" he asked with a smile.

"She always has a wild sparrow on her shoulder—and other birds flock to her. She paints them, and she's eighty-five. She's really wonderful."

"She sounds so. Thank you. But what about you? I fear for you going on alone in the dark. Is your home far?"

Fern laughed gaily. "I'm afraid I haven't had anyone to worry for me for a long time. It rather feels like soap bubbles inside! But no, you needn't worry. It's only a mile or so more up the mountain, and it's a pleasant walk this time of night. Now let's get to Grandma Birdy's where you will have a good rest."

Jacob realized that to press the matter of walking her home would probably touch her pride, so he simply followed her until they came to a small cabin that looked like a wooden dollhouse. Lanterns glowed warmly on the front porch, and a gentle tomcat came running to greet them. "A cat with birds?" Jacob wondered aloud.

Fern whispered to him, "All creatures seem to get along well here." She knocked on the cabin door, and Jacob heard an elderly voice bid them enter. "Grandma Birdy, the missionary's here. His name is Jacob!"

Jacob realized that Grandma must be hard of hearing so he too hollered his greeting as Fern opened the door. The old woman spoke gently from where she sat ensconced on a comfortable-looking chair with a sparrow on her shoulder and a female cardinal on her knee. "Come in, child."

Fern went quickly to hug the older woman while Jacob had to duck to make it through the doorway, but once fully inside he could stand upright even though his head barely scraped the ceiling.

"I'll leave you two to get acquainted. I must go home and see to supper, Grandma," Fern called out.

Grandma Birdy sighed. "Yes, yes. Go on—though your sister might do something to help. . .but I'll not start that trail, child."

Jacob wondered at the comment but had no time to think about it as Fern passed him. "I'll be here bright and early tomorrow, Jacob."

He caught the fresh scent of mint that seemed unique to Fern as she left, and nodded. "Thank you. I'll be ready."

When Fern had shut the door, Jacob followed Grandma Birdy's instructions and pulled baked beans and fresh brown bread from the cookstove. The smells were tantalizing. He sat at the small table and said grace while his stomach growled its approval.

Chapter 5

Fern had so enjoyed spending time with the missionary that she was loathe to tell anyone at home about her day.

She slipped into the small kitchen through the back door of the cabin and lifted one of the clean cast-iron frying pans from its nail on the wall. She started cutting potatoes, adding them and some onion and salt to the pan. She watched Daisy saunter in at the smell of frying potatoes, and her father was soon to follow. Daisy was two years younger than Fern but seemed to have none of the drive that Fern did. Instead, she had no interest in much other than boys. Fern often worried for her. Fern would have rather cooked alone, but she knew her family would want to eat as soon as possible since no one seemed inclined to cook during the day.

"Good evening, Father. Daisy. Where's little Seth?" Seth was the joy of her life. She'd taken over his care when their mother had died at his birth.

"Abed already," her father grunted as he sat at the wooden table. Fern glanced at her dad and noticed the heavy lines in his thin face. He appeared disheveled and far older than his years. She wished she might help him in some way, but it seemed nothing she did had any effect on him.

"I'll take a plate up to Seth when we've finished." Fern spoke her thoughts aloud as she added thin slices of ham to the frying pan. She knew their family was uniquely blessed on the mountain, for Father never seemed to work much but always had housekeeping money on hand. Fern didn't understand it, and she told herself some days that she didn't want to know—like tonight.

"How was yer time with that preacher lady today, Fern?" Daisy asked carelessly while picking a piece of ham from the hot pan.

Fern sighed inwardly. "Deborah Cummings was ill, sadly, so they sent a man in her place."

"A man?" Daisy's hazel eyes opened wide. "What's he look like?"

"Like a man, I suppose," Fern said softly.

"Don't you take no notions in that head of yers, Fern." Her father burped loudly.

"Some city preacher comin' up here. Best let him find his own guide round these parts."

Fern's heart began to speed up but she spoke calmly. "As you wish, Father, but surely you wouldn't want to appear mistrusting to the rest of the mountain. Why, even Bud Bodley took kindly to him."

"Bud Bodley. . .ya don't say? Well, you might as well keep on then. But I don't want yer housekeepin' let go round here. Ya know Daisy gets to faintin' if she works too hard."

"Yes, Father." Fern didn't mind gathering and washing the dirty plates and wiping off the table alone. Her father had given his permission for her to see Jacob again, and she felt a secret joy at the prospect.

Jacob stared at the amazing painting of a robin that Grandma Birdy had done and knew that it was art that rivaled much of what he'd seen in city museums.

"The details are incredible," he said, leaning closer to the work.

"I use a big ol' magnifying glass ta git in real close. I like birds."

Jacob wanted to smile at the plain speaking but instead he leaned over and kissed her rose-petal-like cheek. "Thank you for sharing your gift with me."

"I'm too old for such things as kisses, but Fern Summerson—now she's as beautiful as a bird on the wing."

Jacob smiled. "God has gifted her with beauty indeed."

"Truth well spoken, young man. And tales I could tell you of young Fern. . . ."

"Could you?" Jacob felt his heart thud in his chest and his breathing change a bit. He didn't fully understand the reason why, but any story of Fern Summerson intrigued him.

Grandma Birdy stroked the head of the cat who'd come to rest on her lap, beside a blackbird that had flown in through an open window in the cabin's far wall. Jacob moved to a covered hassock in the mellow light of a kerosene lantern and waited until the old woman was ready to spin her tale.

"Fern would come and sit where you are as a little girl and I'd read to her what books I had. She was especial fond of the dictionary and loved to learn how to pronounce words. You might notice that her speech is a mite different than others round these parts—that comes from hours of our reading together."

Jacob reached to touch her blue-veined hand. "You would have joy in Fern, then, if you taught her to speak so clearly, though what a man or a woman does speaks more loudly in this world than simply what they say."

"Another truth indeed. And I can tell you a secret story of my Fern—one that everyone hereabouts thinks they know but they don't really. Would you care to listen some more?"

"Yes," he said softly.

"Well, my Fern was only but fourteen or so when her mama come to carry another child. Fern's mother was older and the pregnancy was hard on her—sick she was and often. So young Fern had to see to the house and care of her mother, younger sister, and her father when he cared to be about. The night the baby come due, there was a terrible lightning storm and trees were down all over. It was left to Fern alone to bring her brother into this hard world. Her brother came but Fern's mama went with the angels, and Fern was left alone for the whole of a night with a new babe and her dead mother."

Jacob felt his eyes well up with tears for the young girl that Fern was—but still, she appeared light and free as she moved purposefully through the woods. How could a mere child take care of a new baby and deal with the loss of her mother at the same time? And where had her father been? Even with the storm, he should have been there.

But Grandma Birdy was not through. She stroked the sheen of the blackbird's feathers and shook her elderly head. "Her daddy didn't come back for days. Fern tried to send for help through her sister, but Daisy was afraid of the storming that had kept up, so Fern dug her mama's grave alone and then saw to the burying herself. Little Fern. . ."

Jacob swallowed hard, struggling to grasp the horror the girl had experienced. How could the delivering of shoes and candy bring any balm to the hardships Fern had faced? *How insignificant what I'm doing suddenly seems.*

"Now, boy, don't take on so." Grandma broke into his thoughts. "We each are called by the Lord to different tasks—some that seem harder than others—but all equal in faith. Them shoes you got out there mean strength and protection and goodwill, don't forget that."

Jacob stared into the dark-blue eyes that shone bright and clear as a child's. "How do you know about the shoes? I didn't hear Fern tell you and I never said—"

"Sometimes God lets us know what we need in advance, like them shoes. Now, my feet have been bare for near on eighty-six years, and they won't fit the structure of civilized shoes, but I wouldn't mind a piece of hard candy or two when you go to bed your mule down for the night."

"Yes. . .of course. . .I—would you like some jacks as well?"

"Don't tempt me, boy," Grandma Birdy laughed, and Jacob joined her in heartfelt community.

Fern entered the quiet candlelit room where her brother slept and tiptoed to the bed. She bore in her hands a plate of food from supper and a glass of raw milk. "Seth?" she whispered.

His eyes were open in a moment. He scooched up on his pillow and patted his small lap. "Fern, oh, Fern, I was so hungry, but I went to sleep."

She put the plate on top of the quilt and then eased herself down beside him on the edge of the bed. They bowed their heads and prayed for a moment then Seth took up the fork and napkin she'd provided and began to eat with grateful bites.

"How was the missionary lady, Fern?"

"Well," Fern said softly, "it was a missionary man to be exact. His name is Jacob."

"Like in the Bible? Jacob becomes Israel for his name, don't he?"

"Yes, that's right, sweetheart."

"You like him." Seth spoke matter of factly after he'd swallowed a gulp of potatoes.

"I—yes. I like him as a—friend. He'd make a good friend, I think."

"No." Seth waved his fork. "You like him like some girls like boys—maybe not like Daisy—but you still like him, and that's all right."

Fern laughed and cuddled alongside him. "Silly! I saved you some extra cornbread. Would you like it for dessert?"

"Mmm-hmm."

"All right, I'll get it. You finish your ham."

Fern kissed his forehead and went out to the cookstove. But her thoughts were of an emerald-eyed missionary who could shoot blindfolded and still be gentle and kind.

Chapter 6

Jacob tightened the straps on the canvas packs and felt at loose ends. His heart was beating a bit fast, and he knew he was rummaging round in his head as to what to say to Fern when she came. Grandma Birdy had opened a whole other look into the quiet, bright girl's life, and Jacob thought he would probably remember this trip when he was old because of Fern.

He looked up when he heard a soft footfall. Fern stood poised against the coming sunrise on the trail above him. She looked fragile and beautiful, yet inherently strong. Her simple denim dress was nothing of the style he knew, but he also understood that Fern would most likely look beautiful wearing a potato sack.

"Good morning." Her gentle voice broke his reverie, and he left Clod for the moment to go and shake Fern's hand.

"A good morning to you too—Fern."

"Oh dear," she murmured after a moment.

"What?" he asked. "What's wrong?"

She came nearer and peered up into his face then she sighed. "I'm afraid Grandma Birdy's been mentioning me. Am I right?"

He looked at her quizzically. "How do you know?"

"Because you seem different—or the expression on your face seems more sober than yesterday."

He was amazed at her perception and uncertain what to say next.

She smiled and reached out to touch his hand. A feather's touch. . .and then she stepped away. "What happened when Seth was born was for a purpose—though I don't understand it and may not until I get to heaven. But God loves me, and He is good."

Jacob found himself nodding, and his spirit warmed to the strength of faith in this mountain girl.

"I've known many," he said, "who've suffered and become bitter toward God or, more still, who've never had a hard time, it seems, and yet they are careless of any faith. It does my soul good to hear you speak as you do about the Lord." He looked away from her calm gaze. "And it is a great blessing to begin the day with you."

"Yes." She smiled up at him. "Let's go on up the mountain. The other Bodley clan is next."

"Will I be shooting peach cans today?" he asked with a laugh.

"No, things are bit different on the upper Bodley ridge."

"How so?"

She shook her head, her hair shining in the awakening sunbeams. "I think I'll let you find out for yourself."

And with that, he had to be content.

Fern knew a warmness in her heart that the missionary had heard about her mother's death and did not seem to pity her. She wanted his respect, for some reason, but not pity. She didn't bother to examine this further as they climbed through a stand of pines and then came to the Upper Bodleys' ridge.

"Stand down!" An old voice and the cocking of a rifle sounded near. Fern heard Jacob's sigh and hid a smile.

"It's Fern Summerson," she called out sweetly. An old woman appeared from behind a tree, her shotgun braced across her sagging dress.

"Oh, Fern! Forgive me! Ya know my seein's not what it should be and seems ta git worse by the day. Who ya got with ya?"

"The missionary, Jacob Reynolds. Jacob, meet Ma Bodley."

The old woman laughed. "Call me Ma, boy, everyone round here does. 'Cept our hateful kin down below—they probably call me worse!" She laughed again at her own joke and Fern watched Jacob step forward to shake Ma's hand.

"Ma," he said clearly, "it's a pleasure to meet you. And, in truth, the...uh...lower Bodleys had nothing bad to say about you."

"I like yer voice, preacher man. A good, deep voice. And you have the good looks ta match it!"

"I—uh—" Jacob glanced helplessly at Fern, and she smiled.

"You musn't tease the missionary, Ma. But I'll tell you that his hair is the color of russet leaves and his eyes are emerald green." Fern felt herself flush as she gave the personal description and hoped Jacob wouldn't think her forward.

"Thank you, Fern." He spoke gently and her flush grew.

Ma grinned. "You two young things go on out ta the blueberry patch and pick us some berries for breakfast. The pails are on the porch and the snakes should all be sleeping this early. I'll lead the mule to water."

"Snakes?" Jacob asked Fern in a low voice.

"Rattlers," she returned. "But Ma's right—they like the sun best."

"Maybe you'd better let me pick the blueberries."

Fern led him to the porch and picked up two pails, handing him one. "I'm afraid, Jacob, that you have a misconception about snakes and me. First, if you don't bother them, they won't bother you, and second"—she smiled brightly—"one of my earliest memories is running barefoot through high grass and feeling the cold round body of a rattlesnake beneath my bare feet."

She watched his lean jaw tense, and he shook his head. "Bare feet—I'm so sorry that I've never even considered your feet until now. Please—let me get you a pair of shoes to wear or even high boots—you'd be that much safer from snakes."

She felt him studying her bare feet, and her toes curled in the grass of their own accord. "No—I don't want to appear ungrateful, Jacob, but I like my feet to be bare. I'm not worried about snakes—there are worse things in life."

He appeared to think for a moment then nodded reluctantly. "In truth, I have nothing in my packs which would do justice to the daintiness of your feet. And all of my shoes would weigh heavy on your slim ankles."

Fern felt herself blush at his plain-speaking compliments but then she told herself that he was merely thinking of shoes in general. She was sure this was the case when he turned with his pail to scan the surrounding bushes of the property.

"Which direction are the blueberries?"

Fern pointed, half disappointed that he had moved the conversation along. "Over there and back in a bit."

She walked beside him to the bushes, and then they both trod warily through the ground cover. Suddenly Jacob stopped, and Fern saw his lean fingers reach out to gently stroke a pale-pink pouch-like flower that grew taller than the surrounding foliage.

"This is beautiful," he said softly. "I've never seen anything like it before. Do you know what it's called?"

Fern smiled. "You must be drawn to such things as shoes in all cases, Jacob—they're called lady's slippers for their dainty shape. If you look at it from above, it does have the appearance a fancy lady's slipper."

He lifted his head to look at her intently, even as he caressed the flower. "I see that. I was just thinking that it appears to be the only thing that would ever match the beauty of your feet. . . ."

Chapter 7

Jacob knew he crossed a line of propriety when he compared Fern's dainty feet to the worth of the lady's slipper flower, but he'd known no other way to express what he'd been feeling. So now, he listened to the rather disconsolate plunk of blueberries as they hit his pail bottom and wondered if he should apologize.

But Fern began to talk easily of the birds and the trees in the area, naming them with quiet confidence as she filled her pail, so presently his unease passed and he focused on gathering the fruit.

They had been working in companionable silence for about fifteen minutes when he heard a rustling in the bushes and moved closer to defend Fern if necessary from whatever threat there might be. But instead of a wild creature, a girl emerged from the green leaves and smiled broadly at him with unnaturally-colored red lips.

He heard Fern sigh.

"Daisy, why are you here?"

"Aren't you gonna introduce me?"

Jacob saw the consternation on Fern's face as she soberly indicated the other girl with a lift of her hand. "Jacob Reynolds, please meet Daisy Summerson—my younger sister."

"Not that much younger!" Daisy scrambled through the bushes to take Jacob's hand. "Fern just acts like she's old. I'm seventeen. How old are you?"

"Daisy!" Fern said sternly. "Go home. Where's Seth?"

"Oh, the kid ran off somewhere. I was looking for him but then I heard you two moving about."

Jacob watched Fern's delicate cheeks flush with anger. "Daisy! You know it's not safe for him to run around by himself. He's still a little boy, and you are supposed to watch over him while I'm—well, here."

"I can guide Jacob just as easily through the families on the mountain, Fern.

356

Why don't you go look for Seth yourself?"

Jacob cleared his throat. "Why don't we all three look for the child? I think we must have enough blueberries for Mrs. Upper Bodley, wouldn't you say?" He tilted his pail in Fern's direction.

"Yes." Fern nodded, but Jacob could tell by the tension he felt between the two sisters that it might be better to give them a moment alone.

"I'll take the berries back to Ma and meet you both out here in a minute."

He took Fern's pail and headed back the way they'd come.

"Daisy Summerson." Fern spoke levelly despite her anger. "Seth could be in danger, and you are here simply because of Jacob."

"Ohhh! Jacob, is it? Why aren't you calling him Mr. Missionary or something holy like you normally would? Maybe you're a bit smitten yourself."

Fern refused to rise to the bait. "Mind your manners, Daisy. He won't put up with any foolishness, and neither will I."

"Fern Summerson, I think you are—wonderful!"

Fern wrinkled her brow in confusion at her sister's abrupt change; then she followed Daisy's gaze and saw that Jacob stood behind her.

"Do you know," he began in a conversational tone, "that there is a man in that house who cracks walnuts on his forehead?"

Fern laughed. "That's Uncle Sander Bodley. He's a bit. . .unique."

"She means he's crazy," Daisy supplied. "You have to have a dictionary around just to talk to Fern."

Fern ignored Daisy's comment and set out off the path and into the woods. "Seth likes to find different places to play on the mountain," she called over her shoulder to Jacob. "There's no telling where he might be."

They circled around the sidehills and called for Seth for nearly a good hour. Then, out of nowhere, Fern heard Daisy say to Jacob, "Are you married?"

Fern longed to box her sister's ears. Yet, she could not deny that she was interested in Jacob's response, and she could not explain her relief when he calmly answered Daisy in the negative.

"Well, what about a best girl?" Daisy pressed. Fern stopped dead still.

"There," she whispered. "Listen."

In the distance, the sound of a child's scream echoed clear and keen.

"Come on," Fern cried, starting to run. "That's Seth!"

Jacob lay on his belly and stretched his arms to the utmost. "Just take my hands, Seth," he called calmly. The little boy's bruised face was upturned and wet with tears.

"I can't," he wailed.

"Yes, you can, sweetheart," Fern soothed with a catch in her voice. "Jacob will pull you up."

Seth had sobbed out the fact that he'd fallen while pretending to be a squirrel and leaping from rock to rock. He'd slipped and now stood on a rock outcropping with a yawning hollow below.

"All right, Fern. I'll try."

"Good man, Seth," Jacob said. "Now just stretch on your tiptoes and take my hands. I won't let you go." *Please Dear God, don't let me drop the boy. . . .*

Jacob felt the damp little hands clasp at his own and realized that he had not felt such palpable trust in his whole missionary experience nor in his everyday life. He pulled, feeling the muscles in his arms strain, then slowly drew the child up to the top of the rock. He got to his knees and leaned back. Seth ran sobbing into Fern's arms. He extended one thin arm outward, motioning to include Jacob in the embrace.

Jacob was about to move toward Seth and Fern when the rock he was kneeling on gave way and he felt himself falling. He looked down to see the harsh ground rising fast to meet him and thought oddly of Fern's gentle movements—soothing—before he hit bottom and everything he knew was swallowed up in darkness.

Chapter 8

Fern pressed the damp cloth lightly against the raw skin on Jacob's muscular shoulder. He tossed away from her touch, clearly in pain.

"He'll live, young missy. That's what ya should be grateful fer." The old woman, Grandmother Mildred, was the mountain's healer. She had spent some time examining Jacob after the fall. But Fern wasn't so sure of the healer's brusque prediction. *Will he really live,* she wondered. It had been two days since the rock had given way and Jacob had plummeted to the bottom of the hollow after rescuing Seth.

Jacob hadn't regained consciousness and would only toss and mumble when his fever burned hotter. Then he would slip into a troubled sleep for a few hours at a time.

Fern wrung out the cotton cloth in the basin Ma Bodley from the Upper had provided. *I shall have to write to the mission board and tell them about the accident.* Fern had convinced her father that she must nurse the missionary, as she had invited him—or at least Deborah Cummings—to come.

Daisy had run and gotten some Bodley men to carry Jacob back to their house on the upper ridge line. Ma had seen fit to give the missionary her own room, and Fern took up constant watch, with Grandmother Mildred as chaperone. Fern had hoped that Daisy would take Seth home but Seth refused to stay anywhere else but in a trundle alongside Jacob's bed. He refused to leave his rescuer and new friend. At first, Fern had protested, but Seth told her soberly that he wanted to pray over Jacob all through the night, and even though the little boy could barely keep his eyes open past nine o'clock, his prayers were earnest. Fern was loathe to disallow these tender petitions be added to her own.

Please God—let him live. Let him live. . .

She continued to pray and was startled when Seth's voice came, wistful and sweet out of the night. "What's heaven like, Fern?"

She felt her eyes fill with tears at the innocent question. In her spirit, she wanted to refuse to answer, to not dare speak of heaven when Jacob lay so close to death. But she knew that his life was not in her hands to hold back.

"I don't know exactly, Seth," she said honestly, as she always did with him. "I can only tell you that the Bible says we're made new there—new name, new body."

"Well, I know you read to me from somewhere that there are horses there—white ones that Jesus has, and maybe we will get to ride with Him when He comes back. When I go to heaven, I wanna take care of the horses. That's where you'll find me if you're looking." He yawned loudly and Fern smiled.

"All right, Seth—I'll look for you with the white horses. Now, go back to sleep. I love you."

Her last words echoed in the still of the night, and she bowed her head to pray once more. . .

He was burning up, seemingly from the inside out, and he didn't understand the fog that permeated his mind—it was if he were running between two places, wearing out shoes, and then he was falling hard and fast. He cried out to God to catch him before he crashed. . .

Jacob came to himself by slow degrees. The first thing he was aware of was opening his eyes to a small face with a smattering of freckles peering upside down at him.

"Fern!" The face screamed, and Jacob thought his ears would pop from the echoing sound. Then another face stared down at him, with eyes the color of sun-dappled leaves and a bright fringe of honey-blond hair. Hers was a very dear face; he knew it in his heart. He lifted a hand to touch her bright cheek in a soft caress.

"Jacob? Can you hear me?"

He nodded, not wanting to break contact with the smooth skin beneath his fingertips even as he watched the gentle mouth speak softly. Then the little one's face was back again, and Jacob blinked.

"Jacob—you almost got killt after you saved me! Do you remember? I'm Seth."

Jacob tried to speak but found himself hoarse and finally mouthed "Water." The dear face came back, and then she was lifting his head, helping him to drink.

Then he was ready to try and speak. "Fern?" he questioned weakly. "What happened?"

She and Seth told him in simple terms and it all slowly came back to him—pulling Seth up, reaching to gather Fern and the boy in his arms, and then the terrible fall.

Jacob looked up from his sick bed to where Fern stood and slowly shook his head. "How many days have passed?"

"This is the fourth day after the accident. We feared greatly for your life."

Jacob recognized that the soft admission was an understatement, and he whispered his thanks before drifting back to sleep.

Fern hung the paintings with as little banging as possible. Grandma Birdy had sent an armful of her bright bird paintings to lighten up Ma Bodley's bedroom in an effort to give Jacob something cheery to look upon while he recovered. Fern knew that he sometimes chafed at the slowness of his healing, but he'd badly bruised his hip and ribs as well as his shoulder.

"It was God's hand that kept my bones whole," he told Fern one day as she adjusted a quilt over his large frame.

She agreed with a slight smile. "Oh, Jacob, if only you could see exactly how bad of a fall you took. I thought—I thought you would surely die." She looked into his emerald eyes and was about to suggest that he needed more sleep when he reached out a hand to her, palm up, fingers extended.

She shyly placed her hand in his and watched as their fingers entwined together. "Would you have cared so much, Fern Summerson, if I'd passed from this life into the next?"

She swallowed hard, knowing her heart was reflected in her eyes. *But he must go away when he gets well. . .and I must stay here. . . .* She gently withdrew her hand from his and gave him a quiet smile. "I would have cared greatly, Jacob Reynolds." She turned from the bed. "After all, I imagine I would mourn the loss of any missionary as kind as you are."

She listened to his pensive silence then swiped at her eyes and fled the room.

Jacob realized that his temporary bedroom had become sort of a haven for the mountain people as they came in various numbers to ask his advice or "spin him a yarn." And this day, especially after Fern had run out, he was more grateful for company than most. He wanted to try and do the impossible and keep his mind from the honey-haired Fern and not worry about where she was.

Two tiny bird-like sisters whom Ma Bodley introduced as Esther and Abigail Kinney came that afternoon. Ma led the visibly delicate women into the room with the same attention that Jacob imagined she'd show to royalty. He made haste to pull the covers up over his bandaged chest so he wouldn't give offense to their sensibilities.

"We're twins, don't you know, Pastor Reynolds," Abigail pointed out. "But I'm the eldest by four minutes. That matters."

Esther nodded with a smile. "It certainly does. I wouldn't be able to make most decisions without Abigail's mature guidance."

Jacob nodded politely, uncertain of what to add to the conversation. Then Uncle Sander Bodley walked in with his perpetual bag of walnuts, cracked two neatly on his forehead, and handed the meats to the ladies.

"Oh, thank you, Sander." Esther blushed like a young girl, and Jacob realized that the woman had her heart set on Sander Bodley. But what could he do about it?

Jacob felt impulsive for the moment and used his "preacher voice" to speak from the bed. "Love one another!"

Everyone, including Sander, paused and looked at him. Jacob had the absurd notion to laugh but he forged on. "And love your neighbor as yourself!"

Jacob sat up as straight as he could. "Sander, you and Miss Esther are neighbors, right?"

Sander cracked a nut in response, and Esther giggled while Abigail watched in fascination.

"Oh yes, Preacher Reynolds, we've been neighbors for years," Esther affirmed.

"Well," Jacob boomed. "There you have it!"

Remarkably, Sander moved past the bed and handed Esther his bag of walnuts. Esther accepted them. It was as much of an engagement as Jacob had ever seen, and he wondered briefly if he'd done the right thing.

But then Abigail leaned close to the bed and whispered, "I've been trying to accomplish that for years, Preacher Reynolds, and it took you all of thirty seconds. God is with you."

Jacob gave her a smile and felt a stirring in his heart. "Thank you, ma'am. I guess He is."

Fern ran until she felt a stitch in her side and was forced to sit down on an old log. She swiped at the tears that fell freely from her eyes and tried to pray. But it was difficult when her mind was filled with images of Jacob and her cautious rejoinder to his question earlier that day.

Would I miss him? Oh, Dear Father, You know I would miss him if anything happened to him. And You know even more so that my heart has warmed to him—a missionary, a man about Your business. Yet I cannot lie to You, I wish he might stay forever and that we might build a life together. . . Fern opened her eyes, amazed at where the trail of her thoughts in prayer had led her. How could she care about someone so much in such a short while? How could she love— At this she grew frustrated. She was young, yes, but wise enough to know that love must grow and be nurtured. She sighed aloud with confusion and got to her feet. There was no sense mooning about. She needed to go back to Jacob and apologize for leaving so abruptly.

She walked to the path and was surprised to see Lucy Kelley coming toward her. The older woman carried a basket of herbs, and her expression was dour, as usual. But something about the way Lucy held her shoulders—straight—not bowed, intrigued Fern.

"Hello, Lucy. How are you?"

Lucy seemed to struggle to get her reply out. "I—I have been questioning myself—inside like—ever since you and that preacher came by."

Fern felt her heartbeat speed up. Could it be that Lucy might have a change of heart and vision when it came to John? Fern knew she needed to be cautious in what she said. "I was just questioning myself too, Lucy. I think we all do at times."

Lucy sniffed. "Wal, mebbe."

"How's John?" Fern knew it was a risk to speak of the boy, but she felt that she had to take it.

"He's. . .fine."

Fern wanted to cry tears of joy. Jacob planted a seed and God had watered it in Lucy's mind.

"Good," Fern said softly. "I'm very glad."

Lucy nodded. "I must get on to see about supper."

"Of course, have a good day."

Fern watched her go and praised God in her heart.

Jacob realized that he was a novelty of sorts to his visitors, but he didn't understand the full import of what they believed until one of Ma Bodley's sons, Lester, told him the truth later that afternoon.

"Ya shoulda been kilt, Preacher. That fall landed you right in the middle of Devil's Hollow. No one even hunts up that way, but you fell an' wasn't hurt too bad. Or maybe you wuz. . ."

"Lester, what are you talking about?" Jacob's head hurt with the trail of the conversation.

Lester leaned close to the bed and took an experimental poke at Jacob's chest. The boy had an odd expression on his face.

"Maybe yuz a ghost—"

Jacob frowned and now his head was throbbing. "Lester, do I feel like a ghost?"

"No siree, but ya can't tell with ghosts. I heard one story from way back in the mountains about a ghost who walked around at night lookin' for his arm. And he'd be willin' to take what arm he could find from the livin'." Lester rubbed his arm and shuddered. "Now what do you say to that, Preacher Ghost?"

"There are no such things as ghosts," Jacob snapped. "There are demons and angels and there is spiritual warfare—that's it."

"Who-ee, ya got me afeared with such talk, Preacher Ghost, and I am leavin' right quick now." Lester hopped up with a scared backward glance, and Jacob closed his eyes in mute frustration. He had no doubt that some of the mountain people believed in ghosts. Maybe this was a chance for some biblical application.

But that would have to wait for another day, he thought as he slowly drifted off.

He was aware of her presence when the fresh smell of mint permeated his senses. He took a deep breath, muttered her name, and then opened his eyes.

"Hello," he said softly, as if he were speaking to some delicate fawn of the forest that he didn't want to scare away.

"Hello," she returned with a sober expression.

He'd missed her since she'd left earlier, and he realized he'd spoken out of turn asking if she'd miss him. *I probably should apologize*, he mused. But he'd meant it. He'd wanted to know. . . .

"Lester thinks I'm a ghost," he offered, watching her from lowered lids.

She smiled then, and he felt something shift inside of him. It was like a bolt of sunlight touching a corner of his soul. He opened his eyes wide.

"Are you a ghost?" she teased in a light tone.

"You would know better than some, Fern Summerson, that I am but a simple man—flesh and blood—and maybe, sometimes, a fool."

She drew nearer his bed. "Why a fool? You shouldn't say such things about yourself."

"Ah, but it's true. I was a fool to ask you if you'd miss me. It was unfair to put you in that position, and I'm sorry."

"It's all right. But I accept your apology just the same. And I—I wanted to tell you that I saw Lucy Kelley when I was walking. She seemed different. . ."

"Different?" Jacob queried.

"She seemed changed somehow. I think your bold words helped her."

Jacob was quiet for a moment. "I think you helped her too, Fern—by talking with her in the past and being kind to John."

He was about to continue when she nodded and spoke quickly. "I wonder if I might read to you a bit to help pass the time?"

"Of course." He saw that she was unwilling to continue any personal talk, so he folded one of his arms behind his head and grinned at her. "Read on, Miss Fern."

She drew an audible breath and sat down in the chair Lester had vacated beside the bed. "It was the best of times; it was the worst of times. . . ."

He listened to the familiar pattern of the words but knew they were made more sweet coming from her lips. There was a gentle poignancy layered to the story that he knew he'd always remember because she read it to him. . .

And when I'm back in the city, I'll remember her light and sweetness. . .when I'm gone away. . .

Chapter 9

Fern was glad when the day came that Jacob could stand and walk on his own, but he tired quickly.

Grandmother Mildred hollered at him when he would not lie back down. "You'll do as I say, boy. I haven't sat by these last weeks only to see you come down sick again. Besides, yer worryin' Fern."

Fern watched as Jacob sat down abruptly, and hid a smile. "You'll be able to do more as the days go by," she encouraged him.

She noticed that he was rubbing his right side. "Are your bandages just right?"

"Yes, thank you. I'll take it slowly. You have my word."

She felt him look at her searchingly, almost as if for approval, and she couldn't help but smile. "Thank you."

She helped him get comfortable in the bed and covered him with a light quilt.

"I wrote to the mission board in Williamsport last week. Do you think they'll send another missionary to help you?"

"I don't know. See, you understand why I'm anxious to get up. I've got to deliver those shoes."

"Well, as to shoes, you have some visitors," Fern said.

"Come in," she called, and the room hummed with expectation.

Jacob looked up to see Bud Bodley and Ma Bodley shuffle in, their old faces looking rather sheepish.

"What's this?" Jacob asked. "One Upper Bodley and one Lower Bodley. . . Shouldn't you folks be shooting at each other?"

"Well, ya see, Preacher, we is really kin," Bud Bodley admitted. "She's my older sister."

"And he's my younger brother."

"I see." Jacob looked askance to Fern.

"Aw, we got to fussin' and fightin' ever since our Ma died, and there never seemed like a good reason to quit until now."

Jacob arched a brow in question.

"Shoes!" Bud burst out.

"Shoes?"

"Yeah, shoes. We decided since you went to all the trouble you did to pass out shoes and then saved young Seth. . . Well, we decided that we needed to do somethin' in return fer ya. So we been passin' out shoes ta everyone on the mountain—except of course, Fern's daddy."

"Thank you," Jacob said. "But why not to Fern's father?"

"Aw. . ." Ma Bodley shook her head. "You know I don't mean no harm to ya, Fern, or to yer daddy, but Chester Summerson is a tough ol' bird if there ever wuz one, and he won't take nothin' from nobody 'cept maybe money."

"What was that about money?" Jacob heard Fern ask in a curious voice.

"Aw, Mabel, hush up! Fern's right here."

"What is it you're talking about?" Jacob asked.

"Mind ya fixate on gettin' well, Pastor," Bud said. "And don't go worryin' none. Everythin'll be all right fer church service come Sunday mornin'."

"What church service?"

"The one we're havin' right here." Ma Bodley pointed proudly to the wood floor beneath her feet. "Ya can't right git out of bed and hike up the mountain yet, so folks is comin' here to my bedroom for a preachin' service."

"And they'll be wearin' their shoes too," Bud added for emphasis.

Jacob wanted to decline, to say that he couldn't preach from a bed, then he realized he was being prideful. "All right, a preaching service is what we'll have come Sunday."

Fern worked in her kitchen on Friday evening, finally feeling comfortable enough that Jacob was well on the mend and could be left to only occasional needs in care. She couldn't say that she was truly happy to be home, though, as her father was more surly than ever.

Fern had sent Seth to his room to read and was drying the dishes when her father came back into the kitchen. It was a rare thing for him to reappear after a meal was finished, and her body tensed in anticipation of one of his bad moods.

"That preacher ready ta go back ta Williamsport way?" he asked, taking a seat at the table.

"No—he's still on the mend, I believe." Fern kept her voice soft.

"Well, the sooner he's gone, the better. We don't need no religion round here."

Fern put the plate she held down and took a deep breath. "Why do you say that, Dad?"

"Because religion fails people, that's why. What good is it if it can't help pain or sickness?"

"It's no good, I suppose," she whispered. "But God is about relationship, not religion—I think there's a difference."

Her father snorted. "You're a child, Fern. What could you know?"

Fern wanted to retort, *I know what it's like to bring a baby into the world with God's help and how to care for him and how to bury my mother...* But she kept all of this held tightly within. She realized that although she'd accepted what had happened when she was younger, she was angry with her father.

She longed to tell him this but one look at his pale face and sloped shoulders and she knew she could work the anger out with the help of God. So she hung up the dishtowel and bid him a soft good night.

Then she went to her bedroom and tried to read, but she worried for her father and, truth to tell, she worried about the growing feelings she had for Jacob.

She knew too, now that the shoes were distributed, there was little reason for Jacob to stay on. Even his injuries would soon not prevent him from managing the trip back to Williamsport. She sighed to herself at this thought but knew she had no right or claim to think so proprietarily of him.

A quick knock on her door sounded, and Daisy entered with a flounce.

"You could wait until I ask you to come in," Fern said mildly, but Daisy didn't seem to hear. Instead she paced beside Fern's small bed in visible frustration.

"What is it, Daisy?"

"Oh, it's Daddy!"

"Well, what about him?"

Daisy paused in her pacing and didn't meet Fern's gaze. "Well, I might have said that Jacob sort of kissed me...."

Fern swallowed hard. "And did he kiss you?"

"No! Not that I didn't make every effort to get him to! Missionaries are no fun."

Fern ignored the feeling of relief she had and frowned at her sister. "Why would you tell Dad that?"

"Oh, I was hoping it might stir him to go out and defend my honor...you know. Make Jacob marry me or something."

"What? Why Daisy, that's terrible!"

"I guess I know that now. I didn't really believe he'd do anything about it, but here it is nighttime, and he's gone off to haul Jacob up here for a regular shotgun wedding."

Fern began to feel her heart pound. "Daisy, Jacob's just now getting well."

"I know that!"

Fern jumped to her feet and grasped her sister's shoulders. "Stay here with Seth. I mean it, do you hear? I'll run down to Ma Bodley's myself."

"All right, but Fern?"

"Yes?"

Fern watched Daisy struggle with tears. "I'm sorry."

"There'll be time enough for that later!"

Jacob was roused from sleep by the sound of his name being said. He startled, to find a wiry-looking older man sitting in the chair beside the bed. The man's face was eerily illuminated by a kerosene lantern which threw strange shadows on the opposite wall.

"Who's there?" Jacob asked, rubbing the sleep from his eyes.

The man laughed softly, and Jacob felt a tingle of alarm run through him. "I'm Chester Summerson, and I believe you know my daughter well."

"I—yes. She's a lovely young woman."

"So you do know how to talk decent about her anyway. I should just shoot you where you lay but for some reason, she wants to marry you. So, get up."

"What? I'm not—"

"Let's go. If it's a wedding she wants, then that's what she'll get, even if you have treated her poorly by hurting her heart."

Jacob racked his brain, trying to understand this definitely irate father. He realized he didn't mind a nighttime interlude that might include marrying Fern Summerson, but he wasn't about to marry at gunpoint unless he had all the information.

He sat up in the bed and was drawing on a shirt when Fern suddenly burst into the room.

"Daddy, this all a mistake!"

"Not so, girl. Your sister told me that this wolf in sheep's clothing stole a kiss from her and now he's dishonored her name. Daisy wants a wedding—she'll have one."

"Wait a minute," Jacob said. "Daisy? This is about Daisy?"

He felt the hard slap of Chester Summerson across his cheek and bit back the anger that came rushing through him. "Turn the other cheek," he muttered, and just as soon as he spoke, the man struck him on the other side of his face.

"Father, stop!" Fern spoke, and Jacob knew she was surprised at the sudden violence.

He lifted his head in the half dark and spoke with authority. "You know, you're not striking God when you hit me."

"Shut up," Chester growled. "And get up."

"Father, he saved Seth! Think. And Daisy told me back at the cabin that she lied to you. He never kissed her."

"Is that the truth, boy?"

Jacob drew a deep breath. "I never kissed Daisy. I thought you were talking about Fern when you first came in."

"Fern? You've kissed Fern?"

Jacob felt the tension in the room ramp back up again. "No—I just thought you were talking about her, not Daisy."

"Well, you won't be speakin' the name of either of my girls, because I forbid you to see either one of them again. You'll do your preachin' Sunday and then leave Summerson Mountain fer good."

Jacob felt his heart pound in his throat—not see Fern again? How could he do it? At once, God brought words into his heart to speak to the older man. Jacob drew a deep breath. "Keeping me from Fern is your right, of course. But you won't be able to keep Fern from God. Just like you couldn't keep your wife from His hand. He has plans for each one of us, and that includes the times we are to live and the time we are to die. There is no way to outrun God. He—"

There was a chilling click in the shadows and Jacob paused, knowing the sound of a revolver when he heard it.

"Neither can that change His plans," he said softly.

"Daddy, no!" Fern rushed at her father and there was the sudden ear-splitting sound of a shot.

Jacob grabbed the lantern and lifted it high. He saw Fern crumpled on the floor and her father holding the gun.

Jacob put the lantern on the floor and scrambled to get down next to her. He turned her limp body over in his arms, calling her name as he was vaguely aware that many other people now filled the room. Jacob lifted Fern and lay her on the bed. He could see the entrance wound of the bullet high on her left shoulder. There was a lot of blood, but Jacob told himself to keep calm as he applied pressure to the wound and called for bandages.

"Ma," he said, feeling as though he were watching the scene outside of himself, "tear up as many sheets as you have. I've got to stop this bleeding."

He continued to apply pressure even as he investigated the exit wound on the other side of her arm. "The bullet went clean through," he muttered. "Thank You, God."

Fern moaned faintly, and Jacob looked around at all of the Bodleys standing about. "Clear the room and send for Grandmother Mildred. And Ma, please take Fern's father from here and take the gun."

Within moments, Jacob was alone with Fern. He could hear her father's dry sobbing from the other room.

Fern opened her eyes and stared up at him. He smiled encouragingly. "It's all right, Fern. It'll be all right."

"I—he was going to shoot you and I—"

Jacob blinked back tears. "And you jumped in front of the gun for me—to take my place. Oh, Little Fern. Oh, sweetheart. . ." He whispered the last words but she had slipped back into unconsciousness. He was relieved when Grandmother Mildred came.

The old woman bustled him out of the room and Jacob obeyed reluctantly, praying all the while.

Chapter 10

ern drifted in and out of consciousness. She longed to call for Jacob but couldn't seem to form the words. She was dreaming that she saw her mother's face very close and then receding once more, and she cried for her piteously, like she did the night Seth was born. Her mother called back to her, beckoning from a bright light, but there was something inside of Fern that bade her remember Jacob, and then everything was dark. . . .

Fern opened her eyes to sunshine and the light seemed very bright. "Hello," a deep voice spoke. She turned her head to look up into Jacob's pale face. His cheekbones stood in stark relief to the bruise-like circles beneath his eyes.

"You look tired," she whispered up to him.

"And you look beautiful," he returned with palpable ease. "Does the arm hurt much? Grandmother Mildred gave you some tea that she said would help."

Fern shook her head then asked simply. "My father?"

"He's up at your cabin. Lester Bodley goes and checks on him and brings him food. I thought I'd maybe try to talk with him sometime. . . But anyway, I picked you some lady's slippers." He held up a mason jar full of the tender flowers, and Fern rewarded him with a smile.

"It seems like such a long time ago that we set out to deliver the shoes," she whispered.

"It was never about shoes," he said. "God had a plan for us to meet. That's what matters." But Fern had closed her eyes and slipped into a deep sleep.

Word got around that the preaching service would be put off for a week until Fern was better. In the meanwhile, Jacob would make sure she slept and then set out to practice building up his strength in walking the surrounding trails, using a piece of ironwood as a cane of sorts. Seth frequently kept him company and Jacob had grown to appreciate the chatter and interest of the little boy.

"Were you scared Fern was gonna die?" Seth asked as they walked about that morning.

"Yes, terrified."

"How come my father shot her? Why would he do that?"

Jacob ruffled Seth's red-gold hair. "Your father is a man whom God loves. But everyone makes mistakes. He didn't mean to shoot Fern."

"That's good, I s'ppose. Say, you're not going to leave, are you, Jacob? I sure would miss you."

Jacob didn't answer right away. The question seemed to bounce around in his head and then in his heart. *Am I going to leave? How can I leave Fern and these people whom I've come to care about? But I have a job back in Williamsport with the mission board. . .*

"You thinkin' hard, Jacob?" Seth asked, breaking into his thoughts.

"Yes, Seth, I suppose I am."

"Well, I'm going to run down to Mr. Clarey's store and get a penny's worth of candy. Grandmother Mildred gave me a penny this morning."

Jacob reached into his pocket and handed Seth a nickel. "Here, get some extra and we'll share later."

He watched the boy scamper off through the woods and then turned to look where the trail rose above him. He rubbed absently at his ribcage and ignored the pulling sensation that he felt. Instead, he began to climb the trail, feeling convicted in his spirit to go and visit the church on top of the mountain.

Fern allowed the wound in her arm to be dressed daily though the pain was bad. Today was no exception. Grandmother Mildred was gentle though firm and the minor ordeal was soon over with. Fern wanted to ask where Jacob was but knew she couldn't expect him to be by her side every minute, so she sat back and ate the piece of blueberry buckle Ma Bodley brought her. Then, her young body strong in its healing, she drifted back to sleep once more.

She was walking through a house, one she'd never been in before—it was fine and palatial. All the windows that lined the rooms were open, and a slight breeze lifted the silken draperies, billowing them out like ladies' skirts. She knew she was alone in the house; the sound of her bare feet on the highly polished floor made a strange echoing sound. She passed a wide, graceful staircase, and the silence was suddenly punctuated by the noise of a single marble dropping down the stairs. It rolled from the last step and across the floor to stop at a pink pair of women's high-heeled shoes. They sparkled as if covered in the morning dew, and Fern felt drawn to them, intrigued somehow. She sat down on the floor beside them and reached out with tentative fingers to touch the satin shoes. She lifted one carefully and tried to place it on her foot, but the shoe was too big. In fact, it seemed to enlarge as she held it. She looked quickly to the other one on the floor and despaired because she knew that it was too big as well. It seemed that she was failing somehow—unable to fit the elegance of the too-large shoes. She reached for the still marble. It disappeared as she touched it, becoming a single soap bubble that drifted away on the breeze from the open windows. She dropped the shoe then let her head rest on her bent knees as she sobbed softly into the light. . .

Jacob knew he was probably running a risk in visiting the chapel on the mountaintop. After all, the land belonged to the man who'd just tried to kill him. But he strode on, feeling his shoulder and ribs beginning to ache in earnest. He was sweating when he finally cleared the crest of the mountain and swiped his damp hair out of his eyes.

The church was whitewashed and had a small bell tower and a red door. He limped over to it and mounted the two steps. He tried the latch on the door, half expecting it to be locked. But it wasn't, and he slipped inside.

The vestibule was cool, and he drew a deep breath of pleasure at the sanctuary from the heat. He knew, of course, that a church was where God's people were, not necessarily a building. But the little place seemed quiet and cool to his spirit. He pushed open the swing door and entered the main sanctuary. He was surprised to see another man kneeling at the altar in front. He quietly slipped into one of the back pews in an effort not to disturb the other man.

The windows of the small church were open and sunlight poured inside. Jacob was surprised to see a piano at the front and a nice painting of Jesus as the Shepherd. He had just closed his eyes to pray when the man up front began to sob. Jacob was unsure of what to do, but then the same conviction that drew him to the chapel in the first place led him to his feet and up the aisle. He placed his hand on the thin shoulder of the man and spoke quietly.

"Can I pray with you?"

The man looked up, squinting at him, and Jacob recognized Chester Summerson. It took all he had not to take his hand away from the older man. Disgust filled him as he thought about the hatred the man had for God and all of those around him. But then, Jacob's own answer to Seth rose up in bold words in his consciousness. God loves this man. . .God loves him!

"Mr. Summerson? May I sit awhile with you?"

Chester blinked up at him, and the older man's lip quivered like a child's. "You don't know who I am or what I've done."

"But God does," Jacob said thoughtfully. "And I bet you haven't been in this place in a very long time."

Chester swallowed. "After my wife died, I wanted to tear the place down with my bare hands—board by board."

Jacob nodded. "But you didn't."

"No. . .but you was right last night about me hatin' the Lord. This—this was her favorite place to come. Sometimes—sometimes when the girls wuz young we'd come here and pray for them, for our family. . . ."

"God still hears those prayers." Jacob eased down into the seat beside him.

Chester turned to him. "Then why did he take my wife that way? Why wasn't I here?"

"Well, where were you?"

Jacob knew that he had met the source of grief in the other man when Chester hung his head.

"I wuz doin' what I do so often now. Runnin' moonshine. Gettin' men addicted to the stuff so they had ta pay me what I wanted. I keep my still back in the woods. Preacher, I'm an evil man."

Jacob smiled. "We're all evil men, Chester Summerson. Every last one of us. That's why we need Him." Jacob gestured to the painting. "The Good Shepherd, who knows all about the habits of his sheep—good or bad."

There was a stillness in the air of the chapel, one that spoke of peace and forgiveness and humility. It stirred in Jacob's heart. "I bet Fern would love to see you."

"Nah. . .nah she wouldn't."

"Here now, you can't have it both ways—forgiven and not. I know she would love to hear what you've told me. I could even come with you, if you'd like."

Chester nodded after a few quiet moments, and Jacob got to his feet, amazed at how the Lord worked.

Chapter 11

Fern still couldn't believe that her father had come to a place of repentance in the little chapel on the mountaintop. Even now, as she sat on Ma Bodley's front porch to take some sun and fresh air, she found the conversation with her dad and Jacob to be something of a dream. She had been sitting up in bed, and her father had stolen in close beside her to kneel at her side. He had sobbed out his pitiful tale and begged for forgiveness. Fern had touched his graying head and looked up at Jacob with tears in her eyes. Tears of gratitude. Now, she could almost feel the same sense of wonder and disbelief as Jacob came to sit beside her in a matching bentwood rocker.

"Well, the day after tomorrow is Sunday," he stated as if pointing out something she didn't know.

"Yes, and I'm sure you'll be wonderful at preaching God's Word." She forced the words out, knowing where the conversation was headed. "And, after Sunday, I suppose you'll be leaving us," she said, trying not to be bleak.

"That should be so," he agreed.

She tried to hold back sudden tears. "Well, you helped my father, you saved Seth, and you've done so much for me."

She glanced at him and saw that he was looking at her with his emerald-green eyes, shuttered by thick lashes. "I gave very little," he said. "Compared to the beauty you've given me."

She watched his gaze drop to her bare feet and her toes curled automatically against the wood of the porch, but then she let out an "Ow!" and sat up straighter.

"What is it?" Jacob asked.

"Just a splinter, I think."

He got up, grabbed a basin hanging on the porch wall, and ran to the well. He was back in moments, kneeling at her feet with his wet handkerchief and gently prodding at the sole of her injured foot. He found the splinter of wood and carefully eased it out. Then he started to wash her feet.

"Oh, Jacob, you don't have to do that."

"I want to minister to you, Fern Summerson."

She shivered as he touched the delicate arch of her foot and brought his hand-kerchief to tease at each of her toes.

"I could say that a pair of shoes would help prevent splinters," he said in a teasing tone. "But the truth is, I'd rather wash your bare feet than have you bound in a pair of boots."

Fern felt herself blush. "Thank you."

"Anytime, madam. . .anytime."

Jacob stared out at the sea of familiar faces, the faces of the mountain people he had come to know and care for. . .and in some cases, love. He let his eyes dwell on Fern, whom he'd helped up the mountain to the chapel himself, and then looked at Chester, who was regarding him with clear eyes and a lift to his head.

Jacob had tried to think of what to talk about. Normally he'd have no problem asking God for a word, but this day was different because tomorrow he'd leave Summerson Mountain and probably never see Fern again.

He cleared his throat, unsure of what he'd say, but suddenly, he had everyone's distinct attention.

"Good morning," he began, hoping something sensible would come out of his mouth. His gaze locked with Fern's and he said. "God doesn't care if you are happy."

Great. This is just going to be great. . .

"No, not if you're happy. But He does care if you have joy. See, there's a difference between the two—happiness is fleeting. It lasts a brief time, but joy is transcendent—it's able to shine through sadness and hardship and hatred. Joy allows us to move on in life even when life seems too hard. Joy is what gives us strength. The Bible says 'The joy of the Lord is your strength. . .'" He paused as the church door squeaked open. Lucy and John Kelley stood there. Jacob motioned them in with amazement. He struggled for a moment to find his voice and then continued. "And I must tell you all that I have joy in your presence. . .I have learned far more than I have taught you. My own life has been blessed in ways that will last for all of this life through seeing the strength and unity in your joy. I came here to bring shoes; I found joy and love. . . Now let us sing hymn number one hundred sixty-two. The first and third verses."

Fern watched Jacob with tender eyes as he finished the service then stood outside in the sunshine to shake hands with all who passed. When her turn came, she held out her hand steadily and he engulfed it with his own. "Would you wait a moment inside, Fern? I would walk back with you, if you don't mind."

She smiled and slipped to the back of the group. Her heart warmed that he would want to spend a bit more time with her even though he was leaving the next day. She tried to focus on the words of his sermon—that joy would help her through hard times. And surely Jacob's leaving would be one of the hardest things she'd ever experienced.

Soon the small crowd had melted away and Jacob came back into the church. He stretched out his hands to her and she shyly placed her own in his. "Fern," he whispered. "How I will miss you."

She nodded, unable to control the tear that spilled down her cheek.

He gently wiped at her cheek, and she felt him look deep into her eyes, his own dark emerald with intensity. "Fern, I asked you once before if you'd miss me. I'll take the risk of speaking out of turn again, but I must know—will you miss me? Because I love you with all that is in me."

Fern hesitated, longing to tell him the truth but unsure if she should. She knew she had no right, but then felt a gentle affirmation in her heart: *Tell him. . . Tell him the truth.* "Oh, Jacob, I will miss you with all my heart! And I love you too!"

He smiled and gathered her close, gentle with her injured arm, and then his lips found hers in tender agreement.

Epilogue

The news of Fern and Jacob's engagement spread like wildfire on the mountain. Not only was Summerson Mountain getting a new preacher, but also a new couple to rejoice with and find joy—especially in preparation for a summer wedding. Another missionary, Daniel Gideon, was sent from Williamsport to officiate the ceremony, and when he got back to the mission board office, he had one thing to report: "The bride wore white, carried a bouquet of lady's slippers, and was beautifully barefoot as she walked down the aisle."

Kelly Long is the author of the Patch of Heaven series and the historical Amish *Arms of Love*. She was born and raised in the mountains of Northern Pennsylvania. She's been married for twenty-six years and enjoys life with her husband, children, and Bichon.

Hope's Horizon

by Carolyn Zane

Chapter 1

April 1843

Hope Dawson stared out the bay window of Maudie's Milliner Shop in wonder. It seemed to her, as she absently swept up a pile of felt scraps, that the crazy assortment of people parading down Main Street in Independence, Missouri, grew stranger and more circus-like every day. For a moment, she propped her chin on her broom handle and peered through Maudie's special Fancy Hats display.

Out on the street, a red-faced tenderfoot was struggling to get his team of oxen to pull his wagon out of a deep ditch. Hope shook her head. How did he plan to make it across the country when he couldn't make it across the street? Unimaginable.

Luckily for him, a rescuer in the form of a young—she squinted as her mind took a brief flight of fancy—knight in shining dungarees stepped up to save the day. Thumbing his hat back on his head, he calmly assessed the situation, soothed the oxen, directed the tenderfoot's next steps, and quickly, handily, and oh-so-manfully managed to get the wagon back onto the street.

Hope drew in a deep, bubbly breath as she watched him shake the grateful man's hand and then saunter in her direction. *Uh-oh.* Grabbing her broom, she began to sweep. It wouldn't do for him to catch her spying. Not that she'd ever see him again, save for perhaps the occasional dream. Most likely, he was one of those on his way to Oregon Territory. She glanced up as he grew near. Gracious, he was magnificent. The ladies who watched him from across the street seemed to agree. As he passed the shop, he glanced into the window and caught her staring. A lopsided grin revealed a deep dimple in his left cheek and a perfect set of straight white teeth.

Embarrassed, Hope quickly returned his smile and then began madly sweeping again. What must he think of her, so brazenly staring that way? Another peek told her. . .not much.

He was gone.

Ah well. Daydreaming was all fine and well, but she had brims to trim and ribbons to roll if she wanted to keep the job that helped feed her growing brothers. The good Lord knew, hats didn't make themselves. Hope sighed and returned to her sewing table. As she tacked an ostrich plume on one of Maudie's more ostentatious Fruit and Flowers designs, the cowbell over the door jangled and a man stepped into the shop.

She smiled brightly, smoothed the wrinkles from her faded apron, and hoped the stains beneath her armpits didn't show too much.

"Hello and welcome," she called. The man looked somewhere north of forty, for his hair had all but vacated his crown and what was left was threaded with gray and slicked back with a generous application of pomade. The buttons of his silk vest strained to stay attached over his considerable belly, and he carried a silver-handled walking stick that was perhaps not simply for show.

"Hello there," he called back jovially, and his fleshy face broke into a friendly smile.

"How may I be of service?" Hope asked as he scanned the wall displays. The pine floorboards creaked under his substantial weight as he thumped over to where she stood.

"I'm Julius Ditsworth." He thrust forth a meaty hand. "And you, my dear, are?"

"Hope Dawson," she replied as he gave her arm a vigorous pump.

"Hope, I'm here to purchase a special occasion hat for my mother. Money is no object."

Hope doubted there would ever be a time when a member of her family could utter such a phrase, but it was exciting to hear after two weeks of no sales here at the shop. "Very well, then," she said, reciting the verbiage Maudie insisted she use to impress the wealthier clientele, "Perhaps if you told me about the special occasion, I might be able to show you the proper complement of hats."

"Certainly! We are celebrating our departure with the wagon train leaving from Elm Grove in just two short weeks. Perhaps you've heard tell? Folks are calling it the Great Migration of 1843."

"Indeed, I have heard." Hope knew that hundreds of folks, impoverished by the economic depression that had begun in 1839, were flocking to Independence to purchase the supplies they'd need before they began the six-month trip to the Oregon Territory. The land of milk and honey, some said, where robust health and fertile soil abounded and was being given away. With nothing left to lose, scores were trading ties to the people they loved and what little they still owned to gamble on the opportunity to start fresh. "In fact, I've heard of pretty much nothing else for the last few months."

"I'd imagine so," he said with a chuckle. "There will be nearly a thousand people in our company, and my mother insists on looking her best."

"Of course." Hope nodded, although she could hardly fathom anything more ridiculous as one trekked through the wilderness. "We have an assortment of traveling hats," she informed him and ran through several plain and utilitarian choices until she finally noticed he'd stopped listening and was pointing at the flamboyant project Maude had given her that morning.

"That one, there." Brows arched, his eyes lit up and he whistled with an appreciation that Hope couldn't be sure was simply for the hat as he slanted his gaze back at her.

"Oh, that hat is not quite finished."

Folding his hands across his belly, Mr. Ditsworth took a moment to study her and seemed to note with interest the fact that her dress was a decade out of fashion and completely threadbare in spots. He shrugged. "I'll be happy to wait and will pay extra for the privilege."

"Now?" The hat required another two or three hours of work at least.

"However long."

Hope shot an anxious glance at the clock. "I have to close the shop in a moment, but if I come in early tomorrow, I can probably have it ready for you before noon."

"Splendid. Now, you go ahead and close here, and we can discuss the particulars over supper."

"Supper?" Hope frowned. What particulars could he be talking about? And why over supper?

"There is a very nice place, right next door. Since you are willing to work so diligently on this lovely hat for me, I'd be remiss if I did not return the favor by buying you a meal at the very least."

Ah. So that's why he'd considered her worn dress. The dining room at the Riverside Hotel was one of the nicer places in town. As she groped for an excuse to decline, her belly growled noisily, betraying her resolve.

"Please?" Mr. Ditsworth held up a hand. "Provided, of course, that your husband wouldn't mind."

"Oh," she demurred. "I'm not married."

"No? A beautiful woman such as yourself? I'd never have guessed."

She flushed. The fact that her family depended on what little income she contributed had something to do with that issue.

"So. I'll expect you just as soon as you are finished here." He smiled at her with such winsome expectation that Hope didn't want to hurt his feelings, especially if the sale of a rather expensive hat was in the balance. Maudie would have a fit if she found out Hope had foiled a good deal.

"I—" Flustered, Hope gnawed at her lower lip. "I suppose that would be all right." The dining room at the Riverside would certainly be a safe enough place to share a meal with a stranger. And truth be told, she was very hungry.

And one less mouth to feed tonight at home would be a good thing.

William Bradshaw was in the mood to celebrate. He'd just been hired on as a scout by the Oregon Emigrating Company, and nothing sounded better to him than a big slice of apple pie a la mode. Ice cream was nonexistent on the Oregon Trail, and the dining room at the Riverside Hotel was rumored to have the best in Independence.

As he handed his menu to the waiter, he noticed a young woman, close in age to his own twenty-three years, he guessed, sitting awkwardly across from a talkative man William assumed to be her father. She looked as if she was desperately trying to keep up, as arms a-waving, he pontificated.

William grinned. He knew what it was like to have to sit there while his father was on a harangue about something.

She must have felt his gaze because she caught his eye and tried to bite back a smile that tugged at the corners of her mouth. His own grin broadened. Ah yes, she was the pretty girl he'd seen earlier, sweeping up in her shop. Wheat berry blond hair and enormous blue eyes. Light blue. The color of the sky on an overcast day. They were quite striking.

And her father looked familiar. He'd seen him somewhere before. . .but couldn't put his finger on it.

In short order his pie arrived, and, as William tucked in, two men flew through the door leading to the adjoining Riverside Saloon, landed on a dining room table, and crashed to the floor. Fists flew, women screamed, men shouted, glass shattered, and tables were overturned.

As a chair whizzed past, William leapt to his feet and headed into the thick of it.

"Don't worry, my dear!" Julius Ditsworth cried to Hope as he stood and sent his chair tumbling. "I shall return momentarily. I'm just going. . .to. . .to. . . ." With that terse lack of explanation, his walking stick thumping, Mr. Ditsworth disappeared into the melee.

Left to her own devices, Hope wondered if she should follow him or hide, but the mounting chaos had her deciding on the latter. Options being few, she ducked behind a coatrack near the window to wait it out in relative safety. From between a fur stole and a wool overcoat, Hope watched as the young man who'd smiled at her earlier climbed up on a table and shouted for the chaos to stop. Unfortunately for the crystal chandelier, nobody listened until he drew his gun and fired a shot.

Everyone froze in a startled tableau and silence—underscored by the tinkling of falling crystal—reigned. But it wasn't more than a second before an angry accusation had the fight back in full swing.

He rolled his eyes, holstered his gun, leapt off the table, and proceeded to wrestle one of the fighting men to the ground. The sheriff arrived just in time to corral the other brawler and arrest them both for drunk and disorderly conduct.

As the staff set the room back to rights, the young man that Hope had been watching noticed her behind the coats.

"Are you all right, miss?" he asked and grinned as she poked her head from between the wraps.

"Yes. I think so." Although, she had to admit that the twinkle in his eyes rattled her more than the fight had.

"Allow me," he said and helped her emerge from her hiding spot.

"Thank you so much." She reached up and smoothed her hair. "Gracious. I wonder what brought that on."

"Apparently, a man won a horse in a card game. The other fella says he cheated."

"Ah. Seems like the town's being run over by this kind of thing lately," she said. "Never seen so many people with spring fever."

"Most of them will be gone in a week or so. I reckon a lot of 'em are here to hook up with the Oregon Emigrating Company. Heading off to claim the free land being given away out west."

"Is that why you're here?" Hope asked, willing him to say no.

"I just hired on with the OEC as a scout, so I'm an employee more than an emigrant."

"Oh." Hope couldn't stem her disappointment. "So, you'll be leaving."

"Yes. In just about two weeks. I'm William Bradshaw. And you are?"

"I'm Hope Dawson." She took the hand he offered and blinked up at him. He was just about the cutest young man she'd ever seen, with his breathtaking smile, thick dark brown hair, and hazel eyes the color of apple cider. She glanced down as her hand was enveloped by his firm, capable ones, so callused from hard work. "Sounds like a wonderful adventure."

"I'm sure it will be. You're from around these parts?"

"Born and raised. I live near here with my parents and five brothers. I'm the only daughter. I. . ." Hope felt as if she was blathering on but couldn't seem to stop herself. Maybe being tongue-tied with Mr. Ditsworth for so long had the dam of words suddenly overflowing. "I work across the street as an apprentice for the milliner."

"Can't say that I know what that might be." A slow grin revealed that adorable dimple. "Sounds impressive."

Smiling, she glanced around, feeling shy. "I make lady's hats."

"Oh. Guess I'd have no use for you."

"I. . .pardon?" Hope's perplexed expression had him chuckling.

"That didn't come out right now, did it? I just mean I'd probably never have occasion to buy myself a lady's hat—" he tried to explain, bashfully thrusting a hand through the thick hair that fell over his forehead.

Hope laughed at the absurd idea of him in one of her hats and was warmed at how flustered he suddenly seemed. "Not for yourself, certainly, but you might want to buy one for your wife. They make lovely anniversary or birthday gifts." Realizing that it sounded as if she was fishing for his marital status, she dropped a nervous glance at the floor.

"Oh, I'm not married. So, I guess my hat-buying days are still ahead of me."

"Ah. Naturally." She was debating whether to suggest that he come into the shop and look over their small assortment of men's hats when he took a step back and said, "Well, I s'pose I should get you back to your supper."

"Oh. Yes. Of course," she said and nodded, suddenly remembering she was not here alone. He gestured for her to lead the way to her table.

Mr. Ditsworth was still noticeably absent as William held her chair for her. "It was nice meeting you, Hope," he said.

"Likewise," she murmured as he moved back to his table.

At his departure, she sat alone, feeling quite conspicuous, and wondered at the etiquette for such an eventuality. Should she search for her dinner companion? Had he been hurt? Perhaps she should notify the waiter that he was missing? Just as she was really starting to worry, Mr. Ditsworth returned.

"Ohh," he moaned as he sank into his seat, looking as if he been through the wringer.

"What happened?" Hope asked, worried at his rumpled appearance.

"I twisted my ankle as I aided in the capture of those two good-for-nothing thugs."

"Oh, goodness, I'm so sorry."

"Now don't you worry yourself on my account, dear girl. I'll be just fine," he said and tucked his napkin into his collar. "Luckily, I'm fleet of foot, or the damage could have been so much worse. And fortunately, I managed to help several elderly patrons to safety. I suggest we put this whole debacle behind us and enjoy our supper. Now." His smile revealed several gold caps. "Where was I? Oh, yes. I was telling you about—"

As Mr. Ditsworth went back to regaling her with myriad tales of his adventurous life, Hope could feel William watching her. And smiling.

Chapter 2

Hope dearly wished Mr. Ditsworth had not insisted on escorting her to her door, but as he'd grandly informed her, "Julius Ditsworth values the gentlemanly customs. My mother sent me to a finishing school for young men when I was still in short pants."

As he mopped the sweat from his brow with a monogrammed handkerchief, Hope wondered what the important man at her side would think of her home.

Life hadn't always been this hard for Hope and her family. Only a few years back, her parents had owned a big farm with a nice house. But then Daddy was hurt in a farming accident that left him crippled and nearly blind, and they'd lost the house and land in the depression. Now, they lived in the shanty behind her uncle's house, which clung to the edge of the riverbank as if truly—as her father often quipped—afraid of becoming a houseboat. These days for extra money, Mama took in laundry. But lately, she couldn't work much because the ague fevers had her in bed more often than not.

Hope glanced at Mr. Ditsworth as he talked over the shrill hum of the cicada's serenade. Off in the distance, the waning light revealed the occasional flash of lightning bugs flitting among the weeping willows as the Missouri River flowed languidly by.

When he finally paused to take a breath, Hope blurted, "Mr. Ditsworth, we've arrived! Thank you so much for the lovely supper, and honestly, there is no need for you to walk me to the door." She fervently wished he'd release her hand from where he held it firmly in the crook of his arm and let her run on ahead. Unfortunately, he was ever chivalrous.

"It's no problem, my dear. The evening is yet young."

"Hope ith home!" Hope's four-year-old brother, Peter, shouted from his perch on the front stoop when he spied them drawing near. "An thie brung a man with her." Shyly, Peter scrambled to his feet at their approach and groped for Hope's hand. "Howdy, mithter."

Hope reached down and swung him up onto her hip. "How's my sweetheart today?" she asked and nuzzled his dusty neck. Though Hope loved all her brothers dearly, Peter held a special place in her heart.

"Who'd ya brung home, Hope?" The small boy gently petted her cheeks.

"Peter, this is Mr. Ditsworth. He bought one of my hats for his mother today."

"How do you do?" Mr. Ditsworth said and solemnly shook his sticky hand.

Peter grinned. "I do fine."

The squeaky screen door slammed open as the rest of her younger brothers—Silas, Eli, and the twins, Amos and John—burst outside to see what had Peter so excited.

Hope was embarrassed, having a man as sophisticated as Mr. Ditsworth see her ragtag family and their crumbling home. Nevertheless, Mr. Ditsworth didn't seem to mind the attention and one by one, shook hands with each boy.

"Hope," Mama called from the porch, "why don't you invite your friend inside to join us for a sit down and a cup of sweet tea?" Looking pale and far too thin in her oversized work dress, Hope's mother held the screen door open.

"I don't mind if I do, ma'am," Mr. Ditsworth said. And, before Hope could protest, he puffed up the steps after her eager brothers. They didn't get many callers, and having someone as clearly dignified as Mr. Ditsworth join them for tea was exciting stuff. "I bought a beautiful hat from your daughter this afternoon, and she kindly agreed to join me for supper, so of course I had to escort her safely back to the bosom of her family."

"Isn't that nice," Mama murmured.

Hope could see the surprise in Mr. Ditsworth's eyes when he stepped into the small main room and glanced around. Stale aromas of liver and onions that had to be stretched to last three meals too long, sweaty brothers, and a stove that belched smoke because the flu was clogged, permeated the air. A ladder led to where the boys slept up in the narrow attic loft, and the closet-sized room under the loft was for Mama and Daddy. Hope slept on a straw mat in the family area, near the stove.

Despite the cramped quarters, Daddy invited Mr. Ditsworth to have a seat, and after shaking her father's hand, to Hope's surprise, their guest settled himself quite comfortably on the best of their shabby chairs. Her brothers gathered round on the floor, and having a captive audience, Mr. Ditsworth began to regale them with tales of a magical place called Oregon.

Her father and mother smiled indulgently as the spellbound boys pelted him with questions, both excited by his fanciful stories and fascinated by his grand demeanor. "Boys, it's summer all the time there, but rains just enough for the trees to bear fruit year-round. And there are lush forests and enough game to hunt and fish to catch. . .why, all kinds! Salmon and trout as big as you there, boy!"

Peter puffed out his scrawny chest. "Catfish too?"

"Sure! They probably grow on trees! This place isn't called the Promised Land for no reason! They have everything! And they are giving it away to anyone who is brave enough to go."

"Anyone?" Peter placed a grubby finger on Mr. Ditsworth's knee.

"Yes sir. And once you arrive, all a body needs to do is show up at the claim office and they'll hand you the deed to three hundred and twenty acres. When I get there, I plan on building a huge house and opening a general store. I've got friends in the import and export game, and I'll have a thriving business in no time. I'll give jobs to young pioneer lads such as yourselves. They can help me set up and eventually, I'll give them a stake in the business."

The boys were all practically sitting on the man's feet, they strained so far forward. "What about Injuns, Mr. Ditsworth? Ain'tcha afraid of Injuns?"

"Oh, I'm not afraid," Mr. Ditsworth declared. He sat, legs spread wide, his broad belly balanced between his knees. "You just have to show 'em who's boss." The boys all giggled excitedly. "I've had many such adventures, but this one promises to be the most exhilarating yet, I tell you!"

And he did. For over an hour.

Eventually, his eyes landed on Mama's Bible. "Yes," he sighed, "the good Lord has blessed me and mine abundantly."

Papa nodded at this. "The Lord is our shepherd and benefactor in all things," he agreed.

"Amen, sir. Amen." Before he called it an evening, Mr. Ditsworth thanked Hope for her charming company at dinner and her family for making him feel so welcome. With a windy groan, he rose to his feet and moved to the door. "I've so enjoyed your company this evening and, as a single man, other than my mother, I don't know many folks in this neck of the woods; I'm much obliged for the fellowship." He made a slight bow then paused. "You know, I believe I have something I cannot take with me that I would like to give the boys, if I may. I would be happy to drop by tomorrow evening, if it poses no problem."

The boys' eyes grew round.

Hope smiled as her parents gave their permission, but she couldn't for the life of her understand why Julius Ditsworth would want to bother.

In the week that followed, Mr. Ditsworth was nothing if not a persistent guest, and Hope and her family couldn't help but be charmed by the slightly pompous, yet endlessly entertaining and generous Mr. Ditsworth.

The next time he called, Julius gifted Hope's mother with a delicate vase filled with Lenten roses and Virginia bluebells. For Hope's father, it was a selection of smoked fish that he boasted had been imported to Missouri from the shores of Maine. For the two older boys, pocketknives, and for the younger boys, clever hand puzzles. His visits quickly became regular and looked forward to by the entire family.

Hope was fond of the eccentric Mr. Ditsworth, but she suspected that there had to be more to his visits than simple loneliness. Certainly, he couldn't be courting her, as he was equally affectionate with the entire family. Besides, he was easily as old as Papa and rich enough to court society ladies that moved within a league that Hope never dreamed of being part.

No, it wasn't until a few two short days before he was to leave that it all became startlingly clear.

Mr. Ditsworth arrived with a bouquet in his hands and a box of sweets for her family and asked if it would be possible to have a word with Hope's father in private.

As they all waited for information on the front porch, the low murmur of the men's voices was barely audible through the rickety front door. Hope sat on the top steps with Peter on her lap and watched her brothers skip stones in the river. Her mother peeled some tired-looking apples the church brought by last week. Overhead a yellow warbler darted by as Peter asked, "What do ya think they're talkin' 'bout, up there, Hope?"

"I don't suppose he wants to talk to Papa about my hat-making skills, so I just can't imagine."

Finally, Mr. Ditsworth emerged, all smiles, and asked if Hope would mind joining him for a walk along the river.

Puzzled, Hope agreed. And, it was soon apparent that it wasn't another hat, Julius had set his sights on. No, he wanted Hope to join him on the Oregon Trail.

As his wife.

Chapter 3

Hope could only stare in shock at the pleading look in Mr. Ditsworth's eyes as he presented his case.

"Your father has given me the favor of his approval. And when we arrive in Oregon, I will build you a dream house and then immediately build another for your family. Within a year, we'll send for them, and together we'll all live in prosperity."

"Mr. Ditsworth," Hope finally managed around her heart that had leapt into her throat, "I'm just— Well, I'm simply— This is, why, this is all so sudden."

"You don't have to say yes today, my dear. Please, take a night to sleep on it. I'll be back tomorrow to receive your answer. And please understand, I'm not expecting an instant love match here," he said, suddenly fumbling with his handkerchief and mopping his neck in a way that was boyishly shy.

Hope forced a wobbly smile, feeling at once awkward, nauseous, and tongue-tied.

"I know these things take time," he continued. "I understand. In fact, my mother, who would be your chaperone and mentor on the journey, has asked that we wait until we reach Oregon before we wed, so that we might have a proper ceremony, surrounded by the majesty of the new world and the friends we will make along the way. By then, perhaps you will feel more inclined to maybe, eventually, love me."

Hope blinked at the spots suddenly floating before her eyes. *Love him?* She did not love Mr. Ditsworth. While it was true she liked him well enough, she never, not for a moment, ever thought of Mr. Ditsworth and romantic love in the same equation. Frankly, she'd never had time to think much about marriage at all. Papa and Mama needed her too much for her to consider leaving and starting a family of her own. Never mind that most young women were engaged or courting by the time they were her age, Hope was in no hurry. Eventually, she believed God would send the one she should spend her life with.

As if he could read her mind, Mr. Ditsworth licked his lips and took her hands in his giant, meaty ones. "I would treat you like the princess you were born to be, and I have assured your father that I will send for your entire family just as soon as their new home is complete." Breathlessly, he sank to his knees and winced as his joints popped like gunshots. "All your lives will be changed for the better. There will be no end to the abundance I can provide for you all, and one day, hopefully," he looked shyly up at her, "our own children. Hope Dawson. Will you marry me?"

"I. . .I don't know what to say," Hope stammered as her knees threatened to fail. Although why she was surprised was silly, in retrospect. Why hadn't she realized Mr. Ditsworth was courting her? Because, if she were honest, it was because she hadn't wanted to ponder such a possibility. She didn't love him. And she certainly wasn't attracted to him. "Mr. Ditsworth—"

"Julius, please. Say nothing, my dear. Take a night to sleep on it. You can let me know your answer when I come by tomorrow evening."

Seemingly unable to bear the awkward suspense another second, he struggled to an upright position and bid Hope adieu with a kiss on her hand.

How was she going to turn down his generous proposal? she wondered and stood staring after him. Because she knew, as tears began to sting the backs of her eyes, that there was no way she could marry him.

Later that evening over a very meager supper, Hope held Peter on her lap and looked into his innocent face. Then she glanced around at her sweet family. Each one was so dear to her. And, though they all loved each other to distraction, love didn't fill their bellies. None of the boys was filling out the way they should be. Currently, Eli didn't have a pair of shoes and wouldn't until Silas outgrew his. And Papa needed medicine, and Mama couldn't possibly make ends meet by herself. They needed her. Desperately.

But if Hope simply stayed here, when would they ever be able to climb out of the pit of poverty in which they found themselves?

Was Mr. Ditsworth the answer to her constant prayer?

Late that night, after the boys were all asleep, Hope knocked lightly on her parents' door. "Papa?"

"Come in, sweetheart," her father softly called.

"What is it, honey?" Mama asked as she sat up and lit the lamp.

"I've been thinking about Mr. Ditsworth's offer."

"Ahh." Papa patted the bed, and Hope crawled between her parents and snuggled down.

"Why did you give your permission, Papa?" she whispered up at him.

Papa sighed and bunched his shoulders. "Honestly? I had a feeling he was court-ing you from the moment I met him. So, I started to pray. I asked God to give me clear sight in this matter, and that's a big job, considering that I'm nearly blind." His smile was rueful. "And honey? You deserve so much better than I have been able to provide. And oddly, I have such peace whenever I think about you going to Oregon."

"Really?"

"Yes. It's strange the way the peace fills my soul. Mr. Ditsworth seems a decent sort, and he's made all kinds of generous promises to move us all to Oregon next year, promises that I won't hold him to. But this is not about any of that. I simply felt the Lord urging me not to say no. And as He says in the Good Book, 'My thoughts are not your thoughts, neither are your ways my ways.' So"—he pulled Hope's head to his shoulder and stroked her hair—"the final decision is up to you. If you want to go, I feel the Spirit nudging me not to say no. And, if you want to stay home, that is just fine too."

Big fat tears rolled from Hope's eyes and splashed onto her father's nightshirt. She wished he'd forbidden her. Now, she had no choice in the matter.

For the sake of everyone in her family, she knew she must marry Julius Ditsworth.

That night, as Hope lay in her own bed, she swallowed the huge lump in her throat and tried to convince herself that her complete lack of romantic affection for Mr. Ditsworth would eventually change. She also sent up a prayer of thanksgiving that soon her young brothers and parents would have a real home to call their own, full bellies, a doctor's care, and a new life rife with opportunity. Mama might finally recover from the ague and Papa could have surgery, and they could all stop feeling the terrible stress of poverty.

So. If dredging up an affection for Mr. Ditsworth was what it took to give her family everything they so desperately needed, then she would put every ounce of her heart into the task and determine never to look back. Somehow, she would find a way to love Mr. Ditsworth.

And as she dried a wayward tear, she tried not to think about the completely wonderful William Bradshaw who would be leading her, and her betrothed, to Oregon.

The next several days were a flurry of preparation for Hope, and in the blink of an eye, the morning of her departure arrived and with it, Mr. Ditsworth in a hired buggy. The goodbyes to her family were beyond hard, and thankfully, Mr. Ditsworth was silent as they drove to the Carlton Inn where he'd been staying while he pre-pared for their journey, to pick up his mother.

"Every other hotel for miles is booked solid, due to the emigration influx," he explained apologetically as they approached the older, rather ramshackle Carlton Inn. "Normally, we'd have stayed at the Riverside. Oh. There's Mother now." Mr. Ditsworth directed the horse to pull under the portico.

Hope glanced around spotting an angular, hawk-faced woman with the voice of a rusty bagpipe. "What took you so long?" she demanded as Mr. Ditsworth helped Hope from the carriage.

"Hope took a moment to bid her family goodbye," Mr. Ditsworth hastily explained.

The woman harrumphed as he propelled Hope forward. "Mother, I'd like to introduce you to Hope Dawson. Hope, this is my mother, Mrs. Agnes Ditsworth."

"Hello." Hope wondered if she should attempt to embrace the forbidding woman and opted not to, as the woman reared back, causing the chicken wattle at her neck to cascade over her tight collar.

Her first impression of her future mother-in-law was that Agnes Ditsworth was most likely seventy, hoping to be taken for fifty. Two bright red spots of rouge streaked her pale white cheeks and the hairs that sprouted beneath her chin had been well powdered. A salt-and-pepper bun was pinned at her nape, and other than the heavy baubles that dangled from her pendulous earlobes, her new Fruit and Flowers fancy hat was her only adornment.

She peered at Hope through a set of handheld Lorgnette glasses that magnified her beady black eyes. After a thorough inspection of Hope's best dress, she swung her head toward her son and stared at him over the rims of her glasses.

"This"—Agnes's tone was droll—"is she?"

Mr. Ditsworth nodded and tugged at his collar button.

Nostrils flaring, Agnes exhaled on a windy gust. "Boy!" she snapped at a passing hotel employee. "Load my luggage into the carriage immediately." She neither noticed nor seemed to care that the young man was already loaded down with another patron's bags. To her son, she demanded, "Julius. Hand me into the carriage."

The trip to the livery stable to pick up their wagon was thankfully short. When they arrived, several men loaded Hope's meager belongings into the only crevice left vacant in the covered wagon. Once Mr. Ditsworth helped his mother up onto the high bench seat, she peered down her nose at Hope and announced, "I have priceless antiques that I cannot leave behind. There is no room for you inside the wagon. You'll be walking."

Mr. Ditsworth took Hope aside and, with an expression that begged her pardon, he murmured, "I am so sorry. Mother. . .takes a while sometimes, to warm up to people. I promise, we'll figure this out."

"It's all right," Hope reassured him. "I don't mind walking." To be honest, the idea of sitting with Mother Ditsworth was far more daunting.

His relief was palpable. "Don't worry. We will not be traveling very fast, and I hear that most everyone is walking, so you'll be in good company until my ankle heals and I can let you ride." After several false starts, Mr. Ditsworth eventually managed to get his new mule team to the crowded Main Street in downtown Independence.

As a newly hired scout, it was William Bradshaw's duty to make sure the dozens of wagons from Independence made it on time for the May 22 departure from Elm Grove. That day, everyone was gathering for a quick rendezvous before they began a thirty-five-mile journey to join the rest of the OEC.

William's supplies had already been loaded into a company wagon which was waiting for him there. For now, he had everything he needed for the next day or so packed into his saddlebags. All that was left to do was get a nose count.

Already, Main Street was overrun with wagons. Families, cattle, chickens, dogs, and all, it seemed, were anxious to be on their way. Too anxious, to William's way of thinking. Half these men, he thought, as he scanned the crowd from the back of his horse, had no idea what they were in for and—

Wait a minute.

For the first time that morning, he smiled.

Was that Hope Dawson walking next to her father's wagon? Well, would wonders never cease? Suddenly his day got a whole lot brighter. In fact, so did the next six months. Having Hope on the trail would make the entire journey so much more interesting.

Yes, sir, he thought, this was going to be a great trip. Unfortunately, he'd be far too busy to visit with her right away, but he'd be sure to make time, once they arrived in Elm Grove.

Chapter 4

William shifted in his saddle as the wagon carrying Hope's family finally pulled into the grove on Sunday evening, May 21. It had only been two days since they'd left Independence, and already her whiny father and his cantankerous mother were notorious among the travelers. Sighing, he watched them clumsily search for, and finally locate, a vacant spot to camp. Hope's father had no sooner unhitched his mules than they ran.

With a weary groan, William nudged his horse and set off after them. Hard to believe Hope was related to those two characters. And what had become of the five brothers she claimed to have? And her mother? Odd that they would all be left behind in favor of the old lady. Made no sense.

He still hadn't had time to talk to Hope yet.

On the road, after two very hectic days, William was only able to grab a quick bite before he headed to bed. Tonight, once he'd rounded up her two mischievous mules, he might have a chance to finally say hello. And speak of the devil, there was one mule now, knee deep in a nearby stream. Once he had them both roped and following docilely along behind, William nudged his horse in the direction of Hope's camp.

The grove was currently teeming with nearly a thousand people and over a hundred wagons. The grass on the prairie had finally grown long enough to support the livestock they'd need on the trip, and everyone was eager to hit the trail.

There was a definite festive feel as a small town blossomed out in the middle of previously vacant pasture land. Arriving from everywhere, wagons, tents, and fires had popped up over the last week, surrounded by excited children and bewildered animals. Somewhere in the distance, someone was fiddling. A harmonica joined in, and the sounds of laughter and people dancing the Virginia Reel filled the air.

Let them have their fun now, William thought, as he led the mules through the giant camp. Soon enough reality, harsher than they could imagine, would set in.

As he arrived, he found Hope busily building a fire pit, while her father stared at the empty mule harness in his hands. Clearly he was flummoxed as to the next sensible step. Hope's grandmother scowled at her new surroundings from her perch behind the buckboard.

"Hello," William called as he dismounted. Hope was even prettier than he remembered as her head shot up and she swept her thick blond hair over her shoulder.

A delighted smile transformed her face as she glanced first at him and then at the animals. "William! You found our mules! Thank you so much!"

"Yup," he said as he untied them from his saddle horn. "Why didn't you tell me you would be joining the OEC?"

She smoothed her hands on her apron and shrugged. "Probably because at the time, I didn't know."

"Last-minute decision?"

Hope inhaled a deep breath, held it, then blew it out with a nod. "Yes. Very."

"Well, I'm really glad you're here." He smiled into her amazingly clear blue eyes for an extra beat before turning to her father and handing over his missing animals. "Nice to see you, sir. I'm William Bradshaw. Evening, ma'am," he said and nodded at the forbidding crone perched above in the wagon's seat. He tipped his hat. "I just stopped by to welcome you all aboard our train bound for Oregon."

"Thank you kindly, Mr. Bradshaw," Mr. Ditsworth said and grasped his hand.

"I had the privilege of meeting your daughter back in Independence," William said. "I'm so glad she'll be heading west with us."

"Daughter?" Mr. Ditsworth glanced around, puzzled.

"Hope?" William smiled, convinced now the man was eccentric. "Your daughter?"

Mr. Ditsworth inhaled sharply and then suddenly began to cough. And he coughed. And he coughed until he seemed unable to breathe at all.

Had the man sucked in a bug? William wondered, beginning to worry.

"Daughter?" Agnes gawped down at Hope, clearly appalled. "You told this young man that you are Julius's daughter?"

"I. . .no!" Hope cried.

William looked back and forth in confusion between the old woman and the heavyset man who was now busily attempting to unbutton his collar.

"Well, obviously you haven't made it clear that you are betrothed!" Suspicion sparked in Agnes's words. "Would you care to explain why you spoke to this man, unchaperoned, back in Independence?"

"That's because"—Hope's voice was agitated as her attention was split between Agnes and the shade of purple currently staining the older man's cheeks—"that's because, uh, we, we only recently became betrothed and I —" Hope patted him on his back. "Mr. Ditsworth? Do you need me to fetch you some water?"

Betrothed? William frowned, his confusion growing. Why would she refer to her father in such a formal manner? Then again, wasn't Hope's last name Dawson? "I can run for the doctor," he offered. The man really did not look well at all.

"Mr. Ditsworth?" Hope turned to look at Agnes in alarm. "Please, help him!"

"He'll be fine! This happens all the time. Give him a moment," Agnes snapped and, tilting her head back, peered down the considerable bridge of her nose at William.

"Are you sure?" William glanced at Hope for confirmation, but her panicked expression made it clear that she was out of her element.

"Yes! Now, if I may continue?" Agnes demanded. "My son, Julius, has graciously agreed to marry this"—she waved a dismissive hand at Hope—"this woman and take on her impoverished family as his charitable burden next year."

Completely nonplussed, William hoped the shock he felt was not registering on his face.

Hope was betrothed to *this* man? Hope and Julius Ditsworth?

Why on earth would a sweet, lovely woman such as Hope ever willingly commit herself to life with such spoiled, boorish, completely helpless people as the Ditsworths? Certainly her family couldn't wish this for her, no matter how impoverished they might be. He blinked as this information scrabbled around in his brain like a puzzle piece that refused to snap into place. Nothing had ever struck him as a less likely combination than Hope and this Ditsworth buffoon.

"Now, Mother," Mr. Ditsworth gasped. His attack was subsiding some but not enough to come to Hope's rescue. Apology and dismay warred with a lack of oxygen in the worried glance he cast about. "Mo. . .mother, I—"

Agnes cut him off. "Julius has always had a predilection to save the world," she said and sniffed. "He is generous to a fault, a fact that has cost us our magnificent home and a considerable portion of our family fortune. And so. Here we are. Off to claim a piece of paradise for this indigent hatmaker, a fact over which I have no control at this stage in my life." With a parting glare at Hope, Agnes climbed into the wagon and snapped the canvas flap shut, abruptly dismissing them all.

Hope stared after Agnes's departure for a moment before turning back to Mr. Ditsworth. "Sir, are you all right?"

Weakly he sucked in a labored breath and nodded. "Yes," he squeaked. "Thank you."

"Well then." Hope cleared her throat and turned to William. "Mr. Bradshaw, allow me to introduce Mr. Julius Ditsworth, my, er, my"—brow furrowed, she struggled to sum their relationship up in a suitable term—"my. . .well, as of last week, my fiancé. Mr. Ditsworth, this is Mr. William Bradshaw. We met briefly, also last week, when he inquired as to my well-being during the brawl at the restaurant."

Eyes watering, face now a calmer shade of puce, Mr. Ditsworth nodded and attempted to smile. "Ah," he choked as he sagged against the wagon's front wheel. "Thank you"—he coughed some then managed—"for your kind concern for Hope as I entered the battle to ensure her safety."

Realizing his mouth had fallen slack, William gave his head a small, clearing shake. Mr. Ditsworth had been one of the first people out the door that evening and hadn't returned until after the sheriff had made the arrests and left. "Yes. Well. I'm sorry for the, uh"—William gestured loosely between the older man and Hope—"the 'daughter' confusion, there. Very nice to meet you, sir."

"Same." Mr. Ditsworth lifted a limp hand and then let if fall to his side.

"And you, ma'am." William doffed his hat at Hope, both in respect to her status as Mr. Ditsworth's betrothed and in resignation that his brief dream of courting the beautiful young woman had evaporated. "Because we traveled so early on a Sunday, the reverend is going to hold a worship service over by the stump tonight. You're invited."

"No, thank you." Julius shook his head. "I think we'll be retiring early tonight. Another time perhaps."

William got the feeling that Hope had been going to ask what time, but disappointment at Julius's dismissal had her mouth closing. "As I'm working for the company, feel free to let me know if you folks might need anything."

"No need," Julius assured him. "Certainly, we'll face nothing on this excursion that I can't handle."

William shot a dubious look at the overloaded wagon and ill-suited livestock the pompous man had chosen for the task of hauling it all west. "Yes sir," was all he allowed before smiling at Hope and taking his leave.

"You know that fella you were talking to over there?" James Nesmith asked as William rode by his campsite a little later.

"Ditsworth?" William reined in his horse and, crossing his forearms on the saddle horn, nodded at Julius Ditsworth.

"Yeah." James nodded. "Remember how we were talking at the board meeting about troublemakers? Well, he's one of the ones gonna give us fits."

"How so?"

"I ran into him at the mercantile, and he wouldn't listen to a thing Gus told him he needed. He cut corners on staple supplies. Rumor has it he's from money. Don't understand why he'd take the risk of not being properly supplied. 'Specially if he is traveling with two women. I let him know that he and his family were not the responsibility of the OEC and that if he turned up short he was on his own."

"What'd he say?"

"He laughed and invited me to mind my own business." Nesmith snorted. "Acted like all he'd need was a fistful of cash out on the trail. As if there'd be a general store just around the bend right when he'd be needing it."

"I get the strangest feeling I've seen him somewhere before, but I can't say how." William scratched his head.

"I'll ask around. Maybe one of the other men can tell us something."

"Do that. And let me know, just as soon as you hear."

Chapter 5

May 30, 1843

Dearest family,

It took six days for the entire wagon train to cross the Kansas River. While the first wagons wait for the last to cross, we set up a site on the western bank that someone has dubbed Camp Delay and the name has stuck.

This evening, I write to you from under the vast prairie sky, which is beginning to twinkle with starlight. It's early yet, and so I'm sitting in my little tent, just outside the wagons that have circled for the night. The center of this ring acts as a corral for the livestock. Outside, our traveling city is cooking, reading, mending, visiting, and like me, writing to the families they so sorely miss.

As a little boy's laughter pealed from the campfire next wagon over, Hope paused and smiled. William Bradshaw was whittling a small slingshot for the Hembrees' young son, and they sat, heads together, deep in conversation.

"I'm gonna get a bear!" six-year-old Joel Hembree bragged.

"I imagine you could," William said and, with a quick glance over the boy's small shoulder, grinned at Hope. "David got himself a giant, didn't he? Just make sure you say your prayers first and that I'm standing behind you with a shotgun when the time comes."

"Yessir!"

Bending over her journal, Hope swallowed at some of the terrible homesickness that plagued and wondered how Peter was doing without her there to snuggle him and soothe the occasional bad dream.

There is a boy who reminds me very much of you, Peter, and our friend William is teaching him to use a slingshot. Just today, he knocked a tin cup off a rock at twenty paces.

The child was so proud he'd bragged to Hope until Agnes chased him off.

404

*I have my own little tent that is easy to pitch each night near our campfire.
Because it is a simple length of canvas draped over a rod held up by two forked
sticks, it has no doors and I can gaze up into the heavens and imagine that the
same moon is also shining on you as I say my prayers.*

Agnes was already tucked into her feather bed up in the overstuffed wagon, and
Mr. Ditsworth was comfortably situated in a hammock strung between the axels
underneath. Walls of canvas hung from the wagon bed to the ground for him, creating some privacy. Earlier that week, Mr. Ditsworth had offered the hammock to
Hope, but Agnes had thrown a fit.

"Julius, you know your asthma would never permit sleeping on the ground, out
of doors! Besides," she informed Hope, oblivious to the fact that her voice had been
compared to the screeches of a beginner's bugle by their wagon master, "his piles
have been acting up from sitting all day long, driving the wagon. So, if you are going
to expect him to shoulder the burden of getting us all the way to Oregon, he needs
his rest!"

While she was at it, Agnes had also insisted that, "For propriety's sake, Hope's
tent should be two dozen paces from our wagon each night. We can't have people
getting the wrong idea, Julius being a single man, and Hope being. . .what she is."

Hope paused in her musings to listen to Agnes's and Julius's sonorous slumber
rattling the wagon, and again, Joel's giggle rang out. As she glanced over, she could
see the carved wood taking shape in William's hands. He was so good with the boy.
Endlessly patient and playful, even after a long day on the trail.

So unlike Julius. With a heavy sigh, Hope tapped her pencil against her chin
as she thought about how to describe the Ditsworths to her family back home.
Certainly, she couldn't tell the ugly facts, as Julius and his mother had become more
infamous than ever during the difficult river crossing. Their complaints had been
never-ending, and they'd already honed their helpless act in ways that would horrify
her parents. Somehow, she needed to convey the less flattering aspects in a positive
light.

She was deep in thought when William approached and hunkered down next
to her.

"Hey there."

"Oh! Hello!" Hope hated how breathy her voice sounded, but there was just
something about William Bradshaw that made her feel giddy as a kid goat.

"Don't forget, we have to travel six miles before the company meeting tomorrow
at noon," he said, keeping his voice low as Joel had just been sent to bed. "You should

probably get some sleep. Big day tomorrow."

"I know," she nodded as his easy smile had her heart rate accelerating. A sudden surge of shame heated her cheeks. Something about her reaction when William was near made her feel bad about her relationship with Mr. Ditsworth. "It's just nice to have some time to—to, well, to—"

"To finally stop working and relax?"

"Yes!" she said, then looked guiltily around and whispered, "Yes."

"They do keep you working. And walking."

"Ah, well." Hope shrugged. She was used to hard work. And besides, Mr. Ditsworth would eventually take her entire family under his wing. Complaining wasn't an option. "I see you have a new little buddy," she said switching the focus to something more appealing.

William picked up a stick and poked at the dirt as he chuckled. "Yeah. He's a great kid. I remember learning to use a slingshot when I was his age. Six is a great time of life."

"I know. My younger brother, Peter, turned five just before I left. I miss him."

Slowly, William's head bobbed. He broke a piece off the stick and pitched it. "You'll see him again."

Hope nodded and sighed as she picked up her own small stick of wood. "But he'll be older, won't he? Different."

"Yeah. That's the human condition. Getting older. If we're lucky. Don't worry. You'll see all of your brothers again, soon enough."

Feeling a forbidden surge of affection for him, she glanced at the starlight reflecting in his eyes and bashfully returned his smile. She had no right to be thinking about how striking the angles of his handsome profile were or how the timbre of his voice made her insides swirl. "Yes, I'll see them all again." Then, she forced herself to say, "Thanks to Mr. Ditsworth."

"Yeah. Thanks to Mr. Ditsworth." He stared at her for a moment before he tossed the last piece of his stick to the ground and pushed himself to his feet. "Early start tomorrow. Don't forget."

"I won't. Night," she murmured. Unfortunately, she could never forget an opportunity to spend more time with William

"Night," he whispered back and disappeared into the shadows.

By noon, the sun was high overhead and beating down on the heads and shoulders of many folks that couldn't find space to stand under a shade tree. A quick glance over the throng had Hope guessing that most of the nearly one thousand emigrants

were attending Captain John Gantt's first meeting. There was a definite feeling of electricity in the atmosphere. In the high golden grass at the edges of the assembly, children's playful squeals were underscored by the barking of excited dogs and the occasional cries of a fussy baby.

Even Julius and Agnes had risen from their naps to attend, although Hope noticed that they both appeared to be quite cross and were already sweating profusely in the heat of the day. She stood between them and wished for all their sakes that the meeting would be brief.

When Agnes was cranky, everyone suffered. Especially Hope.

She caught a glimpse of William standing patiently nearby as little Joel tugged on his arm, swinging and lolling and giggling. She watched with longing as he teased the boy and tried to envision Julius ever enjoying a child the way William did. Despite the heat, she found herself smiling with nostalgia. Peter used to pester her that way on wash day.

William looked up and caught her eye and she froze. What was it about him that caused her heart to lurch with such excitement? With a helpless glance down at little Joel, William looked back at her with a shrug and shot her a *what-are-you-gonna-do?* grin.

Returning his smile, she shrugged and realized with regret that the warmth that flooded her belly was not from the sun. William Bradshaw was such a nice man. It would be so lovely, she mused, feeling a twinge of melancholy, if Julius had even some of his energy. Or his warmth. Or, and she hated herself for this thought, his handsome face.

Air whooshed in a long blast between her lips. One day, William Bradshaw would make some lucky woman a wonderful, hardworking husband and father. Then again, eventually Julius would too, she stoically reassured herself. He was a good man. He would be a good husband.

Once they'd settled Agnes in a place of her own, of course.

Down front, on an impromptu stage constructed of several wooden crates, Captain John Gantt, former fur trapper and scout of the Pacific Northwest Territories, stood in the sunshine and addressed his subjects. He had to shout so that he could be heard by those in the very back.

"Good day, and thank you all for coming. I can't believe it's already June first! With the long—and very successful, I might add—Kansas River crossing now thankfully behind us, the timing is perfect to formally organize." When the polite applause died down, he continued. "Folks, we need to keep in mind that an emigrant train is simply a moving community. Anything that goes on back in your hometown will certainly occur here as well. There will be births, deaths, courtship, and marriage."

In her peripheral vision, Hope felt William glance at her. Of its own volition, her gaze caught his, and immediately she felt Agnes bristling at her side.

Chagrined, Hope took a small step closer to Julius. *Gracious.* Agnes's expression fairly shouted that anything that could be construed as flirtation, even an innocent smile, was unacceptable. And, of course, that was true. She was betrothed to Julius. The man who had made this journey possible.

But it wasn't as if she was flirting with William. At the mention of courtship and marriage, he'd simply looked at her because he was recently surprised to discover that she was engaged. And naturally, she'd glanced back. As she chewed the inside of her cheek, Hope knew she had no business allowing William to take up so many of her thoughts. She was engaged to be married, for heaven's sake. The merest suggestion of impropriety on her part was so wrong. For her to esteem William too much went against everything her parents taught her was proper and godly.

Though she tried to set her attentions on Mr. Ditsworth, she couldn't help but notice Alison Naylor, daughter of Dr. Naylor, who, at the mention of courtship was boldly staring at William with a winsome expression. Alison had already made it quite plain on several occasions that she'd welcome William as a suitor.

Filled with melancholy, Hope sighed and batted at a persistent horsefly that insisted on making friends. She needed to focus on what Captain Gantt was saying.

". . .and so, some folks will get along well with their neighbors, others will not. There will be those who work hard and always appear when needed and. . .there will be the shirkers." A groan went up, and Hope felt the glances of several people standing nearby directed at her fiancé.

"Quarreling," Captain Gantt continued, "is a fact of life as we are often tired to the point of exhaustion. So, it's in our best interest to have a diplomatic form of government that can solve issues as they arise. Right now, one of our more pressing problems seems to be the cattle."

"That's because there are too many of the stupid beasts!" Agnes muttered loudly enough to spark a surge of heated discussion rippling through the crowd.

"There was no limit on the number of cattle a member of the train could take to Oregon," Jesse Applegate called out as he strode to Captain Gantt's side and faced the audience. "And, if you all want beef and milk in the new country, you'll have to help protect them. I've already lost several head to Indian poaching. That's food you may all have to depend on later in the season, to keep us all alive."

"They're slowing us down," Julius complained, and Hope felt her cheeks prickle as more folks turned to stare at her grumbling fiancé. "Well, it's true. We'd all make it a lot faster if we didn't have your wayward herds holding us back."

"The cattle are not what is slowing you down," Jesse Applegate shot back. "Your wagon is too heavy. Lighten the load and you'll speed up."

"Oh, you'd like that, good sir," Agnes retorted, spittle flying as she vented. "I should sacrifice my authentic Hepplewhite chairs and my hand-carved mahogany bedroom set so that *you* can force men—like my son, Julius, who is in delicate health—to guard your filthy animals! The dust they kick up is enough to kill my poor boy!"

"Then, may I suggest that you folks find a new place in the train to travel. Away from the cattle and dust."

"Yeah, maybe a place back in Missouri," one cattle man said, and a surge of laughter swelled. Hope studied the worn spots on the tips of her shoes and prayed that her bonnet covered the shame she felt glowing in her cheeks.

"Well, I never!" Agnes whirled and began to push her way through the crowd toward her wagon. "Julius?" she screeched over her shoulder. "We do not have to stand here and endure insults hurled at us in jealousy!"

Sour faced, Julius huffed after his mother amid some good-natured catcalls and heckling. He seemed to have completely forgotten about his fiancée, and for that, Hope was relieved. If she followed them back to the wagon while they were this riled, she'd have to break out the polish and labor over each enormous piece of furniture until the sun set. Watching Hope work seemed to soothe Agnes when she was in a mood.

Though. . .if she didn't follow them now, what chores would Agnes invent to punish her lack of loyalty? Hope stood deliberating as Captain Gantt carried on, unfazed by the Ditsworth departure.

"It seems we've moved to the crux of the issue a little sooner that I'd hoped, but first, we need leadership to govern. Right now, we'll hold an election, and the man with the most votes will become captain of the company under my direction. Second most votes will hold the title of orderly sergeant."

Conversations sprung up immediately as Captain Gantt invited the men who were interested in running for these offices to step forward.

William seemed to sense Hope was trying to decide whether she should stay as he approached. "You aren't going to want to miss this."

"Why?" Hope tried to don a bright smile, but the Ditsworths' disagreeable behavior and her own disloyalty to them had left her feeling deflated. "What's happening?"

"The leadership is going to run for office, and it should be"—his grin was wide—"pretty interesting."

"Oh?" she asked, puzzled. She'd always found the elections process tedious.

"Watch," he said and pointed over to where several men were gathering up front.

"Why aren't you stepping up?" Hope asked. "I'd vote for you." Then realizing what she'd just admitted, she added, "And, I'm pretty sure Alison Naylor would."

"Who?"

"Alison? Dr. Naylor's oldest daughter? The pretty young lady who is slowly making her way over here."

Seeming not to grasp the subtle hint that he may have an admirer, William shook his head. "I'd never run for one of those positions. You'd have to be crazy to want to deal with the constant complaining of nearly a thousand people."

Hope glanced at Alison. Yes. The girl was openly staring at William. *How forward*, Hope thought, feeling suddenly churlish, but then wondered why Alison's obvious interest in William should irritate her. Certainly, it was none of her concern who pursued William. However, pondering that issue would have to wait. Captain Gantt was introducing candidates one at a time and giving them a moment to extoll their leadership qualities.

"Now," Captain Gantt boomed as the last candidate finished his spiel, "I'll need each of you fine men to turn your backs to the people. At my signal, all of you"—his arm swept out across the crowd—"please line up behind the candidate of your choice."

Laughter swelled and people began to discuss the merits of each contender. Captain Gantt removed a small brass trumpet that hung from his belt and brought it to his lips for one long blast.

"C'mon," William said and reached for Hope's hand. As he tugged her down front, Alison happily fell in behind them.

Chaos and hilarity instantly ensued as folks surged to line up. The sheer numbers drove the candidates further into the prairie until each began to lead their supporters in long, coiling serpentines through the grasses. People settled their hands at the hips of the person in front of them and, sensing the building excitement, dogs gamboled to and fro and little children shouted and rushed to join the fun. As they marched, crickets leapt, and overhead, curious birds wheeled in the clear blue sky. Even the livestock stopped grazing long enough to stare at the insanity. Little Joel was clinging to William's belt and laughing like a loon as he stumbled along between William's boots.

"Running for office is a little more literal on the prairie than we see in town,"

William said, pulling Hope close so she could hear over the din.

"I think I prefer this," Hope said, chin to shoulder, and discovered his nose was mere inches from her cheek. Her heart skipped a beat, as she whipped her head forward again.

"Me too!" Alison chimed in, clutching the back of William's shirt and barely avoiding collision with Joel who was limp from giggling.

Everyone laughed as the leader of another line tripped and fell. Like dominos, his constituents all went down with him and rolled in the grass with hoots of glee and grunts of pain. Joel broke free and joined the children dogpiling those unfortunates on the ground.

The entire event reminded Hope of the lively barn dances held back home, and despite the Ditsworths' earlier behavior, she felt bubbles of happiness rising. She hadn't felt this light since before her mother had fallen ill.

Giggling, they all continued to stumble along, William holding Hope by the hips and Alison and Joel holding onto him until Captain Gantt blew his trumpet a second time. Though the blast signaled the end of the election, William left his hand lightly at Hope's back as he steered her through the crowd to the meeting area again. Undeterred, Alison stayed with them and chattered genially about a dance and potluck supper that some women were discussing for an upcoming wedding on the trail.

"Oh! Wouldn't that be so much fun?" Alison was such an outgoing, vivacious girl that—even though she was an incorrigible flirt—Hope was finding it hard to dislike her. She guessed eventually William would too. They'd probably pair off and find happiness. The thought made Hope feel more than a little lost.

Captain Gantt blew a long note then announced that Peter Burnett won captain of the company. James Nesmith was elected orderly sergeant. The new leadership immediately launched another vote and the wagon train was split into two groups. Those with more than ten cattle would form the Cow Column, led by Jesse Applegate. Those with less than ten cattle would form the Light Column under Bill Martin and be further divided into marching platoons to which four leaders were appointed. To William's surprise, he found himself one of those leaders and handed a list of his families.

"Looks like you're with me," he murmured as he scanned the list and then glanced at Hope with that endearing grin of his.

Awash with relief—and a thrill she dared not contemplate—Hope peered over his shoulder and read the names printed there. *Payne. Ditsworth. Shively. Beagle. Dodd. Foster. Hill. Hembree. Naylor.*

Her spirits took an irrational dip at the sight of Alison's surname, but she instantly chided herself. Just because William was the only real friend she'd made on this journey so far didn't mean he couldn't forge a—she swallowed hard—romance with Alison.

Homesickness had plagued her something fierce, and only William and little Joel had kept her going on the days she wanted to quit. Still, that did not mean she should interfere with William making his own friends.

Perhaps, Hope reluctantly thought, she should not only welcome Alison's friendship, but stop feeling sorry for herself that Mr. Ditsworth would never provide the spark of romance she hoped for in her own marriage. He was saving her family. That was enough.

Chapter 6

By the third week of their journey west, William was required to help the Ditsworths for one reason or another nearly every day. Though, because of his growing affection for Hope, he found the chore less odious than he might otherwise. She was not only beautiful but amazingly patient with her loathsome mother-in-law. By now, William would have told the old biddy off. But not Hope. She was kind, hardworking, funny, sweet, and—though he knew it was wrong to envy another man—everything he wanted in a bride.

No other woman on this entire wagon train held a candle to her.

It was also not beyond his notice that the selfish Ditsworths rode all day, every day, while Hope walked. Despite their abuse, Hope managed to remain in good spirits and was a strong, capable servant to them both.

Not that Agnes ever gave Hope a word of encouragement, let alone any time to rest.

One blustery cold morning as William rode by on a routine check of his platoon, he noticed, to his disgust, that Hope was limping. He took it upon himself to spell her for a bit.

"It's nothing,." She self-consciously brushed off his concern. "Just a little hole in the sole of my shoe."

"Let me see," he'd instructed, leaving no room for argument. Clearly, she was in pain. He dismounted and knelt at her side. Yep. She had a problem that was only going to grow as she walked. "You need to have these shoes repaired and start using your backup pair."

The flush of her cheeks was completely endearing as she admitted, "I only have one pair."

He tried not to let the irritation he felt at the Ditsworths' lack of preparation show as he stood. "What about Agnes? Can you borrow a pair of hers?"

"I've thought of that, but even if she would consent, I'm afraid her feet are too small and narrow and her shoes are quite"—she seemed to grope for a diplomatic

413

word for *horrible*—". . .fashionable."

William looked down at his boots and tried to imagine her feet swimming in his extra pair. That would only make matters worse. "C'mon," he ordered and led her to the side of his horse. "Up we go." Hands at her slim waist, he lifted and before she knew it, Hope found herself seated in his saddle.

"But what about you? Don't you need to check on the other wagons in your care?" She seemed at the same time concerned and secretly relieved. The way she always put the comfort of others first delighted William's heart.

Grin rueful, he gathered the reins and began to lead Hope and his horse alongside his platoon. "Nope. Nobody ever seems to need my attention as much as the Ditsworths."

"Oh." The word was small, yet packed a wallop of embarrassment. "Why do you suppose they are always lagging so far behind?"

William was taught early to never speak ill of anyone, so he glanced back at Julius dozing in his wagon's seat and lagging a good quarter-mile behind the rest of the train before carefully choosing his words. "Most likely because his mules and horses are too small and untrained. That, and his wagon is overloaded." Not to mention the fact that the unhealthy man and his quarrelsome mother seemed far better suited to parlor life.

Hope bit her lip. "Do you have any idea how we could help him be less of a burden?"

"Short of dumping all of that heavy furniture and finding him several good teams of seasoned oxen?" William shrugged. "No."

Hope sighed. "I'm so sorry."

"Not your fault." He glanced up at her, and she bestowed him with a smile that seemed to break through the clouds that had been gathering on the horizon all afternoon. There was a definite chill in the air, and as they walked, off in the distance, thunder rumbled ominously. "Sounds like we're in for it, huh?"

"Think it will rain?" Hope asked as she squinted at the rolling clouds.

"The sky is sure black. After a while, we'll ride up and talk to Captain Gantt about making camp early tonight."

Hope nodded, and her eyes slid closed as she smiled. William could tell the idea of an early night was all right with her. He resisted the urge to reach up and pat her hand. To entwine their fingers and give her a reassuring squeeze.

He sighed, frustrated. She needed rest and deserved so much better than the man to whom she was betrothed. Unfortunately, she was convinced that Julius Ditsworth was the answer to her family's dire needs. Any intervention on his part would be wrong. Soon she would be married. And he would do well to keep that unhappy fact in mind.

A distant clap of thunder gave William the niggling feeling that the weather was echoing the ill-wind of Julius Ditsworth.

They'd no sooner circled the wagons and made camp that afternoon when the first fat drops of water plopped on the brim of Hope's bonnet. Huge, water-laden thunderclouds roiled, and the prairie winds had tumbleweeds on the run. Women gathered their skirts and held onto their bonnets as the canvas on the wagons began to flap. And when the first bolts of lightning ripped across the sky, children squealed with fear and excitement.

Then, all at once, the heavens opened and the deluge began. All hopes of building a fire and cooking supper were dashed, and secretly, Hope was thankful. One less chore she had to cope with that day. She ignored Julius and Agnes's bitter complaints about the hardtack and jerky and was simply grateful they had anything to eat at all.

As the gale struck full force, Agnes took her tiny meal in the relative safety of her feather bed inside the wagon, and Julius crawled into the canvas cave he'd fashioned beneath the wagon and bundled up in his hammock.

Thankfully, William rode by as Hope was losing the battle with her tent. Every time she drove a stake into the hard ground and attached a corner of the canvas, the wind would tear it up and whip it away. She spent more time chasing than pitching.

"What are you doing clear out here?" William shouted above the wind.

"Agnes prefers that I be two dozen paces away from our wagon at night," she shouted back. At his puzzled expression she added, "For propriety's sake."

William rolled his eyes and jumped off his horse. "In that case, let's get your tent set up under the Naylors' wagon. It'll serve as a wind break, and you can get out of this storm."

Hope nodded as the rain battered their faces. Sounded good to her. She was already soaked to the skin. Thanks to William and Mr. Nesmith, her tent was soon pitched between the Naylors' wagon wheels, halfway under the wagon proper, where thankfully, the ground had yet to be saturated. William helped her inside.

"You going to be all right in here?" His expression was doubtful as he glanced around the small space and listened to her teeth chatter.

"Yes, thanks to you, I'll be fine." She beamed up at him, even as she shivered. There were others in his platoon who needed his help. The Ditsworth faction took up far more than its fair share of his time.

"You're freezing," William said and peered at her face with a concerned frown. "Your lips are blue." Placing his hands on her arms, he proceeded to vigorously rub some much-needed heat into her body.

"N—no, no. P—please," she stammered, as the frigid air made her shudder. "Go. Once I get into my bedroll, I'll warm right up." The fact that her bedroll had already wicked up its weight in water was not something she felt like burdening him with right then.

"At least take this," he said and quickly retrieved an oil lantern the Shively family had tucked into his saddlebag for someone in need. "It will give you light and hopefully help heat your tent some."

"Oh, no, I couldn't," Hope breathed as he lit the wick and the glow illuminated his handsome face. Here he was, taking care of her when her own fiancé couldn't be bothered. "Won't you need this?"

"Not as bad as you will. Besides, I have another." He backed out of the tent and pushed himself to a standing position. Water sluiced off his hat as he bent to peer inside at her. His sweet smile had her pulse suddenly throbbing. "I'll be back in a while to check on you."

"Thank you." The thought of his return warmed her, even as the water from her bedroll seeped into her skirts and chilled her to the bone. Because the small lantern threw some decent heat, Hope decided to huddle close and work on her journal.

June 6, 1843

I have never experienced anything like a thunderstorm on the prairie. Rain falls in torrents and, if the complaints being shouted outside are any indication, it's leeching through even the most waterproof tents and canvas. The wind blows with brute fury, but nothing compares to the peals of the thunder. Since there are no trees or buildings nearby to absorb the shock, it's completely deafening. Imagine having a shotgun repeatedly going off beside your head. I'm thankful that William is so capable. Without his help, I don't know how I should be contending. Right now, he is helping secure Julius's skittish mules. All it would take to send them into a panic is a close strike, as our mules seem to have even less common sense than most.

She'd no sooner closed her journal and stored it away when William appeared once again. His sunny smile seemed to warm her entire tent.

"Ahoy there," he called and knelt in her doorway. "I brought you a couple things." Reaching into his saddlebag, he drew out a dry, well waxed canvas tarp and thrust it at her. "Let's spread this over your damp bedroll. Together they quickly unrolled it and pushed it into place. "And here," he grunted, "you can borrow this wool blanket and an extra shawl from Mrs. Hembree." From his saddlebags, he pushed the dry blanket over her lap, and she blissfully burrowed in. "And, wait just a moment for the best part—" he said, a grin in his voice as he disappeared. He returned in several minutes with two steaming cups of coffee.

"Where did you get this?" she cried, as the wonderful aroma filled the small space.

"Dr. Naylor has a small stove that we set up under an awning over on the other side of the Hembree wagon. A few dry buffalo chips and a miraculous answer to our prayers, and we got fire. He's brewing some for everyone in our platoon to ward off the chill. Says it's a precaution." He sat on his heels inside the opening of her tent and took a big gulp of the steaming coffee.

"Oh my goodness, yes. I'll have to do something nice for him soon." Feeling guilty about her bad attitude toward his daughter, Hope wrapped her hands tightly around the hot tin cup. She'd reach out to Alison as soon as possible. As she sipped, she could feel the warmth begin to return to her extremities.

"I should get going," he finally said, and Hope felt her spirits plunge. "Besides, I know it's probably not too seemly, me being here with you like this unchaperoned." His tone was wry as he referred to Agnes's decree that Hope remain modest. Rain poured off the brim of his hat and splattered mud everywhere as he gulped the last of his coffee. "So, I'll just be on my way."

Hope looked at the mud clinging to his nose and cheeks then glanced around at her soggy, dripping, wide-open-to-passers-by tent, then burst out laughing. They were both as bedraggled as drowned rats, and their entire camp was on the verge of washing away. Hardly the most romantic of scenarios, even if she hadn't been already engaged to Mr. Ditsworth. The humor of the situation was contagious, and soon they were both doubled over with the ridiculousness of Agnes's idea of propriety in the face of veritable monsoon.

"Yes, well," he managed as Hope wiped tears from the corners of her eyes, "I really do need to be on my way. I have more folks to check on before I turn in. I'll be camping with the doctor on the other side of the Naylor wagon, so if you should need anything, just holler, all right?"

Hope smiled at the sweet concern on his face. "I will. I'm already feeling much more comfortable, thanks to your kindness."

He ducked his head. "It's nothing. Take care."

The next morning, the storm's devastation was revealed in the gray light of pre-dawn. Tents had overturned and blown away, but thanks to William's quick thinking, Hope's was not among them. Several of the wagons' canvas covers would need some serious repair, and one wagon in another platoon had overturned. Luckily, no one was hurt. Everyone suffered food damage. Many bags of flour and cornmeal had been soaked through and needed to be dried out or used right away.

And then, there was the poor horse that had been struck by lightning and killed. Unfortunately, it had been one of the Ditsworth spare horses. Not only that, the trauma of the lightning strike had spooked their mules and they were nowhere to be found.

Though the rain was still driving sideways, a hunting party led by William had left before sunup to look for the many animals that had bolted, including the Ditsworth mules. Mr. Ditsworth—so overcome with anxiety at losing the better part of his team—was nursing an asthma attack in his bed.

No one in the entire wagon train had slept at all, save for the occasional babe held in its mother's arms. Everyone had stories over the sputtering morning fires, of shivering the night away in beds that could be wrung out enough to create a lake.

"How are you this morning?" Alison asked when Hope emerged from under their wagon to organize Julius and Agnes's breakfast.

"Thanks to your father's hot coffee and the generosity of everyone in our platoon, I'm fine." Hope smiled warmly. "You?"

"Wet. Cold. Wishing I was home."

Hope looked closely at her. *Really?* That was exactly how she felt. "Me too! And though my home was nothing to brag on, it was a castle compared to my tent, and always warm and dry."

Alison giggled. "I know! I think there is nothing I own that is not dripping wet. And I have the kind of hair that turns into sheep's wool in weather like this. So, my lips are purple and my hair looks as if it endured a lightning strike. . .and. . ." Her face scrunched with the kind of laughter born of trauma. "Oh my."

Knowing that she had fared no better, Hope began to laugh and soon, they had their arms around each other's waists and were giggling with the humor and the horror of it all.

Until Agnes poked her head out of the wagon and scolded them both for interrupting her beauty sleep.

And then? They only laughed harder.

Thus began Hope's lifelong friendship with Alison Naylor.

Chapter 7

June 8, 1843

The cattle are churning the water-logged ground into a deep soup that the wagon wheels send flying everywhere. When the sun appears, I imagine we will be airing our clothes and bedding out and cleaning the mud off everything for days. We only traveled five miles today.

June 9, 1843

More never-ending rain. Everyone is most miserable, and the only respite I've enjoyed are the occasional visits from Alison Naylor, or today, when William dropped by with Joel to pick me up for Bible study with the pastor. We traveled six miles.

June 10, 1843

After we traveled five miles in driving rain, we made camp early. Alison, William, and Joel gathered during a brief break in the rain for a game of rummy and some conversation around the lantern. We are all becoming fast friends. It's quite clear that both Alison and Joel are besotted with William. I'm glad that Alison seems happy enough to allow Joel and me to spend time together with them, or I believe I should die of loneliness.

She didn't mention that Mr. Ditsworth took for granted her hard work and didn't seem interested in according her the affection of a normal fiancé.

Sunday, after a morning church service, the weather let up enough for the company to push forward for most of the day. As was becoming their habit, William picked Joel up after lunch and they'd join Alison and Hope and walk together for an hour or so. When Joel wasn't riding on William's shoulders, he'd jump from puddle to puddle with the glee only a six-year-old understood. But when he ran out of puddles, Hope glanced up to catch him running off after

Alison, who'd been summoned by her father.

"Joel!" Hope called. "Where are you going?"

"I'm gonna go with Alison!"

"No. Dr. Naylor needs Alison for a few minutes to help him dress an injury. Your mother says you need to stay with us."

"*Awww.*" Shoulders drooping, Joel slogged over to trudge between Hope and William. "But I wanted to see the blood and stuff."

"Nah," William grinned over at Hope, and she couldn't help but shiver with pleasure at the obvious spark of interest in his eyes. "That's not something anybody needs to see. Especially a junior whippersnapper like you."

"Swing me!" the boy demanded as he grabbed each of their hands. It was a game they regularly played to keep the boy amused.

"One," William said and grinned at Hope.

"Twwwooo," Hope said, grinning back.

"*Threeeee!*" Joel squealed as they lifted him up and swung him forward. This frivolity only occupied him for a moment before he grew bored and asked, "William? You gonna marry her?" He pointed at Hope.

Startled, Hope stumbled, and William steadied her by the arm.

"Joel!" she chided, mortified. "What on earth makes you ask that?"

"Cuz you like him." The boy's freckled face was innocent and his toothless grin, winsome.

"I. . .well, oh my, I. . ." Oh dear! Had her affections been that obvious? A lump of terrible guilt lodged in her throat.

William watched her with an amused expression. "Is that true? Do you. . .*like* me?" he teased. But he studied her closely for her reaction.

"Well, of course I do," she snapped, sounding sharper than she'd intended, but the child had completely caught her off guard, and she didn't like the feeling that a little boy could read her most secret thoughts. Gracious, if a child could see how much she cared for William, certainly everyone else in this rolling city could too. "And I like *you*, Joel. And *Alison*. But I'm not going to marry you." She swallowed hard. "Or William."

"How come?" Joel's face was scrunched with curiosity.

"Because," she exhaled heavily, "I'm going to marry Mr. Ditsworth."

"Ewww!" Joel cried and jumped feet first into a nearly foot deep puddle. "Ewwwie!"

Rain clouds scuttled across the wide prairie sky, but it wasn't the cool breeze that had gooseflesh rising on her arms.

William threw back his head and laughed as Hope elbowed his ribs. "Hush up," she hissed. "And, Joel, mind your manners."

"Why?" Joel demanded. "Why you gonna marry that old man? He's ole and ewweie and mean."

Hope's gaze skittered off toward the horizon as she struggled to recall all of the reasons that had been so sensible back when she'd agreed to marry Mr. Ditsworth. Joel's question was fair. She could also see it was one that interested William. And, now that she'd had plenty of time to ponder the issue, she wasn't sure she had a good answer. "Well, because I promised him."

Joel gaped at her as if she were addlebrained. "But, *why?*"

"I guess because he's going to take care of me and my family when we get to Oregon. And that makes him a good man."

"No, it don't make him a good man!" Joel informed her as he leapt over a prairie dog's hole.

"No," William corrected. "It *doesn't* make him a good man."

Hope shot him a droll look and William just grinned. She fought the impulse to slug him. And kiss his cheek.

"Right," Joel gifted William with a sunny smile. "He ain't a good man."

"*Isn't.* He isn't a good man."

"That's what I said."

"No. That's what I said," William told Joel as he swung the child up onto his shoulders. "So, want to tell me about your feelings for your future husband?" William broached after a few minutes had passed in silence.

"I don't want to talk about it." Hope sighed. Her feelings were all in a muddle. What had been so perfectly clear as she'd begun this journey was now one giant question mark.

"That's fine." William bit back some laughter at her grumpy expression. "But you're going to have to figure out the answer one of these days pretty soon. The step you are about to take will be permanent. You need to make sure it's the right one."

Hope's eyes slid closed. He was right. She had absolutely no affection for her future husband and wasn't sure she ever would. And that, she was beginning to realize, was a big problem. Couple that with the growing affection she held for William, and she knew she was headed toward serious trouble.

Redoubling her commitment to her family's future, she would work even harder to forge a friendship with Mr. Ditsworth.

"I never, ever, ever thought I'd want it to rain again," Hope muttered to Alison and William by the fifth week. They were all hot and itchy and sweating as they trudged along. All that lay ahead was a long, flat, dry prairie between them and the Platte River.

This, they'd been warned by Captain Gantt at the last all-company meeting, would be the longest stretch of road they would traverse without water. They'd have to go thirty miles—most of it in a single day—before they would reach the shores of the Platte.

The warm temperatures had people and livestock alike feeling lethargic.

"I'd really love to find a shady spot and take a nap right about now," Alison said and yawned broadly.

William nodded. "Hard to believe we were swimming to Oregon just a week ago."

"Remind me? Why were we complaining?" Hope asked. Her nose was burnt, and her eyes ached from the constant glare even under the deep brim of her bonnet. "Tell us a story, William," she suggested. "Tell Alison about why you live in Oregon and why you left." Hope knew some of William's history and wanted to learn more.

"What?" Alison cried and squinted at William. "You *live* in Oregon?"

"Yeah. Oregon City. My father runs a lumber mill there. My family has lived there for a few years now."

"So you have made this trip before?" Alison asked, jaw sagging.

Hope giggled at her shocked expression.

"Twice." He shrugged. "Once with my family in 1839, then last year I came back to the states to try to rustle up some young men to come work in the lumber industry as loggers, sawyers, and builders."

"And you knew this already?" Alison accused Hope, hurt at being left out of the loop.

"Yes, but I still have questions. Like, aren't there already enough men living there? Why did you need to come all the way back to the states?" Hope asked.

"Rumor has it that the government will be issuing free land to anyone brave enough to make the move. Three hundred and twenty acres for every man. And it doubles, if he's married."

"Really? Gracious," Alison said. "That would be a good reason to get married, huh?"

A thought so terrible it stopped Hope in her tracks struck her like a bolt of lightning. Both William and Alison paused and turned to look at her.

"Hope?" William asked. "Are you all right?"

Even in the warm sun, Hope's skin felt suddenly cold and clammy. "You don't—" She swallowed and groped for William's arm. "You don't think that is why Mr. Ditsworth wants to marry me, do you? For the extra acreage? Is it possible he has no intention of helping my family? Maybe he just told me a story so that he could get all that free land?"

They'd come to a full stop now, and she was leaning heavily on William's arm as Alison dabbed at her face with the ties to her bonnet.

"I dunno, Hope," William said gently. "But if that's his reason, the man would have to be a fool."

Alison opened her mouth to speak but then thought better and closed it.

Hope whimpered as the terror that she could be right washed over her. She'd come so far and struggled so hard and committed her life to a loveless marriage, all for the sake of her family. Mr. Ditsworth *had* to follow through on his promise.

"Hope," William said, "any man in his right mind would simply marry you because you're *wonderful*. Sweet. Kind. Beautiful—" He suddenly seemed to realize what he was saying and—and to who—and fell silent.

"Really?" she asked in a tiny voice. Agnes had made it clear she didn't share that sentiment. And Mr. Ditsworth hadn't really shown all that much interest recently in returning Hope's earnest efforts at forging a friendship. Probably because Agnes took every opportunity to belittle her in front of her son.

Alison heaved a sigh, and cupping her friend's face in her hands, looked Hope straight in the eyes. "Of course, you goose. I bet William here would marry you in a second, if you weren't already engaged. Right, William?"

William dragged a hand over his jaw and looked at the ground. "Yeah. In a second."

"I thought so," was all Alison said. But she was smiling.

Early the next morning, the wagon train was intent on getting to the shores of the Platte River, and breakfast had been forfeited in the interest of time.

"They say we've traveled nearly thirty miles already," William said as they squinted out over the flat, dry sunrise.

"It's true," Hope agreed, feeling more than a little drowsy. "Thirsty miles."

William laughed. "I said thirty miles."

"Yes. I'm. . .thirsty."

They stopped walking and clutched each other's arms for some hilarity before they sallied forth. And then, a short time later, a cry went up from the front of the company.

"*Water!*"

"Yes, look! It's a river! It's. . .the. . .PLATTE!"

Several teams of oxen, smelling the water, began to trot then gallop as their wagons bounced haplessly after them.

"Water!" William said and hugged Hope tightly.

"Water," she breathed as she returned his fierce embrace. *Oh, if only she were free to love William. How sweet this moment would be.*

Chapter 8

July 5, 1843

Dearest family,

Crossing the Platte River's south fork was exciting. At various intervals, dozens of wagons were lashed together and then long ropes were tied to the axels of those in the front. Men crossed ahead on horseback with the other ends of these ropes so they could pull our procession from bank to bank.

Hope paused as she contemplated how to convey the rest of the Ditsworths' sorry voyage. Yesterday, the morning of their turn to cross, several OEC board members—including William—approached Mr. Ditsworth advising him to leave Agnes's furniture behind in the interest of safety. And, though Mr. Ditsworth agreed, Agnes would have none of it.

"Absolutely not! I will not leave off my priceless cargo so that some other scoundrel can abscond with it. Julius, I refuse to leave anything behind. I'm staying with my furniture and that is final."

As usual, Agnes had her way.

Everything went beautifully at first, and Agnes was quite smug until they reached deep water and their top-heavy wagon began to sway so dangerously the lashings failed. Though their remaining sets of mules and horses made a valiant effort to stay abreast of the other wagons, there was nothing they could do in the face of the river's strong current. Their wagon broke loose and began to turn in wobbly circles.

Terror stricken, Agnes clutched Hope by the shoulders and rattled her half senseless as she shrieked, *"Do something!"*

Mr. Ditsworth froze.

"Heeelllllp!" Agnes screamed and stood up on the buckboard, her fancy Fruit and Flowers hat listing at a perilous angle as she wildly waved at the folks who stood staring on both shores. "Help us! Now! Get over here and help us!"

Unfortunately, by that point there was nothing anyone could do but watch in horror as the Ditsworth wagon slowly rolled over and sank. Having grown up at the edge of a river, Hope was a strong swimmer and managed to help the sputtering Agnes to the surface. Mr. Ditsworth popped up downstream in the throes of an asthma attack and promptly sank again.

Several Indians who had been hired to help with the crossing bravely dove into the river to rescue the thrashing Ditsworths. Without a second thought, William dove into the water and grabbed ahold of Hope. Together, they swam to shore. William made sure several women loaned her dry clothing and provided hot tea. He hovered nearby, fretting until people began to whisper, before he left to continue helping the others make their crossing.

Sadly, Hope was not the only one to notice that the Ditsworths offered not a single word of gratitude for their lives or the hospitality offered them by the others in their unit for shelter that night.

The following morning, a group of men retrieved the Ditsworth wagon and dried it out. Although worse for the wear, some of the furniture had been salvaged. Unfortunately, one of their horses had not been so fortunate. They had so far lost three-quarters of their team, leaving the weak animals that remained to pull double duty.

Now, in the fading twilight, Hope looked down at her battered and bare feet and was grateful to be alive at all. With the exception of her journal, her personal belongings—including her only pair of shoes—had all been lost. Wrapped tightly in its waterproof pouch, William found her journal hooked on a snag about a mile downstream.

We made camp on the opposite shore, and the entire train has lingered for five days now. Someone gave the nickname "Sleepy Grove" to our campsite, as everyone is exhausted.

Since she couldn't think of anything remotely positive to write beyond that, Hope set her journal aside and cut another long strip from her blanket and bound her feet again. She could tell after only a few days that she wouldn't have much of a blanket left, at the rate the wool was wearing out.

"Hey," William's deep voice startled her, and she quickly covered her feet with the tattered hem of her dress.

"Hello," she said and, taking the offer of his hands, stood.

"The men are having a dance to celebrate the end of this crossing, and I thought maybe you and Alison might want to go watch with Joel and me. They're kicking up a lot of sand and getting crazy, so none of the women are joining in, but a crowd is gathering to watch."

"I'd love it!" she said, excitement suddenly coursing through her veins. "But I—" Her face fell as she realized that she should invite her future family. "Let me ask if the Ditsworths want to join us."

"Oh." William rubbed the bridge of his nose and shrugged. "Sure."

Though it was the last thing she wanted to do, Hope lightly knocked on their wagon's side. "Mrs. Ditsworth, there is a celebration happening down at river's edge, and I'd like to go. Do you want to join me?"

"You think I give a fig what you do with your spare time?"

"Well, being that you are my chaperone—"

"Go away," Agnes moaned.

Mr. Ditsworth was already snoring quite loudly beneath the wagon, so Hope opted not to disturb him. Feeling suddenly giddy with freedom, she and William rushed off to gather Alison and Joel and several of their other friends.

William had been right. A bunch of men were kicking and flinging sand to the tune of a vigorously played fiddle, and the gathering crowd urged them on with hoots and applause for some of the more athletic stunts. A little higher up on the shore, on firmer ground, several couples began to dance.

"Hope, will ya dance with me?" Joel cried, tugging on her hand.

"It would be my honor," she said and whirled him onto the impromptu dance floor. The child had boundless energy, and when Hope began to flag, his very pregnant mother cut in and danced the little boy away.

"I see your partner has been stolen." William hooked his thumbs into his belt loops.

Flushed and breathing hard, Hope laughed and said, "Thanking my lucky stars. He'd like to plumb tucker me out."

Looking crestfallen, William rocked back on his heels. "Too bad. I was hoping you'd give me a turn on the dance floor."

Hope's heart skipped a beat. "Well now, if you promise not to make me swing you, I might have just enough energy for a turn or two with you."

His dimple bloomed, and Hope found herself happily in his arms for the next three songs.

By the time they'd reached Fort Laramie, Hope was walking barefoot much of the time. As they covered amazing terrain that included the strangely formed Chimney Rock, her feet had grown tough. But even so, stepping on a sharp rock or patch of stickers brought tears to her eyes. Mr. Ditsworth still claimed that his ankle was too weak for him to walk, and Agnes would never dream of offering her seat to Hope. So, she walked.

July 14, 1843

Today at noon, we arrived at Fort Laramie. The fort's walls are about fifteen
feet high and surround a large yard. Everyone was relieved to learn that the
fort has a forge and a carpentry shop for blacksmithing and wagon wheel repair.
Unfortunately, there is little for sale, which has been hard on the ladies.

Agnes had been the most vocal and long-winded in her disappointment, so
Hope opted to spend the day out of range. As she and Alison sat, mending a pile of
worn clothing, William appeared with little Joel at his side.

"Hope!" the child cried, "William brung ya a present! Guess what it is! Just
guess! We bartered with an Injun!"

Surprised, Hope shook her head and smiled up at William with breathless
expectation. "I have no idea."

"You're gonna love them! They're for your feet!"

Grin wide, William glanced at the sky. "So much for the surprise," he said and
brought his hands from behind his back.

Hope gasped with delight as he handed her a pair of soft deerskin moccasins,
adorned with delicate beadwork. "They're so beautiful! These—" Tears of gratitude
burned the backs of her eyes. "These are for me?" He was so incredibly thoughtful.

Without wasting another second, she slipped them on her feet. "I think I'm
standing in heaven," she whispered with a sigh and, before she could give any
thought to the propriety of her actions, Hope threw her arms around his neck and
soundly kissed his cheek. "Thank you," she blubbered and pressed her face into his
shirt. "I love them."

"Yeah," William flushed bright red. "Me too."

"Ewww," Joel shouted at Alison. "Didja see that?"

"Yup," Alison was grinning from ear to ear. "I sure did."

On the eighteenth of July, just a few days beyond Fort Laramie, while they
were traveling over road deeply rutted by buffalo traffic, Joel, looking for some
amusement to break up the monotony, climbed up on the tongue of his father's
wagon. Bracing his hands on the rumps of the oxen in front of him, he called
them by name and encouraged them to "Get up, now," just like his dad had been
doing for weeks.

A sudden jolt threw him off, and before anyone realized what had happened,
both the front and back wagon wheels passed over his body.

Chapter 9

The next day, at two in the afternoon, William found Hope walking alone at the very end of the wagon train. The sorrowful expression on his face must have given him away, because she fell to her knees and let out a keening wail that broke his heart.

He sank down beside her and pulled her into his arms. Later, he couldn't say how long they sat, rocking and crying and holding each other tightly and discussing the horror of losing a sweet little boy like Joel, but the wagons had vanished over the horizon before they had the wherewithal to carry on.

By the time they made it back to camp, several of the men had already dug a small grave. Someone found a large rock to serve as his headstone and carved Joel's name and the dates that bookended his life. Little Joel Hembree had the devastating distinction of becoming the first fatality on the '43 train.

Unfortunately, he wouldn't be the last.

In the days that followed, the only thing Hope could bring herself to scribble in her journal was:

HOT. HOT. HOT. DUST. DUST. DUST. No water. Animals and people very thirsty. Poison watering holes. So very tired. I miss Joel terribly. His mother had a baby girl the week after he died. They named her Nancy Jane, and she is a doll.

By the beginning of August, they'd finally passed Independence Rock and made it to the Sweetwater River where everyone enjoyed a reprieve from the heat, with the exception of Mr. and Mrs. Clayborn Payne who died within hours of each other from an inflammation of the bowels. They left four children, all girls, all under the age of five.

Though the Payne family had been among the wagons assigned to William's group, Hope didn't know them all that well. Even so, the news was devastating as she considered the health of her own parents. Would she ever see them again? Nuzzle Peter's sweet neck? Grasp hands around the table as her father blessed the food?

Overwhelmed, she headed down river to a shady spot, where she could sit by herself and pray.

"Hey. We were beginning to worry about you." William tied his horse to a low branch and made his way to the water's edge where Hope had clearly spent an emotional afternoon soaking her feet. In the twilight shadows, he could still see that her eyes were red-rimmed and her face was blotchy. "What's this?" he asked as he sat down beside her. Bending his forefinger, he tipped her chin up. Her smile was wobbly.

"Just feeling bad for the Payne family. I know they suffered ever since we left Fort Laramie. And"—she sniffed, and several tears splashed on her hands—"I really miss Joel."

"Yeah. Me too."

"And my family."

He only nodded.

"And this morning, we lost our last horse. Mr. Nesmith had to shoot it after it stepped in a hole and broke its leg. Sometimes"—she hiccupped and tried to smile—"it's just all too much, you know? I mean, why the Ditsworths? Why nearly all of *their* animals?"

"Yeah. I know." He wished he had a magic cure for the misery she felt, but only time could heal these hurts. The only thing he knew how to do was listen as she poured out her feelings for the next hour. He handed her his handkerchief and she mopped at her face. "Thank you." Her voice was rough from crying so hard. "I'm sorry. You didn't need me to dump all this on you."

"What are you talking about?" he asked gently, wishing he could embrace her without guilt. "It's part of my job description."

"Oh really? Listening to me blubber is part of the job?"

"Well, if it isn't, I'll add it." He grinned and absently picked up one of her moccasins and noticed that the sole had worn through in several spots. "Guess these weren't made for long distance."

"They've been wonderful, and I'm grateful." Wincing, she lifted a foot out of the river and gingerly probed her heel with her fingertips.

William could see the pain in her eyes. "Let me see your foot."

"No." Weakly, she giggled and dropped her foot back in the water. "Besides, it's not proper, a man, all alone with a woman, looking at her bare feet."

William snorted. "The propriety police are asleep back at camp. Show me your foot. I'm not leaving until you do."

With a sheepish sigh, Hope lifted her foot out of the water and William inhaled sharply. "You've got an infection."

"It's nothing."

"Hope. It has started up your ankle. You need to see Alison's father. Now."

"I'll be fine."

William stood, grasped her arms, and pulled her upright. When she attempted to put some weight on her foot, her quick intake of breath said it all. Without ceremony, he swept her into his arms.

"What are you doing?" she squealed and clutched his neck.

"I'm taking you to the doctor," he said as he strode to his horse. "And then? I'm going to have a word with your fiancé." Although, he'd need a minute to calm down before confronting Ditsworth. Because at the moment, he was tempted to do the man bodily harm.

Before William went to meet Ditsworth, he took Hope to the Payne wagon which—along with the Payne girls—was now under his care. Alison was sitting with the newly orphaned children and feeding them dinner at the campfire. Her relief at seeing Hope ride up with William was obvious.

"I've been so worried," she cried, as William set Hope on the ground. The two girls embraced for a long moment and when they'd finished, William lifted Hope into the wagon.

"Alison," William said, "would you please run and get your father? He needs to look at Hope's foot. She's got a pretty nasty infection, and I don't want her walking."

"Of course!" Alison rushed off and returned moments later with Dr. Naylor.

After he'd thoroughly cleaned and inspected her wound, Dr. Naylor turned to William. "Keep her off her feet. I'll go get some leeches and apply them to the affected area. They should fall off within an hour or so."

"Really?" Hope looked helplessly from Alison to William. "Leeches? I hate leeches!"

"It's for your own good," William assured her. To Alison, he said, "Will you tuck the baby and the toddler up in with Hope for the night? The bigger kids can sleep in the tent with me. I'll be back soon."

William didn't tell Hope that the Ditsworths had seemed far more concerned for their comfort than hers when he told them she wouldn't be returning for at least a week.

Agnes was especially put out by the idea that she'd have to shoulder chores she'd always relied on Hope to handle. "How do we know she's actually lame?" she crabbed. "The girl could be feigning this injury to get out of cooking for us."

Outraged, William didn't trust himself to give the woman a civil answer, so he looked instead at Julius. "Your fiancée needs rest. You've been working her half to death. She'll be riding in the Payne wagon until her infection is completely healed and not a moment sooner."

Agnes whirled on her son. "Julius! Are you just going to stand there and take this? How dare he address you in such a disrespectful tone! Go tell Captain Gantt to fire him!"

William left them mid-argument and smiled. Poor Julius Ditsworth would certainly lose that battle.

By mid-August, they'd crossed over the Continental Divide and officially entered Oregon Territory. They'd traveled over nine hundred miles from Missouri, and Fort Bridger was behind them. It had been two weeks that Hope had ridden with the Payne children, and her foot was nearly healed. The children, all too young to understand what had happened to their parents, were very emotional and clung to her with a desperation that broke her heart.

Already, Hope was in love with each of the towheaded moppets and did everything she knew how to ease their suffering. Thankfully, the baby and the two-year-old slept much of the time and seemed to be thriving. The older two were fussier and demanded to be taken to their real mother. Alison would spell her as often as she could, and William was a great help in the evenings.

Though she knew it was wrong, Hope couldn't help but pretend that they were a little family during these sweet evenings together. Once the babies were down for the night, the four-year-old would crawl up onto William's lap and nestle in while he recited a bedtime story near their campfire. Hope and the three-year-old would move in close, cuddling under a blanket and listen with interest to the low, soothing timbre of his voice. His stories were fanciful and more for her benefit than the kids'.

Hope fell ever further under his spell as they would smile at each other over the tops of the girls' drowsy heads, and she wished she could capture these moments in her heart and save them for the time when she wouldn't be able to see them again.

Finally, after putting off the inevitable for as long as possible, Hope took advantage of Alison's help and returned to the Ditsworths to lend a hand. Though the girls were camped only a few wagons away, Hope hated being away from them as she listened to Agnes unleash an overdue tirade.

"So," the old woman huffed, her raisin-like eyes narrowed with loathing. "You've finally decided to grace us with your presence, have you? It's about time!" She darted a look of pity at her son who was seated in a nearby chair, head tilted back, mouth open, snoring in a way Hope was sure would summon moose. "Julius is suffering from an acute case of the piles, because he's had to handle *all* the work in your absence," Agnes hissed. "Why don't you try earning your keep for once and fix the poor man something to eat?"

Eager to avoid further confrontation, Hope found their cast-iron pot and quickly threw a bean soup together.

As she worked, she could hear William nearby, attempting to communicate with a handful of curious Shoshone Indians, who'd come through their camp looking to trade. After she'd hung the pot over the fire, she stepped around the wagon to watch. One of the young Indian men noticed her and stepped away from his friends to stare with unabashed interest.

Suddenly uneasy, Hope moved back toward her fire. The young brave followed. Eyes darting, he stood for a moment, as if to piece the Ditsworth puzzle together. He seemed to decide that Mr. Ditsworth was Hope's father as he approached with ceremonial deference and waited. When Mr. Ditsworth didn't immediately wake, the Indian grabbed him by the shoulders and shook.

"What is the meaning of this?" Mr. Ditsworth sputtered.

The Indian answered in his native tongue, augmented by broad hand gestures.

William watched for a moment then stepped to Hope's side and spoke urgently. "Alison needs you to spell her back at the Payne wagon right way. Kids are fussy and asking for you. Go ahead. I'll make sure nothing burns." Gesturing at the pot of soup she'd hung over the fire with one hand, he nudged her to get moving with the other.

"Why do I get the feeling you're trying to get rid of me?" She glanced at the Indian. "You'd better not be planning on eating my supper," she said in a light tone, trying to keep the tension she felt from spreading.

"You're on to me," he said. "Now get. I think I can hear the baby crying from here."

"I'm going," she said over her shoulder. "Just leave some soup for the rest of us."

"Yeah." He waved, but his focus had shifted back to Ditsworth and the Indian.

"What's he going on about?" Julius blustered.

William cast a sidelong glance at the brave. "He wants Hope." Reaching for his neck, he rubbed at the tense muscles knotted there. "He says he'll give you a horse in return for her hand."

"No fooling?" Julius Ditsworth held up one finger and pointed at the lone horse. "*One?* Only one?" He laughed and held up three fingers. "For her? *Three* horses!"

William vigorously shook his head and hissed at Ditsworth who obviously found the entire discussion uproariously funny. The man was a complete imbecile. "*No!* Don't tell him that!"

"Aw. I'm just joshing." Face red, belly bouncing, Julius laughed himself into an asthma attack.

With a silent scowl, the brave stalked off and less than a minute later had mounted his horse and galloped off without a backward glance.

"See there?" Julius finally gasped. "He'll never give up three horses for one lousy woman. We're well rid of him if you ask me." He dabbed at his eyes as he watched the brave disappear into the shadows.

William looked at Ditsworth in utter disgust before turning on his heel and leaving.

The next day was a long travel day and, as the Payne girls took their midday nap, William climbed up beside Hope and drove their wagon.

"William?" Hope asked after they'd traveled several drowsy miles in companionable silence. "Why did you send me back to the wagon last night when that Indian boy was talking to Mr. Ditsworth?"

"He thought Ditsworth was your father. And"—chin to shoulder, William raised a brow at her—"he was trying to trade his horse for your hand in marriage."

"That Indian boy wanted to *marry* me?" Hope gasped in amazement.

William chuckled. "Can't blame a guy for trying. He was willing to give up a very fine horse in trade. But personally? I'd have come up with a whole lot more than just a good horse for you."

Embarrassed, Hope averted her eyes from William's flirtatious expression. "Oh, is that so?" She shouldn't be feeling so fluttery over his attentions and she knew it.

"Sure. Pretty thing like you should have a big old house with a wraparound porch and an amazing view of the Willamette River."

Studying his earnest face, Hope grew thoughtful. "You have big dreams, don't you?"

"What makes you think I'm dreaming?"

Hope shrugged and was relieved to hear the baby stirring in the basket between them. Listening to William talk about the big house with the river view turned her feelings suddenly melancholy. She reached in and rubbed the baby's stomach. "You don't think he'll come back for me, do you?"

"The Indian? Don't know. We've traveled twenty miles today. So, it's doubtful. And if he does? I'll send him packing."

That night, as they made camp, the familiar cry of *"Indian!"* rang out. Off in the distance, a lone Shoshone brave rode, leading three excellent horses toward the Ditsworth wagon.

After dismounting, the brave pointed at his three horses then pointed at Hope who was in the middle of fixing supper for the Ditsworths. Tossing her spoon in the pot, she was suddenly filled with dread as she noticed that Mr. Ditsworth was looking at the horses with interest. "William!" she cried as panic crowded her throat. There were two wagons between them. *"William!"*

Agnes rushed to her son's side. "Julius! Strike a bargain! If we are going to make it to Oregon, we'll need healthy animals like these horses. And certainly, Hope hasn't been much help now that she's doting on those orphans."

Shock had Hope's head reeling. Agnes wanted to sell her? She'd known the woman had no love for her, but Mr. Ditsworth looked as if he was listening.

Undecided, Julius vacillated. "I don't know. . ."

"*Do it!* Take the trade! I never did approve of this match. You'll meet someone from a better family down the road." Addressing the Indian, Agnes gestured to Hope. *"Take her!* Shoo! Go on, now!"

The brave shrugged and handed the horses to Julius who looked them over with growing greed in his eyes.

"*William!*" Hope finally found her feet and started to run. Her heart was pounding a mile a minute, and terror had her screaming now. *"William! William! Help!"* She had no faith Mr. Ditsworth would come to her rescue.

But William would!

Blindly she careened around the wagon and crashed into William who'd heard her call and come running. His handsome face was filled with concern as he caught her by the arms and demanded, "What is it? What happened?"

"Agnes is trying to sell me!" Her breathing was labored, her skin clammy. Wrapping her arms around his waist, she buried her face in his shirt and vowed to never let go. "To that Indian man! He gave Mr. Ditsworth three horses and now I'm supposed to go with him!"

"Get into the wagon. Now. And close the flaps." William's tone was grim as he pointed to the back of the Ditsworth wagon where some of Agnes's furniture would shield her from view. Gently, he nudged Hope on her way and sent a passing boy on his horse to fetch Captain Gantt. When the Captain arrived, his expression grew ominous as William told him about the bargain Julius Ditsworth was making.

"Go get James Nesmith. Tell him we need a peace package as soon as possible. I'll"—Captain Gantt sighed—"try to deal with this." He gestured to the young brave.

James returned with William carrying a loaded saddlebag, and in broken sign language they tried to convey that Hope was not for sale at any price.

But the brave's face grew hard and his body rigid. Furiously, he shouted at Julius in his native tongue as the older man turned tail and hobbled off to hide.

"Yep. He's offended," William murmured as he laid the peace package at the brave's feet. It took an hour of fast talking, but finally, after presenting the young man with a large parcel of tobacco, several shirts, gun powder, and some glass beads, he gradually became mollified and, taking back his three horses, was on his way, dignity restored.

To Julius Ditsworth, who cowered behind his wagon, William hissed, "I'll deal with you later."

Then, he lifted Hope out of the wagon and onto his horse's back and swung up behind her. As they wended their way back to the Payne wagon, William wished he could hold Hope like this, nestled against his chest, his arms wrapped firmly around her, forever. The idea that she was committed to that Ditsworth fool was nearly more than he could bear. He tightened his grip around her waist and inhaled the sweet, warm scent that was uniquely Hope.

Lord, he prayed silently, *please show Hope the truth. Please release her from her promise to that terrible family. And forgive me for the feelings I have for another man's woman. Amen.*

When she was safely back with Alison and the children, William said tersely, "Captain Gantt has requested a word with me."

Still badly shaken, Hope merely nodded. "Thank you," she whispered. "For everything."

"*Ditsworth!*" William kicked at the man's wagon wheel. "Get up!"

Agnes thrust her head out of the canvas cover. "What is the *meaning* of this?" she demanded at William's combative tone of voice. "It's is now past eight p.m. *and I was asleep!*"

"Not that it's any of your business, but Captain Gantt wants to talk to your son. *Now,*" he growled. "Don't make me come down there and drag you out."

Julius crawled out from under the wagon, disgruntled at being rousted out in such an undignified manner. "What's going on?"

"Come with me and find out," William ordered. "I've saddled your mule. Let's go."

It was clear by his precarious ride over to Captain Gantt's camp that Julius Ditsworth had little affinity for animals. Or direction, for that matter. He'd wrapped his arms around the mule's neck and clung for dear life as they crashed through campsites, scattering chickens and people along the way.

When they'd arrived, William dragged him off the mule and thrust him into the firelight of Captain Gantt's camp. Several men were seated in a circle, waiting.

"Ditsworth," Captain Gantt said. "Have a seat." He gestured to a stump that had been set up for this purpose. Meekly, Julius complied. "You know, ever since I first laid eyes on you, like William here, I had the strangest feeling I'd seen you somewhere before. After we left Fort Bridger, it dawned on me. I sent one of my men back, just to be sure." He reached into his back pocket and pulled out a folded sheet of paper and smoothed it out on his thigh. "Recognize this?"

Julius took one look at the WANTED poster and sagged. There was no way he could run, and he knew it.

"Looks like you owe a lot of folks a lot of money."

Julius remained silent.

"Says here, you're supposed to be in jail for gambling fraud, tax evasion, and embezzlement. And, being that we're going to arrive at Fort Hall tomorrow, I'm going to arrange to have a US Marshall escort you to California with me and the California bound portion of the wagon train. Once there, we'll put you on a boat and send you back to Boston to pay your debt to society. Any marital agreement you've made with Miss Dawson is now void. She'll be traveling to Oregon with Mr. Bradshaw, and once there, they'll decide what to do about the destructive impact you've had on her and her family's lives. We will be leaving tomorrow morning two hours in advance of the rest of the train. You'll have no further contact with Miss Dawson. Have I made myself clear?"

Julius nodded and sighed.

"Good. Any questions?"

"Yes. Will my mother be joining me?"

"Well, sir, as I can't imagine a more fitting punishment for you, the answer to that would be a resounding yes."

Chapter 10

Gone? What do you mean, they're *gone?*" Hope stared at William in confusion. She'd noticed that the Ditsworth wagon had not yet joined their group for the evening and was growing concerned.

"Alison? Can you watch the kids for Hope?" William thumbed his hat back and scratched his head. "We're going to take a little walk."

"We are? But why?" Hope glanced around. Something was rotten in Denmark.

"I need a word. Alone."

Clearly curious, Alison merely nodded at them and gathered the children for supper.

Once they'd moved away from the wagons and found a log to sit on under a small grove of trees, Hope said, "William, please. What's going on? Where are the Ditsworths?" She'd chewed the inside of her cheek nearly raw with fear.

William exhaled deeply and, turning to face her, reached for her hand. "They left early this morning and headed to California with Captain Gantt and his party."

"*What!*" She gave her head a clearing shake. "No. No, no. They are going to *Oregon* to stake a claim. Two, once Mr. Ditsworth and I—" She swallowed at the lump in her throat. "William. Where are they, really?"

"I'm telling you the truth, Hope."

"*No!* I don't understand! *California?* But. . .but. . .how will I catch them? They have to be miles away by now!"

"Hope—"

"It's *not* true!" she cried and leapt to her feet. "How could they do this to me? Did I do something wrong? Was I not good enough for them?" She began to pace as tears threatened her composure. "I always worried that Agnes would convince Julius that my family was not worth the effort. Is *that* what happened?" Hand to her forehead, she stared off into the sunset and tried to reconcile what William was saying.

"No. Hope, no." William stood and went to her. "Honey, it was nothing you did.

It was me. I sent them away. Captain Gantt and I—"

Whirling around, Hope stared at him in disbelief. "You did *what?*" Her mind reeled with the myriad betrayals. How could he do this to her? How could Mr. Ditsworth? "Why would you *do* that? Who is going to help my family now?" She began to feel faint as she paced. "My mother is sick, and the boys are starving. Papa can't work, and the depression is killing them all! And now they don't have my income—I know Julius was not a perfect man. But at least he was willing to help my family!"

"Hope. He was going to sell you!"

"No! It was *Agnes* that wanted to—"

"Hope!" he interrupted. "There's more."

"No! I don't want to hear another word!" She was sobbing now. William had ruined her family's only chance at happiness. What on earth would she do now? She was hundreds of miles from her family and homeless.

"Hope, please—" he reached for her arm, but she shook him off. Nothing he could say would alter the fact that she was alone and destitute.

"No. Don't touch me!" Blinded by her tears, she paused for a moment and buried her face in her hands. "This is all my fault. I was never in love with Mr. Ditsworth, and I let my feelings for you get in the way which was so. . .*wrong*. He probably *knew!* He'd been so generous, and I betrayed him. I'm horrible," she whispered. Guilt flowed from her eyes and dripped off the tip of her nose. "I'm so sorry. I'm just—" Utterly dejected, Hope could only offer a listless shrug. "Please, forgive me." Before he could say anything that would make her feel worse, she whirled and ran back to the wagon. She needed Alison. And the babies. And her parents. And Peter.

But most of all, she needed a heart-to-heart with God.

That night, as Hope lay in her bed, she spilled all the terrible secrets she'd been harboring for so many weeks.

She confessed that she was secretly relieved to be free of the horrible Ditsworths. She confessed that she had sinned by allowing herself to fall in love with William while she was engaged to another man. She confessed her hurt and confusion that William had gone behind her back to send Mr. Ditsworth—her only hope for her family's happiness—away. She confessed the terrible fear of being alone that gripped her belly and made her feel as if she might be sick. And lastly, she confessed that she'd been selfish. She'd depended on her marriage to Mr. Ditsworth to save her family back in Independence and not on God. That wasn't fair to Him. Or Mr. Ditsworth. Or William. Or herself.

And, once Hope had admitted every ugly truth to the Lord, she begged His forgiveness and placed her family, and her future, in His hands.

She'd no sooner murmured, "Amen," than she fell into a deep, exhausted sleep.

The following evening William spotted Hope sitting by herself away from the wagons. The setting sun cast a rosy glow over the distant hills and cooled the sweet mountain air. He'd left her alone all day, thinking she needed the time to figure a few things out. As he'd ridden he spent the day praying and asking God to give him the words she needed to hear. He could only pray that it was the same thing he needed to say, because he was hopelessly in love with her.

She glanced up at his approach.

"Hey," he said.

"Hey."

He knelt beside her, and they were silent for a long moment.

"You said there is more," she finally whispered. "If you want to tell me, I'm ready to listen."

William exhaled heavily. "Julius Ditsworth wasn't actually moving *to* the Oregon Territory. He was fleeing *from* the law."

Her brows shot up as William went on to describe the number of felonies Mr. Ditsworth had committed. "He was a con man, Hope. And you weren't the only person he'd conned. He sold his mother's mansion out from under her and spent every penny of her bank account, and I don't think she knows it."

"Really?" Humiliation filled her eyes.

"I'm sorry."

When the tears started to flow in earnest, William took her in his arms and let her cry. When she'd finished soaking his handkerchief and finally pulled herself together, William said, "And there's more."

"More?" Hope limply waived the handkerchief and gargled up some watery laughter. "I don't think I can take any more."

"Well, I'm praying that this will be good news." He took her hands in his and gently ran his fingers over her wrists.

Sniffing, she nodded. "Go on."

"Hope Dawson. I am in love with you." Her eyes widened, and he could feel the pulse at her wrists quicken. "Have been from the minute I laid eyes on you back in Independence at the Riverside Hotel. I thought Ditsworth was your father, and I hoped you were going to Oregon. When I discovered you were betrothed to that snake, it nearly killed me. You know, he ran out of the dining room before the sheriff showed up. Probably because he figured if he was recognized, he'd have been carted off to jail with the other two."

Hope's mouth fell slack, and he could see the realizations dawning.

"Every day since we left Independence, I've been praying that God would show you the truth. The truth that you didn't belong with the Ditsworths. The truth that you were destined to end up with me. And that you'd fall in love with me too. And maybe even help me raise the Payne kids and someday have a few of our own. And"—he paused and squinted off into the distance—"even if that never happens, I hope that one day, when you look back and consider why I had to send Julius Ditsworth away, you will understand. And forgive me. And know that I'll be there. Waiting for you. Because I love you and know that we're supposed to be together. I've felt it from the beginning."

When he'd finished his speech, William leaned forward and gently kissed her lips before standing and walking away.

Hope stood, staring after him as he left. "William! Wait. . .please. Wait."

He stopped and slowly turned around. "I said I would." The dimple she loved so much blossomed. "Forever."

"No!" she cried as she ran to him. "Wait *now!* I want to tell you"—when she reached him she fell into his waiting arms—"I love you too! I think I always have but couldn't let myself think it. . .because I was engaged."

He swept her up, swung her in a circle, and as she was talking and trying to explain her feelings to him, he cut her off with a kiss. A real kiss between a woman and the man who loves her.

Epilogue

Hope and William married on the Oregon Trail the very next week. Alison was a happy witness and, after the ceremony, she'd organized a lavish potluck dinner and dance to celebrate. She also agreed to take the Payne children with her for the night, as Hope and William had committed to take on the ready-made family as their own.

Joel's mother gave them a quilt that was supposed to be good for blessing a couple with lots of children. "You will be wonderful parents to those little babies," she said, her eyes full of tears.

Within three months they arrived safely in the Willamette Valley, and William introduced his new family to his old family. And though Hope had known William would provide for her and the children, she was stunned to learn that her new husband was the son of a sawmill owner and timber dealer and wealthy in his own right.

The home he'd built was spacious and beautiful with a wonderful view of the river and a wraparound porch, and had *four* bedrooms.

"I built it with my future family in mind. Never did I imagine I'd be so blessed so soon," he confessed as he led her on a tour of her new home. "Wait here," he said, his smile wide. "I have two wedding gifts for you." He disappeared for a moment and returned with a beautiful pair of leather shoes. Bending on one knee he said, "Give me your foot, Cinderella." Hope laughed as he slipped the new shoes on her feet, and there were tears in her eyes as she urged him to stand. "And the second gift?" she asked, still marveling at the wonderful turn her life had taken.

"I've sent word to have your family brought to Oregon next summer, and my father and brothers are going to help me build them a house."

Hope stared at him in wonder. "You are truly the answer to my father's prayer."

"What about your prayer?"

"Oh. . .*yes*. You are more than I could ever have dreamed of. And I have a gift for you too. It's very small, but I think you'll like it." She gripped his hand in hers and said, "This spring, we'll be adding another baby to our family."

William stared at her for a moment before he whooped with joy and spun her in a circle. There were tears of happiness in his eyes as he held her close. "If it's a boy," he whispered, "let's name him Joel."

Author of over 35 novels for numerous publishers, **Carolyn Zane** lives with her college sweetheart and husband, Matt, and two of their five offspring in Oregon's beautiful Willamette Valley. Though the nest is not exactly empty yet, after a few years of homeschooling and juggling carpool, Carolyn is delighted to finally return to her office to write full time. Her sabbatical has thus far produced one married daughter, a delightful son-in-law, a second daughter bound for college, a son in the Air Force Academy who hopes to become a pilot, a third daughter currently writing her own novel, and her baby and second son now in high school and threatening to get his driver's license.

Brand–New Romance Collections from Barbour. . .

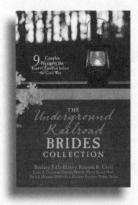

The Underground Railroad Brides Collection

Join the journey as nine couples work along the Underground Railroad between 1849 and 1860, determined to bring freedom and justice to all. There is hope for the future when people come together to fight evil and when men and women find love in the midst of great challenges.

Paperback / 978-1-68322-632-1 / $14.99

The Backcountry Brides Collection

Travel into Colonial America where eight women seek love, but they each know a future husband requires the necessary skills to survive in the backcountry. Living in areas exposed to nature's ferocity, prone to Indian attack, and cut off from regular supplies, can hearts overcome danger to find lasting love?

Paperback / 978-1-68322-622-2 / $14.99